JASON HARDGRAVE

THE CALL

The universe has a funny way of thrusting unexpected events upon us in the middle of the night. This occurrence is typically marked by a harsh ringing coming from a digital device. Someone disrupts the silence of the night with their efforts to communicate. Sarah Triv let out a groan as she fumbled for her tablet. As she picked up the device, she saw it was her father, Richard. At that hour, he wouldn't call unless it was important, and a wave of worry washed over her as she accepted the audio transmission. "Hey, what's going on?" Sarah asked.

There was a momentary pause before she heard her father's voice over the open communication channel. "Hey, Sarah. I'm sorry to wake you at this hour. Something incredible is happening, and you should be a part of it." Sarah was now fully awake, but she still felt the effects of the barrel-aged scotch ale from hours earlier. She pushed aside the dull ache in her head as she readied herself for the news. She was certain she wouldn't be able to go back to sleep after this conversation.

"You have my full attention," Sarah said.

"Earth Initiative wants to recruit you and your team for a specialized mission and needs you and your skills within a new frontier. They believe you are the person for the job," Richard replied.

"What's this opportunity? Please, clue me in," Sarah insisted.

"The inter-system tracking network detected something interesting traveling through the Sol system. A large asteroid appeared that will be striking Europa in seven days," Richard explained. Sarah was still hazy about why this pertained to her. Europa had a surface that was entirely covered with an unbroken crust of ice. Then the pieces connected for Sarah as realization washed over her.

"This is your shot to get out there!" Richard said in an encouraging tone. Sarah realized it was much more than that.

"They want you and your team to be the first. There is a pristine, unexplored ocean under all that ice. That asteroid will unlock the door!" Richard said, unable to contain his excitement.

Sarah had read about the microbial life that had evolved in the Sol system under the Europa ice. She knew about the existence of water on that moon, but Europa's surface temperatures had prevented oceanic exploration. But here was her chance to explore an uncharted alien ocean.

Richard continued, "Sarah, can you get your team together for a briefing in one hour?"

"Yeah, we are on our way," Sarah replied

Sarah's fatigue vanished as her excitement set in. To study undiscovered ocean life on another planet was once just a distant fantasy. She enjoyed working in Earth's oceans, but something always fascinated her about the stars. She was a marine biologist and already had success in the field with her studies on the adaptations of the orca populations near the coast of Argentina. Their recovery was hard, and it took nearly two hundred years for them to come back from the brink of extinction. Although almost everyone in the 2240s wanted to save the population of orcas, it was not until humanity terraformed and colonize parts of Mars that the pressure from human activity eased for many species of wild animals. Sol TV did a story about Sarah's research at the time and presented it as an example of how far humans had come with their conservation efforts. She had become a rising star in science. Fame wasn't something that she had wanted, but it seemed to rekindle human awareness about how special the natural world is. A few years after that, Sarah led a research expedition to study life in the deep volcanic chain in the Galapagos Rift. The trip wasn't nearly as glamorous as working with the cetaceans, but it furthered research of archaebacteria that used chemo-synthesis to create energy without sunlight. That research might have gone unnoticed if not for a single researcher who saw Sarah on the news and followed her work. Using her discoveries, he had harnessed the energy conversion into a new type of Bio-Reciprocation-Incremental-Lepton reactor or BRIL reactor that could be used anywhere sunlight was unavailable. Her name was, again, closely associated with the groundbreaking discovery.

Yeah, I have had wonderful luck in my career, Sarah thought. This luck was likely the reason that she was selected for this mission. That, and her father, Richard, was an elected member of the Earth Initiative council.

"EV will go nuts when he hears about this," Sarah said to herself as she tapped the communication panel.

Evengii Balabanov was a handsome Ukrainian man in his mid-thirties with a short-groomed goatee and mustache, whose jawline appeared to be cut from steel. He had short black hair that was spiked on one side. For that early morning meeting, he wore a pair of jeans, an un-tucked button-up shirt, and a black leather bomber jacket.

Evengii always knew he belonged in the water. The sea had captured his imagination at a young age, and he had followed that passion. Almost everyone called Evengii EV. His friends often joked that he could swim better than most sea creatures and he possessed fantastic endurance. EV's aquatic spirit led him to become one of the best submersible pilots alive. Occasionally he piloted a starship or aircraft, but mostly, he flew through the water. From personal watercraft to the massive submersibles that were sent on missions for many years, EV was adept with them all.

That morning he strolled into the orbital station briefing room twenty minutes late and saw that Sarah, Richard, and Kiah were already talking.

As EV entered the room, Kiah gave him a warm smile. Kiah Spearman was a familiar face on the team, and her role was typically a marine biologist, and she had started her career as a software engineer. Over the years, she had kept her computer skills sharp, but her sincere passion was for the marine life they studied. Kiah, Sarah and EV had bonded over their love for the ocean, and this had developed into a deep and lasting friendship between them.

"Sorry I'm late, but you caught me by surprise," EV explained. He nodded to Sarah and whispered, "Last night's party was grand!" Sarah cracked a smile.

"We have another surprise for you this morning," Sarah explained as EV slipped into the chair beside her.

Richard started, "Alright, what we have is a once-in-a-millennium opportunity, folks. Our friends over at inter-system tracking have identified an asteroid that has been sneaking about the Sol system. They detected it only a few hours ago, and mapped its trajectory. The asteroid looks like it's on a collision course with Europa, and the impact will occur just north of the Pwyll crater in just over seven days."

EV interrupted, "Sounds like a blast, but where does our team come in? Sarah and Kiah are at their best when they are surrounded by ocean life, and I'm just the lucky pilot that gets to escort these fine scientists around."

Richard dismissed the interruption with a slight wave of his hand as he addressed EV directly, "That asteroid will punch a colossal hole in that ice, creating a door into an abyssal unknown. I just thought a couple of marine biologists might want to look around down there. Think you could give them a lift, EV?"

The realization swept across EV's face as it shifted from uncertainty into excitement. "They want to send our team under the ice?"

Richard continued. "Earth Initiative is sending a research team to take advantage of this historic opportunity. At my recommendation, the council offered your team this mission because of your experience and combined skills. Make no mistake; this might be an unprecedented opportunity to study extraterrestrial life within our own solar system."

Scientists had known about life on Europa for almost two hundred years. Early exploration had collected surface ice samples containing several types of preserved bacteria and microscopic organisms from this moon of Jupiter. Later probes sent to Europa attempted to unravel its secrets, and found living microorganisms within the water samples they had collected, but these discoveries were only seen as a marginal success. Europa's ocean was a lightless environment where solar energy was non-existent, leading scientists to believe that ocean life relied on deep underwater tectonic and volcanic activity, similar to what Sarah and her team had researched recently on Earth. Sixteen kilometers of dense ice lay between the moon's surface and the ocean below, making further study nearly impossible without a significant financial investment. Additionally, humans had been creating folds in space to traverse the expanse. The greater the distance, the more energy was required to create these folds, but slowly, humans started discovering other worlds within nearby star systems. A few of these new worlds held a wide variety of life that researchers could readily study and make groundbreaking discoveries. Because of these two factors, scientists had left Europa virtually untouched. This new impact event would create a giant hole through the Europa ice sheet, providing an opportunity for science to reach this previously unreachable ocean.

Kiah Spearman chimed in, "Are we sure that we can get everything ready in time? That window seems pretty short, and we are literally about to dive into the unknown."

"You will have some backup. It will be more than just the three of you going, and Earth Initiative is locking down the other candidates in the next day or so as they confirm their participation. The team will be fairly small, but the EI are putting together their best for this mission. People they trust to get you in there safely," Richard explained, then continued. "EI will also provide the team a leviathan class submersible with a stage four BRIL reactor, and will equip the vessel with a Swift Sphere and Bobb to assist with detailed exploration. The asteroid's crater will refreeze just a few hours after the initial impact, and that is why we must act fast. The mission duration will be six months. After that time, you will rendezvous at the original impact site for extraction. Based on what you find down there, they might send in a second team, and you might have the option to remain if everything is going well."

With a worried hint in her voice, Kiah said, "It still sounds like we are pushing it." She shot a questioning glance at Sarah.

"There is danger; no question about that. There will only be one passage to the surface. If an emergency arises once your team is in the water, it will be hard for others to reach you, depending on your depth. You will be on your own down there." Richard cleared his throat and started again. "A specialized team will monitor progress from here at Earth Dock and will be in communication with your team on Europa. They will be available 24/7 over the com channel and will alert me the moment your team encounters anything interesting."

Kiah still looked concerned for a moment, but then it seemed to fade. Sarah knew her well enough to know she could not resist this opportunity for exploration.

"When do they need to know?" Sarah asked as she leaned across the conference table.

"By noon; otherwise, they will need to look for another team to pull this off. The timetable is tight. EI is already at work, fabricating the equipment you will need and rounding up the rest of the crew," Richard replied.

Kiah and EV both gave the nod to Sarah.

"We're in!" Sarah exclaimed.

PREPARING TO DEPART

Sarah noticed the green notification icon on her tab, indicating she had received a message. She swiped her tab open and saw that the dossiers for the entire Europa team were attached. She whisked her red hair away from her green eyes as she studied the profiles over her morning coffee.

Commander Jake Riley was the first profile in the data packet. Jake had a sandy hair crop top in his photo and looked like an action movie star. He was fully equipped with a small scar that bisected his left eyebrow and a neatly trimmed beard. She thumbed down through his qualifications that listed EI (Earth Initiative) service aboard several star cruisers and flight time in an AB5 gunboat used in patrols of colonized star systems. Although Earth hadn't seen a war in a couple of centuries, and no technologically advanced life had ever been encountered in any of the systems humans had explored, most people still felt it was necessary to keep a small military presence in each inhabited system. This was just in case humanity was ever attacked by unfriendly aliens that didn't like humans spreading throughout the galaxy. Jake also was an accomplished diver and had recent experience cleaning up radioactive waste that had been dumped in the later 20th century off the coast of Europe. The profile said that he was thirty-seven.

Sarah flipped to the next profile and saw the familiar face of Kiah Spearman. In the photo, Kiah wore a dark red knit top with her long blond hair flowing over her shoulders. Sarah had given her that top a few years ago for her birthday and was pleased to see her wearing it in the profile photo. Kiah still had that sense of adventure in her sky-blue eyes. Sarah had been on many missions with Kiah in the past, and they were the closest of friends. She was great with software systems in addition to her vast marine science knowledge. She seemed to remember every species that they had ever encountered. When she put her mind to something, Kiah was an unstoppable force, and Sarah had come to rely on her during their missions together.

Sarah proceeded to the next profile and saw Evengii Balabanov. EV was another of Sarah's close friends and had frequently been a pilot with her teams for the past ten years. She always loved his sense of humor, and he was always rock solid and reliable. He always got them where they needed to go and back safely. Sarah flipped past EV's familiar profile.

Sarah then saw the next profile of Dr. Benjamin Rapner, M.D. He was a dark-skinned gentleman with black curly shoulder-length hair pulled back into a short ponytail. He looked young, and the profile said he was thirty-one years old. Skimming the text, Sarah saw he was a noted prodigy and had been a medical doctor for many years. He had also worked on extraterrestrial botany while living on the colony world of Septimus. Sarah remembered Septimus was about sixty light years from Earth. His skills would be a necessary addition to the crew, and the more Sarah looked through his record, the more excited she was that he would be joining their team.

Sarah took another sip of coffee. Coffee was a luxury and something that was precious to her. At one point in Earth's history, coffee was grown in abundance, but after the great climate shift, the trees became increasingly rare. People shifted to other drinks that contained caffeine, and to most people, coffee became a remnant of the past. To Sarah, it was still a delight. It was now a niche market and was hard to find. The aroma permeated the room, and Sarah let it wash over her as she inhaled deeply.

The next profile was Ashley Martab. Purple and silver streaks accented Ashley's long, black hair as it flowed around her torso. Her hair complemented her elegant face and light brown skin tone. She was an officer and an engineer who worked for Earth Initiative, a specialist in the NIC printing processes. Sarah thought to herself that this was an interesting choice since most of their equipment was going to be pre-printed before they left Earth Dock. Then Sarah remembered how far away help would be if a situation were to occur under the ice, so having someone on board that could design and implement custom equipment just might save their lives. The more Sarah read about Ashley, the more impressed Sarah was with her history.

Using a Nano-Ionic-Compression printer, or NIC printer, was easy enough. These machines could create any object that was already designed and in the NIC database. NIC printers was a staple of modern technology and used reformable matter, more commonly known as NIC matter. The specialized material could create just about any solid object with exact detail down to the atomic level. The printers could fabricate circuit boards and other electronics that would range from personal tabs all the way up to star ships. NIC printers were also capable of printing in a wide array of textures and colors. They could replicate material nearly identical to wood, metal, glass, plastic, ceramic, and rubbers. The one key difference was the material had the ability to be incomprehensibly light-weight and strong. NIC matter was tightly controlled by Earth Initiative because of the potential to create almost anything. Safety protocols were in place to ensure individuals didn't print things like weapons or dangerous items that they weren't qualified to possess. A few specialized engineers had the freedom to pretty much create anything they could imagine. These individuals had access to NIC gloves that allowed them to sculpt the atoms with a wave of their fingers. Ashley was one of these rare individuals, and it was noted in her record. She also was an expert Swift Sphere pilot with many hours of flight time. She was currently under the command of Jake Riley.

Specialist Dyami Swiftwater rounded out the group. Dyami had long jet-black hair pulled back behind his ears, framing his angular facial features. He wore a light blue shirt that complemented his darker complexion. Around his neck, he wore a long necklace of carved wooden beads in the form of various animals. The lines on his face were soft, but Sarah guessed they were becoming more distinctive as he aged. The profile said that he was forty-seven. Dyami was a deep-water environmental control specialist. She found it strange that it was noted in his profile that he would also be acting as a culinary professional for the mission. Dyami was also under Jake Riley's command and currently working for Earth Initiative.

Sarah remembered that they all were about to be working in a potentially dangerous environment in confined quarters and found a bit of solace in the fact that Jake, Ashley, and Dyami had worked closely together before, based on her review of the records.

Just then, Sarah's tab chirped, and she saw the notification alerting her to the time of the final briefing. Their team would launch from Earth Dock the day after tomorrow. The leviathan class submersible was due to finish printing in the dock in the next few hours, and Earth Initiative had scheduled rigorous testing the following day.

Sarah could already feel her anticipation building. They would embark on an adventure of a lifetime, and the tingling sensation of the unknown toyed with Sarah's mind. What would they find under all that ice?

PEGASUS

"Ah, you must be Sarah," a deep voice echoed off the walls of the large orbital dock hangar.

Sarah turned around and saw a man just under two meters tall approaching her. She recognized him as Commander Jake Riley. "Yes. I'm Sarah Triv," she said as she stowed her tab to meet Jake's outstretched hand with her own. "You must be Commander Jake Riley. It's a pleasure to meet you."

As the two exchanged pleasantries, Dyami and Ashley appeared behind Jake. "Sarah, I want to introduce you to Lieutenant Ashley Martab and Specialist Dyami Swiftwater. They will be accompanying us on this mission. They are the finest people I have ever served with. I have trusted them with my life on multiple occasions and convinced them to come along for the ride."

Sarah nodded with an understanding look, then turned to introduce her crew. "Commander Jake Riley, this is Kiah Spearman and Evengii Balabanov." Jake extended a handshake to both of them.

"Oh, call me EV," Evengii said when it was his turn.

Just then, Richard strolled up with a satisfied look on his face. "The Pegasus is almost ready and loaded," he said.

"Pegasus?" Jake questioned.

"That's what Earth Initiative called our ride," Kiah explained.

Richard motioned the group to follow him. The hangar within the orbital dock was beyond massive, with several large areas actively being used to print medium size star ships and large pieces of star cruisers being assembled in the outside docking ring surrounding the station.

Before long, they saw the Pegasus seated in her berth. She had a sleek hull full of flowing curves and graceful arcs. The sub was large, but it could easily cut through any ocean. From where the group stood, they could see the transparent surface of the front-facing NIC glass that looked into the bridge and the marine lab just below that. The bridge had a bulbous hammerhead shape that was almost entirely transparent, and sat on the top bow of the ship. It was evident by the design that this was a vessel built for exploration. Large water scoops faced forward and ran along both sides of the hull, and the flowing contours made it clear where the paths connected and formed a large output at the sub's stern. This piece of engineering was the primary propulsion system for the Pegasus, where massive amounts of water flowed through to propel the craft forward. Most of the upper decks were also NIC glass broken only occasionally by glossy white panels that connected to the lower frame where the moon pool dock was located. The moon pool dock was a seal-able opening at the bottom of the Pegasus that allowed crew and craft to enter and exit the water while the vessel was at any depth. Two parallel stripes of black ran from stem to stern along the moon pool dock, and in between was the word PEGASUS in bold sans-serif lettering. The entire craft was over forty meters long and about four stories high.

"Wow! She's gorgeous!" EV exclaimed, his eyes widening.

Jake turned to him and asked, "Have you ever piloted a sub like this before?"

"Yeah, sure, at least something almost identical. It's very rare to see one out of the water and in pristine condition. She is radiant!" EV responded, enchanted by the vessel before him.

As they walked along the starboard side of the ship toward the stern, Sarah saw the dock crew loading the last of the food and supplies into the Pegasus using the rear ramp that was extended from the moon pool dock. She recognized Ben from his profile photo, who was already there helping load the medical supplies. When he saw the group, he walked over to greet them.

"This lovely group must be the rest of the crew! Hi, I'm Ben Rapner! I'll be your doctor for the next several months," Ben said with a smile.

Jake shook his hand. "Nice to meet you, Doctor. Your record is very impressive, but I have to say that I was a bit surprised you wanted to join this mission."

"You can call me Ben. Earth Initiative said they needed me for this one, and I have always wanted to join an adventure like this. But, until now, my family and career have always taken priority. Being here now is both exhilarating and terrifying!" Ben said.

"Ben, we are lucky to have found you. You have all the required skills and were at the right place at the right time," Richard commented.

"I'm glad to be here," Ben added.

"You'll do great. It's a pleasure to have you on board, Ben," Jake replied.

Each of the crew greeted Ben before he turned back toward the Pegasus. "She's pretty amazing!"

"Well, rather than just admiring the outside, let's take a peek inside," Richard indicated the crew should follow him up the rear ramp and into the ship.

The crew made their way to the ship's briefing room adjacent to the bridge. As they entered, a small curved panel rose from the floor to greet them. Richard tapped a few keys on the waist-high panel, and a glowing blue holo-display appeared with the schematics of the Pegasus. Status boxes also appeared with various indicators blinking in a myriad of colors.

"I'm sure that everyone here has reviewed the mission briefing, but I want to go over some quick final reminders. Commander Jake Riley will take the lead on this mission, and has full command authority."

Jake and the crew nodded their understanding.

"However, this is also primarily a mission of discovery. Despite Sarah's civilian status, she will be the first officer." Richard continued, "There are six weeks of food supplies aboard the Pegasus and a small hydroponics bay adjacent to the environmental control room," as Richard spoke, areas of the schematic lit up. "The Pegasus will need to rendezvous for resupply after six weeks, and Earth Initiative will establish a passage to the surface. With some luck, they can build a small outpost below the ice sheet."

Richard looked around to see if there were any pending questions. "I will stay on Earth Dock with Reg and Samantha, to communicate and monitor your progress from here. Even through the ice, we should be able to keep in communication with you at all times. Each of you already received your objectives and will need to report on the status of each as the mission progresses."

Richard then turned directly toward Jake, and with as much seriousness as possible, said, "Commander, rarely ask for personal favors, but please… bring this crew home safe, especially my Sarah."

Jake leveled his gaze at Richard. "I understand, and will ensure their safety."

Jake turned to the crew, "This is a civilian mission, and I don't expect you to use military jargon. But I expect everyone to treat each other with respect and follow the chain of command. From what I have seen in your profiles, we have an impressive crew, and I expect nothing less than your very best. Now, let's see what's out there."

The crew spent the following two hours checking and rechecking systems, gear, and food reserves, ensuring everything was in place aboard the Pegasus. Every crew member brought a civilian outfit and any items they could fit into a medium-sized duffel that they stored in a personal locker within their quarters. In addition, each crew member had a standard ship suit, a standard wetsuit, and other masks and underwater gear they might need. Each article was printed and perfectly fitted for each person. The equipment also included two Sea Wings. These personal watercraft could pull a diver through the water, significantly increasing their swim speed. They would not be usable in deep water where the pressure alone could kill a person but were included if they found life within the shallower depths of Europa. After confirmation that every piece of equipment had been brought aboard and adequately stored, the seven adventurers were ready.

Just before the scheduled departure, Ben's family appeared at the dock to see him off.

"You be careful out there," Angela Rapner said quietly. "I'm not losing you, so be safe."

Kasidy was just a few steps away, admiring the Pegasus and dreaming about the adventure her father was about to embark on. Her brother, Tyler, just stared blankly. "Whoa, DAD, you're going in THAT?! The top looks like a hammerhead shark!" his daughter Kasidy yelled gleefully. She was eleven, and his son Tyler was six.

"She is pretty cool, huh? We are taking her to Europa," Ben replied.

Tyler scoffed, "Yeah Kas, it's why we are here."

Ben leaned over and kissed his wife. He knew the six months would go by fast as he kept busy, but it would be a different story for Angi as she stayed behind. Tyler was having difficulty fitting in at the school on Earth Dock and was afraid of the family's move to Earth. The upcoming move was the family's second move in just under a year. Angi had received an excellent opportunity to teach in San Francisco. Ben's passions were Angi, his kids... and his plants. Just a few days ago, Ben had gotten the call about Europa. He had the skills the crew needed, and somehow Richard had convinced him they needed him to go. He was excited about the adventure, but his decision didn't go over as well with the rest of his family, except Kasidy. She asked new questions about the trip every available chance.

"Do you think there are any sea watchers on Europa?" Kasidy asked excitedly.

"Probably not Kasidy. They're probably only native to Septimus... But I guess you never know," Ben shrugged with a smile.

"Dad, do you have to go?" Tyler whined.

"Tyler, I know this is hard, but they said they need me on this mission, bud," Ben replied.

Tyler slowly walked over and then gripped his father's waist and squeezed tightly. "I'll see you soon, buddy, but this is only for a few months. You guys get settled, and before you know it, I'll be back," Ben said in an affirming voice. "Besides, we can talk to each other over the coms, and you can give me updates on the High Flyers' scores."

"Alright, fine..." Tyler said as he examined his left shoe.

Angi leaned over and whispered in Ben's ear, "I will take care of them; you just take care of you... I love you."

"I will. I love you too," Ben turned and started heading toward the Pegasus.

"Avoid the cheese, Dad. I am sure your friends would not survive the night locked in that sub with barking spiders," Kasidy called after him.

Sarah had been waiting for Ben before entering the sub and was so caught off guard by the comment that she broke out in a huge laugh that echoed through the hangar. "Some family you have there, Ben," she said with a huge grin.

"Oh yeah, they are really wonderful!" he tried to say sarcastically, but meant it with great affection. Both of Ben's children waved as the two disappeared into the Pegasus.

LAUNCH

"Get set people, we are headed out!" Jake exclaimed, as Ben and Sarah entered the bridge.

The bridge was pristine, and Sarah noted the strong 'freshly printed' smell as she entered. The command deck was spacious and modern with the curved front glass flowing from floor to ceiling. It was equipped with up to seven stations, including the captain's command chair. There were two forward stations situated evenly to the left and right, followed by the captain's chair that was directly centered on the bridge. The forward stations had full swivel chairs with 360-degree holo-controls that followed the user's motion. The chairs could also retract flush into the floor. This allowed for incredible versatility within the space and allowed the crew member to use the station from a standing or sitting position. Reinforced NIC glass was common throughout the structure of the entire Pegasus, and the bridge held an especially impressive view. Glass formed all the way around the hammerhead shape atop the ship. If you stood on either side, you could look all the way down the hull to the stern of the vessel. Where the hammer shape ended, there were two more consoles that were attached along the outer walls. They were flowing curved desks with monitors and various control displays. Each of the back stations could be operated by a single person or could be configured to include an additional chair and workspace for another crew member.

Ben activated one of the second seats along the starboard side and sat next to Kiah at her science station. Every chair was equipped with a five-point harness and he strapped in for the journey ahead.

"Captain, I have checked and everything is aboard and visually verified," Sarah reported.

"Excellent!" Jake exclaimed. "Let's huddle up!" as he swiveled in his chair to face the rest of the crew. Everyone focused on Jake as he began to speak. "Looking at each of you now, I know we have the right people for this mission. I see dedication and determination inside each of you. Despite only knowing some of you for a short while, I can tell we have a fine crew." His face reflected his calm. "We are about to embark on a journey of great discovery that could reshape humankind's understanding of life within our own solar system. Very few individuals will ever experience the type of mysteries that could unfold before us. I can see in each of your eyes that you all appreciate the magnitude of this." He paused for a moment. "Now, let's get to Europa and find out what is below that ice!"

EV gave a very enthusiastic fist pump. "Yes!"

"That's the spirit!" Jake let out a laugh and smiled.

Outside, hundreds of magnetic ropes descended from the shuttle, Resolute, and connected their tips to the hull of the Pegasus. The shuttle reeled in each of the ropes as the Pegasus was smoothly lifted off the deck and locked into place underneath the transport shuttle's hull, as they were secure for transport. The Pegasus was built to fly through the water, not space, and lacked astrological propulsion. That being said, her hull was designed to withstand enormous pressure and would keep the crew safe in the vacuum of space. This jump through the Sol system would be the crew's first step on this long journey. The Resolute lurched forward, with Pegasus perfectly tucked underneath, as it cruised to the jump point at Earth Dock. Only stations had enough power to fold space and send ships to other points within the same star system. Jumping between systems required coordinated efforts between multiple stations within both star systems.

On the bridge of the Pegasus, the seven crew members were strapped in and watching through the forward NIC glass as the Resolute prepared to navigate the fold created in space by the station and make the jump. Jake saw a dot appear on the main heads-up display that overlaid the front glass, with the flashing tag indicating the current position of Europa. The flashing tag blinked faster as they approached the fold. Finally, a massive circle appeared on the glass, outlining where Europa would appear in just a few seconds. Jake could hear the captain aboard the Resolute start the countdown. "Transition in 5, 4, 3, 2, 1.... Mark." Jake could feel the spin up and pull as the shuttle flew through the fold that tore through local space, using the signal on the other side as a guide.

Jake felt the rush as his body traversed the gap. There still was nothing like the thrill of instantly leaping across space to a new place. He had been holding his breath and slowly exhaled as the rush subsided. With her icy beauty, Europa filled the front glass of the Pegasus. The angelic moon was stunning, and wore a very light green dress of ice that gracefully covered her entire surface. The ice looked like it had folds and contours just begging to be explored. Jupiter lay just over her horizon, peering over the shoulder of Europa with the sunlight illuminating the pair as they journeyed together within our solar system. The crew admired the view as they each caught their breath.

"Everyone still with us?" Jake asked, after a long pause.

The crew sounded off letting Jake know they each were ready to start this adventure.

"Good," Jake replied. "The asteroid is due for impact in just under ten minutes. After that, EI intel suggests it will be another few hours before it melts a hole through all that surface ice. That gap will get the Pegasus into the water. We will need some luck here, so hopefully Tyche will provide," Jake finished.

Just then, the massive space rock, Tyche, came into view through the front glass. The front display marked the object with a red indicator flag, and a countdown timer appeared underneath. It looked deceptively small through the front optic, but the crew knew how destructive this object's impact would be on Europa's soft green icy surface. With a nickel-iron core, the Tyche impact would be tremendous.

"Let's get a better look." Jake tapped on the console to the right of his chair and connected to the observer drone camera that was launched to watch the event. The heads-up display overlaying the entire front NIC glass changed, displaying the video feed from the drone. The crew watched in awe for a few minutes as the rock hurtled toward its target. The 'burn' time for Tyche would start very close to the surface since Europa was only layered in a thin atmosphere, but it would be enough to really heat things up.

The countdown was ticking down to the final seconds, and Sarah found that she was holding her breath. "3, 2, 1..." A sudden flash instantly filled the screen, and the drone lost its feed. The front NIC glass automatically became tinted to protect the crew's eyes. In a very literal sense, this was starting the adventure with a BANG, thought Jake as he smiled.

The darkness faded from the front glass just as a compression wave hit both ships. The ships clung together like scared children but pressed forward through the void of space. The Resolute spooled up its chemical engines, heading toward the site of the impact.

Sarah and Jake started to talk about the mission ahead, and Ben listened, occasionally chiming in. Kiah, however, became lost in her own thoughts. She thought about how this trip had happened very suddenly. Sarah, EV, and Kiah had been stationed on the Earth Dock for about a year before this mission came up. Sarah had recently thrown EV a birthday party at a favorite local bar, and Kiah was invited. She had brought along her boyfriend, Melindro. She had met Mel six months ago, and things had been going very well. That night he proposed to Kiah, and she remembered how he looked stricken when she said she would need to think about it. She knew she would want to marry and have children someday, and he seemed like the perfect guy. But she also knew she didn't want to stop exploring the universe, and that calling would lead her away sooner or later. She rued over the fact that it was sooner. A brief thought that she might not see him again skipped through her head, but she quickly skipped it out again. This moment was not the time for doubt, and she could not give in to that thought.

Just then, EV said, "Damn!" in a long-drawn-out exclamation. The crew looked as a giant plume of ice and water vapor started to extend into the far reaches of space. Europa's gravity was even less than Earth's moon, and with the thin Europa atmosphere, the water particulates would not stop any time soon. The sunlight was glinting off the ice crystals making each crystal shine and glimmer in the darkness of space as the cloud expanded. The cloud looked like it was completely made up of diamonds.

"It's breathtaking," Ashley said in close to a whisper.

"I hope this isn't the most impressive thing we see on this trip," Jake said, as he smiled.

"Even if it is, this trip still might be worth it," Kiah replied.

"Kiah, are you getting readings from the impact site and do you have an estimate on how long it will take for the hole to form?" Jake asked. Kiah was on the science consoles to Jake's right and received the sensor data on her screens.

"Yeah, it looks like the projections were right on the mark," Kiah confirmed. "We should be able to enter the water in the next hour or so."

"Great! What do you guys want to do until then?" EV laughed.

THE BALLET

The two intertwined ships began their final approach toward the massive crater. The Pegasus was just about to start her first mission and the Resolute was just dropping off a friend before flying to Jupiter Station for her next assignment.

Space gave way to the thin Europa atmosphere as they descended into a massive cloud of erupting vapor from the superheated impact zone. Ice particles bombarded the Pegasus obstructing any view as frost crusted against the NIC glass. The rush of air shuttered against the hull, and the noise was deafening. Water vapor of vastly different temperatures rapidly expanded all around the pair of ships. EV knew that the Resolute's pilot was flying by instruments as they approached the drop-off point through the elemental chaos. As they dropped further into the 'hole' the fog became thick, and darkness enveloped both ships.

"Skipper, helm shows we are now sixty meters over the ocean pool," EV reported.

The crew could hear the wine of the shuttle's engines as it maintained its altitude and prepared to lower the Pegasus. As smoothly as it was secured before, now the Pegasus descended into the alien ocean below. Europa's water lapped in a slow-motion dance across the Pegasus's hull as it displaced the great sea. The moon's gravity, ever so slight, made the entry as graceful as a ballet. Water slowly surrounded the Pegasus as she nestled into place.

"EV, report," Jake ordered.

"Skipper, we are clear. The Resolute is letting us go now," EV reported.

With a 'thunk' the crew felt the mag ropes disengage. There was a momentary weightless feeling as the Pegasus slipped into the slow waves. Ocean currents began to flow, for the first time, over the great leviathan class submersible.

"Alright, just as we planned EV, take us down twenty meters and hold," Jake ordered.

"Aye, Skipper," EV said, as he entered the commands into the navigation console.

"Oh, and while you are at it, can we pop on some outside lights? It might be nice to see where we are going," Jake added.

As EV keyed the control, the Pegasus lit up like a torch in a dark cave. Light spilled into places that had only ever known darkness. The water was surprisingly clear, considering an asteroid had come through only minutes earlier. There was not much to see except the immense sheet of ice looming above them, with a massive asteroid-sized hole punched through it. There were no visible signs of life outside. The Pegasus slowly descended to twenty meters under the opening. The crater was already beginning to freeze as ice formed over the ocean's surface.

Jake knew another surface support vessel would be along shortly with equipment and parts to begin constructing the new ice/ocean interface outpost, ensuring a passage to the outside surface. This passage would be their way to resupply and swap crews once their six months were completed. For now, they would remain around the crater and ensure everything was operating normally. The intent was that the Pegasus would remain on Europa for the rest of her days, exploring these waters. The crew would give their TV interviews, which each individual was obligated to provide in exchange for some public funding. This mission was a scientific curiosity, and most people would be following this story. Luckily after these first interviews, the crew would be left to do their work. Any discoveries would be subject to review and approval through EI before being released to the public. Once the mission was completed, the crew would be debriefed, and only then could they share their journey with everyone.

"Skipper, we have reached twenty meters and are holding," EV reported from the front-port navigation station.

"Excellent, EV! Crew report!" Jake exclaimed.

From the back-port engineering station Ashley piped, "Gravity decking online, pressure on the hull is nominal, reactor is stable and all checks are green."

Sarah reported from the front-starboard station, "No signs of motion or larger lifeforms yet. Water readings show some bacteria and microbes that are consistent with the previous water samples taken from Europa, but nothing else yet, Captain."

Kiah chimed in from the back-starboard station, "The crew from the support vessel Marybeth reports they will be starting work within the next few minutes and don't see any current difficulties with keeping the passage open above us."

"Excellent! Kiah, please send a message to the Resolute's captain to thank him for the ride," Jake ordered.

"Yes, Captain, message sent," Kiah said.

Jake turned to face Ben and Dyami, seated at the stations along the back of the bridge. "Ben, I want you to go check out the hydroponics and ensure nothing got jostled around down there. Dyami, please head down to environmental and ensure the air recycler and water filtration systems are working correctly. We might want some air to breathe and water to drink tonight."

"Yes sir," they both said in unison as they headed to the door at the back of the bridge.

"Oh, and don't forget Ben, we have interviews with Sol TV in just under two hours, so be sure you are up on the bridge and ready," Jake said. Ben nodded his acknowledgment as he left the room.

"That was some ride," Ben said to Dyami as they left the bridge and walked to the lift. "Have you traveled in space much?"

"Some, but I've most recently been working around the oceans on Earth," Dyami replied. Then he added, "How about you?"

Ben shrugged, "Yeah, my kids were born on Septimus and we had been there for years until recently. We came back to Earth because of my wife's job. While on Earth Dock, I got the call for this mission. I have to admit it was a bit unexpected."

Dyami nodded in understanding as they both stepped into the small lift. "What does your wife do?" he asked.

"Right now, she's an ancient languages professor. Angi is brilliant and has been pulled in various directions throughout her career. I think teaching is her way to settle things down," Ben said with a grin. "What about you, are you married?"

Dyami suddenly had a distant look in his eyes and replied softly, "No. Not anymore."

The lift smoothly came to a stop on the second deck and both men exited. They walked silently for a few seconds until Ben and Dyami reached their respective locations. Dyami broke the silence to return the conversation to business, "Ben, let me know if there is anything you need me to adjust with the water flow and temperature cycling to the hydroponics lab."

"Thanks, Dyami. I'll let you know," Ben replied.

Pressing the button to his right, Ben cycled the door to the hydroponics lab and entered. The half-pipe hydroponic garden started below Ben's knees and arched toward the lab's ceiling. Ben had engineered this growing configuration for his old home on Septimus and was relieved and pleased that it seemed to work well aboard the Pegasus with only slight modification. Each plant was set on a horizontal tray that hung from a curved platform. Ben could easily reach each piece of potentially grown food in this configuration.

Ben keyed the com, "Captain, hydroponics looks good."

Ben heard the faint hum as Dyami turned on the water filtration from the adjacent room. He saw water running through small tubes as it entered from the next room. Tubes spread to individual plants on the platform. The whole system kept the individual plants perfectly watered and their environmental conditions adjusted based upon their real-time needs, using the formulas Ben had calculated for optimal growth.

The Pegasus was built to utilize the hydroponics lab to produce fresh fruits and vegetables to supplement the dry goods. Future meals might include spinach, tomato, mushrooms, potatoes, and green chili if his plants could survive and thrive within the environment Ben curated.

Ben thought about his time working in the garden at his family's old home. He thought about Angi, then reflected for a moment on his decision to come on this mission. Life had its challenges, and Ben had been feeling the need for change. When Richard had contacted him, this seemed like the opportunity he had been looking for. Now, being so far from home, he felt unsure. Maybe it was something he had seen in Dyami's eyes. Change can have unexpected consequences that leave an individual longing for an unreachable past.

On the bridge, Ashley was ready to deploy a remote drone. She pressed the green launch indicator on the console under the heading 'Bobb'. A video monitor on her console came to life as it received and displayed the live video feed from the remote drone. A screen indicator began flashing (five meters port, default) as the drone positioned itself along the midriff of the Pegasus on the port side. Ashley stood up and walked over toward the port window on the bridge to see if she could visually confirm the craft was in the correct position. Through the window, there was black, with the exception of an intimidating ice sheet above. However, Ashley easily spotted the Bobb drone, with its red and white fishing bobber colors and egg shape, being easily distinguished from the rest of the dark scene. It was easy to see how the Bobb drone got its nickname from its appearance.

Ashley shivered as she looked out through the icy water just centimeters from where she now stood. She turned back toward her station and saw EV standing there, peering at her console. Ashley shot him a questioning look, and EV retreated without a word. It was obvious his curiosity had gotten the best of him. Ashley didn't let it show but she smiled a bit inside at his child-like wonder.

Ashley returned to her station and began the transfer of Bobb's controls from the Pegasus to Earth Dock. Through the console, Ashley heard Richard's voice pipe through. "Great, Ashley, confirming we have control of Bobb." Bobb swiveled around the Pegasus and began inspecting the craft from the outside. Richard did a quick visual verification of the ship in her new environment. The video footage from Bobb would be part of the Sol TV broadcast later that evening.

SOL TV LIVE FROM EUROPA

"Tonight, Sol TV is proud to present an exclusive interview with the crew exploring the icy depths of Europa," a disembodied TV announcer's voice said as opening news animations filled the broadcast feed. "In this special presentation of Sol TV, we will take a closer look at their mission and speak with the crew aboard the Pegasus." The screen flashed over as the animations ended, and a familiar face greeted the audience.

"Hello, I am Frank Stone, and thank you for joining us this evening. If you have been following our story over the last few days, you will remember that this mission was only made possible by the giant asteroid, Tyche, that recently impacted Europa. This asteroid burned a hole through the thick ice sheet covering the moon's entire surface. Today, I am happy to report that the Pegasus and her crew have completed the first step in their mission and are now in the Europa Ocean," Frank reported.

Frank shifted into a more serious tone. "Tonight, we will bring you exclusive interviews with the crew. Joining me now via com feed from the bridge of the Pegasus, Captain Jake Riley. Thanks for joining us, Jake."

The broadcast displayed a split screen with Frank on the left and Jake to the right. "Thanks, Frank. We are excited to be here," Jake replied.

"So, let me ask you, Captain, have you found anything yet?" Frank said, as his tone shifted again into excitement.

"Well, we haven't seen any alien whales, if that is what you were hoping for, Frank," Jake cracked a smile. "But we have already confirmed finding some microbial life. We need to do some tests to determine if we have any new discoveries. So, it's too early to tell."

Frank nodded, but had a mild look of disappointment. "Captain, please tell me more about your goals on this mission."

"Well, the current plan is to stay around this initial area, near our insertion point, for a day or two to see if we have any hits on our microphones, motion sensors, or visuals that would indicate where we might look for new lifeforms. Then, if we don't find anything that sparks our interest around these parts, we will be diving farther into the depths," Jake replied.

Frank nodded, "How far down can the Pegasus go? I mean, you have already found your way through a massive ice sheet. How much deeper is the ocean on Europa?"

"Well Frank, this ocean is another sixty kilometers deep. So, it's a very long way down into the abyss," Jake replied.

"Captain, correct me if I am wrong, but the Marianas Trench on Earth is just over ten kilometers deep in most places, and you are talking about six times that depth?" Frank had a concerned look on his face.

Jake nodded in confirmation. "That's correct, Frank. We have tested vessels like the Pegasus in similar conditions on other worlds, so we are confident that she will take us where we need to go."

Frank looked relieved. "Excellent, one last question for you, Captain. What is the plan if you find a new lifeform?" Frank asked.

Jake paused for a moment choosing his next words. "Well, that will depend on what we find. I guarantee this crew will do their best to document and learn all we can. We intend to study, without unnecessary interference, any life that we find on this beautiful moon. We are metaphorically only going to leave footprints."

"Thanks again for your time Captain. It has been a pleasure to interview you tonight," Frank wrapped up the interview with his smooth practiced lines.

The graphics and disembodied voice returned. "Coming up, we will ask a few questions of Ben Rapner, the doctor serving aboard the Pegasus." The broadcast flashed a picture of Ben with his family as the voice-over continued.

"Finally, we will have an exclusive interview with Sarah Triv. She will speak to us about her mission aboard the Pegasus." Scenes of Sarah on a small boat surrounded by relaxed orca filled the screen as the voice-over continued.

The graphics came to a close, and the voice echoed familiar words. "Exclusively on Sol TV"

"Welcome back to Sol TV. I'm Ara Ayad," Ara's name flashed across the broadcast. Ara was beloved, a comforting presence on Sol TV for over a decade.

"I'm here tonight with Doctor Benjamin Rapner." Ara turned slightly to face the display in the studio. "Thank you for speaking with us, Ben."

Ben's face appeared on the broadcast screen next to Ara. It was apparent to most viewers that Ben was nervous as an awkward smile possessed his face.

"The pleasure is mine, thank you," Ben replied.

"Ben, correct me if I'm wrong, but you will serve in three capacities on this mission. Can you elaborate on that a bit more?" Ara's words were smooth and comforting as she conveyed a sense of calm.

"Yeah, I'm hoping that my primary role here will be the biological study of undiscovered life," Ben continued, smiling uncontrollably for the camera. He still felt awkward, but at this point, his smile was on full auto-pilot. Ben continued, "In addition to that, I will help grow some of the hydroponic fruits and vegetables we will be dining on. Also, I am a practicing physician by trade and will fill the role of medical officer." Finally, Ben regained enough control to turn his smile into a more subtle and distinguished nod as he finished speaking. After that awkward volley, Ben relaxed, focusing on Ara.

"Wow, sounds like you have many responsibilities on this voyage, and they will need you out there. Do you think you will need to treat any of the crew as a medical officer?" Ara asked.

"Well, we all hope not. But everyone is glad to have a doctor around when they need one," Ben replied.

Ara nodded to Ben reassuringly as she spoke again, "You're right about that. But, before I let you go, I just have one final question tonight for you, Ben," Ara paused for a few seconds to capture the moment. "Ben, what do you hope to find on Europa?"

Ben carefully considered the question. "I want to find an undiscovered tapestry of life here on Europa, each thread woven into a part of the larger picture. I want to find something amazing here that helps us gain knowledge of where we fit with other living organisms in our universe. It's important to me to share those discoveries with my children and anyone longing for that deeper understanding. I'm fortunate and truly humbled by the opportunity to be here."

Ara let the full impact resonate with the viewers. Ara softly said,

"Thank you, Ben." as the broadcast faded to black.

"Finally, tonight, we have a very special guest," Ara Ayad appeared again on the broadcast. "Many of you will remember Sarah from her enchanting relationship with a pod of orca off the coast of Argentina," Ara said with a warm smile. "Joining me now from Europa is Doctor Sarah Triv. Welcome, Sarah."

Sarah appeared on the screen with a warm, confident smile. Sarah had seen her share of media attention over the years and knew animal conservation efforts everywhere benefited from these types of interviews. But, to Sarah, the cause was always more important than the attention. "Thank you very much, Ara. I'm so glad to be speaking with you again."

"Sarah, before we start talking about your mission aboard the Pegasus, I am sure many viewers are wondering how Keenan is doing?" Ara asked.

The broadcast cut to a two-year-old video clip showing Sarah in an orange ocean kayak with yellow flared graphics. Just below her, beneath the ocean's surface, was a massive adult male orca. In the clip, viewers saw the enormous mammal leisurely swimming upside down, showing his underside to his friend Sarah. His white belly was flanked by distinct patterns of black in the nearly still water as he slowly swam by. Smooth rocks distorted by the Atlantic were the backdrop to the majestic scene.

Sarah smiled fondly, as she remembered the many personal encounters she had with Keenan. The relationship wasn't something she had expected at the time and she tried very hard to study but not interfere with the animals she researched. However, Keenan was a bit too curious and smart for Sarah's evasive tactics and would gently work his way toward any ship she was aboard. He always did so carefully, as if he understood that he needed to show his peaceful and inquisitive nature to Sarah. Day after day, the trust and respect blossomed. Keenan seemed to know their friendship would be special.

"Ara, I was able to visit him a few months ago, and he and his family are doing really well," Sarah said as she reflected on that moment. "They added a new family member in July, and now Keenan has another new baby sister named Lulu."

Even though Ara had previously heard the news, joyful emotion still washed across her face. "That is wonderful. Thank you for sharing the update," Ara said, expressing her gratitude. "Now you're on a new mission, Sarah. Can you tell us more about the work you will be doing aboard the Pegasus?"

Sarah paused for a moment to refocus and started. "Of course. Things have happened pretty fast, and it feels like I have barely had time to take it all in," Sarah explained. "For a long time, science and story writers have wondered what was possibly living here on Europa. To be here now is a truly humbling experience. I'm not sure what we will find on this journey or if there is any great discovery to be made out here. But what I do know is that I will come back with some answers." Sarah paused for a moment. "Ara, I am here to find new life, and I hope that dream becomes a reality on this mission. Often the universe unveils something miraculous, and I hope I know where to look when a mystery is revealed." Her excitement was tangible, even over the broadcast.

"Your stories have touched me, Sarah, and I truly hope you find what you are looking for in the depths." Ara nodded, vicariously taking in Sarah's situation. "You have been a wonderful guest, as always. Is there anything else you want to add before we go?" Ara asked.

Sarah thought about that for a moment. "I would like to say thank you to everyone involved in making this journey possible, including all your viewers. Without everyone's trust and support, this mission wouldn't have happened. Thank you all for allowing me an opportunity to unravel the mysteries of this beautiful place." Sarah spoke through her heart, hoping that showed in her words.

"We all look forward to the stories you will tell once you return. Thank you again for your time, Sarah," Ara concluded.

The interview was over and the camera indicator light shut off as Sarah stood silently in the Pegasus briefing room for a few moments. *It's time to find out what's out here*, Sarah thought as she left the room.

PASS THE SALT

The Pegasus crew decided to meet in the galley at 18:00 for dinner. The outside environment held no indication of the time, so everything was synced to the time at Earth Dock, using Greenwich mean time. It was perpetually dark in this vast unexplored ocean, except for the light that came from the Pegasus.

In order to utilize the grown food that would come from the hydroponics bay, someone on board needed to prepare the evening meals. Dyami loved cooking and had volunteered for that duty aboard the Pegasus. There was something he found fulfilling in serving a hot meal to the crew. The galley was well equipped and wrapped around a large round white dining table with comfortable, matching swivel chairs. Dyami softly hummed a tune from his childhood as he cooked the meal.

Just before the hour, the crew from the bridge made their way down the hallway, past the crew quarters, and entered the galley.

"It has been pretty quiet outside since we arrived. We have not seen anything move or heard any sounds apart from the activity on the ship," Sarah explained to Ashley. "However, many times in an open ocean, so far away from land, you won't see much activity. It's a bit like being in the middle of a desert."

Ashley had a slight hint of disappointment on her face. "Yeah, I know. It just seems a bit anti-climactic that we come blasting all the way out to Europa, and all we have seen is ice."

Sarah smiled and asked, "Have you had the opportunity to do animal research before this mission?"

Ashley shook her head. "No, none at all. I usually end up stuck in front of an engineering console. It can be hard to pry myself away at times," Ashley said.

Jake followed the two women as they entered the Galley. His eyes lingered for a moment on Ashley.

"Yeah, nature documentaries make the search for animals seem easy. But more often than not, it requires patience and even more patience," Sarah said as she slid into a chair.

Ashley filled two glasses with water from the tap and handed one to Sarah as she took a seat. Jake also filled a glass and sat across from the women.

"Do you think anything will respond when we start mimicking other marine animal sounds?" Ashley asked as she looked at Sarah.

"Maybe, if we are lucky. It would make sense that an ocean animal would respond to new sounds within their environment. Many marine creatures use sound for communications or to locate food over long distances. In fact, a blue whale's song can carry over sixteen-hundred kilometers in good conditions. The whales even know how much time has passed by the distance the call had traveled. I'm hoping that we can attract a curious passerby," Sarah said.

"I'm not sure how far the sounds can travel here. There are many factors, like the water salinity, that would play a role in how far the Pegasus can send our calls," Jake said.

Sarah nodded in agreement and grinned as she remembered something. "Yeah, I always loved listening to music and even learned to play the cello when I was a child. One night after a particularly frustrating day waiting for any animals to appear, I was sitting out on the stern of the ship listening to some music. As I looked over, a small group of sea lions suddenly appeared. They seemed to move, almost in a dance, matching the rhythm of the music. It was magical, and I can still see them when I close my eyes. They moved in perfect unison." Sarah closed her eyes for a second, the room falling quiet.

"Do you think they were responding to the music?" Dyami asked.

"I'm sure of it!" Sarah said.

A timer went off on Dyami's tab, and he pulled a salmon from the oven. A wonderful smokey aroma filled the room, but it did give Dyami pause, making him wonder how it would smell in the morning. He would need to check the air scrubbers after dinner.

As Dyami plated the food EV and Kiah strolled into the galley and found empty seats.

"So, are we going to introduce the local wildlife to Johann Sebastian Bach tomorrow?" EV asked, chuckling to himself.

"You know me too well," Sarah shot back. "I have always gotten a good response from Suite No. 1 in G Major. Back me up here, Kiah," she pleaded with her other longtime friend.

"EV you know Sarah has documented evidence that shows that music does attract certain species," Kiah said.

"That's true. All I'm saying is we could mix it up a bit; maybe the life here likes metal," EV joked.

With everyone seated and food distributed, Jake took a moment to say, "Thank you all for your hard work today. Everything was executed exactly as expected, and it's because of everyone's fine attention to the details. I know that each of you cares about our success here, and after today we have shown we can take the necessary steps to get the job done. I'm proud to be a part of this crew." Jake turned toward Dyami, "The only thing unexpected is how good this food is. You impress me every single time, Dyami. Thank you," Jake nodded to his friend.

There was a stunned silence as individuals who had never tried Dyami's cooking, realized his culinary abilities. "Wow, Dyami! Where did you learn to cook like this?" Kiah asked. "My mother taught me most of what I know," Dyami explained. "I make do with what I have in the kitchen, but it is easy when you start with items you have cooked many times," Dyami said as he indicated the plate in front of him.

"Kiah, I have seen this guy make a single can of corn taste good with a few twigs and some dirt," Jake said as he grinned.

"Actually, that was just salt," Dyami admitted as he chuckled.

"Well, whatever it was, it tasted better then it should've," Jake said as he joined the laugh.

"So, Captain, what is the plan after dinner?" Sarah asked.

Jake cleared his throat before saying, "It's ok to call me Jake, especially at dinner. The dining room is a place where each of us can relax and express our thoughts. But again, just be respectful, and I'm sure that will not be an issue with this group." Jake continued, "To answer your question, Sarah, after dinner, I want to do one more check of the systems and sensors. That might seem like overkill, but I want to be sure everything is working properly before we close our eyes tonight." Looking over at Dyami, Jake added, "Dyami, I know you have been busy up here, but how are you on your checks down in environmental?"

"They look good; everything is in the green. If the air mix or pressure has any problems, the ship will send out an alert. I'm keeping an eye on it but expect everything to stay in the nominal range," Dyami reported.

"Excellent! Reg at Earth Dock is on Bobb patrol through tonight. He will alert us if he sees any activity on the drone camera," Jake finished his thought. "Anyway, enough business for now. Does someone have a good story I haven't heard before?" Jake looked over to the four individuals he hadn't served with.

"I have one for you," EV piped up.

"By all means," Jake smiled.

"So, my friend Mark and I went up to the mountains to fish. It had been a gorgeous day, but we didn't catch one… damn… thing… We had decided to call it a day and returned to our tents. After we wrapped up with dinner and some fireside time, we turned in for the night. It must have been a few hours later because I was in a deep slumber, but then I heard this noise that startled me awake. It was a loud cracking and another distinctive sound…." EV made a low deep breathing sound that seemed to erupt from his diaphragm, imitating what he had heard. "I knew right away it was a bear! At first, I lay there, hoping that it would just wander away. Then claws…. scraped against Mark's tent." At this point, EV acted out the scene, "Then I hear a loud, frustrated ROAR. I nearly leapt out of my skin. I jumped out of my sleeping bag and stumbled to my feet, cracking my head against the lantern. I tore open my tent and saw this massive grizzly ripping apart Mark's tent. There was red everywhere, and I'm freaking out! Without thinking, I started shouting and running toward the bear, desperately trying to scare it off! The bear took one look at me and bolted into the woods dragging Mark's tent behind it," EV pauses. "My mind was this blur as I was trying to figure out if Mark was being dragged off into the woods by the bear. I mustered up all the courage I had and was going to run after the bear to save my friend. Then, I hear a voice behind me say, 'I guess I shouldn't have left out that bottle of ketchup,' as Mark wanders back into the camp," EV said as he finished his story.

Faces of horror turned into laughs as Jake, Ashley, Dyami, and Ben realized the entirety of the situation. Even Sarah and Kiah laughed despite hearing that story for the one-hundredth time.

"EV, I still love that story," Kiah said, grinning from ear to ear.

"Yeah, I thought Mark was a goner but he apparently had gotten up before the bear arrived. Then when he came back, he just started watching the show," EV grinned.

"So, what about you, Jake?" EV asked. "Tell us how you got here."

"You really expect me to follow up after a story like that? Seriously? Anyway, to answer your question, I started after attending Earth Initiative Academy. I just sorta followed the path and started flying missions for the EI when I was in my twenties. Gunships mostly, doing sector patrols," Jake continued. "At first, it was great! Flying cool ships with a galactic backdrop is a cadet's dream. But after a while, I started to realize that there wasn't much out there. Every day started to look the same," there was a slight twinge in Jake's voice as he remembered the many dull hours in space alone. "So, I got a transfer back to Earth and started requesting assignments where I felt like I could make a difference. I guess someone appreciated what I was doing, and I ended up here."

By then, everyone had an empty plate in front of them and appreciated their full bellies and the interesting company.

"Well, I'm going to get a few more things done before I pass out," Jake said as he picked up his dishes and placed them in the wash.

PING

S arah was the first to get up the next morning and grabbed water and a nutrient bar before heading to the bridge. These extra chewy bars would be a staple of morning life aboard the Pegasus. It was just before 06:00 and the only sound was the airflow from the environmental fans. Almost all the rooms and crew quarters were lined with windows, but the only light was coming from within the Pegasus and a few exterior lights that reflected off the ice sheet above. Much of the outside world was hidden as this light faded into the depths. Nothing moved outside beyond a few stray bubbles. The science and engineering stations displayed various readings, but even they didn't disturb the quiet of this morning. The two front bridge stations had their holo-control projectors shut off while the crew was away.

Sarah approached the front of the bridge glass and peered out. She marveled at how fast this mission had occurred. She literally was standing on the bridge of an advanced submersible staring off into the alien ocean of Europa. What was once just a writer's fantasy was now her reality, and she savored the moment.

"Good morning," Dyami said softly as he wandered onto the bridge.

Sarah smiled and said, "Good morning, Dyami. I hope you slept well."

Dyami came up beside her and peered through the glass into the ocean beyond. "I couldn't stop thinking about what might be out here. This is the most exciting mission that I have ever experienced. Do we have anything yet?" he asked with some hope in his tone.

"Nothing yet. It has still been pretty quiet..." Sarah's words were interrupted by a blip of noise from the science station.

The com channel cracked. "Pegasus, we just picked up some movement outside," Richard's voice said as it came through the feed.

Sarah rushed over to her station at the front of the bridge. Her station's holo-controls came to life, and she could already tell the sensors had lost the signal. She was too late. She stared at the readings, wishing that whatever 'it' was, 'it' would return.

The sensors had an extensive range, about a kilometer, with both motion sensors and life detection sensors. They could even pick up tiny electrical fields given off by animals. The technology was based on the abilities of sharks, which had been finding prey using electrical impulses for millions of years. Once again, mother nature had provided an almost supernatural sense that later humans emulated with technology.

Sarah decided to retrace the encounter through the sensor logs. As she stepped through the timeline, she saw something come up just within the range of the sensors. Then it leveled out for a very brief time, only to return to the depths a moment later. The whole encounter lasted just four seconds.

"What did we get?" Jake asked as he approached Sarah's station on the bridge.

"We picked up some motion on the sensors! Only for a few seconds, but it was something!" Sarah beamed with excitement.

"What do you make of it? Do you think it is worth following?" Jake asked, quickly taking note of the arrival of Ashley and EV on the bridge.

"Yeah, I think so," Sarah said excitedly. "We didn't get anything clear, but something definitely moved!"

"Alright, in that case, I didn't come here to sit around," Jake stated. "Let's ride out and see what's down there!" Jake said as his excitement started to build. "EV take us down to where we detected the movement," Jake ordered.

"Aye, Skipper," EV replied as he slipped into his chair.

The Pegasus glided down through the cold clear water. Sarah watched like a hawk for anything to reappear on the sensors. She knew they would find something. She could feel there was something here. Europa held so many secrets, and she wouldn't go home until she knew what they were.

There was more silence.

"We have reached the position where the signal was," EV reported.

"Alright, let's hold for a minute and see if our shadow shows up," Jake said. He closely examined the frigid water through the front NIC glass. It wasn't likely he was going to see anything before the motion sensors picked it up, but that would not stop him from trying.

The outside remained still and without any signs of life, only icy water was beyond the glass. The entire crew had gathered on the bridge in silence. The crew held their breath as they all waited for something to happen. The excitement of discovery hung thick in the air.

Still, nothing.

Jake softly broke the silence in almost a whisper, "EV, descend another kilometer. Let's see what happens if we go a little deeper."

The Pegasus descended even further through the black. She was the only speck of light in the whole ocean, diving into the dark depths of the raven's eye.

A sound emanated from the sensors, and the chime broke the silence. "Ping!" There was something here! The red blip appeared just inside the sensor's sphere. "It's alive!" Sarah gasped, as she saw the bioelectrical signal.

"EV, stay on it!" Jake shouted with excitement.

Again, the blip disappeared back into the depths.

Even further, the Pegasus descended. They were approaching seven kilometers in depth the next time the signal returned. This time, it wasn't alone.

"Captain, I am picking up three signals now," Sarah beamed.

"There you are! EV, slow our descent," Jake said with a grin.

"Aye, Skipper," EV acknowledged.

"Keep her steady; we don't want to scare our guests away," Jake instructed.

Sarah's face suddenly turned from glee into a look of concern. "Captain, I'm detecting over a hundred lifeforms ascending directly below us," Sarah said with shock.

"EV stop us here," Jake barked. The crew was on the edge of their seats as the event unfolded. As Sarah watched her display, the entire sensor sphere below the ship lit up with signs of life, all approaching frighteningly fast.

Richard's voice came through the com channel again, "We are sending in Bobb!"

Bobb, the drone, descended past the Pegasus to intercept the signals and try to get a first look at what they were. Sarah felt nervous excitement and tension build in her stomach. This was the moment of discovery. Suddenly, Bobb spotted them, and the camera lens was filled with the creatures as they rushed past in a blur. Every creature flew passed Bobb as they headed toward the Pegasus. Their silvery white skin flashed in the light as they gracefully swam around Bobb. They were about the size of a shoe box and had a fat torpedo shape. Each had three emerald-colored orbs that might have been eyes on their head. Additional details were hard to make out as they flashed by.

The alien creatures rose from the depths, surrounding the Pegasus. They had four aquatic wings along each side of the body and beat in rhythm as the creatures moved through the water. Intricate skin patterns in deep greens and blues were unique to each individual and fanned out upon each wing. In addition, they each possessed a small tail that ran underneath their back wings along their lateral line, and it steered them smoothly through the water, matching the shades of blue and green.

Each creature seemed to regard the Pegasus briefly before descending into the blackness below. They moved with such grace and speed that Sarah was awe-struck by their coordination and beauty.

As quickly as it had begun, the encounter ended. Jake watched as the last few stragglers descended into the deep ocean.

"That was exhilarating!" EV said as the last of the creatures sank below the sphere of the sensors.

Sarah looked over to Kiah's station as she examined the video footage of the encounter. "No one has seen anything like these creatures," Kiah said excitedly.

"Can we get some water samples and..." Sarah was interrupted as the sensors on her console lit up again. The creatures ascended again, but this time they were further aft. Again, the wave of creatures came up and then headed back into the depths. This grouping was smaller than the last, but still hundreds of animals.

"Sarah, what do you make of their behavior?" Jake asked as the second group disappeared from the sensors.

"I have no idea. It is far too early to know," Sarah said after pondering the question for a moment.

"You don't think they are just coming up to check us out?" EV asked.

"Anything is possible. Dyami, can you see if we can catch something interesting in some localized water samples?" Sarah asked.

Dyami was already headed to the lift as she spoke. "Let me guess; you are looking for some alien leavings. Correct?"

Sarah smiled, "It's almost like you read my mind!"

"I will call you if I find any E.T. poop," he chuckled as he walked off the bridge.

Dyami used the lift and descended to the marine lab that was located on deck two. The lab was directly under the bridge. It also had NIC glass that wrapped around the front of the ship, and a person could see the surroundings just about as well as from the bridge. Two large aquariums lined the interior walls where the lab narrowed. These specialized aquariums could be accessed by the lab and a specialized access lock along the outside of the hull.

Dyami was glad to see two small glass tubes containing samples of outside water already waiting for him. He had the foresight to key the sample collection command from the bridge during the encounter. This might be the hard data they needed to prove they had found a new alien species.

Dyami collected the samples and loaded them into the bioanalyzer. The process only took a few moments, but as the scan progressed, Dyami felt his own excitement build.

There were alien cells in the water! The genetic analysis came back as 'unknown species'. The cells were made from primarily carbon and had many resemblances to life on Earth and other colony worlds. However, there were very distinct differences, and further genetic testing would be required to unravel how this creature fit into the animal kingdom.

Dyami keyed the com to the bridge. "We are going to have to figure out what to call these," he said with excitement.

DINNER AND A SHOW

"I'm not sure we should name it that, EV!" Jake exclaimed.

"Aw, c'mon, 'loopen' is the perfect name for those things," EV argued.

"Well, that name is definitely memorable," Dyami said, then remarked, "We can always change it later when we learn more about this species."

The crew had seen a total of seven 'loopen' groups throughout the day. Each group ascending and diving close to the Pegasus. With each new encounter, the Pegasus crew and the Earth Dock team became increasingly excited by the encounters and cataloged the video and sample data carefully for further study. At one point, nearly every team member at Earth Dock was crammed into the control center, trying to get their first glimpse at the new alien species.

There were a few interesting things of note. For example, there was heat emanating from the animals. It could have been that the animals were warm-blooded, but because of the frigid water and the creatures' small size, it likely meant that the creatures needed to eat often. Sarah also had a different idea about where this heat could be coming from and wondered if they would find the answer by following the groups back toward the depths. For the remainder of the day, the Pegasus held at a depth of ten kilometers.

"It's amazing to see them move so quickly through the water," Kiah commented. "Seventy kilometers per hour is no joke for a creature of that size. That is the fastest body size-to-speed ratio we have ever seen in a marine animal," she remarked. "What is even more impressive is their ability to maintain that speed for any length of time."

The crew sat around the dining table discussing the day's excitement as Dyami prepared the evening meal. He loved the company in the kitchen at that time of day as he worked. The casual conversations always brought the crew closer together as savory fragrances filled the air.

As exciting as the day was, Sarah's mind was already at work on their next problem. As the other crew started the meal, Sarah's mind was fifty kilometers away. Where in the depths did the loopens come from? Did they have any predators? Were there any additional considerations needed before they dived further down? It was startling to see so many creatures at a time in the first encounter, but the more she thought about it, the more it made sense. Many animals in the ocean resided in large groups for protection.

"Sarah, do you think we should try to capture one of these creatures for further study?" Jake asked, breaking Sarah's train of thought.

Sarah shifted gears and thought about the question. "I'm not sure that is the right approach. They may be more intelligent than we realize, and we don't want to be seen as aggressive," Sarah finally said. "We should find out where they are coming from and be mindful of their environment. Considering the outside water temperature, I'm also not sure they can live long-term at this depth."

Jake raised an eyebrow, "What makes you say that?"

"As we have descended, the temperature of the outside water has risen ever so slightly. We expected this since tectonic activity is probably how life survives this far away from a star in total darkness. That, mixed with Jupiter's variable gravity on this moon, makes it possible for liquid water to exist here at all," Sarah said as she imagined the landscape. "Europa redefined what humans thought of as the goldilocks zone where life could possibly live within a star system."

"So, you think they only come up briefly because it's too cold?" Jake asked.

"Yeah, I think they are spending most of their time keeping warm below. The evidence seems to support that," Sarah concluded.

"So, what is your recommendation for tomorrow?" Jake asked. The crew gave Sarah their full attention.

"That is a good question," Sarah said and paused momentarily to come up with a good answer. "I think we should follow the loopens down to see where it takes us. We can always stop if something else catches our attention."

Jake nodded in agreement. "Any other thoughts?" he asked while he looked around the table.

"I know we have jumped in the deep end already on this trip," Kiah said. "But encountering so many animals today, and so quickly, has led me to wonder if we need to proceed with more caution. I mean, what happens when we find the creature that eats loopens or the creature that eats that creature? There are many unknowns down here."

Kiah had said what they all were thinking. Jake's primary concern was keeping his crew safe. "The Pegasus is a stout ship and could even take on the jaws of a great white without scratching the paint. However, we need to keep our eyes open, and I don't intend to take any unnecessary risks with our lives on the line out here," Jake said.

The crew all nodded. They had come this far, and it reassured them that they were on the same page.

"I do wonder if they have any good seafood around here?" EV blurted his thoughts aloud.

"Yeah, eating the wildlife is not going to be on the menu anytime soon," Dyami said.

EV laughed, "I was only kidding. I could never eat a creature as cute as a loopen."

The more time the crew spent together, the more they worked as a cohesive team, and Jake noted the camaraderie around the table as the meal finished.

After dinner, Ashley went to deck three to the moon pool and docking area at the lower stern of the ship. The loading ramp was now sealing the moon pool as they traveled. This ramp plate would retract to reveal an opening to the ocean below when they were ready to use the Swift Sphere for their explorations. A pressure field was active along the pool's surface and ensured the ocean water and any particulates it contained would be kept out of the closed environment of the Pegasus. Ashley wanted to ensure that everything was prepped in case they needed the sphere for tomorrow's explorations.

She was almost done with her checks when the bulkhead door cycled open, and she saw Jake walk in.

"Hey there," he said smoothly as the door automatically closed behind him.

Ashley felt a familiar smile wash over her face. It was the smile she seemed to have every time Jake was around. "Hey yourself," she replied, hoping not to reveal her underlying feelings.

"I just thought I would check on you down here. The others have gone back to watching the sensors on the bridge, and I came to see how you were doing," Jake said as he leaned on a smooth section of wall across from where she worked.

"It's going well. I was checking all our equipment and making sure it was ready to go," Ashley said as she nodded toward the Swift Sphere suspended in the moon pool area.

"Hey, listen," Jake started. "I appreciate you coming with me on this mission." Jake knew that Ashley didn't want to talk about losing one of her close friends in an accident a few months back. He was here to support her and let her know she never had to be alone. Jake had known Ashley for the past eight years, and during that time, he came to rely on her more than any other person. She always seemed to have a solution to their problems inside that wonderful head of hers.

"Yeah, you couldn't get rid of me on this one," Ashley joked as she pulled away a strand of hair from her eyes. Ashley smiled softly to herself. "I was not going to let you go off on some grand adventure and take all the credit."

There was a brief awkward silence.

Jake tried to come up with another topic as Ashley broke the silence, "So you are just going to let EV name everything around here?"

They both broke out in a laugh and then another small silence. Unspoken feelings filled the air between them. They both were distracted by their own feelings to recognize those same feelings in the other.

"Yeah, maybe we should let Sarah name the next one," Jake said in response as they laughed again.

The brief conversation concluded; both parties wanting it to last longer, but neither able to see past their own current emotion to find a new 'safe' topic.

Jake left the docking area. He felt a wave of joy and excitement every time he got to talk with Ashley. He knew that he had begun to have serious feelings for her but also felt that pursuing any relationship beyond what they already had was not appropriate. She was still under his command, and that came before any romantic feelings he could have about her. As time progressed, those feelings were becoming stronger and more difficult to ignore. A difficult choice lay ahead, but for now, Jake was determined to succeed at this mission.

FREE FALLING

The morning saw the return of loopens. As before, the crew saw a few single scouts ascend the water column before larger groups followed. Were they communicating or just reacting to the environment around them? Sarah could not be certain.

One of the groups was over two hundred strong, but most were closer to one hundred animals. Sarah could not tell if some might have been the same animal, surfacing again and again.

"EV, please take us down," Jake said after the morning observations were recorded.

"Sarah, let us know if there is any reason we should stop," Jake added.

Sarah kept a close watch on the sensor displays. Before they started the morning descent, Sarah had created a separate sensor mapping she could keep an eye on that filtered out most of the readings coming from the loopens. She could flip between the two displays to keep an eye out for anything else, especially any larger creatures.

After three and a half hours, they reached twenty kilometers below the ice/ocean interface. Nothing seemed to change except the depth and pressure exerted on the hull by the outside water. Jake indicated to push on.

Another ten kilometers deeper, and another three and a half hours went by. The crew was now just over halfway to the bottom of the Europa Ocean, another twenty-eight kilometers below them.

There were increased loopen sightings, and more and more, Sarah felt like they were the ones who were being watched. But it was still amazing to see the grace and speed of these creatures as they jetted around the Pegasus as she descended. As the Pegasus got deeper, the loopens seemed to stay longer. Some now even seemed to play around the ship.

Another two hours passed, and it looked like the crew would not find anything new on this day.

"Alright, let's see what Dyami has for us tonight," Jake said. His hunger would not let him go much longer without an investigation of the smell that was coming from the galley.

Breakfast and lunch were always pre-packaged meals and maybe some juice, so the crew especially appreciated Dyami's culinary talents during the evening meal. Jake had always loved Dyami's cooking and thought of them more as home-cooked meals than the packaged meals he ate while away from a mission.

Ben was the last to join the rest of the crew in the galley. Ben had experienced a wonderful day. In comparison, the rest of the crew had been staring unblinkingly at the sensors waiting for something to magically appear. Ben had been down in his hydroponic garden adjusting and readjusting his optimal grow settings and checking the mycelium growth of his portobello mushrooms. Everything was growing well! In just a couple of short weeks, they would have fresh produce that was locally grown. He also looked forward to using the com feed to talk to his wife and kids later that day. Yeah, it had been a good day.

"You guys look bushed," Ben said as he entered the galley.

"Yeah, the loopens are fun to watch, but it was a tedious journey after a while since we didn't see anything else. But, the loopens sure are cute," EV said.

They all smiled. A few of the groups had come close enough to see them clearly from the bridge over the course of the day. Reviewing the videos of the little silvery white critters with varying patterns was enjoyable all by itself.

"Even from the little we have seen, they appear to be social creatures. We haven't detected any vocalizations coming from them, but the way they swim makes me think they are communicating," Sarah said.

"Yeah, I have seen a reaction with the membrane around the eyes as they change direction," said Kiah. Kiah grabbed her tablet to show the video but caught Jake's slight frown.

"We can work later. How about we enjoy each other's company for now?" Jake said softly. "I just find that unplugging a little can really help us focus when we need to," Jake did not want to quell her excitement but knew how easily work could become part of every minute of every day.

"What do you like to do for fun, Kiah?" Jake asked as he looked for a new subject.

Kiah thought about it for a moment then replied, "I enjoy participating in murder mysteries in VR with my mom."

Ashley suddenly looked intrigued, "Have you tried that new mob assassination story, uh, uh, what was it called?" She tried to remember the title.

"Ashen Planet?" Kiah asked.

"Yeah, that's it! Can you believe they killed the cop's wife in the second season?" Ashley was clearly excited about the new topic.

"Hey guys, I haven't gotten that far," EV pretended as he cocked a grin.

"Shut up, EV, I know you have experienced that series at least twice," Sarah interjected.

"Yeah, but I have not gotten that far in my third play-through," EV said with a big grin.

The crew slowly dispersed to finish the evening checks as the meal concluded.

After dinner, Ben went to the briefing room to call his family. As he strolled into the dark room, the automated lights came on. He eagerly walked to the controls and popped on the video com feed. "Hey guys," the video feed sparked to life.

"Hey, Dad! Have you found anything cool yet?" Kasidy asked excitedly.

"I can't let you in on the details yet, but it has been exciting!" Ben exclaimed.

"Dad. Daaad," Tyler said as he shoved his face into the camera lens. "Mom said we're moving next week, and my last day of school is tomorrow. Is that true?" Tyler said.

"Yeah, if your mom told you that, then it's true," Ben replied.

"Are you going to make Mom carry all your stuff to the new house?" Tyler asked, in a dead serious tone. Ben could tell that his six-year-old son thought that was unfair.

"Yeah, I'm sure she will have the movers to help her," Ben said. "You know she will be able to assert her will and get the job done."

Tyler smiled and giggled. It was good to see him smile. Ben smiled back and saw Tyler had pulled his leg about making Angi do all the work.

"ASSERT HER WILL!" Tyler yelled as he ran off. "ASSERT HER WILL!"

Angi now appeared on the screen and asked, "What did you just tell him!?!" She gave Ben her critical eye. Then, Ben saw through the game and realized she also had pulled his leg. She broke into laughter after Ben cracked a wide grin in relief.

"Yeah, you had me there for a second," Ben said as he scratched his head.

"I won't be mad at you as long as you come back to me safe," Angi's emotions were a mix of happiness and worried as they rippled across her face.

"I'll be ok. This is a great crew, and they will take care of me," Ben said, trying to reassure Angi. "I see that Tyler seems a bit chipper," Ben's voice showed his appreciation for his wife.

"Yeah, he is doing ok. He has been excited about speaking to you all day," Angi said.

"Listen, Angi; I don't want you to feel like I ran away from our family during this transition. They really needed me on this, and Richard can be very persuasive. You are doing a great job with the kids, and we are so very lucky to have you around. I just felt like I needed to tell you that," Ben said.

"I know, Ben. This was not a great time for you to leave, but I understand why," Angi said.

"I don't know what I would do without you in my life," Ben admitted.

Angi nodded, "We have a responsibility to each other and the kids."

Just then, Tyler popped back into the picture and said, "Hey, are you guys talking about me?"

Ben grinned and said, "Yeah, you caught us." He feigned death for a moment as Tyler laughed.

"I'm going to need to go soon," Ben said apologetically.

A pair of "No's" erupted from the kids as they protested the potential end of the video call.

"Ok, ok," Ben said. "Before I go, do you want to sing?"

"YEAH!" Tyler shouted. Kasidy seemed a bit reluctant, but then saw the joy on her younger brother's face.

Ben started, "Children of mine, I care for you. Deeper than the ocean, vaster than any sea," By this time, the children began singing too. With some variation on the lyrics they could remember. The family sang together, and despite being across the solar system, they reveled in this moment they shared. The children smiled as they finished the song, and Angi held a long gaze.

"We love you!" the kids shouted as they waved goodbye.

"I love you too. Be sure to take care of your mom until I get back," Ben said.

"I love you, Ben. We will speak soon," Angi said as the com feed clicked off.

Ben stood in the briefing room for a moment. Even with the video calls, he knew he would miss his family. The next six months would be their longest period apart.

LOOPENS

"Captain?!" Sarah said as the entire sensor sphere lit up below them.

Jake looked over the readings and gasped. What they had found looked like a city, glowing solid red on the sensors! Networks of life signs filled the display. Many were loopens, and they were darting in and out of a colossal structure. A vast array of threads was attached to the natural rock, forming a massive system of terraces from fine strands of green web. These structures towered up to three hundred meters from the seabed. A glowing orange pool under the colony wrapped around a series of thermal vents. Loopens could be seen coming in and out along pouches in the green web.

Along with the loopens, a host of other small creatures were detected around the massive superstructure. Sarah flipped her display to show a thermal readout. The pockets held in heat, and warm loopen bodies appeared as warm streaks that darted in and out. Just then, a wave of loopens came flying around the Pegasus. As they swooped past, they dove below the web structure to the thermal vents, staying long enough to warm up their bodies before finding an empty burrow.

Jake put his hands to his mouth in astonishment.

No one said anything for several minutes as they watched in amazement.

"These readings are incredible!" Richard exclaimed before a long pause. "Are you still reading me?" Richard said through the audio com. His audio signal was still strong even at their immense depth.

"Yeah, we are here. I'm just a bit speechless. I knew something like this was possible, but I just didn't expect it," Jake admitted.

Bobb, the drone, descended ahead of the Pegasus toward the structure. The Pegasus was receiving the video footage and could see the wonder these loopens' called home. As Bobb approached, iridescent rainbow creatures that looked like tiny perfect feathers only two centimeters long with no eyes could be seen swarming around a few of the loopens. Then, several moments later, the loopens swam away, looking refreshed.

Green pods hung underneath the structure. As Bobb's light reflected on the pods, they glistened a dark green and purple. Nestled along these pods were very small loopens only twenty centimeters long. They had a green hue that helped them blend into the backdrop.

"It's a nursery!" Kiah gasped.

Details were coming together rapidly as the crew watched the video feed. A warming light from the orange pool below illuminated the whole structure, presenting the scale of the entire scene. The amount of activity was comparable to a large coral reef. Fantastic creatures, sixty centimeters long with transparent wings, floated just above the orange pool. They were very flat and thin and seemed to hang there, flexing their wings occasionally. The creatures moved delicately through the water and appeared as if they were made of frosted glass.

There were even more creatures lurking in the shadows below. Red tails thrashed as they disappeared after encountering Bobb's light, leaving only ringlets of bubbles in their wake.

There were countless different loopen behaviors exhibited, and different sizes of loopens seemed to co-mingle. Perhaps mothers and daughters? Perhaps fathers and sons? Or perhaps something yet to be discovered and an extraordinary mystery within the chronicle of the universe.

"We hit the jackpot with this find! Where do we start?" EV asked.

"EV, can you get us down even with the structure, maybe on one of the sides? Somewhere we can park where we won't disturb the loopens?" Jake asked.

EV checked his displays to determine where they could get close without disturbing anything. He laid in the course. "I think we can pull up around here, Skipper," he said. The holo-display showed the projection of where the ship could anchor.

"Let's do it EV," Jake said.

EV smiled and punched the throttle to get the Pegasus moving toward the alcove.

The outside hull of the Pegasus seemed to glow orange as light from the pool below reflected off the white NIC material. Smoothly the Pegasus glided into position guided by EV's expert hand. As the ship dropped down, the forward spotlights illuminated the green webs and nest pockets that were the homes of the loopens. Tiny unknown creatures scurried away from the artificial light that projected from the ship.

"Captain, I think we should just stop and observe for a while," Sarah said as she turned to look at Jake. "Sometimes just sitting can help the environment get familiar with your presence. Let's see what happens."

Jake nodded. "That sounds like wisdom coming from experience. EV, let's hold here," he ordered.

The Pegasus held its position, tucked away in a small corner of the great web structure. After a few moments, curious loopens poked their emerald eyes out from nearby pockets, and other creatures started going back about their business.

The crew was silent as they concentrated on the discoveries unfolding before them. The external microphones picked up a wide array of sounds, and the audio was fed to the bridge. Slow, long clicks were layered with ethereal chimes in haunting harmony. The hypnotic sound would start for a few minutes and then softly end, only to begin again after a few more moments.

"Ashley, we are recording this, right?" Sarah asked softly.

Ashley nodded. The entire crew stood on the bridge, listening to the outside world.

Other sounds also tangled into the mix. There was a low grunting sound and a hint of something so high-pitched that only a few of the crew could actually hear the sound.

"What's our next move?" EV asked quietly.

Jake looked over to Ashley, and that was the signal Ashley had been waiting for.

"Ashley, you ready to go for a ride out there?" Jake asked.

"Remember, just observations and simple sample collection," Sarah urged. Sarah felt the trip might be premature, but this was Jake's call.

Ashley smiled and nodded.

Ashley and Jake left the bridge and stepped onto the lift. Ashley pushed the indicator for deck three.

"I want you to take it easy out there. I know we have seen these things for a few days now, and they seem friendly, but I want you to be safe," Jake said.

Ashley nodded, "Yeah, I will take care."

"I know Ashley, I trust you," Jake said.

"I will stay close by," Ashley said as she looked at Jake.

The two exited the lift and walked to the moon pool dock. Today would be a good day to take the Swift Sphere out for a spin.

SWIFT SPHERE

Ashley sat in the cockpit and pulled the release handle, sending the Swift Sphere plunging toward the Europa Ocean below.

The Swift Sphere was basically a NIC glass bubble with a gyroscopic cockpit containing holo-controls. A pair of multi-directional A7 water propulsion thrusters were held in place by magnetic rings, giving the Swift Sphere speed and agility as the craft dove under the moon pool dock. Ashley put on her pressure gloves and 'felt' the control stick slip into her right hand. The stick was not physically there, and a projection was the only visual indicator of its location. Ashley could release the control when she needed to move around more freely in the cockpit, and it would vanish.

Ashley kept the Swift Sphere movement smooth and slow. She was an expert pilot but still focused intently on her control inputs. The sphere illuminated the immediate surroundings, and two focused lights pointed forward. Ashley felt the thrusters' precise handling and crisp response as she increased the throttle. Goose bumps ran along her arms with the thrill of being out here. This could be her opportunity to make a significant contribution to the mission, and she was not going to let the crew down. Light projected forward and illuminated the alien seascape as Ashley cruised to the closest web pocket.

"How's the sphere handling?" Jake's voice cracked in from the com channel in the cockpit. The crew was receiving the video from the sphere and could talk to Ashley as she explored the unknown.

"She is outstanding! Water density is nearly identical to Earth's oceans, and low gravity doesn't affect her performance. The ride is so smooth!" Ashley exclaimed.

As Ashley approached a few of the nest pockets, she noticed a few strands of the green web were coming off. "I'm going to see if I can collect a web sample," Ashley said as she adjusted her heading to intercept the loose material.

Ashley tapped the command, and the Swift Sphere's arms deployed smoothly. She adjusted her grip and took control of the arms and hands through her gloves. She pushed a control, and a fresh specimen canister appeared in one of the hands. With another control flip, the canister used suction to trap a material sample. Ashley released the controls as the canister retracted into the arm, and the arms retracted flush to the craft.

As Ashley looked over, she noticed web coming from a group of passing loopens. The web threads were released from their tails as they weaved the material into the structure. It was confirmed they were the builders of this great wonder.

"Looks like we found our architects," Sarah's voice came through the speaker as she noticed what Ashley was looking at.

Then something strange happened. A loopen with a skin marking that looked like a kid flying a kite came right up to Ashley in the Swift Sphere. The loopen just sat in front of the sphere, bobbing slightly as it held its position. Emerald green eyes looked as sharp as glass. The creature hovered there for a moment, then another. It seemed to be staring directly at Ashley. Finally, the creature slowly lifted a fin, and with a very soft whisk of the tail, the loopen fin touched the sphere.

Ashley suddenly felt her mind slip. It was like she awoke from a daydream, but Ashley never remembered losing her focus. As suddenly as it had happened, the feeling vanished. She was suddenly hit with a small sense of disorientation as she regained her focus.

The loopen casually swam away, flicking its fins as it glided off.

"Ashley? What was that?" Jake's voice came through the audio com.

"I'm not sure. I…" Ashley seemed to lose her breath. She felt like she had just missed something.

"Are you ok?" Jake asked, trying to confirm.

"Yeah… yeah… I'm good now." Ashley paused, then added, "Sarah, what do you want to see?"

"Are you sure you're ok?" Sarah asked through the com.

"Yeah, I just lost focus for a moment," Ashley replied.

"Well then, let's go check out the nursery. Just take it slow," Sarah said.

Ashley maneuvered the sphere around and descended under the structure where they had seen the very young loopens nestled. As she approached, she noticed it looked like an upside-down forest of dark green and purple pods. Each strand had several interconnected pouches and was about two meters long. At the base, it looked like some type of plant, but the shape seemed familiar.

"Oh, cool!" Sarah's voice exclaimed through the audio com.

"This thing looks like it is part loopen or something. What am I looking at here?!" Ashley asked.

"Ashley, can you hold a light by one of the pods?" Sarah asked.

Ashley keyed the control, activating a light on each of the sphere's hands in robotic palms. She then keyed the lights from the sphere to fade as she took control of the arms. Next, she carefully positioned a plant pod between her sphere and the light source. The egg illuminated from behind, and the loopen was clearly seen through the egg casing. Ashley was just a nose away as she peered through the sphere's bubble.

Ashley's mind slipped again. Loss of time... Just for a moment. She struggled to regain her focus. She couldn't reconcile what had just happened.

"Ashley!?" Jake's voice sounded concerned.

"Yeah... I... I'm here," Ashley replied.

"Why don't you come on back? We can put our heads together for a while and hit it again tomorrow," Jake suggested.

"Yeah, that might be a good idea," Ashley replied as she tried to recall the moment before she lost focus. Maybe it was just not enough sleep and all this excitement.

Ashley noticed an empty pod as it sank. It was close to the sphere, and she circled to take the sample. The arms again extended and vacuumed the specimen into another collection canister. Maybe Ben or Sarah could find out what this thing truly was.

From the bridge, the crew had been monitoring Ashley's progress, and they could now see her lights returning through the front bridge glass. As it returned, the Swift Sphere was tiny next to the vast loopen colony.

"Sarah, it looked like that loopen made purposeful contact with Ashley. Have you ever seen a creature exhibit behavior like that?" Jake asked.

"Yes, but very rarely. Encounters like that are usually from very intelligent creatures. I had an encounter once with a Pacific octopus, where she seemed to look into my soul. Those encounters stick with you the rest of your life," Sarah said softly.

Sarah and Jake headed to the lift and proceeded to the marine lab on deck two.

Ben was already there waiting for them. "We are prepped to transfer the samples," Ben said as Jake and Sarah approached.

Ashley maneuvered the Swift Sphere in front of the glass of the marine lab. Ben gave her a wave and a thumbs up, showing the Pegasus was ready to transfer the samples into the marine lab. A tiny cylindrical hatch pushed into the Swift Sphere storage compartment from the Pegasus and locked into place. Quickly the samples were transferred into separate sealed compartments aboard the Pegasus. The crew would be able to analyze the material in sealed containment.

"We got it!" Ben said as the Pegasus confirmed the transfer.

"Great!" Ashley said through the audio com. "Let me park this thing."

Jake walked to the lift to meet Ashley in the moon pool dock and took it to deck three. When he got there, the dock was already preparing for the sphere extraction. The gravity clamps moved into position and lowered to the moon pool's ocean surface. The Swift Sphere suddenly appeared below the pool's mouth, and Ashley smoothly maneuvered into position. There was a slight hum as the gravity clamps activated and the sphere was lifted. The pressure field did its job, not allowing any water particles to enter the Pegasus. The indicator light on the console glowed green, and the sphere was hoisted smoothly into the dock.

"That was some ride!" Ashley beamed.

Jake smiled back and responded, "Yeah, it sounded like you had fun out there!"

The Swift Sphere was an engineering marvel but was awkward to get out of. Jake offered his hand to help Ashley from the cockpit. As Jake touched Ashley's hand, both felt more than just the touch. That was enough to throw them both out of balance, and Ashley landed in Jake's arms. The tension was tangible as they both struggled with this unexpected embrace. They released each other and stood awkwardly for a moment.

"Let's go see what you found," Jake broke the silence as he walked to bulkhead door.

Neither could think of a comfortable topic as they headed to deck two. They each felt the connection but were not sure what to say. The tension remained as they entered the marine lab. Ben and Sarah were too preoccupied with the findings to notice their tension as Jake and Ashley walked up behind them.

After a time, the computer displayed the results of the initial scan.

The results were unexpected, and Ben had a wide eye expression that swept across his face.

"Well, the pods are different from the loopens, but share much of the same genetic material," Ben said after quickly reading the genetics results. "There is still a lot here we have yet to understand. I think that it will be interesting as we observe them for the next few days and maybe find out more about this area and how these species interact."

Richard's voice piped through the audio com feed, "Hey Sarah, take a look at what Bobb found."

Sarah connected her display to the video feed from Bobb. Richard had piloted Bobb to the spot where Ashley had examined the pods. Through the feed, the crew saw the creature inside starting to push its way through the shell of the pod. It was the same pod Ashley had observed earlier. As the creature emerged, the pod popped open and started falling away to the ocean floor.

The creature was a loopen but with one distinct difference. Red marks outlined its tiny wing-like fins. No one spoke as the event occurred.

"Sarah, Ben... can someone tell me if that is a weird coincidence, or... what?" Jake asked.

They looked at each other for a moment. Ben shrugged, and Sarah said, "I'm not sure what to make of that."

As they watched, the newborn loopen started swimming and disappeared into the other pods.

"It looked unharmed. Maybe this was just its time to hatch?" Sarah suggested rhetorically.

"You could fill a room full of things we don't know," Ben said.

After a few more moments, the crew saw no sign of the unique loopen, and Bobb returned to the Pegasus to recharge.

ENCORE PRESENTATION

Dyami noticed his meal was not the only thing heating up in the galley that night. Two people kept exchanging glances, and he knew something was about to change. However, he was going to ignore that for now. "Kiah, so you are saying those pods are more closely related to plants, but they are gestating the loopen young?"

"Well, the evidence seems to support that. Maybe it's some symbiotic relationship," Kiah explained. "Plants have used pollinators for reproduction for millions of years. Many species on Earth rely on another species for reproduction. So the loopens could have been evolving with the pods for a long time," Kiah explained.

Ashley's face flushed slightly at the current topic of reproduction. Only Dyami noticed the reaction.

EV twitched his eyebrow and stared at Kiah for a moment.

Kiah laughed. "My explanation was not that bad!"

EV had a way about him that seemed to put everyone at ease, and paired with Dyami's culinary talent, the evenings were something they all looked forward to. Kiah was starting to see Jake's previous point about Dyami's cooking. He had a knack for cooking anything and making it taste amazing.

"You know, I have been wondering, why do the loopens have eyes if there is not much light down here?" Ben asked, suddenly thinking aloud.

"Interesting question; I was thinking about that when I was looking over the thermal feeds. They could be using some form of infrared vision. Several animal species have that ability on Earth, including many species of fish," Sarah commented. "Maybe we could come up with a test and figure out what they actually see."

"You know, it would be easier to answer some of these questions if we had a specimen. Perhaps we could find one that has recently passed," Kiah suggested.

Jake nodded. "Yeah, that might be a possibility. We should keep our eyes open for those types of opportunities."

"I wonder how they deal with loss," Sarah pondered.

After dinner, Ashley was ready for some shut-eye. It had been a long day, and she felt like her brain needed rest. Ashley's quarters were one door down from the captain's quarters on the port side of the Pegasus. She crawled into her bed and almost immediately fell into a deep trance-like sleep.

Ashley found herself in a dream. Her consciousness became aware that the surroundings were malleable. The scenery around her could be altered, and she could fly. It was not the first time that Ashley had experienced a lucid dream, but the detail in this particular dream was very vivid. Ashley brought herself to a specific beach by the Hocaniio preserve. It was a place where she vacationed with her friends. Ashley had come with her close friend Vanessa, and she had suggested that they also invite Jake along. The three were sharing a beach house and enjoying the Pacific.

This dream was so realistic, and Ashley embraced joy as she saw her close friend, Vanessa, once again. However, Ashley knew this was just a dream, and Vanessa was gone. All that remained were Ashley's cherished memories of her, locked within the time they had spent together. Ashley felt the tears stream down her cheeks as the scene shifted again to a sunset on the Hocaniio beach. Something changed inside Ashley, and a calm wave of peace washed over her spirit.

Ashley opened her eyes as her strong emotions pulled her from sleep. Then she realized there was a presence with her. The room was still dark, but there was the feeling of something... or someone... there. Ashley blinked, allowing her eyes time to focus. A red glow emanated from somewhere in front of her. Ashley blinked again. She could see through the window in her quarters, looking into the ocean. The light was emanating from somewhere beyond. It moved ever so slightly, and Ashley's heart pounded in her chest. She could barely breathe.

After a few moments, Ashley stood. The light slightly bobbed.

Thoughts flew through Ashley's head as she tried to plan her next move. Her first thought was that she might want to call for help or to turn on the lights, but she quickly vetoed those courses of action. She didn't want to frighten whatever was out there. It might run or possibly attack.

She slowly approached the NIC glass that separated her from the ocean beyond. The entire time her eyes were fixed on the red glow coming from the outside. The light began to take shape, and Ashley saw the red outline of a tiny pair of fins. The fear immediately faded as a sense of awe filled Ashley.

The little loopen with red-tipped wings sat just outside the NIC glass where Ashley stood by the window. The streaks of red that appeared along its wings glowed with red bioluminescence. It just looked like it was hanging out.

Ashley was speechless as she watched the little organism float outside the window for several more minutes. She wasn't sure, but it looked larger than it had before. Ashley had finally decided her next move. She slowly got dressed and softly called Jake on the com. She whispered into the microphone, "Jake, I think you need to see this."

After a few more moments, the door cycled, and Jake slowly stepped through as he took note of Ashley's presence by the window. The lights were still off, but the hall light spilled through the open door. "Hey, what's going on?"

Ashley whispered, "We have a visitor."

Jake felt a sudden rush. Then he noted Ashley's calm stature and quietly entered the room. The door slipped closed behind him. As Jake's eyes adjusted, he saw the red glowing wings. "What? How?" Jake stammered.

"I don't know. Maybe it followed Bobb back to the Pegasus?" Ashley said as she kept her voice low. She was not sure how much sound would transfer through the glass.

"How did you find your way here?" Jake asked the tiny creature.

Another moment passed while they pondered what to do next.

Suddenly the decision was made for them, and the little creature swam away and out of sight. Jake and Ashley stared out the window for a time, wondering if the little creature would return.

They sat together for the next two hours, staring into the dark, making no sound, just enjoying the silence and each other's company before finally falling asleep.

WHERE'S BABY

Bobb finished charging in the early morning and was back in action. After Ashley's report about that night's encounter with the loopen, Richard had been on patrol with the drone for several hours, looking for where the loopen might have gone. Unfortunately, the search did not yield any results. So, without a lead, Bobb resumed mapping the massive loopen nest.

After breakfast, Ashley didn't waste any time heading to the moon pool dock. All that she could think about was finding 'Hot Wings' again. That is what she decided to call the visitor that suddenly appeared the previous night. The red markings around his wings were very distinct and hadn't been observed in any other loopens. The name just seemed to fit the cute little creature. Since the encounter, Ashley felt some kind of connection with him, but all she could do was hope he would reappear. She climbed into the Swift Sphere and ran her checks. The indicators were all green, and she pulled the release, slipping through the pressure field into the Europa Ocean.

Ashley slowly maneuvered around the front of the Pegasus and throttled up once she was clear. In a few moments, she was headed to the spot where she had first encountered Hot Wings in the nursery. This place was the best place to start looking for him, and the rest of the crew agreed to that plan over breakfast. Ashley began an arc down and around to the underside of the loopen nest. She pulled back on the throttle as she approached the coordinates. The gyroscopic motion of the sphere around her gave her the best viewing angle to see where the egg had been the day before. The sphere's light caught every curve of the web that supported the structure. Within the patch of pods, there was still the void where Hot Wings had been born.

"I see some smaller loopens hanging out between the pods, but none look like Hot Wings," Ashley reported. She felt a pang of disappointment but had known it would probably not be that easy to find him.

One of the priorities for the day's explorations was to learn more about the orange pool that lay just below the loopen nest. It had the appearance of lava with a bright glow, but Sarah said it was something else. The substance was concentrated around the volcanic thermal tubes that were numerous in this area. Ashley figured this was as good a place as any to continue the search for Hot Wings. However, she remembered they had seen larger creatures in this area, and she had to proceed with caution.

Ashley descended and reoriented her perspective down toward the orange glow. A multitude of loopens were gathered around the orange pool and were feeding on the glowing substance. Ashley cruised the Swift Sphere just above the surface of the pool. The pool's surface slowly gleamed and rippled as it pulsated with surprisingly intense glowing light.

"So, the loopens eat glowing orange gelatin. That figures," EV said through the audio com.

"Ashley, can you get a sample of the material?" Jake asked.

"Yeah, I'm on it," Ashley replied.

Ashley took the controls and the arms extended with a fresh collection canister. Ashley guided the arms and scooped up a sample with one smooth motion. The material had the consistency of a thick gelatinous paste.

"Alright, we have the gel secured," Ashley said.

"Thanks, Ashley. I wanted to look more at the..." Sarah started.

Just then, a small loopen crossed over the pool to where the Swift Sphere was positioned. It glided right up to where Ashley was. That is when an attack occurred. Shadows gave away the positions only an instant before the two attackers were revealed. Two intercepting streaks of red appeared. Knobby scaled ridges formed into a large horn that arched just behind the creature's head, flowing into a powerful snake-like body. Their entire body acted as a single fin as it twisted through the water. They moved with frightening speed like a serpent through the frigid ocean water, leaving ringlets of bubbles in their wake. Rows of razor sharp teeth set deep into their jaws were built for one purpose, to rend flesh. These creatures closed the gap to their target. Each animal was about two meters long.

The exposed loopen suddenly seemed to realize its miscalculation and started to flee. The other loopens in the immediate area also scattered.

The two red horn-heads were closing the distance to their prey as powerful muscles rippled through their serpent bodies. The loopen was quicker and gained an edge as it fled for safety. It just needed a few more seconds before it would be in its nest. A few loopens that were further from the action seemed to watch as the scene occurred. The red horn-heads seemed staggered momentarily, but then the final trap was sprung. More shadows moved just before two more red horn-heads appeared, blocking the fleeing loopen's escape. There was nowhere else to go.

"No!" Ashley yelled as her heart leapt.

The moment was quick, and the loopen lost its life. Death is a part of every day that life exists.

Several tears fell from Ashley's eyes as the scene finished.

"It wasn't him. That loopen wasn't Hot Wings," Jake said, through the com.

Ashley nodded and wiped the tears from her cheeks. "That was intense. Sometimes nature can be hard to watch." Ashley let out a sigh as she focused on the controls. With a short pause, Ashley asked, "Where to next?"

"Thanks, Ashley," Sarah said, pausing to give Ashley another moment to collect herself. "Do you think you could find some of the rainbow feather animals we saw on our way in?"

"Sure, we should be able to retrace Bobb's path to where we saw them before," Ashley said as she plotted the course.

As Ashley headed back toward the colony, she noticed some of the loopens that were feeding below had carried food to their young in the nursery. Orange streams shot into the water, and the young loopens enjoyed the meals their elders provided. Ashley paused at the sight. The young looked like they were playing as they fed in the streams. They moved with grace in a fluid dance. Their small fins and tails worked in perfect orchestration through the water. They made loops every once in a while, changing direction almost effortlessly.

"My kids aren't going to believe this. Even on other worlds, species still care dearly about their young. It's wonderful to see that some things in nature stay the same, no matter where you go," Ben's voice came through the com feed.

"You're capturing some really good video shots Ashley," Sarah commented.

"Thanks. I feel a big mix of emotions right now," Ashley laughed a bit as she smiled. Tears still filled her eyes, just as much from her joy as from her recent sorrow. After several minutes of watching the loopens Ashley smoothly throttled up. She had a steady hand at the stick and piloted the Swift Sphere to the next destination.

The Swift Sphere rose above the loopen colony and found a familiar sight. In a bustle of activity, the rainbow feathers cleaned the loopens. They took small flakes of dead skin off the loopens, attaching themselves for a while before letting go and drifting away in the slow current. There were hundreds of them, each about the size of a small coin.

"If you can collect one without causing the creature any harm, that would be great. I don't think they will mind," Sarah said.

Ashley again prepped the specimen canister and successfully captured one of the rainbow feathers.

Another hour passed as Ashley explored the top of the loopen colony. She had seen several more groups of rainbow feathers and had even captured video of a blurry snowball object that seemed to melt away after direct light hit it. Another tiny bright yellow multi-legged creature appeared with a shell-like exoskeleton. This place truly was a sanctuary for a wide array of living organisms. Finally, the charge on the Swift Sphere ran low.

"Hey, Ashley. I think it's time to head back," Jake said through the com.

Ashley finally ran out of time and needed to return to the Pegasus. The Swift Sphere needed to charge, and there was no ignoring that fact. "Alright, I'm heading back now," she replied. She plotted a course back to drop off the sample canisters. As she maneuvered toward the front of the Pegasus, she saw what she had been searching for all day.

Hot Wings, as if by magic, had suddenly appeared in front of the Pegasus, following Ashley. Sarah and Ben looked shocked through the front glass of the marine lab as the pair pulled up.

"Hey, look who decided to follow me home," Ashley laughed.

Ashley keyed the command to drop off the samples. Hot Wings seemed especially interested in the glowing orange sample as it retracted into the Pegasus. Ashley had a sudden thought. What if she needed to take care of him? He was, after all, only a baby, and they had observed the other loopens feeding their young. What if he needed her to do the same?

Ashley quickly docked at the moon pool. She practically leapt out of the Swift Sphere and shot to the marine lab. Hot Wings remained by the bow of the Pegasus and examined the canister docking port. It was apparent that he was interested in where the food had disappeared.

"Hey, is it possible to release some of the orange gel into the water for him?" Ashley asked.

Ben thought about it for a second, then split off some orange gel by dividing it into two different canisters. Then, with another tap, Ben released the gel by flushing ocean water through one of the canisters. The material flowed into the water and promptly vanished into Hot Wing's mouth.

"I'm not sure feeding the loopens is the best idea," Sarah said after the event. She had also wanted to see what would happen but felt a bit uncomfortable with the potential consequences of that action.

Ben shrugged.

"Our presence here might have already impacted this loopen. He has already followed me home, and I have a strong feeling that we should care for him," Ashley insisted.

Sarah gave Ashley an odd look for a second but understood her point. Generally, when observing animals, the observer lets nature take its course. However, in this odd situation, Ashley seemed somehow connected to this particular creature. Sarah also reconsidered how the relationship could help the team understand more about these creatures. Usually, mutual understanding is the foundation for trust. Perhaps this offering of food was a step in that direction.

HOT WINGS

The next few weeks were spent researching and documenting the behaviors of the loopens in their environment. Hot Wings continued to hang around the Pegasus most of the time. However, he occasionally disappeared for a few hours, only to turn up again later. Ashley convinced the crew that feeding Hot Wings was a way for the crew to observe and bond with the little loopen.

Ben had discovered that the orange gel was vast colonies of autotrophs that were being consumed by an 'unknown' microbial bioluminescent species. The whole cycle used chemosynthesis to grow, and the material was rich in vitamins, minerals, and protein. The cellular structure of the microbe had unique adaptations for deep ocean life. Ben wondered how the substance might taste, but then thought better than to try some himself. He also discovered that small holes were providing methane directly under the glowing pool. This resource helped the microbial colony grow to an immense size, feeding the entire food chain over thousands of years. Loopens used the gel as their primary food source, and Ben was able to synthesize the conditions and grow the substance in the lab. It's like orange juice for loopens he thought to himself one morning and started to call the substance o-gel.

The red horn-heads were seen on several occasions as they hunted the loopens. Many times, the loopen would escape back to a nest where they could not be reached by the larger predator. The horn-heads hunted in small packs, and despite some success, they often looked as if they were just learning their hunting skills. Often the larger horn-heads seemed to start an ambush but would suddenly break off their pursuit. It was a mystery that Sarah could not quite figure out. They seemed to swim faster and were more powerful than their smaller counterparts but almost never finished the chase.

Hot Wings turned out to be quite a character. He followed Ashley every time she took out the Swift Sphere. There was a deeper bond growing between them, which was evident in his behavior. He sometimes gathered with the other young loopens to feed and play but always returned to Ashley and the Pegasus. She even started to talk to him when he was around. Hot Wings was a great listener and never had any commentary.

"So, what do you think, Hot Wings?" Ashley asked as she waited for him to respond. Ashley was staring down at where she had seen him disappear. She pressed her nose to the glass as she peered down. Something else was moving, and she needed a closer look as she rotated the lights on the sphere. Hot Wings glided into view, then looped back again toward the movement. Ashley's heart was racing as she waited for something to happen.

There was a moment of silence... Ashley held her breath...

Suddenly, a tiny head popped out from behind the sheet of the dark green web. It was very smooth, with a thick curve in the head all the way down to where the web obscured the view. It was a light shade of gray with a dark gray jaw.

Hot Wings swam toward the creature with a few graceful motions, and Ashley was afraid he might scare the creature back into hiding. However, it didn't retreat, instead, standing its ground as it confronted Hot Wings. As Hot Wings approached, the critter seemed to relax. Ashley nudged the throttle of the Swift Sphere and inched closer to the organism, to get a better angle and see its entire body.

The little head swiveled around slightly, mouth open, and took a big bite out of the web it was standing on as it went back to feeding. "Awww!" Ashley let the sound escape her lips.

Ashley saw a brightly colored spiral shell with little legs which stuck out the underside. The patterns of white, red, orange and yellow, blended into an almost hypnotic fractal pattern. It looked like a hermit crab with a tiny alien head. Multiple sets of small claws lined the end of each armored leg joint. It seemed to be at ease when Hot Wings was around. His presence invited interactions that weren't possible without him, and Ashley shook her head at the thought.

"Alright, this is pretty cool! Thanks for the introduction," Ashley exclaimed as she spoke to Hot Wings.

"He is really showing you around the neighborhood," Jake said from the audio com.

"Yeah, this is something else," Ashley's satisfied wanderlust was apparent in her voice.

Ashley collected water samples, and after a few minutes, Hot Wings started in another direction. He stopped a few meters away, waiting for Ashley to follow him. She took the hint and glided to his position. As the pair moved over the loopen colony, other loopens seemed to swim alongside them briefly. It was almost as if they were coming in for a closer look at Ashley, the alien in their world.

Hot Wings started to slow, and Ashley eased the throttle back. There was something there. The creature had a divided tail just behind a shell that wrapped around the first half of the body. The almost completely transparent body was pressed up against the loopen nest. It was tricky to see nestled in strands of web. As they watched the creature's small arms, all ten pairs of them, could be seen through the shell picking through the web for the 'irregularities' it called food.

Ashley just stared in amazement as the creature slowly fed. These beings were beyond anything Ashley could have imagined encountering. She was being personally escorted to each creature living in the sanctuary. "This is incredible, Hot Wings!" she finally said.

The creature moved out of view a few moments later, looking for its next morsel of food in the web. The more time Ashley spent with Hot Wings, the more obvious it became that despite his young age, he was tremendously intelligent.

As the day wrapped up, Ashley returned once again to the Pegasus. As she finished docking the sphere, she noticed Jake standing at the dock waiting for her. It was obvious from his expression that he had to tell her something she didn't want to hear.

Ashley tried to reassure him as she asked, "What's up?"

"Ashley, we are going to need to explore other areas to see if there is anything else out here," Jake said.

"I know. We talked about that as a crew," Ashley replied.

"I know this isn't what you want, but I think we need to leave Hot Wings here. It might not be safe for him out there, and he probably needs to stay with his species," Jake explained.

Ashley knew this day would come eventually, and she sighed, "Yeah, you are probably right. I feel responsible for him." Loopens didn't have an identifiable gender, but she still liked to think of Hot Wings as her little guy.

"I know you do. I know you have felt that way since the first day he found you. I also want what's best for him," Jake lamented with a deep sympathy in his eyes.

Ashley nodded at that. She knew that Jake cared about her feelings and also cared about Hot Wings. She knew that he was trying to do what was right.

"I just want him to be happy, and that is probably with his family," Ashley let the words spill out as she realized that this would probably be the last day she would spend with Hot Wings.

A wave washed over Ashley, and she embraced Jake as the sorrow swept over her. The sudden full physical embrace of him was an overwhelming sensation. What was once an unwavering friendship turned into a sense of belonging. Then, with another wave of feelings, Ashley kissed Jake, and ripples of that pure emotion were launched into the universe. The two had a sense that as long as they had each other, everything would be all right.

VISITORS

To be at the bottom of the Europa Ocean is to experience an eternal night. Other than the Pegasus and the glowing orange pool, there were still no other light sources. It was like being huddled next to a campfire with the darkness surrounding you. Creatures seem to peer in from just beyond the campfire's light.

There were brief times that Sarah noticed something odd on the sensors. However, there was never a visual. Just something right at the very edge. So, it was not surprising when another reading appeared, but this time it lingered.

"Captain, we are picking it up again," Sarah said as she gestured toward the reading with a nod. "Whatever it is, it's pretty big. Maybe about ten meters in length."

"EV, let's see if we can find out a little more. Navigate the Pegasus toward that signal," Jake ordered.

The Pegasus started to glide toward the sensor readings. The craft carefully ascended over the loopen colony as it elegantly passed over the little creatures. The forward lights gleamed off the green web as they passed by. The orange glow faded from the hull as the Pegasus left the sanctuary. Hot Wings had gone on one of his excursions, and that might have been for the best as the submersible slipped away without him.

As wonderful as the loopens were and as impressive as their colony was, the crew had orders to explore the area. They also wondered what else was living down here and hoped the new readings might hold some answers. Richard had informed EI of the plans to track the new signals, and the crew was encouraged to proceed. This was their chance to check out the larger environment. As the Pegasus cruised toward the signal and beyond the loopen colony, there was a sense of anticipation in the air. The ocean floor changed into rolling rock fields with slips of sand between them.

The organism they were tracking was moving slowly away from the Pegasus approach, but the distance was closing.

"Skipper, we are approaching the target now," EV said as they closed the gap.

Through the blackness appeared a white figure in the light from the forward spotlights. The full form was masked by what looked like purple velvet curtains wrapping around the animal. The thick skin had a series of tiny circles, similar to a rhino. They still could not yet see the head of the creature as the Pegasus swam in from behind. As this individual swam, it was clear the velvet curtains were actually the creature's tail, dorsal, and ventral fins. As the Pegasus moved alongside, the crew could see two additional purple pectoral fins, and the creature's head with an elongated nose that ended with a downward tilt along with two symmetrical crests that protruded from the back of its skull. The creature swam with its head extended, its crest flat against the neck. The body was sleek as it arched through the water. Two purple crescent shapes appeared along the throat connecting at the lower jaw. As the Pegasus approached, the creature let out a long deep cry. The sound was so loud the crew could feel it in their bones.

"Whoa!" Kiah exclaimed.

Another bioelectrical field appeared on sensors and was headed in their direction. This creature moved quickly as it approached, and Sarah could tell it was about the same size. It was a second creature of the same species.

"We have another one incoming!" Sarah said.

"Let's stay a steady forty meters to port," Jake ordered. "Give them some room. Maybe with some luck, they won't mind that we're here."

The new creature came into view. Rather than the purple fins, this animal had bright orange fins with a white body and orange crescent markings. It positioned itself between the original animal and the Pegasus and appeared to be pushing the original creature away from the Pegasus. EV slightly adjusted course to match, remaining parallel to the creatures. Another minute passed as the two animals swam.

Then the orange creature turned and charged toward the Pegasus, breaking off after a few meters. It opened a toothless mouth and bellowed. The sound caused the Pegasus to vibrate, even with the gravity decking.

"I think that is our hint that we need to back off," Jake said and seemed to nod to the animal through the NIC glass. "EV, hold our position."

EV throttled down, and the Pegasus came to a drifting stop. "All stop, Skipper!" EV reported.

Sarah, Ashley and Kiah could not contain their excitement as grins possessed their faces. "Wow, did you see that second animal come in and warn us off?!" Sarah asked.

"That was so intense!" Ashley said from her engineering station.

"Those colors were striking!" Kiah said as she bounced in her chair. "Why do you think they have such vivid colors in a place this dark?"

"I have no idea, but I want to find out!" Sarah exclaimed.

"Alright, are you guys done geeking out so we can get back to work?" EV asked as he grinned.

"Not quite, EV, but we will keep you posted," Kiah laughed.

"It looks like they are moving off together," Sarah said. The crew watched as the creatures moved beyond the sensors. By then, the Pegasus had traveled pretty far away from the loopen colony.

"That looked like defensive behavior. Maybe trying to protect its mate?" Kiah wondered aloud.

"Possibly," Sarah said as she pondered that question. "The loopens didn't seem to have any distinct gender, but those two creatures had distinctive colors that point to some differences between the pair."

After a few more hours, the Pegasus had made a wide arc around the loopen colony and looked for something else interesting in the area. Toward the end of the day, the crew found themselves looking at the beginnings of a massive trench stretching far below them.

"I think we are going to hold here for now. I want to get some dinner and tackle this with fresh eyes in the morning," Jake said as he stretched beside his chair.

"I can keep an eye out," Richard said as he controlled Bobb, releasing it from the charging dock on top of the Pegasus.

The crew from the bridge already knew they were in for something special. The smell coming from the galley was divine.

Dyami saw something new that night. Rather than tedious glances, new looks were exchanged, ones of partnership. He would ignore that for now. "So, what are we calling those creatures, EV?"

"How about crown cloaks?" EV replied. "I mean, with that big crest that looks like a crown and the cool fins that look like a wizard's cloak," EV added.

"You really do have a knack for naming things!" Dyami laughed. EV knew he was being a bit sarcastic for fun, and EV liked that game.

That night, Ben had provided the first batch of portobello mushrooms from the hydroponics lab, and Dyami had made them delectable.

"Dyami, I would be honored if I could learn to cook from you," EV meant it but reflected the sarcasm. "Actually, this is probably all Ben's doing, huh? These are the best portobello mushrooms I have ever had!" EV said with his mouth half full.

"Yeah! Thanks!" Ben exclaimed, laughing.

"So, what's the plan for tomorrow? Are we going to see if we can find our lovely couple?" EV asked, unaware of the two people in the room that blushed slightly.

Dyami could tell the dynamic had changed. He knew that Jake and Ashley were about to get past the blockade each had lived with for so many years. He felt a sense of satisfaction they were finally coming together. *Some relationships just can't be rushed,* he thought.

After dinner, Ashley tapped on the door to the captain's cabin. "Hey, Jake, do you think we could talk?" she inquired.

Jake smiled and nodded. "I was really hoping to talk to you too."

"Before you say anything else, I need to tell you..." Ashley mustered up her nerves and took the leap. "I care about you very deeply, Jake. I have always admired you, and you are my closest friend. I can't imagine my life without you. I want to be with you in every way possible, and I realize that means changing our lives. I don't want to lose you as a friend, but I feel there is so much more for us. I think that is how you feel too. Isn't it?"

Jake had made his way across the room and spread his arms to embrace her. He had been nodding the entire time she had been speaking. Ashley could see emotions welling within his eyes. "I would go anywhere with you. I trust you with my life, and I trust you with my heart!" Jake replied.

The pair shared a kiss that felt like an eternity. Lips caressed across one another as they moved with sheer passion. Breaths quickened and fell hot on parallel necks.

"After this mission, we will figure out what to do with the rest of our lives," Jake whispered in Ashley's ear. She kissed him on the neck, and he felt the tip of her nose as she nodded.

There is something to be said about being slow, smooth, and deliberate. Some things you enjoy in your life deserve your entire focus and attention. Tonight, the pair expressed this attention toward one another.

THREE-UNION

"Sarah, I think you better see this," Samantha's voice came through the audio com. Samantha was on the Earth Dock shift that morning. It was early enough that Richard had not yet made it in, and in the background, Sarah could hear her asking someone to contact him. Richard was often on the audio com during the day cycle, but while the Pegasus was stationary, he had returned home to get some sleep.

"There is a pair of bioelectrical fields coming toward the Pegasus," Samantha announced through the com.

Sarah had shot out of the galley and made her way to her seat on the bridge when Samantha's voice chimed through again. "Actually, there are three signals now."

From the console, Sarah saw the two creatures from the previous day were returning, and another life form was approaching from a different vector. *This could get interesting,* she thought.

"What have we got?" Jake asked as he entered the bridge a moment later.

"We have three bioelectrical fields that match the creatures we saw yesterday. They are moving toward us slowly," Sarah answered.

"So, they are coming back?" Jake asked.

Sarah and Kiah looked at each other and shrugged. "They don't appear to be in any hurry," Sarah said.

"Well, let's hold position to see if they come to us," Jake said as he examined the sensors over Sarah's shoulder.

The creatures moved slowly, taking several hours to reach the Pegasus. Sarah noted that all three arrived at nearly the same time. Through the front NIC glass, the crew saw the approach. The two crown cloaks from the previous day swam into view. "Magnify," Jake said as the pair approached. The forward augmented NIC glass overlay changed to a magnified camera view and showed the first pair as they swam in slow circles around one another. Their cloak fins softly touched, intertwining the orange and purple.

"They're beautiful," Dyami said quietly.

Just then, the third creature appeared. The fins were a brilliant shade of green that paired with the other two colors. It joined the others, and the three started to glow and swim in a slow circular dance. A sudden bioluminescence burst came from their fins as the three caressed each other. The three creatures were slowly tumbling around each other as the glow became more intense.

"Captain, we may want to kill the outside lights so we don't disturb them," Kiah suggested.

Jake nodded, "Do it!"

The crew just stared at the mesmerizing sight. As the scene progressed, it was apparent that the light rippled any time the three sets of fins touched. It appeared as a physical manifestation of the contact between the three creatures.

A minute went by before Sarah noticed something else. "It can't be..." she rejoiced. A small and now very familiar creature appeared on the sensors.

Sure enough, it was Hot Wings!

"There's Hot Wings!" Sarah exclaimed.

The little loopen had caught a ride with the green crown cloak and was visible in the glow emanating from the creatures. They hadn't seen him riding with the larger crown cloak.

"What? Really?!?!" Ashley trilled with excitement.

"That crazy hot shot!" EV shouted.

"Ashley, I have an idea. Let's get down to the marine lab," Jake said.

Jake and Ashley met Ben in the marine lab on deck two. As they entered, Ben was already looking through the front glass at the crown cloaks. "What's up?" he asked as Jake and Ashley approached.

"Hot Wings came back!" Ashley said as she barely contained her excitement.

Ben looked a bit shocked. "You mean he swam all this way?" he asked in disbelief.

"It looks like he might have hitched a ride," Jake added, nodding toward the green crown cloak. "Ben, we have already filled the large aquarium with local water, correct?" Jake asked.

"Yes, it was readied before we left the loopen colony," Ben replied.

"Well, let's see if our little friend wants another lift. Please open the water lock on the port aquarium," Jake said as he smiled.

Ben keyed a few commands on his console, and the lock door located on the outside of the port aquarium opened with a thunk. The opening was just large enough that a person could swim through to access the aquarium from the outside.

As if on cue, Hot Wings glided through the lock as it opened, and into the Pegasus aquarium, swimming up to the glass where Ashley stood. There was an expression of great joy on her face as the little loopen approached. She laughed as the improbable seemed to occur again. She had her little guy back. *It's funny how he just seems to show up,* Ashley thought.

Hot Wings glowed as he hovered by the aquarium glass.

"Alright, let's get him settled in. I'm sure Sarah wants to follow our new friends. Ben, can you give him some food and close the lock while we are underway? If there are any troubles or odd behavior with him, let me know immediately," Jake ordered. "He seems intent on coming with us, but he is free to come and go as he wishes."

Ashley reached out and touched Jake's arm. "Thank you," she said with a smile.

He smiled back at her before leaving the room and returning to the bridge.

ELECTRICITY

"Do you mind if we follow them?" Sarah asked nodding to the screen where the three crown cloaks where slowly moving off. Bobb only had minimal running lights as the drone slowly followed the creatures, recording the interaction between the creatures' glowing fins as they touched and shined.

"Sure. Hot Wings is along for the ride in one of the aquariums," Jake explained. Sarah gave Jake a wondering glance but then shrugged a bit.

"Let's follow them! EV, just keep the Pegasus behind the crown cloaks and give them plenty of room," Jake ordered.

The ridges of the abyssal trench loomed like titans in the dark ocean. The inverted peaks of the trench stretched out below the crown cloaks. They descended, gliding through the void, illuminating the shale with a ghostly light. Shadows mingled with their bioluminescent glow along the sharp edges of the rock.

Ashley made her way back to the bridge. When she looked at her display, she gasped. Sensors were detecting a massive high-energy electrical field. It was emanating from further down in the trench. "There is something there!" Ashley reported. "It looks like some type of electrical field is just ahead and it's not biological!"

"Yeah, I see it too," Sarah confirmed.

"What can you tell me about it?" Jake asked.

"It's like nothing I have seen before. The energy spike is massive, but there is some type of distortion," Ashley explained.

"What's it doing?" Jake asked.

"It appears to be stationary, but it is just ahead of us if we maintain this vector," Ashley reported.

The crown cloaks were also heading in that same direction. The Pegasus easily fit through the trench, looking like a tiny child's toy in the vast chasm.

"Alright, let's keep going," Jake said softly.

When the Pegasus got within half a kilometer of the artificial power source, the crown cloaks started to ascend through the water. The crew of the Pegasus could still hear their bellows.

"Keep on the power signal. I want to find out where that is coming from," Jake ordered.

"Alright, we will follow the crown cloaks for a while with Bobb," Richard said. Richard was now at the audio com coming from Earth Dock.

What the crew was unaware of, and the sensors couldn't detect, was a constructed deck lying beneath over two thousand years of sand brought in by the ocean currents. This alien artifact had lain dormant through the ages waiting for the right conditions. The Pegasus sailed through the trench and above the artifact, closing in on the power source. As the Pegasus glided to the center of the clearing, an unexpected event occurred.

Two massive crescent half-rings rose above the Pegasus, surrounding them. They were made from dark metal and beamed in piercing blue lights. A strong energy field was being emitted from the rings, and before there was time to react, the Pegasus was trapped in the conjoining fields. The rings formed a massive cross, overlapping into a half sphere that spanned the entire clearing.

"Report," Jake barked as he tried to assess the situation.

"There is a massive amount of energy coming off those rings. The energy is pulling us toward the center!" Ashley explained. The Pegasus came to an abrupt halt.

"We need to get out of here! EV, reverse course and see if you can get us free!" Jake ordered. Before Jake was done speaking, there was a new problem.

"We have a massive energy spike coming from below us!" Ashley responded quickly.

Below the Pegasus, the ocean floor seemed to twist before opening into a beam of light as bright as a star. A rift between worlds had opened.

MISSING

"What the hell just happened?" Richard shouted. The displays in front of him had flashed a new message that simply read 'offline' with a disconnected icon. Richard cursed and banged his hand on the desk in front of him.

Samantha also stared at the displays with the red offline message. "I have no idea! I am trying to get the signal back now," she said as she furiously punched in commands. "I can't reestablish the connection to the Pegasus!"

"Did something disable the satellite?" Richard asked.

Samantha looked and saw the satellite was still online. "The satellite is still operational," she responded.

After the shuttle Resolute had dropped off the Pegasus, it left a geosynchronous coms satellite in Europa's orbit. The satellite maintained a microscopic tear in space, allowing instant communications. The satellite was still there, but the connection to the Pegasus was severed.

"Can you establish coms with the Marybeth's crew?" Richard asked, trying to think through the panic occurring within his mind. That crew had been constructing the lift and small base to help resupply the Pegasus in the upcoming weeks.

The display turned black for a second before a new message said, 'connecting' with a yellow icon.

"This is Tim," a burly man's voice came through the com feed.

"Tim, we have a situation. Can you make contact with the Pegasus?" Richard asked quickly.

"Let me give them a try," Tim's voice came through.

Moments passed in what seemed to be an eternity.

"No sir. I tried, but I didn't get any response," Tim's voice came through the feed again. "Something wrong?"

"Tim, keep trying! If you get through, let us know!" Richard ordered.

Richard had another thought. He turned to Samantha, whose hands were still racing across the controls.

"Try to link the com satellite directly to Bobb," Richard ordered as his mind raced with the current scenario. Samantha tapped a few keys, and the display flashed the connecting message.

There was a wait of several seconds that seemed like hours as the satellite attempted to handshake directly with the Bobb drone. The display flashed as the input from Bobb's video feed displayed on the screen. It was dark and only a few small floating particles were visible in Bobb's light. Richard used the glove and reached for Bobb's control stick. Bobb didn't move.

"Just a sec, Bobb's systems weren't built to be accessed like this," Samantha said. She flashed through screens as she tried to make the control functions respond to Richard's commands. With a sudden jerk, the controls were routed through. "The controls might be a bit clunky. I had to manually patch the basics," she reported.

Richard was already concentrating on piloting the drone. Most of Bobb's functions were offline. The main sensors and navigation were offline, since those functions were all controlled through the main array on the Pegasus. At least a few things still worked, such as the lights, video, propulsion, and manual controls. Richard's stomach twisted when he saw that the battery on Bobb was nearly depleted.

Richard spun Bobb on its axis and changed vector, following a course that would lead to the Pegasus. Light reflected on the sheer gray cliffs as Bobb descended into the trench. Then a cloud of silty sand lay ahead. Richard continued to push through as the visibility dropped. Then the ocean floor came into view quickly, and despite Richard pulling hard at the control, the slow response time caused Bobb to bounce off the seabed.

Richard let out a frustrated growl as he tapped the controls to ascend and Bobb rose several meters. The last thing they had seen at Earth Dock was the Pegasus approaching the power source, and Richard hoped something had simply interfered with the communication connection.

Bobb glided over some small mounds as it entered a flat expanse on the ocean floor, silt still obscuring most of the view. Richard was sure this was the direction the Pegasus was traveling before the disconnect. Bobb smoothly crossed the flat expanse toward the middle of the clearing. Then Richard saw something.

In the middle was a circular crater in the sand. It was about twenty meters across and looked like an antlion hole. The material looked like it had striations and might have been recently disturbed. Richard did his best to go around the disturbance. Losing Bobb to an ambush predator hidden in the sand would be catastrophic.

Nothing moved except Bobb and the silt falling slowly to the ocean floor as the drone crossed the second half of the clearing.

Richard wondered if he had already passed the electrical signal the Pegasus had detected. There was no way to tell for sure without any sensors. Bobb's light glistened off metal as an alien bay door appeared from the silt and shadows. The large vertical door appeared to be solid metal and was embedded into the cliff face. It was about eight meters high, twenty meters long, and looked ominous after countless years of being exposed to the deep. Then Bobb's light faded as the battery level dropped to zero, and Earth Dock lost its connection to the now-stranded drone.

No Pegasus. Richard had hit a wall.

SOMEWHERE BEYOND

The Pegasus fell through the rift. This trip was not just connecting two points in space with a fold; this was something more. An unimaginable tear through the tapestry of the universe, its threads connecting to destinations unknown.

Sarah felt many lifetimes flash before her eyes as paths she hadn't taken played out in a moment. Realities stretched out before her as they blurred together in a single instant. Her consciousness never processing the details of the worlds she had never visited as she peered through her own eyes into the lives she had never led.

Sarah drew a breath, then another. The crew was still in a fog as they regained awareness of their surroundings. Breath came slowly, lungs struggling to gasp for air. There was deep violet light coming from outside.

"Is everyone alright?" Jake finally asked.

"Yeah..." Kiah and Sarah said in unison.

"I'm alright," Ashley confirmed.

Jake hit the com button on the captain's chair. "Ben? Dyami? You guys good?"

"Yeah, we are here... What happened?!" Ben's voice came through the com a moment later.

"I'm not sure..." Jake said as he looked around.

Jake tapped the com link button on the captain's chair. "Pegasus to Earth Dock, do you read?" There was silence. "Richard, can you hear me?" Another long silence as Jake waited for a response. The button changed from blinking red to a solid red as the communication equipment reported the lack of any signal.

"We're not on Europa anymore!" Sarah said as she noted the starlight coming through the front NIC glass. She realized that light was filtering down to the depth they were currently at. Everything around them seemed almost black except the small crack of violet light filtering from a surface above.

Jake swallowed hard and saw the point immediately.

"Ashley, check all critical systems and any impacts to the ship based on the external environment. I need to know if we are in any danger," Jake ordered immediately.

"On it!" Ashley responded.

Then Jake focused on Sarah, "Sarah, is there anything around us? Do we have sensors?" Jake asked.

The sensors didn't seem to be working properly. "Just a second," Sarah replied.

Sarah noticed the issue and initiated a reset of the sensor system that had crashed during the transition. Ashley was working through her checks.

As the sensors reset, EV reported, "It looks like we are at a depth of three hundred meters, and we are twenty meters from the seabed."

Sarah's sensors sprung back to life. "There are a few life signs in the area, but they appear to be only tiny animals," she reported.

"Any sign of the rings?" Jake asked. The dismay of being lost crept into his thoughts.

"I reset a few systems, and all critical systems are functioning properly. The pressure on the hull has decreased dramatically, and hull integrity is nominal. The Pegasus is safe, but everything else is gone," Ashley said from the engineering station as panic started to set into her voice. "No electrical fields. No satellite. No outpost. No Earth. Nothing!" she said, flipping through the readings frantically.

"The readings from the sensors do not match any known ocean. There is plenty of information but nothing to indicate where we are," Sarah confirmed.

Ben and Dyami entered the bridge.

"Everyone alright up here?" Ben asked as he quickly scanned the room.

"Everything is gone," Ashley repeated as shock set in.

"What do you mean gone?" Ben asked.

"We are lost…" Ashley trailed off.

Ben had a confused look on his face. "Lost?"

"We traveled somewhere beyond known space," Sarah explained.

"What? How can that be?" Ben was trying to wrap his mind around the situation.

"I don't know, but we are no longer on Europa or in any known ocean," Sarah said.

Ben felt dread, and he started to shout, "Where are we? What about getting back to my family? I promised Angi… I promised…"

"We need to hold it together. Let's assess the situation and figure out what happened and where we are," Jake said. He felt the enormity of the situation as consequences weighed on him, but he needed to remain calm and keep his anxiety in check.

"That is easy for you to say. I left my family to help on this mission, and you are saying we are lost!" Ben shouted.

"Ben, I'm sure Jake will do everything in his power to get us home. Clearly, we found our way here. There must be a way back," Dyami tried to reassure him.

Ben's mind was in a whirl. He couldn't find a reason to blame anyone, but fear was taking control. Fear of never seeing his wife and kids ever again. *What can I do?* The thought rang out again and again. *What can I do? Maybe this is all a hallucination or a dream? Maybe that is the simplest explanation?* Ben left the bridge and headed for the medical lab. Maybe he could prove this wasn't actually happening.

Ashley watched Ben leave. Then she remembered that Hot Wings was still down in the aquarium. "Oh no.. Hot Wings?!" she exclaimed.

"Ashley, go check on him. We can't afford another surprise right now," Jake nodded toward the door.

Ashley rushed off the bridge toward the marine lab. As she stepped off the lift and entered the lab's door, she saw he was fine.

"I'm so glad you're alright!" Ashley breathed a sigh of relief. "I can't imagine losing you. We will need to find you a way home, too," Ashley said to Hot Wings.

"Everything alright down there?" Jake said through the com.

"Yeah, he's good. Everything is fine," Ashley replied.

"Good… Ashley, I need you back up here. We need to figure out our next step," Jake replied.

"I will be right there," Ashley replied.

Kiah was white as a ghost, and Sarah tried to console her as Ashley returned to the bridge.

"Since we need to figure out where we are, and there are no obvious signs of civilization in the immediate area, my suggestion would be to surface and take a look around," EV said.

"That's a sound plan. We might be able to determine our position by using the stars around this planet or moon," Jake remarked. "Do you have any other ideas, EV?"

EV thought for a moment. "We should also scout around and see if we can find another crescent ring gate. It was hidden in the sand before, so maybe there is one around here. One of those things brought us here, and maybe it can send us back." EV was unphased by the event. He was accustomed to being on his own with Sarah and Kiah. This was simply another adventure, and they always found their way through a jam in the end.

Sarah added, "That could be very risky. We aren't sure how the gates work, and leaping through another gate might get us even more lost. Establishing our current position should be the priority. After that, we can take the next step based on what we know. I do find it puzzling that no civilization or ruins are within the area. Why would a gateway send us here?" Sarah thought aloud.

"That is a good question, but as you said, let's start with where we are. Let's surface and look around. Unless someone has a better idea?" Jake waited for a moment, but no one spoke.

"Alright, EV bring us up," Jake ordered.

EV punched in the throttle, and the Pegasus rose smoothly within this new ocean.

Dyami nodded his head. He had experienced the tragic loss of loved ones. Over many years that loss eventually healed, and he found comfort with the people close to him. Jake and Ashley were his friends; if anyone could get the Pegasus through this, it would be them.

As the Pegasus ascended, the light became brighter. It changed from a deep dark shade of violet into light pinks and lavender purples.

"Just expose the top sensor tower to the atmosphere, so we can get some readings and switch over to that camera," Jake ordered.

The main display switched to a new video feed from a camera that looked directly at the surface. As the Pegasus ascended, it became apparent that there was more than one point of light. It appeared that two burning orbs were rippling in the waves above them. One was noticeably more prominent than the other. As the camera lens broke the surface, the much closer yellow star came into view. Its light had a hint of ruby brilliance as it burned in the sky. Behind that star, the smaller orb of fire was a massive blue giant. It was further away from their current position but still showed its presence in this daytime sky. The sky itself was a deep violet with a gradation of dark blue.

"Is the atmosphere breathable?" Sarah immediately wondered aloud and started reviewing the data. "According to the scans, the atmosphere consists mostly of nitrogen, twenty-two percent oxygen, and other trace gases. The air is remarkably similar to Earth and breathable," Sarah reported. "However, just breathing here might still have a risk of unknown pathogens. The Pegasus might still be the safest option for air," Sarah added.

"Is there any way to tell where we are by these stars?" Jake asked.

The crew looked for additional details. They saw pink fluffy clouds covering one of the horizons that turned to darker rain clouds further into a storm on the very edge of another horizon. But they only could see the two main stars in the daytime sky. There was also no land in sight, as the ocean stretched as far as the eye could see.

"I'll run it through the astronomical mapping system, but these two stars alone are probably not enough to determine our position," EV replied.

Jake swallowed hard as he faced the events that were unfolding before him. "This mission just turned into a mission to survive. So let's run through what we have and what we know," Jake said.

"First, Dyami, visually inspect the air scrubbers," Jake ordered.

"Yes, Captain. I will check them, and we still can convert water into oxygen and bleed off the CO2 if we need to," Dyami reported.

"Second, I want to ensure that there is no damage to the BRIL reactor and that the Pegasus still has the power we need. Ashley, please run a full reactor and systems check when we are done here. If we are careful, we should have enough biomass to fuel the reactor for several years. The Pegasus is our only lifeline right now. We need to be sure she is in top working order," Jake asserted.

Ashley nodded in agreement.

"Third, we need to assess our water and food situation," Jake said as he ran through the survival priorities.

"I will do some tests, but we probably can still filter the outside water. We have about two-hundred gallons of reserve filtered water and the water left within the recycling system. So we should be good for a while," Dyami said.

"Regarding food, we have just over thirty days of food, including the estimations from the growth in the hydroponics lab. Then about one week of emergency rations," Dyami reported. "I also want to note that it might not be a good idea to starve ourselves too much. We need sharp minds to get ourselves out of this one. But if this is longer than a few weeks, we will need to find other food sources," he added.

"Ashley, do we still have the NIC printer on deck three with a full material cartridge?" Jake asked.

Ashley nodded and said, "Yeah, and related to that, I have an idea for getting back in contact with Earth. It might be a long shot, but it could work."

LUCK

Dyami checked the water filtration and air scrubbers and found they were fully operational within this new oceanic environment. He even ran through the checks a second time to verify the results. Ashley had run several diagnostics on the BRIL reactor and the other various systems around the ship. After resetting a few minor systems, all the status indicator lights were green with the status of 'operational'. Their lives depended on these systems, and the crew felt relieved to find they could still rely on the Pegasus.

The Pegasus wasn't a custom submersible. Many features had been modified for Europa, but with the tight timeline for this mission, there wasn't time to customize many of the schematics for the Pegasus. It was the latest design for this class of ship and still contained certain components that were never needed on Europa. The Pegasus was still equipped with a magnetic rail launcher that had the capability to launch satellites into space. After arriving on this world, Ashley had planned to launch an oceanic scanning satellite that could map large ocean areas and check water and weather conditions that they might encounter. That information might just save their lives, and Ashley knew it. As she thought more about the launcher, she had another idea that just might get them home.

"So, you have an idea on reestablishing communications with Earth?" Jake asked as he followed Ashley into the NIC printing bay.

"Yeah, I remember reading about a prototype communications satellite with astrometric mapping software that had been developed for use with the magnetic rail launcher. It will take some tweaks, but I can get it to work. However, there is still a problem," Ashley replied.

Jake frowned, and his brow furrowed as he realized the situation. "To establish communications, Earth would need to know where we are. They would need to pinpoint a transmitter to our exact star system even to have any chance to reestablish communications."

"Exactly!" Ashley confirmed. "Maybe they have some clue where we are, so I think it's still worth a shot," she added.

Jake nodded in agreement.

Ashley found the prototype blueprint in the NIC database and keyed in the print confirmation. She would tweak and test the final design before launch. The NIC printer started the cycle as beams of light appeared and began to build up the NIC material for the communications satellite. "Alright, that will take a few hours," Ashley said as she watched the aerodynamic shape start to take form.

"Are you ok?" Jake asked after a few moments.

"Yeah, I think so. This all happened so suddenly that I have not had time to process everything that has occurred," Ashley replied. "What about you?" she asked quietly.

"I'm responsible for the crew, and that means bringing them home safe," Jake said as he looked at the floor.

Ashley glided a hand across Jake's cheek and lifted his chin slightly as she locked eyes with him. "It's alright. We will figure this out together," she said in a calm voice.

Jake nodded, but his face still showed great concern. "Why did this happen?" he asked rhetorically.

Even though she sensed the question was rhetorical, Ashley responded. "You couldn't have known this would happen. Sometimes, even with the best plans, even when we take every precaution, things just happen. It is not something that you did wrong. It is just something we must deal with now," she said, pouring empathy into her words.

"You're right, but I'm still responsible," Jake said sadly.

"You are going to do everything you can to fix it, Jake. That is who you are. That is why I trust you. That is why the crew trusts you," Ashley said.

Jake nodded, but he still could feel the pit within him remain.

Dyami entered the medical lab and saw Ben staring off into space. As Dyami entered, Ben didn't acknowledge his arrival. Dyami contemplated leaving Ben to his thoughts and exiting the lab, but instead, he approached. He put his hand on Ben's shoulder and squeezed gently with his thumb. Ben turned, but his facial expression didn't change as he stared ahead, unblinking. Dyami knew from the look that Ben needed more time to process their predicament. So rather than broach the topic directly, Dyami asked, "Do you need any help with your work?"

"I just thought I would check on a few things," Ben replied. After a brief moment of silence, he added, "I needed some work to distract me. I need to help solve this problem."

"Contributing to the solution is important," Dyami said as he gently nodded. "Is there anything I can do to help you?" Dyami's offer was there for Ben, with whatever he might need.

Ben nodded somberly. Their situation was difficult for Ben to fully wrap his mind around. He needed to keep his promise to Angi, but things were out of his control. Periods of denial and panic were counter-balancing, as his emotions skipped between these anxieties. Ben's analytical mind struggled to find any answers within their current reality.

"Are we hallucinating?" Dyami asked.

Ben just shook his head. "I didn't find anything to suggest that." He paused before adding, "I'm collecting air and water samples to test for dangerous bacteria or pathogens. We might need to be able to breathe and swim out there."

"Tell me what I can do to help," Dyami said.

"Just let me work on this alone for a while," Ben said.

Dyami left him with his thoughts but knew Ben would need a good friend soon.

Ashley finished her last few tweaks and picked up the sleek, long shape with a dense solar panel pattern on the outside shell. The satellite was very light. Guidance flaps lined the outside and would help to guide the projectile into orbit. A pressure field would help to ensure the satellite would survive the journey. She loaded the projectile into the launcher securing it in place with the magnetic rail console. Ashley turned to Jake and asked, "Are we forgetting anything?"

Jake kissed her. "Thanks for talking with me earlier," he said softly.

"Jake, you can count on me. I'm here. Whatever you need. Always," Ashley said.

"Let's get this thing launched," he said.

Ashley confirmed the launch, and with an electronic pulse, the coms satellite started its journey. She then reset the NIC printer for the oceanic scanning satellite and started that sequence.

"Alright, lets head to the bridge and see if we get really lucky," Jake said.

At the engineering station on the bridge, they saw that the coms satellite had reached orbit and seemed functional. The entire crew gathered to see the results. After leaving the atmosphere, the satellite identified other celestial bodies and began ascertaining its position relative to Sol. A few minutes elapsed as the satellite's programming worked on the search.

Then the satellite had the answer.

Their position was 31,502 light-years from Earth, currently. The Pegasus was still in the Milky Way Galaxy on a neighboring arm but farther than anyone had ever traveled before by over two orders of magnitude.

The Earth Dock transmitter would need to be configured and calibrated to point to this exact star system for any chance of a communication signal. At this distance, Jake was unsure if communication would even be possible and held his breath as the satellite searched for a connection. The longer the search progressed, the more distant Jake felt from their home. Then the coms satellite returned a blank array of communication options. There was no communication signal received from Earth, or any other type of reachable signal.

"Shit!" EV exclaimed as the news appeared on the engineering station. "Now what?"

"We find a way back as soon as possible. That is the only correct answer," Ben's words were insistent.

"Ben's right. We need to find a way back," Jake said.

"There isn't anything significant here. What do you propose we do?" Sarah asked.

"We remedy that issue. We already have the oceanic scanning satellite printing, and that will give us some idea of the surrounding area and water conditions. We can also print a couple of aqua probes to help us search. They are not as sophisticated as Bobb, but we will make due," Jake replied.

SEARCH

Ashley realized she had fallen asleep at some point as her senses recognized the dream world. A familiar entity was floating within the space. Ashley gasped as her conscious mind pulled her back into reality.

"I gotcha. Everything is alright," Jake reassured her.

She had fallen asleep against him in his cabin as they were reviewing data on her tablet. The Pegasus was still at the ocean's surface, and Ashley heard the water as it lapped against the hull. Violet hue spilled through the NIC window in the captain's cabin as it filtered through ocean water and fragmented into pillars of light.

"How long was I asleep?" Ashley asked.

"Just an hour. Dyami is keeping watch now," Jake said. "You should probably get some more sleep if you can."

Ashley blinked once and then closed her eyes again. "Thanks. I just had a weird dream."

Jake softly rubbed her shoulder as she drifted back into sleep.

The next time Ashley awoke, the light from the window was gone. The suns had set after eighteen hours. The two closest stars mirrored each other's movements across the sky, setting around the same time and leaving twelve hours of darkness ahead.

Jake started to stir as Ashley awoke. Ashley's head was lying against him, and his gray knit shirt was soft against her cheek. She slowly got to her feet and tried to remember where they had left off.

They had learned quite a bit before their minds had demanded sleep. Through the data, they determined the relative position of many astrological bodies and the rotation and tilt of the planet they were currently on, allowing them to know the basics. This planet was larger than Earth, and the gravity was comparable at 1.03g. Water temperature and salinity were similar to many tropical regions of Earth's oceans. The crew also verified the inventory of their supplies. They knew where they were in relation to Earth. But they had no contact with anyone else and no way to know if Earth was looking for them. The crew had to move forward. What other choice did they have?

Sarah had launched the oceanic scanning satellite into orbit once it had finished printing. The last of the satellite's data was coming through just before Jake and Ashley entered the bridge. The front NIC glass was mostly submerged in water, but toward the top, the star-scape was clearly visible. The brilliant array of stars was the Milky Way Galaxy, stretching across an unfamiliar sky. Never-before-seen stars filled the heavens, including young stars whose light hadn't yet reached Earth. Sarah stared out at the nebula that shined in the night sky. The star cluster light reflected on the water world where the Pegasus now resided.

"So that's the only land?" EV asked as he looked at the navigation console. There was a long, narrow string of islands about 32,000 kilometers away. The largest island was only fifty kilometers wide. The Pegasus was at least a twenty-five-day journey away from the islands, and that was in optimal conditions if they moved all eighteen hours in the thirty-hour day.

"What do you think, Skipper?" asked EV as he turned to Jake.

Jake looked at Sarah. "Sarah, do you think Richard is trying to find us?" he asked.

"I know he is searching for us, but I have a feeling it will take some time for him to figure it out. I would have retraced the Pegasus's steps if I were in his shoes. If he did that with Bobb, why isn't Bobb here too? There could be any number of reasons for that, but none of the reasons I can think of are simple," Sarah said.

"What if he finds a way to open the portal again, but we are too far away?" Ben asked.

"I'm not so sure that was simply a portal. I remember we were on Europa before the disorientation. After that, we found ourselves in this new world, far from every other human in existence. There's nothing around here, so far, to indicate a gate on this side," Ashley said.

Jake nodded. "EV, I want you to set up a search pattern for this area. Let's find out if there is another ring gate or other indication of where we might look. In the meantime, that should give Richard time to see if he can send something through the Europa gate again. I think it is our best option before heading in any direction," Jake said.

EV set the navigation and started the descent.

"Kiah, please drop an aqua probe with a camera. I want to keep tabs on where we landed in case someone comes looking for us," Jake requested.

After several hours of searching the area and seabed, the crew did not find anything to indicate any structures or artificial electrical fields were close to where they had landed. In fact, the seafloor in this area was unremarkable beyond the layers of violet water. Even the water's composition was remarkably similar to Earth's oceans. The main difference was the light spectrum coming from the stars above. The bottom was a slowly sloping sandy area, but they found no evidence of metal alloys or anything beneath the sand.

"Let's widen the search area. There must be something around here," Jake said.

The Pegasus and crew continued their search for another four hours when the sensors detected numerous large bioelectrical signals.

GRAZERS

The Pegasus cruised slowly into the rock formation at a depth of sixty meters. The rock pillars had variable heights resembling the towers of a large city. A thick layer of plants covered each rock's face. Twisting roots held each plant tight to the underwater rock faces, ensuring the current did not carry them away. An array of elongated heart-shaped leaves bathed in the suns' rising light. The lavender-colored water was slightly obscuring the true color of the foliage. The brilliant green hue of the leaves was revealed as they caught the spotlights coming from the Pegasus. The scene held a sense of majesty as they approached.

Sarah was the first to see the new creature as it clung to a huge bundle of roots. The animal was substantial measuring nearly twelve meters long, and had a powerful tail. Its dorsal and ventral fins stretched the entire length of the body. Patterns of green blended into black that matched the foliage, and shadows ran across the creatures' flanks. A set of small arms held onto the roots as the duck-billed mouth ate the nearby leaves. Most of the body lay flat against the rock to avoid the persistent current as the animal grazed. A large red hump sat on the bridge of the creature's nose, just before two large eyes that shined metallic gray.

"It can't be a coincidence that the crescent ring gate brought us here. It brought us to another alien ocean filled with life. I hope we figure out why," Sarah said.

The long neck of the creature changed angle as it ate. Leaf particulates floated through the water as the creature ground the material with pachyderm-looking teeth.

There was a sudden crackle from the audio feed in the marine lab.

"Uh, guys..." Dyami's voice came through the com with a slight shrill feedback loop. "Hot Wings escaped!"

Ashley's eyes widened as she saw Hot Wings approaching the creature as it ate. "How the hell did that happen?"

"I hope we didn't just witness the beginning of an apocalyptic event," Jake said as he frowned.

Ashley was running to the Swift Sphere even before the order was given. She needed to get him back. She had to make sure that Hot Wings was safe on this planet...and this planet was safe from Hot Wings. Making her way to the moon pool dock, Ashley climbed into the sphere and plunged into the ocean.

"I'll get him!" Ashley said into the audio com. Ashley felt her heart racing as she maneuvered to catch up. She also noted how Hot Wings had grown; he was about forty centimeters long and moved quickly. As she got closer, she saw Hot Wings alongside one of the grazing beasts. The creatures just seemed to want to eat. As Ashley approached, the creature turned a head slowly to Hot Wings. They stared at each other for a second without moving. Green emerald eyes stared into their big gray metallic counterparts.

As Ashley moved closer, the creature appeared to greet her with an understanding nod. She was not sure what to do, so she just squeaked out, "Hello?" not entirely sure if the creature would be able to hear her through the NIC glass.

The creature seemed to nod a bit and then went back to eating. Ashley felt a slight blush fill her cheeks. She looked at Hot Wings again, "WINGS! Don't push it, buddy!" Ashley saw an expression of joy in Hot Wing's little green emerald eyes.

With that glint of joy, Hot Wings executed his next tactic. Run and find another friend!

"Ashley, Hot Wings is on your port one hundred meters," Sarah's voice came through the audio com. Ashley glided up to another one of the creatures. "We are calling them 'grazers', by the way," EV's voice shot through the com.

"Of course we are," Ashley snickered. Ashley thought about how EV might be enjoying the naming role a little too much. But, in reflection, she was out here chasing one alien species on another alien world, hoping all hell wouldn't break lose.

"I think he might be taking a look around, saying hello to the new neighbors. Hot Wings is a pretty friendly guy," EV suggested.

"Well, one thing is for sure, he seems perfectly happy swimming in these unfamiliar waters," Sarah added.

Ashley had finally caught up to Hot Wings. He was hanging out with another new friend. Ashley had been trying to devise a plan to persuade the loopen to return to the Pegasus. So far, the only thing she could think of was if he got hungry, he might want the o-gel. However, that hope was dashed when Hot Wings started trying to eat the local flora. He opened up his mouth and stuck a whole leaf in. The creature just stared at Hot Wings for a moment, looking at him with interested regard. At that point, Hot Wings coughed up the leaf as green mushy-ooze filled the water. Ashley just smirked. "Not to your liking?"

The grazer looked at Ashley then and bellowed softly. It was a familiar sound. The past echoed in Ashley's recent memories. How was this world connected to Europa? How were they going to get home?

That is when Hot Wings swam off again. This time he just kept swimming for several minutes. Ashley started to worry that he might try to escape, then they ran across something unexpected. Within the rock pillar formations was a small clearing with a sandy bottom, and in the center of the clearing was a raised, flat metal surface. Green roots and heart-shaped leaves wrapped around the outside. However, the top was unencumbered by vegetation. It was apparent that this place was a shrine. Hot Wings was swimming in graceful loops in the middle of the shrine and appeared to be waiting for Ashley.

"Pegasus, do you see this?" Ashley asked.

"I'm not sure what I'm looking at," Sarah said over the com.

"Ashley, can you get a closer look at the platform?" Jake asked.

As Ashley got closer, she started to be able to make out intricate details carved into the dark metal of the shrine. Lines, swirls, arcs, and shapes adorned the top of the level platform. It appeared to be some type of writing or glyphs.

"Kiah, you know more about languages and patterns than any of us. So what do you make of it?" Jake said as Ashley listened over the com.

"It's fascinating. I'm not sure I have seen anything like this. I will see if the computer can decipher the patterns and will run the still shots through the translation algorithm," Kiah said.

"I think the real question is, how did Hot Wings know this was here?" Sarah asked.

"You're right! He made a beeline here right after we greeted the second creature," Ashley replied.

Ashley took several still shots and videos of the surface and surrounding area, in addition to the passive video and scans that the Swift

Sphere was always recording. Finally, Kiah fed all the input back into the computer for translation. Not surprisingly, the Pegasus returned a status of 'unknown language, additional input required'.

"So, what do we do now?" Ashley asked.

There was a long pause over the audio com feed.

"Well, we need to look around the area to see if there are any more of these. This object is our first clue that there is, or at least has been, intelligent life on this planet, and maybe if we collect enough input for the computer, we can start to figure out why we are here and maybe find a way home," Jake said.

"What about Hot Wings?" Ashley asked.

At that point, Dyami's voice chimed in, "I think I might have a solution for that."

Hot Wings suddenly seemed to perk up and jetted toward the Pegasus. "Whatever you did, it got his attention," Ashley sighed with relief.

Ashley looked carefully around the shrine one last time, trying to see if she had missed anything. Why hadn't they seen any signs of civilization when they first arrived? "What is here that I'm missing? There must be something!" she whispered to herself.

Suddenly she thought she recognized a figure etched into the metal surface. The more she looked at it, the more confident she became. The figure was a loopen!

"Hey, I got some o-gel for you, buddy," Dyami said as Hot Wings entered the large aquarium tank, slipping quickly through the water lock. Ashley docked the sphere a few minutes later and headed straight to the marine lab. Jake and Dyami were already there.

"How did he escape the lock if it was shut?" Jake seemed to be questioning Dyami as Ashley entered the room.

"Well, I'm not entirely sure," Dyami paused while he tried to recall what had happened. "I was working with Ben on a general inoculum for this planet's environment. He wanted to be sure we were protected from any potential pathogens if we needed to leave the ship for any reason. I was collecting some additional air and water samples for Ben from the marine lab. As I entered the lab to pick up the samples, I suddenly lost my train of thought. The next thing I remember is my hand on the open lock button. There's some time missing in my memory."

"Ashley, didn't you say you had a similar experience when you first met the loopens?" Jake asked.

Ashley nodded. "Yeah, this off sensation that my memory was missing time," she replied.

Jake seemed to stare into the distance as he thought about the implications. "I'm not going to lie; this scares me." He paused before speaking again. "We seem to have an alien on board that has the ability to influence our minds. In an environment where he doesn't belong. In a survival situation where we actually might need his help to pull through. So far, from everything we have observed, his actions seem benevolent, but we need to monitor the situation closely. I can't have him risking the lives of the crew." Jake saw a grimace on Ashley's face as he said the last part. "Let's just make sure to keep an eye on him."

Ashley turned back to the aquarium and saw Hot Wings in one of the corners eating a fat lump of o-gel. "Well, at least he came back," she muttered. Jake put a hand on Ashley's shoulder as they watched him eat for a few minutes.

"The good news is that Ben came up with a way to grow the o-gel in his aquarium," Dyami explained. "We should be able to keep him fed easily enough at this point."

Jake nodded as the three watched the little loopen.

The day seemed to stretch on forever, but the suns set after about eighteen hours. Many of the crew had been living on nutrient bars and water while they were working. Dyami made a point that he would prepare their next meal, and the crew gathered for dinner.

Jake had a twisted feeling in his gut. They didn't seem any closer to finding a way home. Maybe they would come across some breakthrough, but the more hours passed, the less likely they would be rescued soon.

"What else can I do to help?" Ben asked, his gaze deadlocked on Jake.

"Your work on the general inoculum is your priority. I know you have made good progress. When do you think it will be ready?" Jake asked.

"It needs time. The bacteria and viruses we have found here are foreign and would not likely infect a human body, but my work will ensure we are safe. Even with the rapid sequencing, this will take time," Ben replied. Then he stared Jake right in the eyes. "I need to go home."

Jake nodded. "Yeah, I'm working on that as best I can."

"Just make sure you keep me in the loop. I need to be able to trust you. So tell me everything that is going on. Period!" Ben said.

"I'm involved with Ashley," Jake blurted out.

Ben looked at him hard. "I don't care about that. Is there anything critical that I need to know?"

"Ben, I promise to share every important detail with you and the rest…" Jake trailed off as Ben raised his hand.

"Fine. Just get us home," Ben said.

Jake and Ben were the last to enter the galley for dinner. As they sat around the dinner table, Jake cleared his throat. Jake looked around the table. Despite his discomfort at the topic of his personal life, he felt that he needed to tell the rest of the crew about his involvement with Ashley.

"Everyone, we all need to trust each other on this mission fully, and I'm not going to withhold any information from any of you. That being said, there is a personal matter I need to share with everyone." Jake looked over at Ashley. She nodded in agreement. "Ashley and I have started a romantic relationship. We have known each other for a long time, and we have admitted our feelings for each other. This was going to be my last mission as her commanding officer. I thought we could get through this mission and sort all the details out after, but that was before this current situation arose."

Jake's statement left everyone just staring at him for a moment. Ben frowned a bit at the thought that his loved ones were so far away.

Finally, Kiah said, "You mean you weren't already a couple at the beginning of this mission?"

Sarah chimed in, "Yeah, that is kinda what I thought too."

A shocked look took hold of Jake's face. "You guys thought we were a couple from the beginning?"

Dyami laughed to himself. He had observed Jake and Ashley tiptoe around their feelings for one another for many years. He had easily identified when their relationship took its next step on this voyage. He knew Jake had conflicted feelings about being the superior officer and having romantic feelings toward a crew member. Then, his morals forced him to admit the relationship to the crew.

"We all knew," Ben said abruptly. "Anything else anyone needs to share?"

Everyone seemed to shake their head at the question. Not many other words were exchanged that night, with everyone lost in their own thoughts.

LURKING

The Pegasus had been traveling across the pillared underwater landscape for just over a day, searching for any more shrines or signs of civilization, and that search had come up empty. The entire crew was vigilant for anything that could lead them to the answers they sought. They had seen hundreds of the grazers, including several small groups that appeared to be younger individuals, even a few egg clutches. Sarah wished that there was more time to study these creatures, but the priority was to find a way home.

Violatis was the name the crew gave to this planet. The term came from the light refracted in the ocean, revealing a spectrum of deep purples and violets. The colors were mesmerizing and added a remarkable beauty to this place. As the midday suns beat down on the sea, the crew came to the end of this biome. The intertwined rock and vine landscape gave way to an enormous trench that started with a sheer cliff. As the Pegasus cameras and sensors peered over the edge, it became evident that the ocean floor was not visible. According to the sensors, the other side was over sixty kilometers away.

"EV, hold our position," Jake ordered.

"Aye, Skipper, all stop," EV replied.

Jake seemed to think for a few moments before he addressed the bridge crew. "The way I see it, we can continue searching here or head toward the planet's only islands. We have already found the one shrine in this area but haven't found anything else. If we head toward the islands, that may hold the greatest possibility of finding civilization. Thoughts?"

"Everything that we have found so far has been in the ocean. We found the gate and the shrine underwater," Kiah remarked.

"True. However, even if the gate creators are an ocean-dwelling species, they might still congregate by land. Coral reefs often exist in the waters around islands. They hold the most diversity of life in Earth's oceans," Sarah said.

"I'm with Sarah on this one. We need to be on the lookout for civilization, and beyond that, the islands might hold additional resources that we could use," Ashley added.

"I think that is our best bet," EV nodded in agreement.

"Alright, EV lay in a course for the islands," Jake said.

Sarah turned back to her console and was surprised to find a new signal on her sensors. "Captain, something just appeared in the trench," Sarah said.

Jake stood up and walked over to her console with excitement. "Can you make out what it might be?" Jake asked as he looked over her shoulder at the bioelectrical sensor readings.

"It's hard to get a fix, but whatever it is, it's massive," Sarah said as she looked over at Jake.

"EV hold up for a second," Jake said.

The lights from the Pegasus shined over the great precipice before them as the ship remained motionless. An eerie stillness seemed to settle over the scene. Sarah noticed there were no other life signs in their area. She felt like something was wrong.

"What are you thinking, Sarah?" Jake asked after a moment.

"I'm not sure, but something feels off," Sarah said.

"What do you mean?" Jake asked.

"This could be an ambush," Sarah said.

"What?!" Jake exclaimed as he suddenly felt the tension.

"On Earth, great whites use a particular strategy to ambush their prey. First, they lie in deep water, waiting for a shadow to pass by above. Then, once they spot something, they launch themselves vertically before making their kill," Sarah said.

"You think that is what is happening?" EV asked.

"I'm not sure," Sarah said as she frowned at the display.

"I think we should check it out. I mean, we are looking for intelligent life, aren't we? What if that is them?" Ashley remarked.

An apex ocean predator would need to be larger than any ever discovered to threaten the Pegasus. Ashley was probably right; they should check it out, but that did not stop Sarah's sense that they were being hunted.

Jake looked at the reading again over Sarah's shoulder.

"That's a big reading," Jake finally remarked. "Let's take it slow. EV, bring us parallel to the trench, and we will follow the ridge for a while to see what happens," Jake said.

EV nodded, "It's your call, Skipper. I have the navigation set."

As the Pegasus glided along the ridge, it became apparent the signal was following them.

"Well, we know one thing for sure. Whatever it is, it knows we are here," Sarah said.

"Has it come any closer?" Jake asked.

"Not yet. It seems to be at the same depth in the trench as it follows us," Sarah said as a chill ran down her spine.

"EV, drop our speed by half. Let's see if it comes any closer," Jake ordered.

Sarah looked at Jake nervously. "You think that is a good idea?" she asked.

"It still could be the beings who built the gate, and if it is, we can't just run away," Jake replied.

As the Pegasus slowed, the signal slowed in response.

"Could something be off with the sensors? Maybe an echo?" EV asked.

"The likelihood of that is minimal. I have checked the sensors several times, and they have come back green every time," Ashley said.

"Yeah, I don't think this is a glitch," Jake said.

Several more minutes passed in silence as the crew watched the readings and looked at the cameras pointing toward the signal. Whatever it was, it was shrouded in the darkness of the depths. Jake was debating whether to drop another aqua probe to investigate. They had a limited amount of NIC material, but they could always repurpose it, assuming they could retrieve the probe.

Jake was about to give the order when the Pegasus approached a group of socializing grazers. Most stopped what they were doing to watch the submersible pass. Their attention was focused on the foreign ship gliding through their environment.

There was sudden movement on the sensors as Sarah gasped, "It's coming!"

A gigantic head surged upward from the deep with a broad jaw that narrowed into the creature's rounded nose. Interlocking upper and lower teeth were visible along the closed jawline. Scaley ridges ran just above its black eyes, which seemed small for the creature's size but were still the size of dinner plates. A powerful, thick neck connected the dragon-like head to its body. Two sets of mighty flippers ran along the sides of the body, propelling the creature forward at a frightening speed. A broad tail lashed as it guided the trajectory of the great beast. This goliath was the same length as the Pegasus. The dark back with purple underbelly matched the environment perfectly, camouflaging this ambush predator.

"Shit!" EV exclaimed as he reacted to the sudden attack and steered the Pegasus away from the trench.

"Get us outta here!" Jake yelled.

Everyone's perception slowed as the event took place. The massive creature emerged from the depths faster than anyone could have imagined. Serrated teeth lined the opening jaws as the animal approached. Swirling waters roiled behind powerful fin and tail strokes as the distance narrowed. The eyes roll back into the creature's head as the mouth tore through the intended target.

A cry of pain rang out as one of the grazers was mortally wounded. Teeth suddenly sank into soft flesh, and then the predator gave one swift shake of its massive head, nearly tearing the grazer's tail off with one bite. With that, the initial attack ended. The other grazers fled, retreating back to the safety of the rock pillars. The predator appeared satisfied with the wound it had inflicted and swam back over the trench, staying close to the top of the ridge. The end of the beast's tail lashed out, making contact with the Pegasus as it swam away, a loud thud echoing through the hull.

"That was too close," Jake said with wide eyes as EV guided the Pegasus away from the danger.

"What's it doing now?" Ashley asked.

"It's likely waiting for the grazer to bleed to death before it eats it," Sarah replied softly.

The creature let out a massive roar that carried easily through the water and the hull of the Pegasus. The sound was deafening.

"Well, we aren't waiting around here to become the second course in its meal. EV, take us the hell away from here," Jake ordered.

"On it," EV did not need to be asked twice and moved the Pegasus further away from the carnage.

"That is by far the largest meat-eating predator in recorded history," Kiah said.

The adrenaline was still coursing through their veins.

"You guys ok down in the medical lab?" Jake asked.

"That scared the shit out of me, but beyond that, we are fine," Ben replied. "What was that thing?!"

"A tyrant," Jake replied.

EV nodded.

As the Pegasus sped away, the only detail that was visible behind them was the red blood that had mixed within the ocean currents, obscuring the feeding that Sarah knew was taking place.

STILL OUT THERE

Richard pounded the desk in front of him. **"Don't give me that** line of bullshit. They are still out there!" he yelled.

"Richard, calm down. We need to think about the situation before we send another crew under that ice," Ellie said in a defensive tone. Ellie Donovan was serving alongside Richard on the council. She had met with him to convey her sympathy for the situation, but that was not what Richard wanted to hear.

"Tell me, how long will that take? A week? A month? My daughter is out there right now!" Richard yelled across the table.

"Hang on now. We still don't know exactly what happened," Ellie expressed as she tried to get a word in.

"The Pegasus was sent somewhere. The ship didn't disappear without any trace. We found that door and what looks like metal rings under the disturbed seafloor." Richard said, regaining some of his composure. "Check the footage from Bobb. Something is down there!"

"That is why we must be careful before sending more people. The council will not approve a possible suicide mission," Ellie argued.

"I'll go! Just get me the equipment, and I'll go!" Richard yelled.

"What?! Alone?! You can't be serious?!" Ellie exclaimed.

"It's my daughter, Ellie!!!" Richard bit off the words. He was more serious about this than anything in his life.

Ellie's brows furrowed as she imagined what Richard was going through. She had never seen him so unhinged and could tell he wouldn't stop until he found Sarah again. "You're probably going to get yourself killed…" she said softly.

"Maybe, but I need to try," Richard's voice had a somber tone.

"Alright, I'll do whatever I can to get you the support you will need," Ellie said sympathetically.

Richard nodded and clasped a hand over his mouth, trying to hold it together.

After a moment, Richard said, "Thanks…"

The past few days, Richard hadn't slept much. Instead, he would wake up in the middle of the night, his brain constantly looking for a solution, not letting him rest. Every thought he had was about the difficulty in front of him. Where in the universe did his daughter go? The answer to that question was at the bottom of the Europa Ocean.

This time getting another ship under the ice would be more challenging. Richard was going to need to call in every favor he had. Ellie was right, and he knew he couldn't do this alone. But Richard knew one person would always have his back.

"Sam, I need you to come," Richard pleaded.

Samantha shook her head. "You know I'm too old for this."

"I know I can trust you," Richard explained.

"Sounds like you might need to find some younger people to trust," Samantha suggested. "I just don't want to disappoint you. Not on something this important." Samantha's adventurous years were now wrinkles on her face.

"I do have younger people I trust, but those are the very same people I need to save right now," he said softly.

Samantha sighed. "I know someone who can help you."

"Who?" Richard asked.

"Her name is Anya. She is Evengii's sister," Samantha said.

"His sister? Why was she not mentioned in his family profile?" Richard asked.

"She was adopted by his family when she was five. Her parents were family friends with EV's parents. So when her parents died, she just became part of the Balabanov family," Samantha said.

"You know her?" Richard asked.

"Yeah, I have seen her work." Samantha looked Richard right in the eye. "I truly believe she is who you need. I will tell her you're coming," she said.

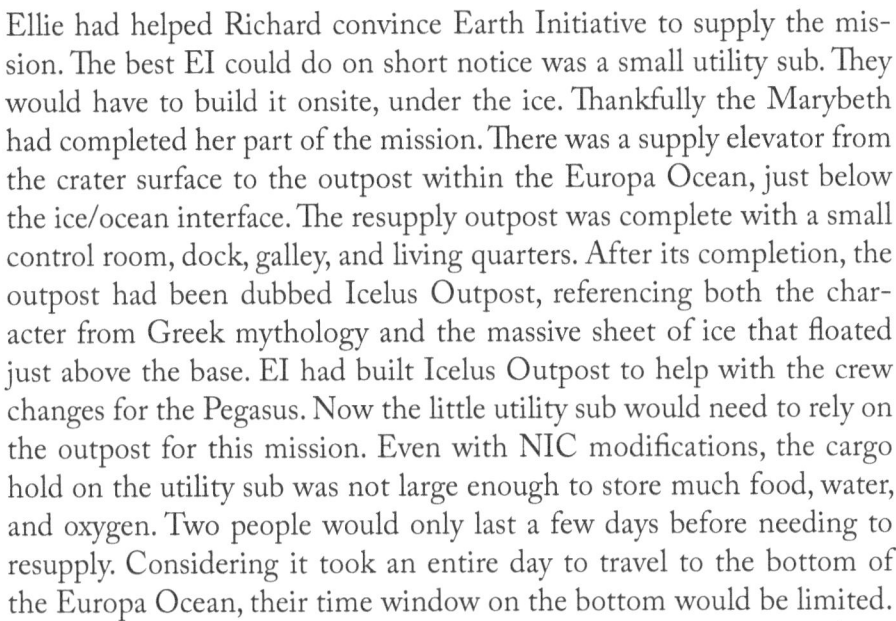

Ellie had helped Richard convince Earth Initiative to supply the mission. The best EI could do on short notice was a small utility sub. They would have to build it onsite, under the ice. Thankfully the Marybeth had completed her part of the mission. There was a supply elevator from the crater surface to the outpost within the Europa Ocean, just below the ice/ocean interface. The resupply outpost was complete with a small control room, dock, galley, and living quarters. After its completion, the outpost had been dubbed Icelus Outpost, referencing both the character from Greek mythology and the massive sheet of ice that floated just above the base. EI had built Icelus Outpost to help with the crew changes for the Pegasus. Now the little utility sub would need to rely on the outpost for this mission. Even with NIC modifications, the cargo hold on the utility sub was not large enough to store much food, water, and oxygen. Two people would only last a few days before needing to resupply. Considering it took an entire day to travel to the bottom of the Europa Ocean, their time window on the bottom would be limited.

After all that was in place, Richard's last task was to convince Anya to come with him on this crazy mission. In essence, Richard would be asking her to cram herself into a tin can and dive into the dark depths with him on a journey they might not return from. "How could any reasonable person say yes to that?" he asked himself. He needed to ask it anyway because there was nothing else he could do.

Richard held his breath as he knocked on the door of her quarters. When the door opened, he let out his breath with a single word. "Hello."

Anya studied Richard for a moment with her blue skylike eyes. "Hello. Sam said that you would be coming," she said.

Richard nodded, "I'm just going to cut to the chase. I need your help."

"Obviously, otherwise, you would not have come to see me. So, my guess is that this has something to do with EV's mission?" Anya asked bluntly.

"It does," Richard replied.

"Is he in some type of trouble?" Anya asked.

"We don't know where he is. I'm going to go look for the crew he is with," Richard sighed. The following words that came out of Anya's mouth just about floored Richard.

"I still owe him one. Count me in!" Anya nodded her head in agreement.

She relished Richard's shocked expression as his eyes widened.

"Just like that?" Richard asked.

"Alright, fine, let's argue about it for a while!" Anya exclaimed. She shot Richard an annoyed look.

"That isn't what I meant," Richard backpedaled, realizing she had said yes before his dumbfounded reply.

"I want a million credits and a nice ship where people need to call me Captain," Anya continued.

"I am not sure I can…" Richard started to say.

"Let's just go before you hurt yourself," Anya interrupted as she walked out the door and headed for the dock.

Richard stood there for a moment in shock. What the hell just happened? Then he realized he better follow her before the answer changed and rushed after her.

THE CAVE

The abyss held a level of fear for the crew as they approached the precipice again. The trench stretched three kilometers below them as the water graduated into darkness. The Pegasus slowly approached the cliff, came about, and glided to a halt.

"Any sign of the tyrant?" Jake asked as he watched over Sarah's shoulder.

"No, I'm not picking up any life signs in the area," Sarah replied.

Jake shuddered, thinking about the first encounter with the great beast. It was large enough that it might be able to tear a hole through the thick NIC outer hull of the Pegasus. This ship was their only lifeline. However, they could not ignore the readings from their sensors. There was an artificial electrical field and something generating power down there. They had sent an aqua probe down to investigate but had lost contact after entering a small cave. With every part of his being, he wished this was their way home and not a massive mistake.

As the Pegasus maneuvered into position, Sarah carefully studied the sensors. There were no signs of the tyrant. Ashley was waiting for the signal before launching the Swift Sphere.

"Alright, you are clear," Sarah said into the com.

Ashley made the plunge, diving below the Pegasus into the trench. It took her a moment to get her bearings and start her descent. After about twenty meters, the cave appeared below her position, along the cliff wall, and Ashley knew from the probe's data that it had to be where the electrical signal was coming from.

"Pegasus, I see the cave where the power source must be located," Ashley said.

"Ashley, be careful," Jake said. Even through the com, she heard fear in his voice.

"I will. Sarah, let me know if you spot anything coming our way. I need you to be my eyes," Ashley said.

"I will let you know the moment I spot anything at all. I have your back," Sarah said into the com.

Ashley felt her heart pounding as she descended into the darkening water of the abyss. The trench wall was composed of clusters of jagged rock formations. The light from the sphere intersected the edges of the stone, and shadows haunted Ashley as she descended. Finally, after what felt like forever, Ashley reached the cave's depth. The gaping maw in the cliffside loomed before her.

"I'm headed in," Ashley said before holding her breath.

The cave twisted into the dark, and Ashley saw several deep cracks in the walls. As she turned a corner, a hunk of dark gray metal was wedged perpendicular to the wall, blocking her path. She pulled back on the throttle, but it was too late.

"Damn!" Ashley exclaimed.

The sphere banged off the metal and ricocheted with a bone-jarring thud. The metal face was smooth, but the edges were gnarled and deformed. It looked like a makeshift barricade blocking further entry into the cave.

"Well, that's something! Ashley, do you see any way to move it?" Jake asked.

Ashley inspected the barricade and saw a piece of cordage looped through a hole where the metal was torn. "Give me a sec. I might have found a way in," she said. She used the robotic arms and gripped the cable. Then, throwing the sphere into reverse, she gave it a firm tug. The metal sheet broke free and scraped along the wall as it fell away.

Ashley pushed forward, moving into an open area not much larger than the sphere itself. Objects that might have been tools lay scattered in one corner, wrapped in artificial netting. As Ashley moved through the space, suddenly, there was a glint as light reflected off a curved dark metal blade. The blade had intricate carvings etched into the handle. The exquisite piece sat on top of a pile of bones.

"Unbelievable!" Ashley exclaimed.

"Oh wow! Ashley, can we take a better look at that skeleton?" Sarah asked through the com channel.

Ashley moved closer to the remains. The bones looked old and were partially buried in fine sand, making it difficult to see the actual form. However, the skull was almost totally uncovered and leaning gently against the rock wall. It was about the size of a human skull and had two crests wrapped around the eye sockets. The jaw was slightly elongated with triangular teeth.

"Do you think this is the being that built the ring gate?" Ashley asked.

"Possibly, but we are still missing something," Sarah said as she examined the video feed from the Pegasus bridge.

"We have not found what is creating the electrical field," Kiah said.

"Precisely!" exclaimed Sarah.

Ashley used the robotic arms of the sphere and gently held the skull for closer examination. A bone crest wrapped around the back of the skull and protruded about six centimeters, arching toward where the alien's neck would have been.

"What's that? Ashley, look to your right just a bit. It looks like something is there," Jake said through the com.

"I don't see… Wait," Ashley paused as she saw the glimmer of metal in a crack between the rocks.

"Can you grab it?" Jake asked.

Ashley moved the right arm and reached into the crack in the rockface at the base of the wall. Unfortunately, she could not retrieve the object. The hand was too large to fit, and the object was wedged firmly in place.

"No, it's stuck. Maybe if I had something to pry it with," Ashley said.

"What about the knife?" Kiah asked through the com.

"That might work! Let me give that a shot," Ashley replied.

Ashley maneuvered over to the knife and picked it up. Then went back to where the metal object was wedged in the wall. She slowly slid the blade through the crack along the top until she hooked around the object and pulled it forward, freeing it from the crack.

The thin flat rectangular object was about thirty centimeters across and fell to the cave floor. The smooth surface that looked like a screen lit up as it did. Red and blue marks and patterns shined across its face. Ashley picked it up, and some of the symbols changed. It seemed like it might be a computer or controller. The symbols changed again. The symbols were strange, and Ashley wondered what they meant. Where did this object come from?

Ashley felt a rumble as the rock wall suddenly shifted, and the cave ceiling collapsed. The outer shell of the Swift Sphere held as the pressure from tons of rock wedged it indefinitely into place at the bottom of the cave. Ashley felt a sudden wave of fear as the outer world plunged into darkness.

The crew saw the event for a split second before the sensors and video from the Swift Sphere died suddenly. On the bridge, Jake gasped and then yelled, "ASHLEY, PLEASE RESPOND! ASHLEY, CAN YOU HEAR ME!"

There was no response.

"ASHLEY!" he yelled again.

"I need options! Someone?!" he yelled frantically, looking for any ideas from the crew.

Over the com, Ashley groaned.

"ASHLEY, ARE YOU ALRIGHT?" Jake yelled.

"Yeah, I'm here," Ashley said. Her words were thin and weak.

"Thank goodness," Jake breathed a sigh of relief. "What is your situation?"

Ashley had hit her head hard on the back of the seat during the collision with the rock slab. She had a splitting headache and felt dizzy. Only a few indicators in the cockpit worked, and there was the sound of water. The sphere was smashed against the wall where the device was found. The split in the rockface was now a large crack where the sphere was now wedged. Ashley tried the controls, but nothing moved. She tried the arms, but they also failed to respond.

"I have a leak..." Ashley replied as she tried the controls one last time. One of the thrusters still fired, but the sphere did not budge "...I can't move."

"How much time do you have?" Jake asked.

"About ten minutes. The water is rising quickly. The hull is cracked," she replied.

"Is there any way you can get out?" Kiah asked.

"Maybe, but I'm not sure there is anywhere to go if I get out," Ashley said.

"Ashley shut off all the lights in the sphere. All of them." Kiah said quickly.

Immediately Ashley realized what Kiah was thinking. "Just a sec..." Ashley grabbed for the NIC cutter and emergency mask under her seat. She unclipped it from the harness and gathered it into her lap. She would need this and didn't want to try finding it in the dark. The emergency diver's mask had a five-minute oxygen supply within two small tanks attached to the mask.

"I'm killing the lights now," Ashley said as she keyed the controls.

The lights immediately extinguished, and Ashley was in complete darkness. Everything was black. Ashley felt the cold sea around her closing in as she felt the water filling around her feet.

"Do you see anything?" Jake asked through the com.

"Nothing yet," Ashley said. She used every ounce of concentration to focus on anything with her eyes as they adjusted. She used her peripheral vision, where she knew her eyes were most sensitive to light. *Damn it, there is nothing!* she thought. Panic started to claw at Ashley's mind.

"Anything?" Jake persisted.

His voice was startling in the silence. "You will be the first to know," Ashley gasped as she grappled with her fear. Another minute went by. Ashley started to wonder if she was looking toward the crack at all. Everything was black. She began to struggle, trying to think of a new plan. This was not going to… Then there was something. A spot of light could be seen and became more apparent as Ashley's eyes adjusted to the darkness.

"There's light!" Ashley shouted. "There's sun light!"

Ashley could make out where the sphere had punctured through the wall exposing a gap in the rockface. She could see the light from the surface, but the swim would be long, and there was the possibility it could be a dead end.

"Ashley, remember to close your eyes when you use the cutter. The emergency mask has an eye shield, but you won't want to lose your vision from the light. You will need it when you make your ascent," Kiah said.

Ashely was still grappling with what she was about to do. The water around her ankles felt cool, but the cold feeling that she might die sent uncontrollable shivers through her entire body. Ashley could see more of the gap in the rockface now. The opening was very narrow in certain spots, but it looked passible. At least the parts she could see. "Ashley, hold on, I'm going to find you," she heard Jake say through the com.

"Ashley, give me a minute to get outside. I'm coming for you," Jake said.

Jake went to the moon pool to get one of the Sea Wings and wet-suits. Sea Wings were a device to pull a diver quickly through the water, and Jake knew that he would be exposing himself to everything within the outside environment. But there was no time for second thoughts and no time for doubt. He had to save her. He quickly put on the wetsuit and scuba equipment, including a full rebreather radio mask to allow him to communicate. He grabbed one of the Sea Wings and went to the moon pool controls.

"Jake, tell me this is going to work," Ashley said. It sounded like her voice quaked, even through the com feed.

"I'm coming for you," Jake tried to reassure her.

He keyed the sequence to release the pressure field on the moon pool. Unlike the Swift Sphere, divers could not push through the pressure field. However, the air pressure in the moon pool dock would be enough to keep the ocean at bay. The console immediately returned an error. 'Potential ship contamination - authorized access required' appeared on the display screen.

"Jake, we lost her signal," Sarah said over the com.

Jake punched in the override command and confirmed with his fingerprint. The field disengaged, and the humming sound the field produced stopped. Jake didn't hesitate. He dove straight into the water leading with the Sea Wing's front triangular point.

Jake looked around, observing several stone pillars but there were no creatures in the area. That was until Hot Wings glided along the hull toward Jake's position.

"I thought you could use the help," Ben's voice came through the small com transmitter in Jake's ear.

Ashley was terrified. Extraction from a Swift Sphere was rare, and she had practiced it only a dozen times. This attempt would be her first in an actual emergency. Plus, she would have to keep her eyes closed while cutting. She needed to be able to see once she exited the craft and could not risk her pupils shrinking from any light. She wanted to be sure she was headed in the correct direction. She unclipped herself from the cockpit harness. She would need to go at any moment.

It seemed like forever as the water continued to rise inside the cockpit. The water was now up to her chest. Suddenly she heard an electrical short. The lights flickered back on for a split second before the systems died. Acrid smoke filled the remaining air space in the compartment, and that was Ashley's cue to go. She triggered the seal on her mask, closed her eyes, and started cutting the NIC glass.

She cut below the water line first. Water started filling the cockpit at an alarming rate. The water rushed over her head in a heartbeat. She continued to cut and to keep her eyes closed. Ashley concentrated hard to ensure the hole would be large enough as she used the NIC cutter to free herself from the sphere. She felt the low rumble as the laser sliced through the shell. Even through the safety guard, she felt the intense heat generated by the cutter.

The sphere interior was full of water. Nevertheless, Ashley held her concentration and patience as she continued to cut. Every second she focused on cutting through the entire shell. If she missed a spot within the cut, she would probably drown.

After three minutes, Ashley finished the cut. She opened her eyes as the tint within the mask faded. To her relief, she could still see the light coming from the surface. She pushed against the shell face, but the fragment did not move. She had missed a spot in the cut, and was still trapped inside. Her time was running out. She quickly braced herself against the seat and pushed at the shell fragment with her legs. She was desperate to create her exit and kicked hard.

The fragment broke loose where she had made the circular cut, and Ashley felt a sudden jarring pain in her left leg. She cried out in agony, her breath fogging her mask. She could not see what had happened but felt a laceration running up her calf and winced with the pain. Ashley took several deep breaths to collect herself. She only had maybe two minutes of air in the emergency mask. After that, she would be holding her breath. Ashley spun around and kicked off the chair with her good leg and swam through the hole in the sphere toward the light.

Ashley pulled herself along the rock face, leaving everything behind. She ascended through the water hand over hand, gripping knobs and handholds as she pulled herself forward. The natural shaft spiraled toward the surface as she pressed on. The further up the shaft she swam, the brighter the light became. Ashley swam hard. The mask beeped, and Ashley held her breath. She now had just over a minute to find her way out.

That is when it became apparent to her that the light was not from the surface and the suns. Instead, a tangle of roots lay before her. Some of them glowed in brilliant light that looked like cracks of sunlight. Ashley started to feel her lungs burn, and the pain in her leg intensified. Panic began to consume her thoughts as she realized she was trapped.

She looked for a way out, any way out. There had to be something. Ashley tugged at the roots trying to move them aside. Nothing moved. Nothing gave way. Ashley's lungs burned like fire as she uncontrollably gasped for air in the mask. Nothing.

Darkness descended on the edges of Ashley's vision as she struggled against the inevitable.

Hot Wings darted in front of Jake's eyes and pulled his gaze to where Jake saw a significant surge of bubbles, maybe a hundred meters away.

"That has to be the air release from the Swift Sphere!" Jake exclaimed.

Jake swam hard as the Sea Wing pulled him forward. The Sea Wing had two handles, one for each hand, and the two propellers along the sides pulled Jake through the ocean waters as he roared forward toward the bubbles.

Hot Wings took the lead and rushed straight to the spot. On the top of one of the stone pillars was an opening within the rock, but a dense twisting of leaves and roots blocked the passage. Hot Wings started thrashing at the vines attempting to find a way through.

"I'm gonna need to cut through! Dyami, get out here with a cutter!" Jake yelled into the com.

Jake removed the knife from a compartment in the right fin of the Sea Wing and began cutting away the roots. Or he was trying to...

The gashes in the roots reconnected and started to regenerate.

"SHIT!" Jake yelled.

"What's going on?" Sarah's voice sounded shrill on the com.

"I can't get through these things! Dyami, I need that cutter NOW!" Jake yelled.

Luckily, Dyami was already swimming to Jake with the cutter in one hand and Sea Wing in the other. He had anticipated Jake might need something and had prepped to assist with the other Sea Wing.

A minute later, Dyami was on the scene and started to cut. The roots cut easily enough with the NIC cutter, but that didn't stop the regeneration. Jake and Dyami saw an opening under the foliage where they were cutting. But as soon as they moved to the next section, the roots grew back.

"DAMN!" Jake swore.

That is when SHE showed up.

CLOSE ENCOUNTER

J ake only saw her for an instant before she slashed out with dual blades, one in each hand. Her torso, size, and some features of her face looked similar to humans, but her fins and tail proved she wasn't. She was a being born from the sea. Jake pushed away as the strike landed among the roots where he had been just a moment before. As he turned back, he saw the blades had cut cleanly through everything they touched.

"Pegasus, we are under attack," Jake yelled.

"Wait," Dyami said through his com.

As she wheeled around for a second strike, Jake saw the strike wasn't meant for him. The slash landed perpendicular to the first, cutting cleanly through the tangle of vines and roots. They weren't growing back, and they weren't regenerating! She whirled around and repeated the process, slicing with precision through the mottled green leaves and twisted gnarled wall of brown roots. She finished the cut and, in one motion, sheathed the knives in the harness that wrapped around her form. Her hands reached through the opening in the vegetation and she pulled Ashley through.

Jake could immediately tell that Ashley was unconscious, and her mask had no air. Jake dove toward Ashley without further thought, yanking an additional air supply line from his scuba tank and plugging it into her mask, pumping air for her to breathe. She didn't take a breath. He could see she was already turning blue.

"ASHLEY!" Jake cried out to her and shook her hard.

She coughed and then took a deep breath.

"Thank you!" Jake breathed a sigh of relief as Ashley took another breath.

"Jake?" Ashley sputtered.

"I've got you. You're alright!" he said softly. Tears filled his eyes as relief coursed through him.

That is when Jake realized the broader scope of the situation and turned.

She swam just meters away. Many of her facial features were similar to humans. Her eyes had wide pupils and were as deep blue as the Pacific. They were larger than human eyes and filled their sockets with grace. Her nose and cheeks had perfect symmetry, highlighted by her face's smooth blue skin adorned with a delicate natural pattern that resembled tiny water droplets. Her lips were full in a slightly darker shade of blue. Different triangular patterns in deep purple ran along the crests above her eyes. Scales adorn the ridges around her eyes in vivid purples and with touches of pink. Another crest lay along the back of her head, and an elegant fin extended further down her neck. The fin flowed around the back of her neck as she moved. She had tiny round ears that sat flush against her head with small slits that might have been gills just behind them. Her torso looked almost human with shoulders and arms that bent at the elbow and had four fingered hands. Her chest and muscles were sculpted like a female swimming athlete. She wore what appeared to be some type of leather that perfectly contoured her skin. The garment started at her neck, ended just below her waist, and effectively slipped through the water. Her harness wrapped around her shoulders and held the dual blades within a sheath. Fine green fiber wrapped around the blades' handles. Her tail started from her hips, the muscle narrowing past her waist, then widening into a single large horizontal tail. The skin was perfectly smooth, and the tail looked almost like a whale's tail with slight ridges along the back edge. The skin was midnight blue around the tail and lightened in color as it disappeared under her leather-like garment.

Suddenly a roar pushed through the water as the sound carried over the lip of the trench. Jake looked over to where the sound came from. It likely came from kilometers away, but he did not want to meet the tyrant that had let loose that howl.

As he turned back, she was gone, only leaving a shadow that identified her position for a moment until it disappeared too.

"Jake, we need to go," Dyami said as he noted Ashley's wounded leg.

"Thank you," Ashley called after the being as she gazed off, wondering if they would see HER again. She had saved Ashley's life.

"Let's get outta here," Jake said as he held the Sea Wing with one hand and Ashley around the waist with his other arm.

The Sea Wing's electric motors pulled Jake and Ashley through the water as the tandem swam back to the Pegasus. Ashley rode along, avoiding using her legs to limit additional blood loss. After a few minutes, they arrived at the moon pool dock. Jake climbed out of the water and helped Ashley out of the water as Dyami helped to lift her from underneath. Ashley almost collapsed onto the floor of the dock. Her head still throbbed, and she felt woozy.

"I got you," Jake said as he scooped her into his arms.

"EV, we are on board. Move us away from the trench and the sound of that tyrant," Jake said into the com.

Just then, Ben opened the bulkhead door to the moon pool dock. He stared at Jake and Ashley, then nodded. "Follow me."

Ben led the way to the med lab, where Jake lay Ashley on the patient bed.

"It looks like you missed the major artery," Ben said as he started to work to clean, fill, and seal the wound with the med regenerator. "You're still going to hurt for a week or more," he said as he dressed the deep gash.

"Thanks, Ben," Ashley nodded to him with gratitude.

"You know you broke quarantine protocol by letting us in," Jake stated in a soft but questioning voice.

Ben nodded a bit. "You and Dyami broke protocol when you left to rescue her. It seems none of us can sit by and watch someone die."

Jake nodded with understanding. "I find it admirable when someone knows when to break the rules. Thanks."

"I'm close on the inoculum, and hopefully, any parasites can be dealt with by using a pair of tweezers. Otherwise, we might have a problem," Ben half-joked.

"Ben, we might have seen a gate builder. She saved Ashley's life," Jake said.

Ben wasn't sure what to say at first. That exciting news could be a fundamental step in the right direction.

"Did you see where she went?" Ben asked.

"No, but we need to find her," Jake replied.

ANGI

The trip was a whirlwind for Richard and Anya. Ellie had persuaded a few on the council, expediting the rescue operation. After a few long days, they made it to Europa with the equipment the council had approved. Included in these items were several pre-printed NIC parts necessary to build a small utility sub, the Crichton. The Crichton was the key to reaching the deepest depths of this ocean. Evidently, after the construction of Icelus Outpost, nearly all the Marybeth's crew had left, and the replacement crew for the Pegasus had not yet been finalized. The only exception was Malcolm Oliveira, a personal friend of Ellie's and a part of the Pegasus emergency rescue crew. It did not take much convincing before he joined this new operation. Malcolm was an expert at logistics and support and was a critical asset. However, with everything else in flux, it left just the three of them in the field on Europa to complete this vital mission, with support from the original crew at Earth Dock.

Because of the sensitivity and secrecy of some of the findings on the Pegasus mission, the disappearance was not made public, and families were not immediately told about the missing crew. The fact that they could be dealing with unknown alien technology compounded the issue, and the council decided they needed more time to investigate before publicizing any news. This fact was also part of the reason that this rescue operation was so small, and additional support teams were left out of the loop. EI had finally reached out to the adult members of the families earlier that morning, with just a message letting them know they had lost communication with the crew, but even that information was still considered classified. However, Richard knew there was one person he needed to speak with directly about the situation. The video channel had barely clicked on before Angi asked, "Where is he?!"

Richard had thought long and hard about his next words. He knew that she needed the whole truth. Trust can be a foundation that two people can share, but it can be so easily twisted in unforeseen ways. His eyes focused on the display in front of him. Angi looked determined as she stared at him through the video com.

"Angi, they have disappeared. We think they are still alive, but we don't know where they are currently," Richard said.

"Disappeared?! To the point, you can't communicate with them?!" Angi's words were filled with anger, dismay, and mostly worry.

"They vanished suddenly," Richard felt the tension. He had trouble imagining what Angi must be feeling hearing those words.

"Vanished?!" Angi shouted.

"I'm personally leading the mission to find them," Richard explained.

Angi just stared a hole straight through Richard. There was a long moment until she spoke again. "You will take me with you."

Richard's first reaction was to protest, but Angi quickly held up her hand. "The only reason you told me the truth is because you need my help. You don't know where they are or how they disappeared. You know I can help you solve that mystery! If you still think they are alive, I'm coming with you," Angi concluded.

"You can't come," Richard said.

"The hell I can't. I'm coming, or I go to the media for support in finding my husband. The only thing I care about is getting him back," Angi hissed.

"What about your kids?" Richard tried to persuade her from a new angle but immediately regretted his words.

"My kids are none of your concern! I need to find my Ben. My kids will stay with my parents," Angi snapped.

Richard sighed. "We are already on Europa. It might take time before I can get another shuttle out here."

"Just do it, Richard! I'm not letting this go," Angi glared at him.

Richard nodded. "Alright, I will work something out, and a man named Malcolm will contact you with the details," he said.

Before Angi abruptly ended the conversation, Richard saw Angi's eyes welling with tears. The com channel went dead, and there was silence in the room. He wondered if he had made a mistake. Angi could be a crucial asset and was adept at solving challenging puzzles. She was currently an ancient languages professor in San Francisco, but even before that, she had been instrumental in solving the mysteries of the Voynich manuscript. She was also well-known and had connections. However, she was inevitably bound to this situation by her missing loved one. They all were.

There was a chime at the door. "Enter," Richard replied.

Anya stood in the door as it slid open. "What did you tell Ben's wife?"

Richard's gaze lost altitude, "I told her what happened."

"And?"

"Do you think we could use her on this mission?" Richard asked a question in response to the question.

Anya chuckled a bit. "So, she invited herself along?"

"Yeah, she did," Richard admitted.

"Richard, you're a damn pushover!" Anya snickered.

"She has just as much motivation as the two of us. Her husband is a part of that crew," Richard expressed.

"Alright, I will give her a shot. But if she doesn't work out, you are the one that will need to send her home," Anya said sternly.

"I will," Richard said, then paused. "Have you found any more clues yet?"

Anya shook her head. "The Crichton is almost ready. The docks assembly drones are close to having all the parts together. We can go for our ride in about an hour."

"The space in that sub will be cramped. We are going down for only a few days at a time before we need to turn around and resupply here. Most of the time will be spent ascending or descending," Richard said. He knew these trips wouldn't be easy, and the long hours of waiting while the crew was still missing would be agonizing. These might be the longest weeks of his memorable life.

"Let's do this so we can get back, and you can buy me a beer. Did you know EI has not yet opened a bar on Europa? In fact, I think EI ignored my request to send some bourbon along for this trip," Anya said.

Richard cracked a pitiful smile. He still felt drained from the last several days, but at least he had slept some since they arrived on Europa. He had been having strange dreams but they were restful enough for him to recuperate his mental fortitude. "Let's go check on our sub."

As they left the crew quarters, they ran into Malcolm. He had finished loading the sub and was finding Richard to report. He stood at attention when he saw Richard. "Sir, the sub is loaded and is ready to depart."

"Thank you, Malcolm. You can just call me Richard. Could I get your help with one more thing?" Richard asked.

"Of course," Malcolm waited.

"I need you to find a way to transport Angela Rapner here. We will need her help," Richard explained.

"I'm on it," Malcolm replied.

AN OFFER OF TIME

Jake looked around the briefing room. Each crew member looked at the still image they had captured of HER on the main holo-display. The only absent crew member was Ashley. She was still asleep in the med bay, recovering from her injury.

"Whoever she is, she saved Ashley. We need to find her," Jake said into the room.

"The sensors could not track her through the rock formations," Sarah said.

"I think that she is coming back," Kiah speculated.

"What makes you say that?" Jake asked.

"She is certainly intelligent, and with intelligence comes curiosity. She was likely observing us when the incident occurred and decided to intervene. She's not human, so we don't understand the behavior, but for her to show up at that critical moment can't be a coincidence. Besides, chasing after her, might seem hostile. We should wait for her to return," Kiah said.

There was a pause as the crew thought about Kiah's words.

"Is there any possibility that she caused the cave-in?" EV asked.

"From the readings and video analysis, I think WE caused that cave-in. The rocks were already shattered, and our disturbances caused the collapse," Kiah said.

"I should have been more careful," Jake said.

"Jake, it's not your fault. We needed to find answers, and investigating that cave was the only option at the time," Ben said.

"Back to the matter at hand. This species might not know how we got here. So how do we convince the residents here that we aren't an invasion force?" EV asked.

"We just need to hope they are friendly and do everything in our power to ensure we have good relations with them. If a technologically advanced species, hell even an intelligent species, has a problem with us on this world, there will be no chance of surviving long term on this planet," Jake said.

"We need to show our humility," Sarah said.

"What are you thinking, Sarah?" Jake asked.

"Well, we don't know anything about them or their culture. We aren't sure how a gift would be received or in what context. The most valuable thing we have is time. We need to show our humility and vulnerability. Someone should stand watch outside of the Pegasus with nothing more than a wetsuit and a tank. We need to meet her face-to-face," Sarah said.

Jake rubbed his chin as he thought about it. "You're absolutely right, Sarah. She appeared once, and we need to let her come to us again," he said.

EV frowned just a bit. "Skipper, just to remind you that we have a limited supply of food. Are you sure we should just wait around here?"

"Yeah, we need their help. In all likelihood they built the gate or know who did. Unless you can offer a better alternative?" Jake asked.

"I'm not a fan of sitting around," EV admitted.

"I understand EV, but at this point, I think it's our best option. It's time to lay our cards on the table and hope for help. So, we wait," Jake finished.

The Violatis general inoculum was finished, and Ben was confident it would protect the crew from most localized viruses and bacteria on this planet. Science had progressed leaps and bounds when it came to curing diseases, but he had worked many long hours on its development. They were just lucky that the microbiome worked similarly across the galaxy. Ben administered the injections right after the briefing was over. Jake was last and lingered for a moment.

"Anything we need to worry about?" Jake asked as Ben inserted the needle into his arm.

"I have done everything I can. We are about to leap in head first into this environment, and I wouldn't let you risk our lives if I weren't sure this would work," Ben said.

"I know, Ben. I appreciate that," Jake stated. Jake patted Ben's arm.

"Anything I can do to help get us home?" Ben asked.

"I know you put in some long hours, Ben. This inoculum is a real accomplishment, and I can't express enough gratitude for what you have done for Ashley over the last few hours. It would be best if you took a few hours off for yourself. After you rest up, come and see me," Jake said.

"I will try, but when my hands are idle, my thoughts will not leave me alone," Ben said.

"I understand. As you know, we will need you at your best when we need to count on you the most. Please consider that and rest while you can," Jake said.

The Pegasus stopped by a clearing away from the trench. The sand in the seabed was a shade of gold, layered under the lavender water. The view was gorgeous, surrounded by the spiraling green foliage wrapped around each pillar in the seascape.

Jake, Sarah, Dyami, and Kiah decided to switch off shifts. Of the seven human crew, the four of them made the most sense to try for contact with the alien residents. Each shift would be about an hour before they would switch and resupply their O2 tanks.

Sarah took the first shift. She put on a wetsuit with fins, an O2 tank, and a rebreather mask with a com link. Sarah smoothly swam into the clearing. Finding a small rock toward the center of the clearing, she stopped. She floated there and waited alone. She refrained from using the com, thinking about how that would appear if she was chattering to herself when SHE approached. The sudden lack of focused activity made Sarah's mind shift into overdrive, her vivid thoughts erupting within the silence.

Sarah thought about her father, Richard. She tried to imagine what he might do in this situation. She thought about Keenan the orca and how she became friends with him without understanding a single word. She hoped she could be that lucky with a friendship here. Finally, she thought about Hot Wings and how he seemed to have adopted the crew just as much as the crew had adopted him.

"How are you doing out there, Sarah?" EV said from the com feed in her ear.

"Just lost in thought," Sarah whispered back. "I sure hope this was the right decision."

"If it makes you feel any better, I don't think we were brought here just to be killed by alien marauders. The alien scientists might want to study us first," EV said. Sarah could tell he was grinning even over the com.

"Quiet," Sarah said, chuckling just a bit. For some reason, the outrageous but possible truth always carried a grim hint of humor.

"Sarah, I respect what you're doing, and if you need anything, just shout. Just don't wave your arms too much; that might be a threatening gesture," EV said.

"Shhh… and thanks," Sarah said.

After the first hour, there was no sign of HER.

Jake wanted to know something before he took his first shift. It had pulled at the back of his mind. He needed to find that alien tablet. After reviewing the data, the Pegasus had received from the Swift Sphere, that tablet seemed to be the source of the electrical signal within the cave.

While Sarah still floated in the clearing finishing her first shift, he dressed in his wetsuit and grabbed an O2 tank. Taking one of the Swift Wings to the cave, Jake thought about the Swift Sphere that was now pinned and flooded at the bottom of that cave. The green roots still appeared to be cut away as Jake entered the passage making his way into the opening.

As he swam further down, he had to abandon the Sea Wing to proceed. He squeezed through, finding a way to slide his body through the tight spaces.

The broken Swift Sphere lay ahead of him. The shell reminded Jake of a ghost as his headlamp moved across the dark scene. He needed to be very careful and avoid another cave-in at all costs.

A glimmer of light reflected back, and Jake examined it further. Indeed, it was the alien tablet, the display dark but the metal glinting in the light. Next to it was the dark metal of the curved blade that Ashley used to pry the device free. Jake saw the resemblance with the blades that had cut Ashley free from the roots. Jake picked up both objects, returned to retrieve the Sea Wing, and returned the items to the Pegasus. Maybe the computer could make sense of the information on the tablet.

Dyami was on his fourth shift, and calmed himself as he swam into the clearing. The area they had chosen seemed peaceful, and the Pegasus sensors had not seen any signs of the tyrant or other predatory animal activity since their arrival. After his last shift, he reflected on his approach to the situation. This time he wanted to feel the living energy around him. Dyami relaxed into a calm state of mind as he looked out. As his eyes became slits, he could see the auras around the life within this world as it shined and glimmered in arcs of all colors.

Dyami had honed this skill ever since he was a small child, and he perceived things that most others could not. The skill did not often show him what to do; it simply applied a new perspective to his situation. Dyami started to become aware of another's existence. The presence was not forceful, existing with a sense of peace, and moving closer to his position. He felt that it had to be HER. SHE was going to make her presence known when SHE was ready.

This watch was Kiah's fourth and final watch for the day. It was getting late, and Kiah swam slowly in the clearing to pass the time. Her mind wandered as she was left alone. To calm her thoughts, she imagined she was in a field at her mother's house, with the mountain meadow gently sloping and the smell of wildflowers. She remembered how the clouds looked that morning, rain clouds below her elevation obscuring views of plains and cloaking the lower part of the mountain. There wasn't a single cloud above her elevation, and everything was crisp in the morning light. She often visualized this place when she needed a respite within her mind.

Kiah felt the tips of the meadow grass as the long soft tops gently brushed against her hands. The thought felt tangible and still very real as Kiah turned as stroked the individual strands in her mind's eye. She felt drawn to this place she so desperately wanted to return to.

Then she sensed something outside her peaceful memories, like a new presence in the meadow. Kiah could feel it now. A gaze that always seems to announce its existence in the back of your consciousness. She slowly opened her eyes and looked to where she felt the gaze. SHE was there.

Kiah took a deep breath and didn't move.

Several moments passed as the two gazed at each other across the clearing.

"Hello, my name is Syuk," was spoken softly into Kiah's mind. The thought was delicate and with a gentle touch as the words slipped through.

"Syuk… can you understand me?" Kiah said aloud, her voice also carrying over the open com channel.

"Yes, I can understand you. I only know the words you intend to share with me. If you wish to speak aloud, I can understand your words through your thoughts," Syuk spoke through her mind but also made a song-like vocalization.

"We still use vocalizations when it enhances the situation or to get someone's attention," Syuk sang through the water. "Meeting a being from a different world is a good reason to sing."

"Nice to meet you, Syuk. My name is Kiah," Kiah's words carried through thought and her voice still covered by her rebreather mask.

"Where did you come from, Kiah?" Syuk sang. Kiah was astonished by the clarity of the words that made sense in her head.

"A planet we call Earth… can you also see that in my head?" Kiah asked

"Only if you wish to share the image in your mind," Syuk sang. "Why are you here?"

"We are lost. We did not travel here on our own," Kiah said.

Syuk started to swim closer to Kiah. Her graceful movements through the water reminded Kiah of how dolphins swam. Her long broad tail made smooth strokes as she approached. The crest fin flowed around her neck. The crests around her eyes perfectly framed her deep blue gaze.

"You came here from Europa," Syuk sang.

"How do you know about Europa?" Kiah asked.

"We both understand that moon. We have a common context. You call them 'loopens'. One was there that day of our initial encounter. They are a mythical creature in our culture," Syuk sang.

"We call that loopen Hot Wings, and he traveled here with us. He is currently on board our ship. Do you know Europa because your people built the crescent ring gates?" Kiah asked. She needed that answer. She knew the Pegasus was listening to the conversation… or at least her part of the conversation.

"Yes… and no…" Syuk sang. "The nature of reality is often more complex."

"Can you help us?" Kiah pleaded.

"Probably, but not in all the ways you hope. We can be friends, but you are probably never going to see Europa again," Syuk sang.

"We need to get back. Is there anything…?" Kiah pleaded.

Syuk, with a sad gaze and slight shake of the head, "We do not have what you seek."

Kiah felt something collapse inside. This news was crushing, and it hit her hard. She tried to push the blow aside but felt short of breath. There still had to be a way, any way. She felt as if her life had just been ripped away from her, and she was lost in a wave of emotions.

Syuk just patiently watched as Kiah struggled with the news.

After a moment, Kiah said, "I apologize. This is our species' first encounter with an entity as advanced and intelligent as you are. I didn't intend to be so bold with my request."

Syuk asked, "How is your friend doing?"

"She is recovering. Thank you so much for saving her," Kiah said.

Syuk nodded a bit, "You are welcome. Will you be here tomorrow?"

"Yes. We can wait," Kiah confirmed.

Syuk seemed to think for a moment. "We call our people Scanii. What is the name of your people?"

"We're humans," Kiah said.

"Well then, Kiah the human, meet me here tomorrow. There is still knowledge we can share, but the suns' are low in the sky," Syuk sang.

"I will see you tomorrow. Thanks for your kindness," Kiah said graciously.

Syuk nodded as she swam strongly away, disappearing into the stone pillars.

CRICHTON

The small utility sub, Crichton, had spent the last twenty-one hours descending. Richard felt nervous tension as time passed. He seemed to be checking their depth every five meters as it felt like they were slowly crawling to the bottom of the Europa Ocean.

On this journey, the Crichton only could accommodate two people at a time. Two seats looked out the front NIC glass. There was one bed that lined the starboard side wall behind the chairs, and opposite that, there was an area to heat food and get water and a small lavatory. That was all the livable space this sub had. There was no place to change and no room for extra clothes. So, all they had was clothes on their backs, and they slept in them. This utility sub was intended for use with a larger ship. Its design was for facilitating tasks in locations where the larger ship could not venture. It was never intended for use much beyond a single day.

Richard now wished they were not confined to such a small craft, but the fact was that Icelus Outpost on Europa did not have a large format NIC printer, so each piece had to be transported from the surface by elevator and assembled on site. They were lucky to have Malcolm, who had coordinated the logistics of the assembly process. Crichton's design was also one of the few able to withstand the enormous water pressure on the bottom of the ocean. It was a minor miracle that they had already made it this far, and Richard knew that their time was running short. However, they needed to find the Pegasus and fast. If they didn't find answers and provide results quickly, politics would become involved again. If that happened, he knew that he would have a fight on his hands.

"Anya, wake up," Richard said from the left helm station's chair.

"We better be there, Richard, and you're not waking me up about the wildlife again," Anya yawned from the bed in the back.

"Yeah, we are here," Richard confirmed.

The Crichton swam smoothly through the trench toward the clearing at the Pegasus's last known position. The cliffs loomed as the sub's light glanced off the nearest rocks, the eternal darkness was disrupted yet again by humankind.

"Have you located the position where Bobb stopped?" Anya asked.

"Just about, we are almost to the clearing where we think they vanished. I already relayed a signal to Malcolm and Earth Dock, and they are observing our progress," Richard explained.

Anya nodded, and Richard removed himself from the pilot's chair and sat at the support station's chair that was positioned to the right.

"Be vigilant. We still don't know what triggered the event. Our goal is to find them, not become lost ourselves," Richard said.

"Yeah, you said that, and I already told you that I understand," Anya said with a hint of annoyance.

"I may be a bit paranoid, but I believe in this case it's justified," Richard stared through the darkness, just beyond their spotlights, trying to sense any danger. There was a secret here, and he had to find out what it was.

Richard checked the sensor readings. "There appears to be some type of metal buried where the sand looks disturbed around the edges of the clearing."

"You said they disappeared after entering that clearing, right?" Anya asked.

"Yeah, everything just cut out after that point," Richard said.

"What the hell is that?" Anya asked in surprise.

A light glanced off of the metal shape in front of them.

As they circled the clearing, they approached the huge alien door. Even after being exposed to the ocean's water for countless years, the door had no signs of rust. Sand had worn some of the metal, but the door was fully exposed with no residual buildup of sand. It also was embedded in the side of a cliff face and was the only artificial structure that could be seen in the light from the sub.

"There is Bobb!" exclaimed Anya.

Bobb was dead. The batteries were depleted. Richard knew they would find out if Bobb just needed a charge in a minute.

The Crichton attempted to charge the Bobb drone wirelessly. Sure enough, Bobb sparked back to life, just enough to dock with the utility sub and start the primary charging process. Richard hoped there might be more data to analyze from the Bobb drone beyond what had been transmitted. Maybe they would find out more information about the disappearance of the Pegasus.

Richard refocused on the bay door, or at least he hoped it was a door. It was impossible to tell what exactly it was or how deep it went since the frame was embedded into a cliff face. But it was their best clue about what might have happened to the Pegasus. If they could get this thing open, maybe they could find a way to bring back the Pegasus. Unfortunately, as he examined it more closely, there did not seem to be any release mechanism or other obvious way to open it.

"So, you're just going to try to cut your way through that thing? What if it's just a giant cube of metal?" Anya asked.

"I'm open to suggestions, but this is one of the reasons we brought this tin can," Richard said as he prepped the NIC laser cutter for the task ahead. The Crichton had several tool arms that could be switched out on each side of the sub, which allowed for a wide range of functions it could complete.

"I'm good with the blunt approach, but it's your fault if we break it," Anya added.

As Richard and Anya positioned the Crichton to make the cut, the bay door suddenly and automatically slid opened, retracting into the walls. There were unmistakable red scales beyond the door as the light filled the area opening before them. Twisting snake-like bodies uncoiled as they glowed from the spotlights. Three horn-heads of massive proportion lay inside, and were easily twenty meters long. Their enormous heads had equally immense jaws as their large black eyes focused on the Crichton.

An unearthly cry rang out.

"Oh shit. We need to get outta here. Now!" Anya yelled.

"Anya, move us away!" Richard exclaimed.

With its thrusters, the Crichton turned on an axis and bolted away with all the power it could muster.

The three red horn-heads pursued as they focused in on the sub. They quickly closed the distance even as the Crichton fled.

As the first creature approached, it lashed out with its enormous head and bit the Crichton. Its razor-sharp teeth scraped along the hull with a spine-chilling screech. Anya screamed in terror as the second creature lunged, grabbing one of the thrusters on the port side of the Crichton and shaking its head violently.

Richard punched the controls as the first creature released its bite and coiled for another attack. Yet, again, it sprang toward the other thruster. Suddenly there was total darkness.

"SHIT!" Anya yelled in sheer panic.

"Quiet!" Richard said through the black.

There was more scraping as the ship bucked under the muscular power of the enormous creatures. Then everything went silent.

Richard felt his heart pounding, and his temple throbbed as the adrenaline coursed through his body.

"I killed the lights and thrusters," Richard whispered.

"What? Why did you do that?" Anya whispered back.

"Their food glows, and I didn't want to look like food," Richard whispered.

They sat in silence, praying that the attack was over. After several minutes Anya asked, "So now what's the plan?"

Richard keyed the controls to bring back up the holo-displays and the control illumination at the dimmest setting. The horn-heads had retreated to their lair after they found the sub unpalatable. The bay door remained open.

"They left, but it looks like our port thruster is damaged," he said, looking through the displays.

"Are we able to make it back?" Anya asked.

"I sure hope so," Richard said.

Anya keyed the control, and the Crichton started to spin in a wide circle. "Hang on a sec," Richard adjusted the thruster settings as he tried to even out the thrust on both sides of the sub. Then using the undamaged Bobb, Richard found another source of thrust.

The Crichton stabilized a bit but was sluggish with the damage. There was also a distinct creaking sound, and Richard felt his heart start to race again. He was unsure how much damage the hull had sustained, and at the depth they were at, the water pressure alone would kill them instantly if the hull breached.

"Anya, we need to leave. Take us up," Richard ordered.

"You don't need to ask me twice!"

RELATIONS

Kiah reported the whole conversation to the rest of the crew after they gathered in the briefing room. The Pegasus could record the Scanii vocalizations, but the translations for the words came from Kiah. The words were translated into her thoughts. The computer still needed much more input before it could accurately translate the Scanii vocal patterns.

"Syuk was able to understand and communicate through the thought and intention of speech. She had telepathically shared that there needed to be the intention to communicate with that individual for the translation to work. She requested me to meet her here tomorrow," Kiah explained.

"Do you trust Syuk? What is your read on her?" Jake asked.

"I'm not sure we have many choices, and I do trust her," Kiah expressed. "There is something about her mannerisms that seem genuine. Her offer of friendship seemed sincere," she explained.

"You said that she mentioned something about Hot Wings?" Jake asked, trying to clarify the interaction.

"Yeah, they knew about Europa and the loopens. She said something about them being regarded as a mythical creature," Kiah said.

"I wonder what that means," Sarah said.

"I'm not sure," Kiah responded.

"Hot Wing's actions have demonstrated his willingness to help us and that he might be one of the most intelligent creatures humans have yet encountered. It makes sense that the Scanii regard them in such a way if they are familiar with that species," Sarah said.

"We need to be respectful of Hot Wing's needs. We can't just lock him up in the aquarium tank… it's not like we have been able to keep him in there anyway," Dyami said.

Jake nodded, "When you meet Syuk, I want Dyami to go with

you. He has a good feel for social interactions and has a good sense about people."

"I think that is a good idea," Kiah said.

The crew was excited about the encounter with Syuk, and there was a sense of renewed hope, except for one individual. Ben wore his genuine emotions under a thin shell, and Dyami could tell something was disturbing him. He had not said a word in the briefing and wore a face that reflected his despair.

After Dyami and the rest of the crew finished, Dyami went to check on Ben. He knew he would probably find him in the hydroponics lab.

"Hey Ben, you look like you could use a friend right now," Dyami said softly as he entered the lab.

After a pause, Dyami asked, "Are you alright?"

Ben started to cry. He had to let it out. Things were just too much. "I missed Kasidy's birthday today. She turned twelve, and I didn't keep my promise to call her on her birthday… I feel so helpless here. This was never part of any plan." Ben started to sob. "I am so alone. I miss my family. I miss my life. The longer we are here, the more I feel like I will never see or speak to them ever again."

Dyami offered a hug, his arms wide. Ben embraced him as he felt his shell melt into deep sadness but also deep gratitude that he was no longer alone. Dyami patiently waited as Ben's tears fell.

"I'm sorry to unload this on you. I really feel lost," Ben said through his tears.

"I understand, and I am here any time," Dyami said softly. Just Dyami's presence soothed Ben with his caring heart.

After a while, Ben collected himself.

"Ben, I don't know the future, but I do know that everything is going to be alright," Dyami said.

"How can you be so sure?" Ben asked.

"Several years ago, I lost my husband and son in an accident. That event nearly broke my spirit and my soul. At the time, the way forward seemed impossible, and I was unsure how I could live without them. Despite my belief that their spirits still exist and help guide me, I faced the reality that they were gone from the physical world. I barely slept and felt my body withering away," Dyami reflected.

"How did you get through it?" Ben asked.

"I got through it with the support of the people that cared about me and the spirits of my family that came before me. Jake and Ashley are more than just my crewmates. They are my dear friends and are guides along the path I walk," Dyami explained.

"Is that why you came here? To help?" Ben asked hesitantly.

"Of course," Dyami smiled. "Sometimes, in a moment, it can be hard to see how things can get better. But if your heart is still beating, there is a path forward. If you have a path forward, then there is still hope. You do not have to hide away your sadness, and I'm here to help you find your way through it," Dyami said.

"I appreciate that, Dyami. Thank you," Ben said.

"Ben, you have already contributed so much to this mission, and this crew still needs your help to survive here. None of us can do this alone, and we must rely on each other. If you ever need to talk, if you ever need a friend, if you ever need a guide, I am here," Dyami's words carried great weight as he meant every word, and Ben felt a deep, genuine connection to him.

Just as Syuk promised, she appeared the following day, this time with a gray-skinned female friend of her species. They swam several meters away from the Pegasus as Kiah and Dyami swam over to greet them.

"Syuk, this is my friend and crew mate Dyami," Kiah said into her mask.

"Greetings," Syuk sang as she nodded, speaking directly at Dyami so Kiah could still hear in her mind. "This is our matriarch Sianda."

Sianda had dark grey skin with a hint of dark blue, and the crests around her eyes had a triangular pattern with the same deep purple that was unique but similar to Syuk's eyes and lined with vivid scales. The fin around her neck shimmered in a rotating variety of complementary colors.

Sianda bowed her head slightly, "Greetings, Kiah and Dyami," Sianda sang as she translated the thought.

Kiah asked, "Would you two be willing to meet the rest of our crew and captain? As you might have guessed by our masks and tanks, we don't live permanently within the water."

"Of course, lead the way," Syuk sang.

Kiah and Dyami swam toward the bridge of the Pegasus leading the way. It was pretty apparent the Scanii were built to travel through the water as they swam. Syuk and Sianda glided through the water effortlessly, but Kiah was intrigued to notice the slight differences in their swimming techniques. Although Kiah and Dyami were in great physical shape, they swam slowly compared to the Scanii. Finally, the four were looking through the NIC glass into the bridge of the Pegasus.

"Sianda and Syuk, this is Captain Jake Riley. Captain, may I introduce matriarch Sianda and Syuk," Kiah said into the com.

"It's an honor to meet you both," Jake bowed his head. Behind him stood the rest of the crew of the Pegasus as they looked on from the bridge.

"Greetings Captain Jake Riley," Sianda 'spoke' so everyone was addressed.

"Please, just call me by my first name, Jake."

"Jake, I am sure you have many questions. Let me see if I can begin to provide clarity by presenting the truth. Our race on this planet has given up technology," Sianda spoke. "I understand the concept of the device that brought you here, but my kin no longer relies on technology. That relic is from a long time ago, and we no longer possess such a device, and our kin does not have the desire to use such a device again."

Sianda paused momentarily to let the thought sink in, "Long ago, there was a war. Our ancestors escaped to this planet through what you call the crescent ring gate. They came here to save that moon from the exploitation of war and never returned. We survived here and thrived here after we gave up that technological power. Now, we try to live in balance with this planet, in peace."

"I understand," Jake said softly after a time. "Is there any way to learn about the crescent ring gate?"

"No one living has that knowledge," Sianda spoke.

"Are there any records or a database?" Jake asked.

"All that is left is the remains of one of the ancient ships. It is the last of the ancient technology that exists on this planet," Sianda spoke.

"Is it possible for us to see it?" Jake asked.

Sianda seemed to regard Jake and the crew for a moment as if to size up their situation. Then, she replied, "Perhaps."

"I understand, and thank you for…" at that moment Hot Wings appeared.

"It's true. A loopen is here on our world," Sianda spoke. The fin along the crest of her head changed into a bright blue color. The crew understood the excitement and awe behind her words.

"Yeah, he kinda followed us here," Ashley explained from her seat on the bridge.

"He followed you?" Sianda asked.

"Yeah, almost as if he belonged with this crew," Ashley said.

"So, you are connected?" Sianda asked.

Ashley thought she might not understand that translation completely, "Connected? Yeah, I guess we are connected."

Sianda shook her head slightly, "We know about them from our history, but to see a loopen is an honor."

Sianda paused for a moment in thought. "My kin are nomadic, and we are headed toward the ancient ship in a few days. The way can be dangerous, but your crew and the loopen are welcome to accompany us on our journey."

"Thank you," Jake said as he nodded.

PLAN

The trip back for Richard and Anya was harrowing, but with each meter they ascended toward the surface, they breathed a little bit easier. Finally, they made it back to the ice/ocean interface and to Icelus Outpost. Richard breathed a massive sigh of relief when they docked. The Crichton had made it back in mostly one piece, thanks to the assistance of Bobb. As Anya and Richard exited, they caught their first glimpse of the damage on the port side thruster. The NIC material had been shredded and looked like it was barely hanging on. The thruster's inner-workings were visible, and Richard was shocked it had even made the journey.

"We got lucky," Anya said as she examined the damage with Richard.

"Yeah, we are going to need to make some repairs before we try again," Richard said.

"We need to do better than that. We need a plan," Anya said.

"Agreed."

Richard heard footsteps behind him, and as he turned around, he saw Malcolm and Angi walking up to him.

"Are you ok, Richard?" Angi asked quickly.

"Yeah, we are…" That is when Angi gave Richard a stern look that silenced him.

"Losing contact with the Crichton suddenly, during that attack, scared the hell outta me. You jeopardized this mission by putting yourselves at risk," Angi growled.

"We were not aware there was that kind of threat from a creature here," Richard explained. "We're trying to find information about where the Pegasus went."

"Richard, we barely know anything about this world or what occurrence caused the disappearance of the Pegasus. We need to be cautious within that area. I want you to at least tell me before you take action like that. There are just a few of us out here. We only get one shot to do this mission right. If someone dies here, EI is going to cancel this WHOLE TRIP," Angi snapped.

Richard looked into Angi's eyes and then nodded. "You're right."

Angi stared briefly before admitting, "I probably would have done the same damn thing you did." Then she pointed over Richard's shoulder to the damaged thruster. "But we can't risk doing that again!" she yelled.

Richard nodded again.

Angi's shoulders slumped a bit. "Finding out that the crew disappeared days ago, and I was not told about it immediately, has really rattled me. It's already been a tough week," she said, lowing her tone.

"For me, too," Richard said.

"We need to figure this out," Angi said.

Malcolm stood there, nearly frozen, and felt awkward at the sudden intense verbal exchange.

"What if we built a depot nestled near the loopen nest?" Anya suddenly asked.

"Huh?" Richard said.

"We anchor a tether near the nest where we can pump down air and guide supplies, then operate from there. Then we use Bobb to scout the unknown and dangerous areas. If something big comes by, we can make a run for Icelus Outpost in the sub. That way, we can lessen the risk and still get the job done," Anya explained.

"Alright… yeah… that might work. It's going to require lots of material and time, and I don't think we have enough for that right now," Richard said.

"Plenty of NIC material will be arriving shortly. There should be enough to build or print whatever we need, assuming you can get the finished materials in the correct place. I planned ahead," Angi said.

Richard looked puzzled. "Wait, what do you mean you brought plenty of NIC material?"

"I pulled some strings and paid for a load to be delivered into orbit. I figured we needed more than what EI sent for this mission. It will be here shortly," Angi explained.

Richard nodded. "Yeah, others on the EI council were trying to keep this mission quiet because of the sensitive information, and I fought for more supplies and staff but was overridden. So I'm glad you came and brought some back up," Richard said gratefully.

"I'll get started coordinating the incoming supplies and assembling or printing any materials we need," Malcolm said as he hurried away.

"What the hell were those things down there?" Angi asked.

"Sea monsters," Richard said as he shook his head. "Big ones!"

"Do you think this depot plan is going to work?" Angi asked.

"We need to be down there to figure this out. I think this is our best shot based on what we know now," Richard explained.

"Yeah, just setting an oxygen and electrical line on an anchor could help. Then, with the NIC cable, we should be able to shuttle supplies to the bottom," Anya said.

"The cable could take a while to print," Richard said.

"That is why I brought one hundred kilometers of pre-printed NIC cable. I figured that would be enough to reach the sixty kilometers in depth at the needed angle. I also brought some ready-made buildings that need basic assembly and whatever modification necessary to be usable at the depth we are working within. Just be sure whatever we build is large enough for the three of us," Angi said.

"Angi, I think you should stay here. Even being here at Icelus Outpost is dangerous," Richard pleaded. "We are already pushing the limits, and I can't risk your life. Malcolm is here, and this is our safest location on Europa."

"Alright, at least for now. But Richard, your backup needs to know the plan to help. So keep that in mind for the future," Angi said.

"We will keep the channel open. We can always use another pair of eyes," Anya said.

Richard nodded.

The freighter Angi had brought had just arrived in orbit along with an automated drop pod-style container delivery system. Richard wasn't sure what strings Angi had pulled or what she had spent for this arrangement. Whatever she did and how fast she did it bordered on a miracle. This particular freighter seemed like it might have been originally headed for a colony and had a pre-built NIC residential module that could be deployed using several interconnecting blocks. With a few adjustments, it could be used at the sixty-kilometer depth of the loopen nest. Their luck continued when they determined that each block could even fit down the elevator from the surface to the ice/ocean interface outpost.

Maybe things were starting to look up for the rescue team.

CAMP

Syuk and Sianda agreed to lead the Pegasus to the Scanii camp.
The camp was nestled against an outcropping of rock that stretched
almost to the water's surface. The camp consisted of many pod-
like tents made from natural plant materials. From a distance, the tents
glowed, and outlines of Scanii figures stood. The light was disappearing along the horizon, and the last sun faded into the ocean waves as
they arrived.

The variety in sizes of the Scanii was remarkably similar to humans.
Sarah thought that she observed two different forms. Syuk and Sianda
appeared female with similar curves and torsos as human women. Then
there was another distinct form that did not appear to be the same as the
females. Their size was similar to the females, and they were muscular,
were wider through their hips, and their tails were very different. Their
tails moved as one structure, but there was a clear gap between the inde-
pendent parts before being bound again near their flukes. This second
type made up the majority of the group.

Each individual had unique crest patterns and coloring around their
eyes. The Scanii skin colors ranged from pale blue in the young to deeper
blue in the young adults to dark grey as they aged. The flowing fin along
the back of their head always appeared in shifting colors, and Sarah
wondered if the crest color changed based on the individual's moods
or feelings.

As they traveled closer to the camp, Sarah could tell the tents were
stuffed with bioluminescent leaves. They appeared only large enough to
fit maybe one to three Scanii within them at a time. Even then, the
quarters would have been tight, and it didn't appear that any Scanii
were actively using them when the Pegasus arrived. It made Sarah
wonder if these structures were only used for sleeping or had some other
purpose entirely.

Several groups watched with curiosity as the Pegasus approached their camp. The Pegasus stopped several lengths from the edge of the camp and held position.

"Do you mind if we consume a meal together?" Sianda spoke to the nearby minds. "I realize you will need to remain in your ship to eat."

"Yes, that would be wonderful," Jake replied. Ben had earlier soothed his concerns about possible cross-species bacterial or viral infections. He assured Jake that interacting with the Scanii would be safe for both species.

Sianda nodded in agreement. "I will gather my kin."

Hot Wings quickly made his appearance after traveling within the ship to the camp. He went up to every individual Scanii and seemed to greet them. He was a focal point of wonderment for the Scanii, and they watched as he moved through their ranks, always letting him approach first. Occasionally, a Scanii would hold out their hand and gently rub his body along the tips of their fingers. Even Syuk and Sianda waited for the little loopen to reach them.

An hour later, the dinner had arrived as all the Scanii gathered. Trays were woven from glowing leaves and presented some type of raw meat. The Scanii wore various colorful outfits that reminded Jake of an electronic dance movement. There were about fifty individuals that gathered around the Pegasus. Some Scanii leaned on the Pegasus as they prepared for the coming meal. Jake pushed aside his feeling of protectiveness toward the ship as he summoned a smile.

A young adult Scanii swam up to the moon pool dock with a tray full of food and handed the tray to Kiah, standing just above the pool's surface along one of the edges.

"Thank you," Kiah smiled.

The Scanii made an echoing laugh of joy as they swam off.

Ben was also at the moon pool, ready to examine everything before the crew tried to ingest any of the alien food. He had an image in his mind of radioactive alien sushi, especially with the food being presented atop the glowing leaves.

"Kiah, I want to scan the food before we eat anything," Ben said, following her out of the moon pool dock with the tray. She turned slightly and let him grab one of the filets from the tray.

Kiah proceeded to bring the tray into the galley of the Pegasus on deck one, and Dyami would also scrutinize the filets to ensure they were edible for the crew. She then proceeded to the bridge, where she knew the remaining crew was already socializing with the Scanii. As she entered, Sarah was in mid-sentence.

"…Yes, our species is from the same star system as Europa," Sarah said.

After entering the room, Kiah could hear the translated conversation in her mind. Sianda sang, "Interesting. There are stories that there was another habitable ocean planet in that system. But the stories are just writings within our history." Sarah stood on one side of the NIC glass as Sianda swam closely on the other side. The world of air and the world of water were separated only by the glass as they conversed. The more they spoke to each other, the more Sarah realized that the name and words she and the crew used were perfectly translated when the Scanii also had a common context for the thing or concept.

"Do the Scanii have a written history?" Sarah asked.

"We still write about many things, including our history. This knowledge is no longer kept in machine data. Now it is kept in handwritten tomes or carved into certain metals. We do not mass produce computers for our use," Sianda sang. "Most of our stories are now from this world. We learn lessons from our past and teach those lessons to prevent those missteps within our future."

"Sounds idyllic. Why did your kind leave Europa to come here?" Sarah asked.

"The story is long, and my memory is old," Sianda sang. She paused before singing, "Our kin came from a place far away from Europa that belonged to a vast empire composed of several races. A civil war raged for decades, a struggle for life and freedom between civil fighters and the subjugating military that rules the stars. Europa was a secret civil fighter research base working on bio-compounds for speculative medicine. But they found more than they ever expected. There was a whole colony of creatures on Europa. The same creatures you call loopens. After a while, our kin started experiencing visions that seemed to be connected to the creatures. They showed us an alternate path, one that led my people here."

"Wow. Where is this empire now? Are they a threat to our Sol system?" Sarah asked.

"We do not know for sure. One of our original kin named Rux stayed on Europa. He told my ancestors that there was one last thing that he had to do to protect Europa. They waited for him to find his way here, but he never did. Most Scanii here thought he prevented anyone from ever finding Europa and the secret base."

"You said Rux was a he?" Sarah asked as she looked around at the other Scanii and wondered.

"Yes, there are fewer males within our species. None travel with us right now. Our group consists of only females and hosts at the moment," Sianda sang. "So, you have never seen the military that rules the stars?"

"No, you are the first space-faring civilization humans have ever encountered," Sarah replied.

"Interesting. The empire never found us here, either. How far out into the galaxy has your species gone?" Sianda asked.

"That might be a matter of opinion in a galaxy this large. Other than our unexpected trip here, humans have traveled no more than one hundred light years beyond Earth. Our travel system requires massive amounts of energy at both locations to send a ship from one point to another. So before we can travel to a new system, an uncrewed ship must traverse the entire distance and collect enough power for the transition. It takes a long time, but after it is done, we can fold the space between the two points and travel instantly to the other side. How far the first gate is from the other determines how much power is necessary to link the two points. The crescent ring gate technology that sent us here is far beyond any travel capabilities we have ever seen," Ashley explained.

Jake gave Ashley a quizzical look, wondering how much detail they should share with their new friends. However, he wanted to establish trust with the Scanii and proceeded to share the details of their journey with the gathering.

"Are you ready to eat?" Sianda suddenly asked.

Jake realized that each Scanii had a filet in their hands but were waiting patiently to eat. Jake flushed a bit and asked over the com feed, "Ben, do you have a conclusion about this food and how it will interact with our physiology?"

Ben immediately responded, "Yeah, you might want to cook it first. But it appears to be edible."

"Dyami, can you bring…" Before Jake had time to finish the sentence, Dyami strolled onto the bridge with several cooked alien filets still on the glowing tray of leaves.

Jake blushed a bit more as he turned back to Sianda, "I hope you don't mind that we slightly altered the food you brought."

"That is fine, of course," Sianda sang.

Each crew member grabbed a filet from the tray, just as they had seen the Scanii do.

"It's just an adventure for your mouth," EV whispered to himself as he grabbed his. The texture was rubbery along the outside and held firm in his hands.

Sianda nodded, raised her food slightly above her head, then took a bite. Her triangular teeth tore through the meat as she carefully ate. The other Scanii followed suit and started to eat. Sarah noted the careful way that they consumed their meal. That is when she took a half bite into her cooked alien flesh that looked like whitefish. The outside was a bit rubbery, but a flaky and juicy interior exploded into her mouth as Sarah's teeth plunged through the first layer. There was a citric flavor, and she felt a tingle in her nose. It was the same tingle she got when she ate pungent horseradish. Overall, it tasted alright, and she was surprised when she found herself taking another bite.

"I hope you're enjoying the meal," Sianda sang.

"Yes. Thank you," Sarah said.

That is when one of the younger individuals asked, "What do you normally eat?"

"Well, we eat many forms of meat and plants," Sarah said. "We even grow some of the plants we eat in our ship."

The young individual became excited as they sang their following words, "Really? Is that something you will share with us?"

Syuk chimed in at this point, "Yes, I would be interested in learning more about your food."

"Yes, I can give you some samples," Sarah said.

"No rush, please finish your meal first," Syuk sang.

Sarah nodded in acknowledgment.

"So, how do you survive with the tyrant and other large predators on this planet?" Sarah asked.

"Why do you call it a tyrant?" Syuk asked. "I understand the context of the creature that you refer to, but it also has another meaning in your spoken word?"

"Yeah, it means an oppressive ruler. Sometimes humans apply negative descriptions to things we fear," Sarah said.

"It is just a creature. It has its patterns. Observing and respecting those patterns is how to avoid conflict," Syuk sang.

"What happens if it deviates from those patterns? How do you protect yourself?" Sarah asked.

"Some die because of the tyrant, that is true. But death is always a part of life. Struggles for survival between creatures is a natural process. I do feel fear, but I do not let it control me," Syuk sang.

Sarah nodded, and she could see other Scanii nodding too. "What is the word you call the tyrant?"

"Rahav," Syuk sang. The translation in Sarah's mind sounded very similar to the sounds Syuk made.

"Rahav," Sarah mimicked back. Syuk smiled without revealing teeth and let out a sound that reminded Sarah of a giggle. Sarah was amazed at the similarities between human reactions and the Scanii reactions. Were they mimicking human responses, just as a reflection would? Or did they come by these same reactions genuinely? It felt genuine, and maybe there was a way to find out.

"Did your ancestors meet other alien races?" Sarah asked.

"The Scanii were not the only species within the empire. Some were even terrestrial like yourselves," Syuk sang.

"Did you communicate with them in the same way as you're communicating now?" Sarah asked.

"Yes, but the Scanii learned the technique from another powerful being. This form of communication was a gift," Syuk sang. Sarah wanted more information about this gift, but Syuk didn't add anything further.

"My turn for a question," Syuk sang. "Where are your hosts? Do you not have any on this trip?"

"What do you mean by hosts?" Sarah asked.

"The gender responsible for gestating young. I hope you treat them well. As humans?" Syuk sang.

"Generally, human females carry the young. On research expeditions like ours, typically, we do not bring our young to protect them from unknown dangers. Individual humans usually vary between two genders, females and males. Some individuals even chose to transition between genders. There is variety within our genders and even our ancestry. However, our society endeavors for fairness and equality for every individual, regardless of gender or race. The pursuit of perfect equality has come a long way within our history and is still something we strive for to this day," Sarah answered.

Even though questions were flowing, Sarah was surprised to find her alien food was gone, only leaving crumbs in her hand. She brushed it away as she noticed something shimmer in the artificial light of the Pegasus. Rainbow feathers floated within the Scanii gathering.

Syuk did not seem surprised by their presence, but Sarah was shocked to see them here since she had only first observed them on Europa.

"You have seen these creatures before?" Sarah asked.

"Yes, they appeared on this world when the Scanii did and are not native. I believe their arrival was unintentional, and we were fortunate they found a niche to fill within this ecosystem. We bring them as cleaners to ensure scraps do not attract unwanted attention," Syuk replied.

"From the Rahav?" Sarah asked.

"No, from others," Syuk replied.

Earlier, Jake had broken off into a conversation with Sianda since he was more interested in where they were going. "So, how far is this ancient ship?"

"Eleven Violatis days travel from here," Sianda replied.

"You had mentioned dangers along this journey?" Jake asked.

"Yes, there are predatory creatures, more dangerous than the Rahav," Sianda sang. "They have hooks on the ends of their many arms, and their ability to suddenly appear makes them exceptionally dangerous. Only recently did we find out about their existence. They kill anything and everything. Many of our kin have been slaughtered by them. They appear like ghosts and will hunt you," Sianda explained.

"Ghosts?" Jake questioned.

"Invisible. There is no trace of them before they appear unexpectedly," Sianda replied. "We have only encountered them very recently. We do not know all the wildlife here on Violatis, but they only have appeared in the last few cycles. The number of attacks has been growing. They are the Axén," Sianda replied.

Dyami was listening to the conversation after distributing the food. He wondered if he could feel these creatures if he looked. Relaxing into a calm state of mind, he looked out. The auras from the Scanii and Hot Wings were intense. There were many conscious minds around, and almost all of them were new to him. If there was anything else around, he couldn't feel it.

Kiah returned to the hydroponics lab to grab some tomatoes for the Scanii. After gathering three fat tomatoes and one giant mushroom, she returned with the samples to the moon pool dock. She thought about grabbing a pepper but thought it might be better to avoid the culinary fire.

As the bulkhead door slid open, Kiah was surprised to find three young adult Scanii sitting along the moon pool edge waiting for her.

"Hello," Kiah smiled.

The closest Scanii let out a slight squeal and held out their hand. The other two Scanii followed close behind. Kiah was unsure but decided to give them one of the tomatoes. They squealed again before diving back into the moon pool.

Kiah laughed at the sight.

The next Scanii that approached was older and held a toothless smile as she swam up. Kiah could tell she still had plenty of teeth but was respecting her by not showing them. She did the same, holding her teeth within her big grin.

This Scanii offered something in return. Kiah graciously took the offering of two large objects that might have been fruit. Then, Kiah let her select between her offerings. The Scanii chose another tomato and the mushroom. As she left, she bowed her head slightly and sang, "Thank you."

Kiah had one more tomato. It smelled wonderful, and she felt the smooth skin as she held the fruit in her one hand. She set the other exchanged items aside.

That is when Syuk appeared just after she finished her conversation with Sarah.

She regarded Kiah with her smile. Kiah found it remarkable how fast this had all happened. Out of desperation, the relationship with the Scanii had formed. *The relationship between our species feels like a genuine relationship between friends,* she thought.

"Enjoy. I love tomatoes," Kiah said as she handed the fruit to Syuk.

"Thank you, I will endeavor to savor it," Syuk took the fruit.

After the meal ended, Hot Wings became the center of everyone's attention. Every single one of the Scanii was enchanted by his presence. As he swam up to the front glass of the bridge, he paused for a moment floating in front of Syuk and Sianda.

The two Scanii greeted the young loopen and offered him a smile.

"Are you able to speak to him?" Ashley asked.

"No. We have never been able to communicate with them in that way. It is said that some individuals can sense their feelings," Syuk answered. "Do you experience that?"

Ashley was shocked and delighted by the thought that might be possible. "Can you show me how?"

Syuk closed her eyes, and suddenly a wave of sensations swept through Ashley. Ashley closed her eyes as the experience started. Joy, playfulness, and belonging all swirled in an amalgam of emotions that she was experiencing. She also felt profound love and was surprised to learn it was directed at her. There was also something else, something deeper. She relaxed and let the feelings flow through her. She felt light, as if she would be able to simply fly. When she opened her eyes, she was no longer standing on the bridge of the Pegasus. She was floating in a space with a warm light that wrapped around her body within the expanse. Hot Wings was there with her, and the experience intensified as another wave of love washed over Ashley. She sensed that this being had a profound and lasting connection to her. No words were spoken as the two shared their emotions within this sacred space. Ashley also felt a strong maternal bond with Hot Wings. The feelings were intense and almost tangible as they swirled through her.

She felt a pull as she returned to her conscious mind and body. Jake's hand was resting lightly on her shoulder. "Hey, are you alright?" he asked.

She smiled warmly at him. "Yes, that was amazing," she reassured him calmly.

Syuk was still less than an arm's length away from where they stood. "How did you do that?" Ashley asked.

"I did nothing. You are connected to this loopen," Syuk replied.

GUIDE

The next morning the Scanii group prepared to depart. They gathered the materials from their pod tents and put pieces together on the water's surface, building a type of raft. The Pegasus had ascended to the surface and bobbed slightly as small waves rolled by. Sarah and Kiah had left the Pegasus in their one-piece swimsuits to swim for an hour and burn off the build-up of tension. Once they finished, they basked on top of the Pegasus in the suns' morning glow. The light felt good, and Sarah couldn't remember the last time direct sunlight had touched her skin. She felt a slight ache from the exercise and the blood flowing smoothly through her loosened muscles. It felt good.

Sarah marveled as the Scanii constructed their travel raft on the surface. Everything seemed to have a place, and the speed and skill made it apparent that the Scanii kin was used to the construction process. Floating items on the water's surface was an efficient way to move heavy objects across an ocean, and she wondered how many times they had constructed such a raft. She also wondered about the technologies the Scanii had given up when they came here. They could instantly cross the stars and forge metal despite being an ocean-faring species. She wanted more details about Scanii's history and how they accomplished technological feats while living in their underwater world. The answers to those questions might take several lifetimes for a human to fully understand.

EV emerged from the hatch connected to the small airlock on the top of the Pegasus above deck one. He was in his gnarly orange and yellow palm trunks. The colors appeared darker in this world's light, but the color intensity was beyond comprehension. "Catch'n the rays?" he asked as he smiled at the ladies. "A bit of sun can really help cheer up any day. I even convinced the Skipper that it was a good idea." EV unfurled an equally intense flower towel and laid it on the deck, ceremoniously setting himself in the center on a bright yellow hibiscus.

"So, what happened with you at the party last night, EV?" Sarah asked.

EV chuckled a bit before he responded. "I was conversing with a few Scanii, and they mentioned the upcoming haul." He nodded toward the raft that was still being assembled. "They asked if I wanted to help!"

"The Pegasus could pull that entire raft as we travel," Kiah said.

"Where's the fun in that? Besides, their civilization gave up technology, remember. I'm not sure they want us hauling all of their homes with our fancy ship," EV said.

"So how were you planning to help them without the Pegasus," Kiah asked.

"SWIMMING!" EV proudly announced. "They said it was alright!"

"Wait?! You'll swim with them and try to pull that thing?" Kiah asked skeptically.

"Hell yeah!" EV puffed out his chest. "They said we will have a good current flowing in our favor and asked if I wanted to join."

"Huh…" Kiah said. "Think you're going to be able to keep up?"

"Maybe, but that is not the best part," EV had a huge grin.

Sarah gave him the pleasure of explaining by asking, "What is the best part, EV?"

"I told them about wake surfing! They wanted me to show them how!" EV said with pure excitement.

"So let me get this straight. You, EV, encounter a new aquatic alien race, and just days after meeting them, you want to teach them about surfing?" Sarah asked.

"It's like you totally understand me!" EV was grinning ear to ear. "I will have to improvise the board, of course. Also, I'm not sure they would want to try it for themselves since they can already swim as fast as dolphins, but they seemed intrigued by human water recreation. In addition, I learned they can breathe just as easily in the open air as they can within the water," he explained.

"Alright, so if you're doing that, who will be piloting the ship?" Kiah asked.

"Ashley said she could handle it until we stop for the first break," EV explained.

"Well, good luck," Kiah said and smiled at him. "Make us proud!"

EV smiled at that. Sarah started to feel the bite of the two suns as their rays began to burn her skin. She hoped the journey ahead would be this pleasant, but something told her the path would be challenging.

About mid-morning, everyone was ready. "Pegasus, just follow along behind us," Sianda communicated the thought to the crew as the kin began to swim.

"Ashley, if you would keep pace, please," Jake smiled at her as the Pegasus glided ahead by her hand.

Up ahead, EV was positioned in the middle of the group as he swam with a brisk arm stroke. He had equipped a set of fins and a wetsuit to increase his speed within the water. He had skipped the O2 tank and anything else that could weigh him down. Despite every advantage he allowed himself, after a minute, he was already falling behind and swimming as hard as he could.

Many of the Scanii pulled the raft forward on the surface of the water as they swam ahead. After about ten minutes of hard swimming, EV found the current that had been promised and started to keep up without as much effort. He still was not pulling any of the weight, and despite being a legendary swimmer, it was still all he could do to keep up with the Scanii, even with the current at his back. On the other hand, the Scanii were leisurely swimming, letting the current do most of the work, and stroking with their tail occasionally.

After another hour, EV was tired and struggled to keep pace with the group. The Scanii he spoke to last night had encouraged him to hold on to the raft for a while and 'hang out' with the young. The young Scanii were swimming 'slowly' by the raft and seemed delighted by their new swimming companion as EV approached. With a few powerful strokes, EV hung onto the raft. He was tired and just kicked with his fins for a while. Many of the younger Scanii also held on as they marveled at the human swimming beside them.

The raft surged forward with the Scanii combined effort. EV held his breath as he observed his surroundings. In front of him, he could see the leading group continuing forward. As he looked down, all he could see was violet water with rays of light shimmering through the ocean. Looking back, he saw the Pegasus keeping pace at a distance. The scene was breathtaking as he surfaced for another breath.

After another minute, EV pulled himself further up on one of the struts of the raft. The material seemed light but strong, made from natural fiber. With an angled shape at the front of the craft, it looked like a narrow surfboard widening slightly where his feet now stood. There were several of these planks that held up the raft. These were the pieces the Scanii had told him about last night. EV pulled his fins off and allowed his feet to feel the streams of water as they passed by the board being pulled along the water's surface. He stood on the board, steadying himself along the raft as he gained his balance in mid-glide.

Individual Scanii jumped from the water and seemed to regard him as he stretched his arms wide, feeling the water move beneath the makeshift board.

EV felt the breeze as they raced forward. The suns were still climbing high in the sky. A moon was visible just over the horizon and resembled a large coin with a bright bronze color. This was the first time a human had ever set eyes on that celestial body as it glimmered with reflected light.

EV felt the thrill of being in the moment. He felt exhilaration. He felt complete.

As the breeze became stronger, EV noticed the dark clouds on the horizon. A gentle rain fell over the ocean, and the waves began to pick up as the raft cruised through falling water.

As he rode across the waves, he smiled to himself, "This is being alive!"

After a few hours, the group had made it to a calm circle of grand rocks. The current was not disturbing the small sheltered alcove. Here they would briefly stop to enjoy a small meal. Many Scanii came over to show their interest and respect for the land-dwelling alien that swam alongside them during this initial journey.

At the midday break, the Scanii generously traded with the Pegasus. They gave several fresh filets to each of the crew. Dyami was on point this time and had fresh peppers and potatoes ready to go with the alien fare, turning it into something that smelled spicy and inviting.

EV returned to the Pegasus to resume his post after the midday meal, and blushed after a few compliments on his swimming performance.

"How was it out there?" Sarah asked.

"Amazing!" EV exclaimed.

"Well, I'm going to try the next ride. Any pro tips?" Sarah asked.

"Have fun out there, Dr. Triv!" EV said as he smiled.

The crew gathered in the galley as Dyami served the midday meal. Sarah and EV were the last to join the group. Through the NIC windows in the galley, the crew saw Syuk and Sianda as they ate their meal close by with several of their kin.

"It looks like you made a good impression EV," Jake said as they sat down.

"Do you think now I will be as popular as Hot Wings?" EV asked.

"Nope!" Jake said as he shook his head.

"That's ok. It was still epic! Thanks for letting me participate, Skipper!" EV exclaimed as he gave Jake a thumbs up.

"We need friends right now, EV. You did really well," Jake felt respect for EV as he put himself out there to further forge their relationship with the Scanii.

Sarah swam up in her one-piece black suit along the raft's edge to the spot where EV had ridden. She knew she could not swim as fast as EV and had even considered using one of the Sea Wings to help pull the raft. Still, she was unsure if using that technology would offend the Scanii, who clearly knew what they were doing and seemed to pull the raft effortlessly without assistance. As she pulled herself onto the platform, she saw Syuk swimming on her back, facing Sarah. Bubbles swirled around Syuk's body as she swam strongly along the water's surface. Syuk smiled at Sarah as she prepared for the next stage of the day's swim. Sarah smiled back, wondering how the journey would go.

"This is a long journey," Syuk sang. "I was wondering if you were up for some company and conversation?"

"Yeah, I would like that," Sarah said. Sarah was finding a comfortable position on the board. She kept her balance and braced comfortably against the raft.

Sianda communicated to all, "Forward!"

The Scanii surged ahead again through the current. The raft quickly moved forward, returning to the deeper water as the sandy bottom faded again into the violet ocean. Syuk swam close to the raft, where Sarah could see her along the surface.

"I still have questions," Syuk communicated through thought. "I want to know about your oceans. Your planet's life developed in the oceans?"

Sarah felt the rush of the breeze around her as she kept her balance on the board as it cut through the water. "Yeah, it did. Humans like to categorize things into groups we can understand scientifically. Humans are in a group called mammals. On Earth, there are still a variety of intelligent mammals that live within the oceans."

"Do you communicate with them?" Syuk asked.

Sarah smiled a bit at that. "In a way. I like to think that there is an understanding without words being exchanged. Mostly it is knowing the moods and recognizing the familiarities in actions between both individuals. They always seemed to be natural stewards of our planet, whereas our species still struggles with that."

"You personally communicated with one of these individual mammals?" Syuk asked.

"Yes. It's actually one of the reasons I was selected for this mission," Sarah said, thinking about Keenan. "I do want to see him again."

Syuk paused, then asked, "Tell me about this individual."

"Well, he is much larger than I am, and his skin is black and white. We call them orcas," Sarah said, holding the image of Keenan in her mind.

"Those are just surface details. Tell me about the individual you know," Syuk spoke through thought.

"He is curious and smart. He is caring, even toward the younger males, and is a leader. He is attentive to the needs of others and listens to his mother and matriarch. He loves to sneak up, and I often don't see him until he is close to my boat. He is brave and an ambassador for his species," Sarah reflected.

Sarah felt the sunlight caressing her skin as she sailed on the raft pulled by the Scanii. She saw many Scanii leaping from the water as they pulled the craft along. She marveled at the teamwork involved in moving the great craft, with ropes strapped to harnesses that were made from some type of plant fiber.

"Are you a steward of your planet?" Syuk asked.

The question took Sarah by surprise. She did not immediately respond as she thought about the answer. "I always try to be. But even today, humans have a hard time not over-using the places we live. I participate in human society, but still disagree with how certain aspects function. I do my best to make positive changes with the people and creatures I interact with. Is that enough to negate the resources I consume... I hope so."

The sentiment just spilled out, and Sarah was surprised to be sharing these thoughts with Syuk. She had felt this way for a long time, but sharing the feelings so openly with another being she just met was new. Somehow it still felt right, especially to this individual who had given up technology's complexities for a simpler life.

Sarah adjusted her balance again on the board as it skimmed through the water. The water sliding along the edges felt cool, and Sarah regarded the open sea ahead. From this view, there was nothing but water ahead, and she enjoyed this fresh perspective, unbound by instruments.

"Do you wish you could change your current life?" Syuk asked.

"Do I have regrets? Yes, absolutely. But I also look back and ask myself this question. Did I do my best with the time and circumstances I had? If the answer is yes, then I can live with what I have done and move on. If not, I tend to never forget it and do everything I can to learn from the experience and never repeat my failure," Sarah felt the words as they flowed.

"Interesting. I often wonder if my kins' path is the correct path." Syuk admitted. "Our ancestors did not pursue technology they knew existed. They laid it to rest. Some of what they knew has now been totally forgotten. Some of our struggles would be easier with that technology, and we tell ourselves that sacrificing those pursuits helps prevent the creation of another oppressive empire. I wonder if they were right or if perhaps there is a different path." Syuk sang. "Now your kind is here, reliant on technology to survive in this world. I only hope your presence is not a challenge to some. Our kin do not always agree."

"How many of your species exist in this world?" Sarah asked.

"About one hundred thousand individuals. The first colony was made up of about nine hundred Scanii, and was formed about two thousand years ago," Syuk responded. "Many Scanii still live near the grandfather ship, where that first colony was originally formed."

"Do any of them pursue technology?" Sarah asked.

"Some. They learn all they can. But without much way to construct very complex machines, most of their time is spent learning written knowledge. They rarely are able to use it." Syuk replied. "Many others remind them of the grim ends they feel technology brings. I think they are brave for their efforts to try to learn and understand in the face of much criticism."

"You empathize with them?" Sarah asked.

"Yes. Some just want to learn. Others, the reasons are more obscure and sometimes frightening." Syuk sang.

Sarah felt a bit of a knot in her stomach at the thought. How would the other Scanii treat the Pegasus and her crew? They were walking into an alien culture that was much more complex than what was represented by this first group of Scanii, and that thought made Sarah nervous.

The day slipped away as the aquatic travel continued. Darkness once again returned as the Scanii found the camp's final location for the night.

After dinner, Dyami was about ready to settle in for the night. All the Scanii had returned to the tents curling themselves inside the leaves. Before sleep, he figured that he should try reaching out once again. He shifted into relaxation and instinctually focused. The presence of the Scanii was still very intense. Dyami focused and saw auras, trying to see beyond, but the energy of the camp was all he could see. He still did not find anything that appeared to be an Axén.

With some relief, Dyami sighed, then went to sleep. There would be more travel tomorrow, and they all needed some rest.

LOOPEN PARADISE

"That should do it," Richard said as he connected the cable supplying power to the small base using Crichton's robotic arm. The base now resided at the bottom of the ocean, nestled close to the loopen nest. They had modified the pre-built residential module that had included two bunks, a full bathroom, and a small kitchen with a table and an emergency battery. This new setup was in addition to their facilities aboard the Crichton. Anya had suggested they call the base Paradise since it was a vast improvement over being stuck in the confinement of the Crichton. It was connected to Icelus Outpost, located at the ice/ocean interface, by a NIC power and supply cable that stretched the entire length of the water column. They had simply attached and dropped the modules and supplies down the line, guiding them to this exact location. So far, they hadn't seen the massive horn-heads by the loopen nest, and Richard was hoping they didn't start seeing them now that they had placed the base here. The small base powered up, and the air pump began pressurizing the new base. This location was close to where the Pegasus had rested while exploring the area.

The supplies Angi had rerouted were from a colony formation shipment. Richard didn't want to ask where she got the shipment or how much she had paid, but he was glad it had arrived and was delivered with Malcolm's help. They quickly had been able to set up with many of the prefabricated components. Now they had a firm foothold on the bottom of this abyssal ocean and could focus on finding the Pegasus.

As the airlock between the Crichton and the base turned green, Anya said without hesitation, "Dibs on the shower!"

Richard nodded as the continuous hours caught up with him. He had been working on securing Paradise Base against the rockface all day. The day before was the long descent. The day before that was the construction of the residential module. *There is no rest*, he thought to himself. Each task came in rapid succession, but he always felt persistent urgency. Time was always stalking him. Every waking hour was devoted to the tasks at hand. Each day he wondered if their efforts would bring back the Pegasus. He hoped they would find some answers soon. The two of them needed rest now, and Richard sent a quick message to Angi, letting her know the situation.

Richard climbed into one of the bunks. He was weary from the day, and with the calming sound of the shower in the next room, he was asleep before his head hit the pillow.

Richard awoke several hours later to an incoming video call from Angi at Icelus Outpost. "Yeah, I'm here," Richard answered.

"How's it going?" Angi asked.

"We have the base in place, and it's operational. The plan is to send the Bobb drone out later today. If we are lucky, the horn-heads are gone, and we can see what's behind that bay door," Richard explained.

"Richard… You did well. Please, get my Ben back… Oh, and Richard…be careful," Angi said quietly.

Richard just nodded across the channel at Angi. "I will. I understand what's at stake," he said.

"I know you do," Angi breathed.

With that, the communication ended, and Richard was again left in the darkness of the room. He seemed to lose track of time and wondered if he had nodded off to sleep again while he sat there.

The door then chimed, and Richard blinked back into focus. "Enter"

Anya stood there. "Hey, I think you'd better check this out."

"What is it?" Richard asked.

Anya nodded for him to follow. Collecting himself, Richard stood and walked to the door. They entered the kitchen area just down from the two bunk rooms. The NIC window beyond had an orange glow from the o-gel growth. There in the window, Richard clearly saw two loopens floating by the glass. Their wing patterns were glowing green in the dark. "They have been like that for a while now," Anya explained.

As Richard approached the loopens, their patterns became brighter and shimmered. He felt an overwhelming benevolence emanating from these creatures as he stared at them. Suddenly he sensed another person. "Sarah?" He couldn't be sure. He relaxed, closed his eyes, and tried to hold onto where the feeling was coming from.

Richard fell into another plane of existence within his mind, guided into the connection by the loopens.

"Hello?" Richard's voice echoed across the expanse. Then, he saw someone else was with him in this place.

"Ashley? Is that you?" Richard's words felt strange in his throat. The words echoed in repeat.

"Richard!? How are you here!?" Ashley exclaimed.

Two loopens swam through the thought-scape toward them. One was Hot Wings, and Ashley seemed to recognize the other loopen.

"Ashley, where is the Pegasus?" Richard quickly asked.

Ashley relayed the coordinates from the communications satellite and had Richard repeat the numbers to her.

"So, everyone is safe?" Richard asked.

"Richard, everyone is alive and safe. It's frightening how far we are from home, and we are anxious to establish communication with Earth Dock. Hopefully, you can talk to Jake and Sarah after we get the com satellite pointed in the right direction. Now that you have the coordinates for our star system, Earth Dock should be able to find us. We have found some pretty extraordinary things and met some extraordinary beings," Ashely reported.

"Is this real?" Richard suddenly asked. His mind was still having trouble processing what was taking place.

Ashley nodded. "Don't forget what I told you. We already launched our com satellite. We are waiting on you now."

Richard gasped as he returned from the journey. Anya was hovering over him. "Richard, don't you dare leave me all alone down here with these aliens!"

"I KNOW WHERE THEY ARE!" Richard exclaimed.

Instantly, Richard was scrambling to record the coordinates on his tab.

Anya saw how wide his eyes were. *You crazy old man,* she thought to herself. What were the odds that Richard would suddenly just know where they were? She then stared out the window at the alien lightshow the loopens were creating. "We can't be that lucky," she whispered to herself.

Richard was already on the com to Earth Dock. "Yeah, those are the coordinates. Plug them in and start a com feed as soon as possible."

On the other end, the technician raised concerns about the power required for such a distant transmission. He warned that it would take a massive amount of energy even to attempt such a connection.

"Get it done!" Richard barked.

The line switched to another figure that now stood on the screen, "We will do this for you, Richard, but I hope you know what you're doing." With that, the line was disconnected.

Anya looked at Richard for a moment. "What was that all about?"

"Anya, I saw Ashley. She told me where they are," Richard said.

"You mean when you passed out on the floor?" Anya asked.

"Yes, it was because of them," Richard said as he pointed to the loopens still hovering by the window.

"You sure you didn't just dream this up?" Anya asked. "You were only out of it for a few moments, and I have seen the stress this mission is putting on you. Are you sure you're alright?"

That is when the video com channel flashed, and Jake's shocked face appeared on the bridge of the Pegasus in front of the rest of his crew. "Richard? Is that you?"

"Yeah, it's good to see you!" Richard cried out in victory.

That is when the message flashed across the screen. It read, (Com Termination Imminent – Insufficient Power).

"We are good. Have you found a way...."

That is when the feed abruptly ended.

Richard didn't know how to feel about what had just happened. That is when Anya broke in with a cheer. "Richard! You old bastard, you found them! Alive!"

"We did, didn't we!" he yelled.

"Hell yeah, YOU did!" Anya yelled back. Despite her usually cool and rebellious persona, Anya hugged Richard hard as a huge smile crossed her face.

"Try calling them back. Maybe we can get a clear signal," she suggested.

Richard tapped at the controls as he tried to reconnect, but the system seemed to still be dead. He tried again, but there was nothing. He changed the channel and signaled Earth Dock, but there was still no response. Then he tried Angi on the local com network, and she picked up. "Richard? What's up?" Angi said tiredly as she picked up the video com feed.

"Angi, we made brief contact with the Pegasus! We know where they are!" Richard said.

A massive wave of relief washed over Angi's face, and she immediately wanted to know when she could see Ben again. "Did you get them back?" Angi waited for the response with bated breath.

"It's a long story, and I will explain everything later, but can you see if you can contact Earth Dock? We lost the transmission, and we need that channel." Richard explained quickly.

Angi tried the connection, but the expression on her face showed her frustration. "It says it can't connect. I'm not seeing anything on the com network except your local transmission," she replied.

Richard wondered what widespread consequences that 31,502 light-year-long distance call had as he remembered the tech's prior warning.

"... Richard?" Richard suddenly realized that Angi was waiting for him to answer while his brain ran through the problem.

"They are very far away, but we know their location," Richard said, hoping that would answer most of her questions. He gave her the few details he knew and how far away they were. Angi listened as he explained and saw a cloud of disappointment darken over Angi's face as she realized not all the news was good news.

"Angi, there might be another way that I can contact them," Richard said, then turned away from the video screen to see if the loopens were still there. They were gone, leaving an emptiness as the moment passed.

Hours later, Richard learned about the gory details that had temporarily knocked out the communications power network because of his long-distance call. The current system was never built to handle an open com channel that stretched across the galaxy. In fact, the only way it had worked at all was because of crafty settings changes the tech had enabled before trying to establish the epic connection.

"When can we try contacting the Pegasus again?" Richard respectfully asked the Earth Dock commanding officer, first dock Admiral Joseph Xander.

"Sir, my men said it would be a week before they could have a communication link up for that kind of transmission. We aren't going to have this connection hooked to the primary network this time," Admiral Xander said through the video com. "Richard, you said that you came across this location information because you saw it in your mind?"

"Yeah, most would have thought I was crazy but the results are undeniable," Richard smiled at the thought and wondered if the loopens would come back.

"You said this was because of these loopen creatures?" Admiral Xander asked.

"Yes, we believe so," Richard replied.

"How extraordinary…" Admiral Xander said trailing off.

More time passed, and Richard started to question if he should look for the loopen that had connected with him. He closed his eyes for the tenth time, trying to find a way to connect with Ashley again. Again, he relaxed, but after several moments nothing seemed to happen. Maybe he needed to take the Crichton out and look for the alien that could link to Ashley.

He sighed as he thought about what to do next.

"Still nothing?" Anya asked.

"No. No luck," Richard quietly replied.

Suddenly a large flash of loopens swam by the window. The creatures swirled around Paradise Base, and each animal glowed and pulsed as they moved in a tight formation. Then they began shooting green web, enveloping the base's hull. *What is happening?* Richard thought.

CONTACT

The morning started with a touch as a soft foot caressed the side of Jake's leg. He stirred slightly as the feeling roused his mind. Ashley lay next to him. They were still fully clothed. It had been long days of travel, and the need for sleep had taken its toll.

Ashley was still asleep, and Jake closed his eyes again. He lay there, drifting back into sleep. His mind returned to rest. Later, for what seemed to Jake like a few moments, he felt a hand rubbing across his back. It felt good. Energy seemed to crawl across his skin as her touch went under his shirt. He smiled, his eyes still shut as he awoke.

"I know you're awake," Ashley whispered.

Jake rolled over slightly and brought his hand to caress Ashley's left cheek as his nose touched hers. "I hope we didn't sleep too late."

"There is still time," Ashley whispered as Jake opened his eyes.

"Just give me a moment," Jake said, becoming conscious of his musk. Three minutes later, Jake returned and smelled fresher. Maybe not perfect, but with marked improvement.

Ashley kissed him deeply as she sat him on the bed. His imperfect aroma made her mind crazy with tantalizing pleasures.

Ashley discarded her top as she fell upon Jake. Skin touching as their bodies met, expanding their sensations as the two lovers fell together. The two knew precisely when and how to move as they expressed their longing and love for one another.

After breakfast, Ashley entered the connected state of mind with Hot Wings. She liked the way she felt emotionally after each interaction. She found it comforting and could sense that Hot Wings felt the same.

Time seemed to move slower in the trance, and Ashley found it a place to relax outside of real-time. That is when she felt another presence.

"Ashley? Is that you?"

"Richard!? How are you here!?"

Ashley felt yet another presence. She realized she had also met the new arrival before. It was the loopen that stopped to greet her on that very first day by the nest. She secretly named him Kite in reference to his unique patterned skin. He swam up with Hot Wings, and Ashley immediately wondered if they were related somehow.

"Ashley, where is the Pegasus?" Richard quickly asked.

Ashley's brain went blank for a second, but she had committed the location to memory in case a chance to communicate the information ever came up. She rattled off the coordinates as quickly as her brain retrieved the data, having Richard repeat the numbers.

"So, everyone is safe?" Richard looked concerned. He had no idea of anything that had happened.

"Richard, everyone is alive and safe. It's frightening how far we are from home, and we are anxious to establish communication with Earth Dock. Hopefully, you can talk to Jake and Sarah after we get the com satellite pointed in the right direction. Now that you have the coordinates for our star system, Earth Dock should be able to find us. We have found some pretty extraordinary things and met some extraordinary beings," Ashely said with pride.

"Is this real?" Richard suddenly asked. Ashley knew she needed to keep him on track and get him back. Maybe real communication would actually work!

Ashley nodded. "Don't forget what I told you. We already launched our com satellite. We are waiting on you now."

"Richard? Is that you?" Jake asked as the video channel connected.

"Yeah, it's good to see you!" Richard cried out in joy over the open com.

(Com Termination Imminent – Insufficient Power)

"We are good. Have you found a way to bring us…" the channel suddenly froze and went dark, "home?" Jake finished his sentence, still hoping for an answer.

The shouting of joy echoed for a moment before the silence set in. "What happened?" Ben's voice came through the intercom from the marine lab.

"Ben, Earth Dock called, but we lost the connection," Jake explained.

"WHAT?!" Ben said excitedly.

"Richard knows where we are!" Jake exclaimed.

"I will be right there!" Ben exclaimed.

A gust of air seemed to fill the bridge as Ben rushed in, with Dyami following closely behind. "Can we speak with them now? How do we get in touch with them?" he asked excitedly.

"Ben, I'm sure they would call us back if they could. Something must have happened that is preventing them from reestablishing the connection," Jake thought aloud.

Ashley speculated. "They probably tripped out some fuses or scorched some wires in the network. Two years ago, EI upgraded the entire com network because of the high demand of the com traffic to the growing colonies. The engineers said it would meet the communication needs over the next twenty years. Without that upgrade, the call probably would not have worked at all. I suspected it would be a long shot, but they know where we are!" Ashley explained. Her mind still felt sharp after her brief connection with Hot Wings and the other loopen, Kite.

"How long does that take to fix?" Ben asked.

"It is almost impossible to guess, but it could be a while before they can contact us again," Ashley said.

"How did they find us in the first place?" Ben asked.

Ashley looked through the front glass where Hot Wings was still floating by the window near her station. "I was connected with Hot Wings and then saw Richard and Kite in my mind. The two loopens had connected with each other and included Richard."

"Who's Kite?" EV asked.

"He was the first loopen I saw up close on Europa. He seemed to welcome me to the colony that first day... Maybe I'm also connected to him," Ashley found the words spill out before she had time to process them.

EV nodded approval at the name.

"You communicated with him through your mind?" Ben asked for confirmation.

"Yes. Richard knows we are alright," Ashley replied.

Ben felt a strong desire to talk to Angi. However, just knowing she was aware he was alive gave him comfort. He felt a spark return to his heart and a sense of progress toward seeing her again. "Thank you, Ashely. Have you tried to contact Richard again through Hot Wings?"

Ashley nodded and closed her eyes, again trying to relax back into the connected state of mind. This time she easily slipped into the trance once again. The path was becoming familiar, and the connection seemed easy to make at this point. She had a strong bond with Hot Wings. Moments later, Ashley seemed to awake from the trance. "Richard isn't there right now, and neither was Kite." Ben felt a pang of disappointment.

Ashley had tried to contact Richard many times over the next few hours, entering the trance with Hot Wings. Ben had been worried about the unknown effects on Ashley's mind but could never find any physical evidence that the connection harmed either species. He also didn't have any scientific explanation for the connection to the loopen. Even the Scanii telepathic speaking process remained a mystery beyond the fact that it obviously worked. Although, Ben reminded himself that he had been distracted by other essential tasks. He remained worried about the food situation on the Pegasus. Dyami had helped him convert part of the environmental section into an extended growing area. They might be able to grow enough food to sustain the crew for the next several months. They had also been exchanging edible plants and meat with the generous Scanii. When Ben had more time, perhaps he could try cultivating some of those plants within one of the aquariums. Ben reflected on their progress over the last several days as they traveled with the Scanii.

"I am glad that you were able to contact the other humans," Sianda sang, looking over to Jake.

Jake enjoyed the midday travel breaks. Ashley sat close to his right, her hip slightly making contact with his.

"Thanks, Sianda. It's not a way home yet, but it feels like a big win," Jake said as Ashley listened.

"Jake, we will be reuniting with part of my family, once we arrive at our camp tonight. There will be someone there I think you should meet. Will you speak with him?" Sianda sang

"Of course, but may I ask who he is?" Jake asked.

"His name is Rynan, and he is the father and protector of my boys. They are the first twin males in over a century, and twin males are traditionally raised by their father." A slight sadness seemed to glint in Sianda's eyes, but then smiled a bit as if anticipating the reunion. "I think it is important that you share your story with him, and you can bring Ashley and Hot Wings if you wish," Sianda finished.

"It would be an honor," Jake replied.

They finished the midday meal, and before heading to the bridge, Jake took a pit stop to freshen up in his cabin. The hot water felt good as he splashed it on his face and scrubbed off the thin dried layer of sweat from eating the naturally spicy alien fillet.

Ashley entered the cabin, "Hey you!"

"Hey!" Jake smiled back.

Jake held her tight. He felt at home with Ashley and didn't want to let her go. He thought that as long as they were together, he would do all he could to make her happy and protect her. "Ashley, I love you." The words were smooth and Ashley felt light as they touched her as she fell deeper into the embrace.

"Ben is expecting me to meet him in the medical lab," Jake said after a minute had passed.

"It's alright. There are some things I also need to check on the bridge. Let's go!" Ashley said as she stood and walked out of the cabin.

The Violatis day had settled into dusk as the new camp had been established just before the suns had set. Rynan and the twins had arrived just ahead of the main group accompanying the Pegasus. Sianda had assured the Pegasus crew that she had had contact with him before their arrival.

Rynan and his two sons had strong muscular bodies but were slightly smaller than the females and the hosts. The sons looked about two-thirds their father's size but were still quite impressive. Despite the marginally smaller stature, Rynan still looked intimidating.

After the evening meal, Jake and Ashley outfitted themselves with tanks and rebreathers to meet Sianda. Just outside the Pegasus, Hot Wings also joined them. The water was nearly forty meters deep and at a comfortable temperature. The evening felt relaxed as they swam to where Sianda waited for them. The camp glowed in the darkness with the bioluminescent leaves. Their current location was an immense natural growth of these bright aquatic plants. The leaves seemed to grow and twist in every direction. This place must have been where the Scanii harvested these plants that filled their sleeping structures.

"Thank you for coming," Sianda sang.

The group followed Sianda and swam to a red cliffside where the light colors seemed to mix in the waves. Four tents were set in a loose formation around a clearing with an altar in the middle. Sianda made the more formal introductions for Rynan and her two sons, Zovair and Ven. Sianda explained that Yamala, the family's host, was ill and would not join them this evening. Hot Wings was first introduced to the family and took the opportunity to rub against the children's outstretched palms. Then Jake and Ashley were, in turn, introduced to the family.

"Sianda has mentioned your journey," Rynan sang as he spoke to the group.

Jake looked around at the faces. "I'm sure you have many questions about me and my people," Jake said.

"I would like you to tell me your story," Rynan spoke. "Where do you come from?"

Jake told the tale that had seen them travel from Earth Dock to Europa to here. He went into detail about how Syuk had saved Ashley and how grateful they were to Sianda for helping them. Rynan listened intently as Jake spoke. "That is quite a tale," Rynan sang after Jake was finished.

"Is there anything else you can tell me about your journey?" Rynan asked.

Jake thought for a moment. "Actually, there is one more thing," Jake pulled an object from a small pack attached to his harness. "We found this where the sphere wrecked. I apologize for not sharing this earlier." He handed the object to Sianda, and she stared for a moment. "I know you said your species had given up on technology, but we found this and some old Scanii skeletal remains."

"Why are you sharing this? And why now?" Sianda asked.

Jake looked at her. "I felt like we needed to establish mutual trust before I shared this discovery." He looked over Sianda's family. "We have come a long way in such a short time."

Sianda looked upon the object. The screen seemed to glow as she touched it. Her hands motioned across the screen as the ancient Scanii text appeared. "This appears to be one of the original computers from the ancient ship," Sianda sang. "None are known to exist in this time… until now. Where did you say you found this?"

Jake explained how Ashley had found the tablet and the blade and how he had returned to collect them following Ashley's rescue. He reported that he had brought them back to the Pegasus.

"Where is this blade now?" Sianda asked.

Jake had also brought the blade and presented it to Sianda. She took the object from him and carefully examined it. Her eyes widened as she recognized the blade. "This is the missing twin to the Solo Blade! This blade belonged to Rux!" Sianda sang as she regarded the relic.

"What does that mean?" Jake asked.

"I am not sure how you found this where you did," Sianda sang. She thought for a long moment as she stared at the blade and tablet in her hand. After a moment, she handed both objects back to Jake. "You found these, and you can present these to the gathering once we reach the city of Tirilean."

A sudden cry echoed through the ocean, and Jake felt a chill up his spine. Then another. The cries were close, and Jake could immediately tell they were coming from the other Scanii kin. Sianda froze for a second, listening. "We are under attack!"

Sianda produced her own two blades from their side sheaths, a blade in each hand. "You stay here! I must fight to save my kin. Rynan, protect our children!" she yelled out as she swam out of the clearing.

Rynan turned to Jake and exclaimed, "Axén are here! Be on your guard!"

Jake handed the tablet to Ashley, who put the device in her pack. He readied the blade as he looked for some cover. There was very little protection in the area. The Scanii pod tents were small, and Jake was unsure if they could fully close. Before he could weigh his options, Jake's radio cracked, and Dyami's voice rang out over the com, "Jake, they are right on top of you!"

Rynan produced his own two blades and took a defensive posture next to his children. Despite this move, he didn't see the threat until it was too late.

The Axén appeared from nowhere as an expansive cloud of ink filled the surrounding ocean. A set of tentacles with hooks the size of steak knives streaked across the water in a flash, emerging from the ink cloud. In less than a blink, Jake saw Rynan twist his body to neutralize the attack. His efforts were too little too late as the hooks slashed across his tail, drawing a large plume of blood, deep red mixing with water. Rynan grunted with the pain and resolve as he readied himself again for a strike, curling his body.

Jake positioned himself to protect Ashley, but they were being backed into the rockface. Ashley grabbed Jake's arm, guiding him forward. They maneuvered to a more defensible position alongside Rynan. The dark ink faded, but the beast was already gone.

Another huge dark ink cloud appeared directly in front of Jake. This time Rynan was prepared and sprang forward, barreling through the cloud. Knocking a creature out of the darkness, Rynan grappled the opponent. The pair fought through the water. The entity could barely be seen as it blended its colors to match the surroundings. It looked just as large as Rynan, but the shape was not defined. A few tentacles and a larger body mass, but Jake could not see much more. Then Rynan slashed, and green ooze filled the water as the blade pierced the Axén body. Jake had never seen such a fearsome fight as the Axén continued to try to overwhelm Rynan despite the beast's mortal wound.

Just then, Jake noticed a flicker in the water. He saw what was happening before the event occurred. Almost instinctively, Jake braced against the wall and pushed off with all the force he had. Lunging through the water, he crossed the clearing as the next dark cloud of ink appeared. Tentacles with razor hooks leapt out of the cloud before Jake could get there. Rynan was winning his fight, but this new attack flanked his children.

The hooks arched quickly toward the boys, catching them off guard. However, Jake's lunge through the water was on the mark, and with the Solo Blade slashing forward, he intercepted the Axén. He roared, putting every drop of strength into the thrust as he plunged the blade deep into the beast. He twisted the blade and ripped it from the body, severing tentacles as it exited, leaving a massive wound. Green ooze poured from the gaping hole as the beast lurched, becoming a writhing mass of muscle. A wicked howl filled the water, and Jake felt the last spasm as death took the creature.

"JAKE!" Ashley screamed through the com.

The warning echoed in Jake's ears. A third creature appeared behind Jake as the dark soup filled the water again. Jake turned to face a new threat, but a deep pain in his side revealed that he was too late. The hooks drove deep into his fragile body. Before he could react, the tentacles retracted, ripping a hole through his abdomen. Then hooks came for him again, and pain shot through him as they plunged into him. He felt the strength draining from his body, and with everything he had left, he looked over to where Ashley would have been, but the haze from his own blood in the water shrouded his view.

With every fiber of his being, he didn't want to leave her. Then the world slowly spun to black.

THE FIGHT

Rynan finished off the third creature. Ashley swam as fast as she could toward where Jake should be. His body was obscured by blood in the water. Horror struck her hard as she saw his wounds. She forced herself through the panic. The only hope for saving his life was to get him back to the Pegasus. Hot Wings swam close by as she began pulling him back to the ship. It was so far away, and he would bleed out long before she got there, but Ashley had no choice but to try. She pressed her hands tightly against the gaping wounds as she tried to pull him forward. She only had two hands, and they were not enough to cover all the holes.

Ashley cried out as she felt the situation slipping away. She needed a miracle to save him.

Just then, Dyami appeared with a Sea Wing. He hooked Ashley's arms as she held tight to Jake, and they flew toward the ship. Jake breathed shallowly, his eyes twitching quickly behind closed lids, his mask fogging from perspiration.

The journey was just two minutes, but each moment was agonizing as Jake seemed to be slipping away. They needed to be at the ship already. "BEN, HE NEEDS HELP!" Ashley said with sheer panic in her voice.

"I'm waiting at the dock. Get him here as quickly as you can!" Ben said.

Jake awoke and found himself lying on a soft bed. It was weird that everything else was shrouded in darkness. Jake tried to speak, but the words were caught in his throat. He moved, and there was no pain. His body was warm and numb. The sensation felt strange. He looked down; his body was dressed in his favorite clothes. Nothing appeared to be injured.

Jake sat up and looked around. A vast emptiness stretched out before him. There was something there, a presence of some kind. Hot Wings appeared from the shadows. Light cascaded from a hidden source above, streaming into pillars as if it had refracted through water. Jake stood up and walked toward the loopen.

As the realization dawned, Jake's mind knew this must be where Ashley spoke of, her connected state of consciousness. But how was he here? Why was he here?

Hot Wings seemed to float just above him.

"What am I doing here, Hot Wings?" Jake asked the little loopen.

That is when Jake felt it. Black then white is all he could see. Gradually other primary colors came into focus. He was at his own beginning. This was a trek through his existence. His entire life played out in exquisite detail. Every forgotten moment, every treasured memory, every tragic decision played out as if in real-time. Jake was experiencing it ALL again without any ability to change the speed of this experience. He had no control and was a passenger, able to observe the path he had taken.

As he made his way through every moment again, he remembered how he had felt at the time but also had the context of his now. It was the ultimate reflection of the person he had been and the person he had become. Witnessing all his best successes and worst mistakes forged his soul.

"Wow, check it out!"

A father named Victor regards his ten-year-old son as they stand before the space shuttle Discovery.

"This is one of the first shuttles! This thing saw tons of space flight, at least for the time!" an excited young Jake exclaimed.

"How about it, Jake? Do you want to explore space?" asked Jake's father.

"Yeah, I do. I can't imagine anything I could want more!" Jake exclaimed as he looked upon the Discovery.

"It's good to have dreams. It's how I got what I wanted in my life,"

Victor said.

"What's that?" Jake asked.

"A family." Jake's father smiled.

"Dad, that is so boring. It's easy to have one of those," young Jake said as they gazed upon the ancient spacecraft.

"Someday, you will realize how important family is to you," Victor said.

There was so much joy and pain in that moment for Jake as he watched it all unfold again. Reliving this moment again was bittersweet. The life continued.

"Dad!?" Jake's voice rang out as the mug shattered.

Victor froze as the pieces careened across the floor. The shuttle Discovery print shattered into the far corners of the kitchen.

"I'm sorry, Jake. That was an unfortunate accident," Victor said.

Jake, now fourteen, steadied himself for a moment, "It's just a mug. We can get another by going back to the museum," Jake said.

"Jake, I'm not sure we can go back," his father replied.

"It doesn't have to be right away, Dad. Maybe I will take you when I'm older and have my own family," Jake smiled in response trying to cheer up his father.

"I am afraid there isn't time," Jake felt the impact of those words as his father spoke them.

"What do you mean?" Jake's voice echoed.

"Jake, I need to tell you something important…"

Father's words were clear. "Jake, trust your own path. I will always be proud of you and love you."

Jake's father died on April third when Jake was still fourteen. The rapid neural degeneration took him away swiftly. Sorrow ran through his being, both past and present. Some things can't be fixed. People in our lives die, and voids are left. Jake observed as his mother encountered the void that dwelled in her life. The pain of reliving the moments was almost unbearable in Jake's mind. He felt helpless all over again as the scenes played out in tragic form.

Jake watched as his mom fell into a deep depression for a while. She eventually found a way to live with the fact that her husband was gone, and Jake helped her more than he had realized at the time. The years felt hard, but Jake knew the pain would diminish and life would find meaning again.

Jake relived joining Earth Initiative. By then, his mother was fine living on her own and had embraced her independence.

"People that live must still find a way to live," she had started saying.

Jake had wanted to have his own life in space exploration, and Earth Initiative was the way to do it.

"Hello," Jake's memory was now when he was twenty-nine years old.

"Sir, Ensign Ashley Martab, reporting for duty."

"At ease Ensign Martab. Is this your first assignment?" Lieutenant Jake asked.

"Yes, sir," Ashley replied.

"Well, you probably are pretty anxious about the new assignment. Don't worry. We take care of each other around here." Jake responded. Jake savored the memory of the first time he had met Ashley as it played.

"Thank you, sir," Ashley replied. "May I ask a question?"

"Please proceed," Jake gave a friendly smile.

"Why did you take this assignment?" Ashley asked.

Jake stood there momentarily, collecting his thoughts, "I want to make a difference here on Earth. We have an obligation to make the world livable for all species that are left."

"Excellent, sir. That is the same reason that I am here," Ashley said.

Even then, Jake felt more than just a simple attraction to Ashley. She was beautiful, intelligent, and caring.

Reliving the moment they first met was beyond anything he had ever experienced. The anticipation had built over the years, and seeing her face again filled him with joy. To watch it all play out again with full precognition and no control of the narrative was a wonderful and powerless feeling.

Jake stood looking at the lake that was the view from Ashley's grand-mother's apartment balcony. After a few years, Jake and Ashley became friends outside of EI missions. He loved hanging out with her and always felt comfortable talking to her. She always did her best to spread good in the world, and it was a characteristic that Jake admired.

"Coffee?" Ashley asked as she handed Jake a mug of black delight.

"Yes, please," Jake said as he took the mug. His heart almost stopped. "Where did you get this?"

"What the coffee? Gran keeps some around her cabinet, and the taste has grown on me," Ashley explained.

Somehow by the grace of the galaxy, Jake now held a space shuttle Discovery mug in his hands. This phoenix once again rising from the ashes.

"Oh, the mug. Gran got it for me several years back. I returned it to her for safekeeping when I left for Earth Initiative. Do you like it?" Ashley asked.

"I love it. My dad got me one just like this long ago, but it shattered just before he died," Jake said. He couldn't believe what he was holding, his past sorrow fading into anticipation for the future.

Ashley looked at Jake, "He meant a lot to you. Huh?"

"Yeah, he was something special. I wish he were still around," Jake admitted.

"He is a part of who you are. He still contributes to your life Jake," Ashley said.

"Always," Jake said in reflection.

"I'm sure he was a great man," Ashley smiled as she sipped her coffee.

Jake had wondered at the time. What would his father do? There was a pull at Jake's feelings, and he pushed the emotion away as his current self only observed.

"Thanks for talking me into this," Jake said as he relaxed in the patio chair.

"Thanks for coming. Vanessa and I would have had plenty of fun with just the two of us, but it would have been a shame to waste the third bedroom," Ashley said.

"Jake, you are welcome anytime. Ashley talks all the time about the work you two do. She is really proud of the restoration efforts," Vanessa said.

"The work is hard, but we are making some real progress. Ashley has a real talent for creating new specialized drone models to widen our radiation cleanup area," Jake explained.

"Oh, I know. It's almost all Ashley talks about when she calls. That and…"

"Hey, does anyone else need a beer? I really could go for another beer," Ashley interjects.

Vanessa smiles despite the interruption, "Yeah, that would be wonderful."

"Great!" Ashley says, shooting Vanessa a quick glance as she walks inside the house, leaving Jake and Vanessa alone.

"What was that?" Jake asked.

Vanessa smiled as she turned to look out over the ocean, pretending she didn't hear the question. "It's a beautiful night."

Jake turned to gaze out at the water. The moon reflected across the waves, and the smell of tropical flowers drifted in the air. It was a perfect night, and Jake felt exhilarated and happy.

The two sat in the quiet until Ashley returned. She quietly sat back in her chair, and Jake gazed over the evening's candle as she returned, saying nothing. The warm light illuminated her perfectly smooth brown skin. The shadows and light dancing across her face seemed to reveal her inner being.

Again, Jake's past self felt the overwhelming pull of his feelings for her. Again, he resisted.

Now, Jake wished that he could change the past. To tell Ashley right then that he loved her, not to leave them stranded across the galaxy, not to waste any more time. He wanted to tell them all how precious this moment would be. He knew Vanessa's tragic end. He knew his own.

Jake wanted a life with Ashley. He wanted a family with her. The feelings rooted deep within him as he watched the candle light caress her soul. Was this all that was left? Empty wishes on an uncontrollable past? After all this was over, what would be next? Everything in his current mind wished he could do more than watch the moment slip by.

Jake's blood drained from his body. When the moment came again, he knew he didn't want to die. Despite his will to live, he, again, watched his own sacrifice. Even now, he wouldn't have changed what had occurred at that moment. There were many things that he regretted in his life, but saving the Scanii twins was not one of them. Lives were saved, and he knew this act would help secure the Scanii's trust and support. It was the ultimate price to pay to keep his crew and Ashley safe in this world.

"Jake is gone." The words echoed as they lingered in the room. Ben's voice was somber as he spoke.

Tears spilled from fragile eyes. Ashley wanted to run away, but there was nowhere to go. She wanted to scream, so she did. Everyone had worked so hard to save him, but that didn't change the fact that he was dead now. His lifeless body lay there on the stretcher next to the moon pool.

"He fought till the end," Ben said as streams of despair rolled down Ashley's cheeks. "It was unbelievable he survived as long as he did."

Ashley was crushed, and the overwhelming feeling of loss soaked through her body and soul. She had lost him. She had found the love of her life, but now he was gone. How could she live with that? How was she going to go on without him? Ashley felt the anguish take root. The rest of their lives were ripped away at that moment, every hope of a life together. Even if they never returned to Earth, they were going to have each other.

Ashley felt her legs give way. Ben tried to catch her, but she collapsed hard onto the deck. The sudden sharp pain in her knees was not even registered over the massive emotional blow that was now consuming Ashley. She felt it eating at her, suffocating her as she stared at Jake's lifeless corpse.

That is when she felt something pulling at her mind. Ashley felt her conscious self letting go as she slipped into the connection.

OF TWO MINDS

"Ashley? Is that you? Ashley?"

The voice rang across the space.

"Jake?"

Ashley saw him then. It had to be him. Her voice quivered, "Jake?" she repeated as he approached.

"It's really me. I'm really here," Jake admitted.

"How are you here? I saw you die. Are you a dream?" Ashley stammered.

Jake looked into her eyes and bared his soul, "Ashley, these eyes have seen everything in my life play out again from the beginning. I saw my whole life knowing how it all would end. All my joys, all my regrets. Ashley, I am your Jake." There was a calm in his words and sincere depth in his eyes.

"How are you here?" Ashley's emotions were in free fall. Overwhelming grief was being replaced by puzzlement, and beyond that, a lifetime of hope revolved around that question.

"The loopens are special. Hot Wings saved my consciousness before my body died," Jake reassured her.

"So, are you still… you?" Ashley asked.

Jake just nodded. He was not sure how else to explain it. "Let me show you something," he said.

The scene transformed, and they appeared at the lake, standing on her grandmother's balcony. Ashley studied the man that stood in front of her. She could feel the warmth deep within his eyes. "Jake?" She wanted affirmation this was real.

"Reliving it all again, there were so many times I should have told you how I felt. There were so many times the answers were right in front of me, and I was afraid of that change. Now I have another chance, and I know the past is set. The future and what we do with this time is all that matters now," Jake said.

Ashley had a tsunami of emotion that flooded her brain. Somehow it subsided while Jake stood patiently. "So, you live in here now?"

"Yeah, I live within a part of Hot Wings. His mind is extraordinary, and I can't claim to understand how it works, but we are here together," Jake said.

The thought scared Ashley a bit. She didn't want things to change between them. Everything had changed so fast. "Can I…?" she reached a hand out to touch him.

Jake smiled as he held up his hand. Ashley reached out slowly as their fingers touched. The touch was sensitive and intimate as their fingers kissed for the first time in this new world that was created within their minds. The sensation was just as real as in life. Goosebumps ran across Ashley's arm as she fell into his embrace. She clearly felt Jake's touch across this new reality. This was never a future that they imagined for themselves; it was something that was thrust upon them. But as they held each other, Ashley had the sensation that they were going to be alright. He was still here, and she could feel and connect with him in this place.

"So, what now?" Ashley asked.

"Ashley, there is something else," Jake said.

As Jake spoke the words, Ashley knew what it was. There was no doubt in her mind. "We?! …" Ashley stammered.

Jake nodded.

"How?" Ashley asked.

"One in a million. Maybe one in a billion. But somehow it happened," Jake shrugged.

Ashley felt another presence within the connected space, and she was shocked to discover that she was pregnant. She could now sense the life growing within her. The individual's conscious mind had still not awakened yet, but she knew it was their offspring. Despite the fact they both had been on reproductive suppressants, this child would become part of their world.

Another wave of bitter-sweet emotion washed over Ashley as her whole life changed in the blink of an eye. She would need to care for the child in the real world, a world without Jake. However, this realm of endless imagined possibilities could be a refuge the whole family could share.

She thought back to that specific beach by the Hocaniio preserve.

The scene changed around them as the reality shifted. The surf was warm as the great Pacific ran over Ashley's toes. Loose sand washed against her skin as she walked. She looked out over the vast expanse of ocean. The sunset across the water made the island glow in the golden light. They were alone here.

"Ashley, we can have an existence here," Jake looked down at that point. "I just couldn't let those children die. I saw what was going to happen, and I had to save them. The last Axén... I didn't see it until it was too late."

Ashley nodded. Tears filled her eyes. She was still on the final leg of the roller coaster as her emotions leveled and slowed once again. "Jake." He wrapped his arms around her and hugged her from behind as they looked across the scene.

"It's alright. We still have each other," Jake said.

Ashley felt his arms around her. His loving embrace wrapped around her, and the warmth of his body felt amazing. It was hard to imagine how their lives would be affected moving forward, but they could still move forward together. Ashley let go of all her doubt. She wasn't going to waste this second chance. She couldn't.

"Jake?" she asked.

"Yes?" Jake replied.

"I will always be here. You complete me, and I love you," Ashley said.

JOURNEYS

The loopens were weaving Paradise Base in their green web. Richard had a sudden, horrifying thought. "Anya head for the Crichton. We can't let it get stuck in this building project with no way back to Icelus!" he barked as he headed in that direction.

Richard hopped into the pilot's seat, then sealed the hatches after seeing Anya was right behind him. They undocked from the base with a loud thud from the airlock. The loopens continued to build their nest as the Crichton maneuvered away. Richard watched the nest's construction with a certain hypnotic wonder. The loopens seemed to build with intricate precision and astonishingly left room around the docking bay. Richard wondered if that was a coincidence or if these creatures had an understanding of the airlock's purpose. The depths of loopen understanding might never be known with the unimaginable power that these creatures possessed. This once simple scientific mission was now revealed as a deep dive into the realities that make up our universe.

"Well, looks like we're stuck in this tin can again," Anya said with a matter-of-fact statement.

Just then, a totally milk-white loopen appeared. It floated just outside the front glass close to the Crichton. The wings were elongated, and streamer-looking growths seemed to flank the edges. This individual appeared to be ancient.

"A wizard has appeared," Anya joked as they both stared at the entity.

Richard did not respond.

"Anya to Richard, you still in there?" she asked.

Richard was no longer there as he slipped into a connected mind state. He was somewhere else and someone else. This ancient loopen was guiding his consciousness into a timeworn past. Richard couldn't even imagine how the old memories still existed. He was a Scanii, and his name was Rux.

Looking out through alien eyes is a surreal experience, revisit-
ing memories that are saved from another being's consciousness. The
sequence and speed of events is not controllable by the observer. The
actions of another replayed as if on film.

Rux was alone, the last of his kind on Europa. His kin had left weeks
ago for a new world far beyond the empire's boundaries, far beyond the
reach of the frightening military that rules the stars. His purpose here
was clear. He needed to protect his kin and their secret new home on
Violatis. There was just one last thing that had to be done, a necessary
decision that was not his to make.

Rux felt anxious as he readied himself for the next step. As if on cue,
the gate opened, and a familiar ship appeared through the bright light.
Rux had been expecting them and watched as Yoge departed the craft.
Yoge was a host, neither male nor female.

"Clear water Yoge," Rux greeted them as they approached.

Yoge seemed confused as they looked around. Their eyes steeled as
they examined Rux closely. "Where are your kin, Rux? What is going on
here?" Yoge finally asked.

Rux handed Yoge a data chip. "They are gone. This chip contains all
the information you need."

"Well, call them back. We have further work to do," Yoge expressed
as they tucked away the chip.

"They are not coming back. We have found a new way to exist, outside the conflict, outside the fighting," Rux explained.

"You are saying they all just abandoned the cause, abandoned the
civil fighters?" Yoge asked.

"Yes. There is a more important path that must be followed," Rux said.

"What path are you referring to?" Yoge asked.

"The Scanii can have a future beyond this war. That future needs us.
The creatures here have shown us this path," Rux said.

"The research here is essential to our cause. You can't just abandon
that!" Yoge argued.

"We have already found what we need here. Protecting this place
from outside interference is more important. We can't let the military
that rules the stars discover these creatures. It would be catastrophic. The
chip I gave you provides all the answers. I need your help, Yoge. We need
to protect this place," Rux begged.

"We all have our responsibilities. I'm not going to abandon mine, not even for you, Rux," Yoge responded.

"Yoge, we have known each other for a long time, and I have never asked you for anything. Give me a chance to show you why this is necessary, and more important than the civil fighters. Everyone who lived here saw this truth and agreed. Please, trust me," Rux spoke.

Yoge thought for a long moment. Rux started to sense that Yoge might join them, up until the point a scowl cracked across their face. "No... You can't just leave. This decision is not yours to make, and I want to know where your kin are, NOW!" Yoge was seething as they spoke to Rux. Yoge had no choice; their obligation was to report to command that the scientists were abandoning their cause. Pulling their hand-held weapon, Yoge leveled the spines at Rux.

"Yoge, please. This is more important than you know. You can bring back that data. Please leave now, and no one needs to be hurt," Rux pleaded as he raised his hands.

"I am unsure of the game you are playing here, but you cannot just turn away from our cause like that," Yoge kept the weapon aimed at Rux.

Rux's shoulders slumped. He had hoped to avoid this, but now he had no other choice. He thought that maybe Yoge would understand or maybe even follow them to Violatis. Yoge didn't understand and had chosen their path. Behind Yoge, Rux saw the solution to this unfortunate but anticipated disagreement.

A calm seemed to pass over their face as Yoge slowly lowered their weapon. A loopen entered their mind. Rux wondered what all information the loopen would force them to forget. He tried to see if there were any signs of pain in Yoge's eyes as the loopens removed their memories of this place. After a few minutes, Yoge seemed to fall into a deep sleep, and Rux carried Yoge back into their ship.

Rux pulled the data chip from Yoge's pocket and slipped the chip into the ship's computer. He executed the program that would wipe out location, logs, and data that pertained to Europa from the system. Once the ship docked at central command, the program would transfer to the main computer and ensure that Europa could not be found again. Because of the secrecy of this base, once the memory and data were gone, there wouldn't be a way to retrace the steps to this point.

Rux returned to the control room and activated the gate, sending Yoge and the ship back to the civil fighters and away from Europa forever. *This place will only be found when the time is right,* Rux thought.

It was finally over, and Rux could rejoin his family on Violatis. The loopens were wonderful, but the cold and darkness of this place were no replacement for being with his kin. He had not seen starlight in months now, and the thought that he would be able to see without the artificial lights gave him joy.

Rux knew the path ahead would have its own trials, living without technology, but a life without war was worth the price. At first, it seemed unimaginable to give up the technology, but now he looked forward to things being simpler. Giving up the great power for the chance to live in the peace and harmony that the loopens had shown them was possible. Rux wondered if the technology they were giving up would ever be needed once again.

Rux collected his few possessions and brought them to the portal on a flat metal carrier. This would be all he brought as he leapt across the galaxy. As he set the coordinates to his new home, he thought about the loopens. They were not coming on this journey, but something compelled Rux to set the computer for a second jump that would trigger if the loopens entered the clearing for the ring gate.

Just as Rux was about to leave the control room, a tablet caught his eye. It held the data for many pieces of technology, including the crescent ring gate. His kin agreed to leave it all behind, but something inside Rux urged him to take this last item with him. He reset the coordinates for his arrival on Violatis to a location outside the Scanii settlement. This location is where he would secure this tablet, this last vestige of technology.

Rux traversed the gate, and a lifetime of possibilities unfolded before him in the blink of an eye. His physical body dropped through a seam in the universe as he headed for his final destination. With a surge, he found his way into the alien ocean on Violatis. He had taken the leap and was finally here.

Rux found himself floating above a great abyssal trench as the shimmer of suns light from the surface quickly disappeared into the depths. That light would be fading soon. In the distance, he could see a rockface and began to swim in that direction. As he got closer, he noticed a cave carved into the cliffside. Rux knew that was where he should keep the tablet. Rux swam into the cave and found it opened up into a room. He could detect the walls clearly, echolocating in the darkness. He placed the tablet in an alcove along the cave wall.

Rux decided to make a temporary shelter in this cave for the night. He could set out toward the settlement at first light. He used the flat metal carrier as a door and stored his items as he prepared for sleep. He figured he would be safe in here tonight.

Amazingly, Rux still felt his loopen connected somewhere within his mind. He wondered if it had guided him here. All the loopens had remained on Europa, but he still felt the connection across all space. *Remarkable,* he thought.

The following day Rux awoke. He and the loopen had been connected again in his dreams. He felt refreshed as he opened his eyes in the darkness of the cave. He clicked a few times to get a sense of his surroundings. Today he would make his way to his new home. He remembered his very dear host's face. They were beautiful and had carried many of his children before they were born. He thought about how good it would feel to see them, his mate, and his children. His body tensed into motion after waking from a deep sleep. He swam to the cave mouth and looked out. The warm starlight was wonderful, and he marveled at this new world. Violatis was terrific, and he had never imagined a world with so much beauty.

With a swift thrust, he smoothly swam forward and left the cave. He wanted to scout the area for food and figured there might be something to explore toward the top of the rock wall. He was hungry, and he knew some of the native edible plants because of his kins scouting reports. After months of research, his kin had learned about this new planet. This was the place that the loopens had shown them. His people could thrive here.

Without warning, a monstrous shape appeared from the depths. A massive beast emerged from the darkness. The dragon-like head surged forward, propelled by giant flippers and a muscular tail. It was the largest creature Rux had ever seen. The tyrant called rahav closed in on his position with frightening speed.

With another blink, Rux realized the creature would be on him in seconds. Rux bolted for the cave. With a quick flip, he swam strongly toward the cave entrance. He didn't look back but could feel the great beast closing the distance quickly. Rux had already underestimated this adversary, and despite his own speed, the rahav closed the gap and lunged with it massive jaws stretched wide. Fear gripped Rux as he felt a sharp pain burn through his tail.

He looked down and saw several massive teeth plunging through his lower body. Flesh was ragged around the wounds, and Rux could smell his own blood in the water. *This is it,* Rux thought, as a new pain jarred his entire body. With their momentum, the pair slammed into the wall on the left side of the cave. Rux fell free of the jaws as the rahav howled at the shock of slamming into the rock face. Rux screamed in his own agony as the pain coursed through his body.

I have to try, the thought pounded in his head as he entered the cave and pulled his way along the wall. The rahav circled and made for another pass. The rahav roared as it plunged into the mouth of the cave, stretching as far as it could into the rock opening. Rocks cracked under the weight of the huge beast and, small fragments fell and broke away, but the cave held. Rux slipped just out of reach past the makeshift metal door.

Rux gasped as water flowed over his gills. The fear that had coursed through his body was suddenly replaced by lightheadedness. Blood was leaving his veins quickly, and there was no one to help him. He could feel his strength slipping away. With some effort, he pulled out the curved blade that the host of his children had crafted. He looked upon the blade that was once a treasured gift. Their host gave him this blade, and its twin to their female mate. He reflected on that moment, realizing he would never see them again. Then there was a comforting presence as Rux slipped into the haze that was filling in his mind.

Rux then physically died.

Richard blinked, and Anya sighed in relief. His experience returned to the present and his own body. The vision was in perfect clarity, and he remembered everything. He knew what the Scanii had seen, what Rux had felt, the coordinates that he entered, and the console's operation. Everything!

"So, where did you go?" Anya asked bluntly.

"Anya, I know what we need to do," Richard felt the déjà vu as he spoke. It was a vision he had experienced through another's eyes. There were just three massive horned obstacles that Richard needed to address. He hoped that his plan would work.

Anya seemed to roll her eyes a bit. "Let me guess; the loopen showed you the answers to all our problems."

"Well, not quite," Richard admitted. "We still need to clear out the monsters in that control room. How did you know the loopen showed me how to operate it?"

"Well, I took some observations and mixed them with some luck. Just a roll of the dice," Anya replied. She shrugged her shoulders. "So, what do we do now?"

"I have an idea of how to deal with the horn-heads!" Richard exclaimed.

HONOR

"He's not dead," Ashley repeated as they made their way to the bridge from the moon pool dock. Ben transported Jake's body to cold storage in the med lab, following the rest of the crew to the bridge shortly after.

Sarah looked with concern at Ashley. Jake was gone, and that fact was so fresh that the crew had not fully realized the implications of his death. The dangers of this planet felt more tangible than ever before. Mind-bending things had happened along their journey, but this sudden loss put everything back in perspective for Sarah. She was now in command of the Pegasus, and the gravity of their situation now rested upon her shoulders. She wished that Ashley was right, but Jake's body was an overwhelming fact in this particular situation.

"His conscious self still exists within Hot Wings," Ashley said convincingly. "He's not dead."

"Maybe, but we don't have time for that now," Sarah explained.

Sarah and Ashley entered the bridge. Kiah was on the starboard side bridge station, and her eyes swept the sensor displays for any signs of Axén. The first objective was to determine if they were still in danger.

"Report," Sarah ordered as she peered over Kiah's shoulder.

"They are gone. Or at least I don't detect any more incursions at the moment," Kiah said.

"Tell me we can detect these things before they appear!" Sarah said.

Kiah shook her head, "No, we barely see them on the sensors when the ink cloud appears."

"What about Hot Wings?" Kiah suggested. "Can he sense these things?"

Ashley shook her head, "It's not something that he has indicated. He doesn't exactly talk directly with me. Jake says he shares Hot Wing's perceptions. I will ask him." There was a momentary pause as if Ashley thought it over for a second. After another breath, Sarah realized Ashley was connecting to Hot Wings.

"Hot Wings and Jake can't perceive the Axén before they appeared," Ashley finally said.

Alright, that is weird, Sarah thought to herself. Either Ashley has totally cracked, or she was really talking to Jake. Either way, the outcome was overwhelming, and Sarah suddenly had a tingling in the back of her mind.

"Excuse me, I know this might be an odd time to add more strangeness onto the pile, but I might have a way to detect the Axén," Dyami responded. "Captain," he said with a new respect for the role Sarah now embraced.

Sarah nodded, "Go ahead, Dyami. What have you got for us?"

"Well, you see... I have a sense about certain things," Dyami looked at Ashley. She wore an expression like she already knew what he would say. With a nod, she urged him to continue. "I can see auras. I have been able to see them ever since I was a child. They reveal information about our physical world. I was able to see the Axén before they appeared. I have been tuning into the auras in this world ever since we arrived," Dyami said.

Ashley looked at Sarah, "Dyami's skill has saved us a few times over the years. Including today. Without his warning, we might have all been killed."

Sarah again noted Ashley's persistence that Jake was still alive. Could it really be true? She refocused on the other news that had just been presented. "Are they still here, Dyami?" That was the question Sarah needed an immediate answer to.

Dyami fell silent and closed his eyes for a moment. Sarah saw his posture relax as he focused. His eyes opened slightly into slits as the bridge around him fell quiet. "No, they are gone now," he finally said, blinking and returning his focus to the room.

"You're sure?" Sarah asked.

"Yeah, I'm pretty sure," Dyami said.

Sianda swam to the front of the bridge glass. Her face looked cracked by despair. "Is.... Is Jake going to live?" She looked around the room and noticed that Ben was shaking his head. Her gaze fell, and Sarah sensed that wasn't the only loss Sianda had experienced this day.

"How bad is it?" Sarah asked.

"We lost a few of my kin," Sianda paused, and a further sign of anguish washed across her face. "Yamala, my family's host, perished tonight. They felt ill and had not joined us when we met with Jake... I... I am sorry... Rynan told me that Jake saved my children." Her tone was somber, and Sarah could tell there was an even deeper hurt there. "I left to save Yamala. I heard Yamala screaming out for me as I left." It was easy to see how much Sianda had loved Yamala, and the loss stabbed deep within her heart.

"Jake isn't gone," Ashley said. "Hot Wings saved him." The words seemed to echo across the bridge as she spoke them. Sianda looked up at her questioningly.

"You mean it's true? They have the power to save the mind of an individual?" Sianda asked.

Ashley nodded.

"You can still communicate with him?" she pressed.

Ashley nodded again, "Yes, I can see him and visit him through the connection with Hot Wings."

Sianda's gaze fell again. "Pass along my deepest gratitude for what he has done."

With that, Hot Wings appeared. "You can tell him yourself," Ashley explained. "He sees what Hot Wings sees."

Sianda was struck with a deep sense of awe at the sudden realization. This mythical creature that suddenly appeared now contained the consciousness of the human that had saved her children. She looked directly at Hot Wings. "I honor you, Jake. You have all my gratitude."

Hot Wings just floated by Sianda, looking content.

After a moment, Ashley broke the silence: "Jake said that he would make that choice every time." Ashley clearly still felt a little mixed up about the situation.

Sianda suddenly said, "I must go. I need to attend to my family."

"Come see me in the morning," Sarah called out as Sianda swam away.

The bridge fell silent again as the crew felt the horror and adrenalin turn into stress and fatigue.

"I can take the watch, Captain," Dyami offered. "I can let you know if the Axén come back. You need sleep, and the crew will need to be sharp for what is ahead."

"That isn't going to happen for a little while yet," Sarah was still standing by Kiah at the right front bridge station. She eyed the command chair with an almost haunted look. That was her chair now. She felt an overwhelming sense of responsibility emanating from that chair and what it represented.

Ashley spoke softly by Sarah's left ear, "Sarah, I know this is hard, but you are now the rightful Captain of this mission. Jake and I agree that you are the best choice for our current situation."

Dyami nodded his approval.

EV looked over from the helm station and smiled. "You have my vote every single time."

Ben was sitting at the science station that was previously Kiah's station. "You work on getting me home to Angi, and I will have your back all the way, Sarah."

She nodded back to him. That was still the mission, to get back to Earth somehow.

Kiah stood up and hugged Sarah. "Sarah, you always have my support."

Sarah walked over to the chair and stood in front of it. She turned to address the crew. "I never wanted this, not like this. All I can say is I will do everything I can to protect this crew. You each have performed brilliantly on this mission." Sarah made eye contact with Ben as she spoke those words. "You have reached out with your mind and found new ways," she looked over at Dyami. "You have been kindred spirits," she looked at EV and Kiah one after the other, her longtime friends and traveling companions. "Now, we must continue and find our way home." Sarah sat in the chair as collective relief washed over the room. Now they could move forward with the journey ahead.

LIGHT TRAVEL

The crew had been through a rough night, but after getting a few hours of sleep under Dyami's watchful eye, the crew had risen to find the Scanii preparing to leave.

At Ben's request, one of the bodies of the Axén were brought to the Pegasus and stored in the second aquarium opposite from Hot Wing's current home. After a quick autopsy, Ben made some disturbing discoveries about the Axén. The most concerning was the discovery of very corrosive acid within their stomachs. He found it particularly concerning when the compound proceeded to eat through the container, the NIC lab table, and the surface of the floor, before he could stop it with a chemical neutralizer kit.

"Sarah, this could be a danger to the ship. If this stuff made contact with the outside hull, it could mean disaster," Ben explained.

"I will keep that in mind. Keep at it, and let me know if you find anything else. See if you can find a way to combat these creatures if they get too close to the ship," Sarah said.

As Sarah was about to leave the marine lab, she felt Sianda request her presence at the moon pool. Sarah keyed the com, "Dyami, could I have you meet me by the moon pool?" she asked.

"On my way," Dyami said.

Sianda met them both there with the Solo Blade she retrieved from the scene the night before.

"Sarah, take this. Jake had found it, and I believe you might soon need it. Please keep it close," Sianda spoke. She handed Sarah the blade.

"Thank you," Sarah accepted the blade. "Sianda, Dyami has the ability to see the Axén. He has a way of perceiving their auras," Sarah explained.

"Can the ability be taught?" Sianda asked.

"Possibly. I have met individuals that learned the ability rather than coming about it naturally. It usually requires training of the mind and certain physical conditions applied to the body and senses," Dyami explained. "Do you need me to keep lookout today?"

Sianda looked at him. "The Axén generally don't attack while we are on the move. They typically wait and ambush our camps at night. However, we have never observed them here before. Attacks have been occurring with incredible frequency. The first attacks occurred a few cycles ago when travelers were camping by the dunes at night. The Scanii started avoiding the dunes to avoid these Axén attacks, hoping they were a random occurrence from a species we had not yet discovered. Now their range seems to be growing exponentially." Sianda seemed to think about it for a moment. "With your vision, we could cross over the dunes and reach the city much faster. If the Axén are this far out, camping several more nights might carry more risk. If we travel a full day, we could reach the other side of the dunes by nightfall. If we continue through tonight, we could reach the city of Tirilean. Is your vision perceptive enough to keep us safe on that journey?"

"How will the Scanii know where the threat is?" Dyami asked.

"You hold the vision of the Axén location in your mind and purposefully intend to show that information to my kin," Sianda replied. "It is similar to how we are communicating now, only with an image. It is even possible for us to relay that image to the other humans."

Dyami looked at Sianda. "That could work." He thought for a moment, "I will need some sleep. How long before we would arrive at the dunes?"

Sianda nodded, "It will take us a third of daylight to reach them. Is that enough?"

Six hours would be fine, Dyami thought. "That will be enough."

"Dyami, go get some sleep. We will keep watch and let you know if anything comes up. If we are going to make this push, I will need everyone sharp today," Sarah said.

"I will signal you when the convoy is ready to depart," Sianda sang, and Sarah nodded in acknowledgment.

Sarah made her way back to the bridge. The rest of the crew were there waiting to hear the plan.

"Sianda reports that we can get to their city Tirilean if we make a push through the dunes. After last night she didn't want to risk more nightly attacks on the camp. We will push for the next thirty hours and rotate shifts to keep everyone fresh." Sarah sounded smooth and confident. This is not exactly how she felt inside, but her smooth manner seemed to calm the crew. *I hope Sianda is right and we don't meet any resistance,* Sarah thought to herself.

"EV, please engage engines on Sianda's signal," Sarah ordered.

"The Pegasus is ready to glide, Skipper," EV acknowledged.

Sianda gave the command to the convoy to push forward, with the Pegasus bringing up the rear. The ship swept over the grove where the camp had been. The scene was a painting of various colors, light, and shadows. Some leaves still glowed from the deep shade, while others soaked in the suns' rays. Sarah still noted the wonderous artistry of this world but the tragic losses that night tainted her perception of this scene. After a few moments of reflection, Sarah's mind slipped back to the topic of Jake's death. She hadn't known Jake before this mission, but his sudden absence was a shock on her senses. It felt like she had known him for years, and they had been through unforgettable experiences on this mission. Now the crew was relying on her, and she needed to stay strong for them, despite her grief.

"EV, do you think you could get more sleep right now?" Sarah asked. "I can take the controls for a while before we reach the dunes. We will need you at one hundred percent when we get there," she said.

"I really could use the sleep. I'm not sure I slept more than a few minutes at a time last night," EV replied.

"Go rest then… please," Sarah said. "Ashley, you should also grab some shut-eye."

"Actually…" Ashely had an odd look on her face. Sarah had a hard time guessing what she was about to say.

Ashley continued, "I have had more than enough sleep. Time moves slowly when I'm with Jake. Seconds here are hours there."

Sarah's mind popped with a sudden flash. "Seconds here are hours there," she repeated. That kind of time dilation could have many advantages. Complex puzzles in the mind could be slowed, studied, and solved within seconds. If Ashley's mind could sleep there, it would indicate she could keep the watch thirty hours a day. Additionally, if Ashley was correct and Jake was truly there too, it also meant that it was not even one mind working in this state but two. Sarah knew they might need this advantage later.

"Kiah, go get some rest. Ashley and I can cover the bridge for now," Sarah said.

Ashley headed for EV's left bridge station and took the helm. Sarah returned to the right bridge station and slipped into her old seat. She started to sweep the area with the sensors looking for anything out of place on the scans.

Sarah was studying the readings when suddenly a greeting entered her mind "Hey, Sarah. Do you have some time to talk? We could just communicate through thought," Syuk spoke.

Syuk swam smoothly above the bridge to the starboard side of the Pegasus, and Sarah offered her a weary smile as she locked eyes with Syuk. Sarah concentrated a bit and returned the conversation through thought. "Hey, Syuk," Sarah was aware that the conversation was just between herself and Syuk.

"I just wanted to see if you're ok," Syuk concern was conveyed as she spoke in thought.

Sarah replied, "I'm managing. This crew has my back, and we need to move forward. They are relying on me now. I will be ok." Sarah continued to review the live scans as the conversation continued.

"I am here if you need to talk about it," Syuk spoke. Syuk was about to swim off before she was stopped by Sarah's words in the next thought.

"Syuk, tell me a story from your life." Sarah didn't want to be alone. Syuk was an empathetic soul outside of her command and outside of her responsibility.

There was a pause, and Sarah wondered if she had received the query. Then Syuk spoke. "When I was younger, a young Scanii male showed great interest in me. His name was Dac. I have known him all my life. We were inseparable as children and were great friends. During our adolescence, we often played exclusively with one another. As we got older, he told me his romantic feelings and asked if one day I would want to join with him. However, I did not feel the same way about him. He was wonderful and charming, and physically fit. But my interests were in others." Syuk paused again. "Not all Scanii are attracted to the opposite sex." There was another pause.

"That is also true with humans," Sarah offered softly in her thoughts, reassuring her. "What happened?"

"He felt hurt that I did not share his romantic feelings. But he recognized it was no one's fault. Often a lack of fault is of little comfort to an individual when it comes to matters of love. A few days later, he approached me. I felt very awkward, but he reassured me that everything would be alright. Then he sang a beautiful song to me about wanting to always be close friends and how he supported me in my choice. It was a key moment in my life. Watching someone lay their heart out in a beautiful song because they care about you even if you are different than they wish you to be. Eventually, he found others to love. Often Scanii males are intimate with more than one female and host pair. This shared love is often the nature of our species," Syuk explained.

"Do you still see him today?" Sarah asked.

Syuk smiled as she gracefully kept pace with the Pegasus, "Dac and I are still lifelong friends, and you will probably meet him in Tirilean when we get there."

"I was expecting a sadder story," Sarah replied.

"I figured you needed something positive right now," Syuk sang. Sarah could feel the compassion that Syuk was conveying in her thoughts.

"It was perfect," Sarah said. Syuk had once again shown Sarah trust, revealing details about herself that seemed personal and precious. Sarah was still reviewing the scans, and everything looked completely normal. She wondered what was really out there.

"It's your turn. Tell me any story you would like to share," Syuk spoke.

Sarah thought about her answer before she responded. "When I was growing up, we had a dog. Dogs are the animal known for being human's best friend. Domestic dogs rely on humans for all their physical needs." Sarah suddenly felt odd about explaining and trying to oversimplify the complex relationship humans have with dogs to another being that had never seen a dog. Sarah visualized the memory of her dog to share with Syuk.

Syuk seemed to sense this and spoke, "I believe I understand."

Sarah proceeded, "Anyway, my dog Ginger followed me everywhere. She loved and protected me on all my childhood adventures. She was so attentive and used to react to my every move. She was my very first bridge in understanding the creatures in our universe. She was so sweet and even got along with the neighborhood cats. She had a very long life for a dog, but eventually, she died." Sarah paused. "I remember I was sixteen when she died. It broke my heart. I cried many times, even months later. The hurt of losing a friend has always been hard." Sarah's mind returned to Jake's absence. "I need to be alright now. My crew needs me to show strength and guidance now that Jake is…." Sarah struggled for the word, but nothing came to mind for their current situation. How could she even describe the situation she was experiencing?

"You're in pain, Sarah, and I understand your feelings about being strong for your crew. I am here anytime that you need someone to listen." Syuk's thought to Sarah was soothing.

There was a moment of silence as they continued to traverse the vast underwater landscape. The whole caravan passed close to an underwater rock ridge. The red color of the rock reminded Sarah of the desert cliffs in Utah. They were beautiful in the lavender-colored water. Sarah was stunned by the beauty of this planet and saw why the Scanii chose to live here, not to conquer this world but to live in harmony with this place. Giving up everything to come here seemed to make more and more sense to Sarah, and she marveled that Syuk's ancestors took such a significant leap in their lives and the lives of their descendants. They abandoned everything they had ever known to come to live here.

"You're pretty quiet over there, Captain. Are you ok?" Ashley asked from across the empty bridge.

"Yeah, Syuk and I were just talking. Practicing my communication through thought," Sarah said.

Ashley was curious about the private conversation taking place in their heads but suddenly found the irony in that. All her conversations with Jake were private now. Now he could only speak through her. She suddenly wondered what he was doing when she was not there. Was he living lifetimes alone while her time was spent here? Time moved ever so slowly in the real world during the periods she was connected to Hot Wings. The course was set, and there was a calm moment. Ashley relaxed and slipped into the connected state of mind. It was becoming second nature for her to reach out with her mind and enter the trance with Hot Wings.

"Hey, my star," Jake whispered. Ashley found that she was standing next to Jake. Just as she had left him the last time, she snuggled in for a hug and placed her cheek against his neck.

"How much time is passing between the times you see me?" she asked. "Are you always alone once I leave?"

"When I'm here with you, Hot Wing's mind is slowing time for the two of us. His mental concentration allows us this space. When we aren't here, he focuses on the here and now, allowing me to see through his eyes," Jake said softly.

"You have said that before, but how?" Ashley asked.

Darkness suddenly surrounded them. Then three glowing orbs of light hovered in the darkness. Ashley walked toward the orbs. Jake's face reflected the glowing light of the orbs as he gazed down through the perfect spheres. Ashley looked down and saw several Scanii frozen in time as they swam through the water. With wonder, she realized that she was looking through Hot Wing's eyes and seeing the real-time scene in slow motion. "When you aren't here, I see through his eyes in real-time. I don't have control over what Hot Wings does, but he sometimes seems to listen to my suggestions."

"You can make suggestions?" Ashley asked.

"Oh yeah!" Jake yells into the darkness, "Hey, Hot Wings, I bet Sianda needs some company."

Ashley laughed, "I should have figured." Her gaze fell, "We could live out lifetimes in here. Just you and me."

"I'm not sure that would work out well for Hot Wings. I am not entirely sure what his limits are, but he is a biological creature just like the rest of us and experiences fatigue when concentrating for long periods of time. Hot Wings is drained for a while after letting another consciousness connect with him. I can sense what he feels," Jake said.

"What happens to you once Hot Wings is gone?" Ashley said as she realized the implications.

"I will no longer be here. My memories might be passed to another loopen, but I will be gone. This is an extension of my life, but it's not forever," Jake explained.

"How long do we have?" Ashley had no idea how long the loopens lived.

"We have as much time as the future will allow us, just like everyone else." Jake looked into Ashley's eyes. "Loopens can have long lives," he said.

"I am still wrapping my head around this," Ashley admitted. "How will our lives work inside this space?"

"That's a good question, and we are going to learn firsthand," Jake replied.

That is when they both felt it. A sense that Richard was present within the connected loopen consciousness and was looking for them.

Jake shifted the thought, and Ashley followed him through to the mentally simulated briefing room aboard the Pegasus. Richard seemed to be already waiting for Ashley but was shocked to see Jake. Hot Wings and Kite floated just outside the conference room in an ocean created by the mind. Their emerald eyes seemed to shine in this place.

"Jake? How are you here?" Richard asked.

"I died. It's a long story. It comes down to one fact. I only exist here in this place," Jake said.

"You died?" Richard asked, puzzled.

"Hot Wings saved my consciousness, and now I live within his mind," Jake replied.

Richard shook his head, trying to absorb this concept and organize his thoughts. "Anyway. I think I have a way to get you back home. There is a tablet in this certain cave." Jake held up the memory of the tablet. Richard shook his head in astonishment. "You found it already?"

"We still have it!" Ashley proclaimed. "I stored it in my pack! Jake gave it to me!"

"I know how to unlock, access, and interpret the tablet's data. I was shown how in a vision," Richard explained.

Now it was Ashley's turn to look shocked. "You saw it in a vision?"

"Yeah, it has instructions for a crescent ring gate, and I believe we can build it," Richard explained. Then he paused. "Please tell Sarah that I am coming. Where can I meet you?"

"We are headed to the ancient ship, about a day's travel from here. Do you know where that is?" asked Jake.

"If that is where the Scanii first landed on Violatis, then the information is in the Scanii control room computer on Europa. I remember the location looking through his eyes," Richard said.

"Whose eyes?" Ashley asked.

Richard then relayed the news to Ashley and Jake on the elder loopen they named Merlin and his experience through the senses of Rux. Remembering every vital detail, Richard conveyed the story. He also told them about how Angi had insisted on joining the rescue party and how she had brought enough materials to establish a colony or perhaps build a crescent ring gate. Ashley and Jake then took the time to detail their situation with the Scanii and how Syuk saved Ashley. They added the details about finding the blade and tablet and how they were traveling with the Scanii caravan. Then they spoke about Jake's sacrifice saving Sianda's twin boys, Zovair and Ven. The attack of the ghostly Axén and how it had killed Jake's body, but Hot Wings had saved his mind. They also remembered Rux's Solo Blade and its return to Sarah after Jake's death. They had the time here to convey every detail in this space where time moved so slowly with little regard for physical reality. The subject eventually returned to the ancient ship.

"Will the Scanii let us build a crescent ring gate by Tirilean?" Richard asked.

"I hope so, and let's plan on that. This opportunity seems like the way back to Earth, and Sianda will advocate on our behalf," Jake explained.

"Can you meet us there?" Ashley asked.

"Yes, I will be there," Richard promised. "Let's bring the Pegasus home."

DUNES

The dunes stretched out in front of the Pegasus. The main Scanii caravan fell toward the rear as they approached the dunes, allowing the Pegasus to take point. Dyami had returned to the bridge half an hour before they reached the leading edge of the dunes and was steeling himself for the hours that lay ahead. Crimson sand stretched before them as far as the eye could see in the clear ocean water. The sky above the sea was unusually calm as the suns' light embraced the ocean floor through the clear water. Piles of sand crested on hidden rockfaces that reached toward the surface. The scenery felt barren, with flowing curves of sand stretching across the landscape.

Dyami sat flat on the floor in the lotus position. He saw everything through the NIC bridge glass that extended to the floor. He relaxed as he entered his meditative state, his awareness traveling the familiar paths. His eyes slightly opened into slits as he focused on the auras around them. As he looked out, he couldn't see any signs of life, just the smooth flow of the dunes in front of them. The crew smoothly glided along for the first four hours, and Dyami began to wonder if there were any Axén in this part of the ocean or if it was just a myth that this was their home.

Four hours into the journey, he sensed it. Something was there, but he couldn't tell what it was exactly. There did not appear to be any other auras in this area, and he guessed that this was because of the lack of life in this region. The aura he saw looked clouded and dark, resonating the same way the Axén aura had appeared before but with subtle differences.

Dyami focused on the nearest location, sharing the image with the Scanii, who in turn shared the vision with the rest of the crew. EV moved the Pegasus toward the position. The bridge remained quiet as they approached, and Sarah held her breath. Soon they were close to the location, and the Pegasus eased to a stop.

"It's there," Dyami said as he indicated a position in the sand holding the vision in his mind.

Two female Scanii hunters outfitted with carapace shields and a long-curved blade approached the location. "EV, bring us closer," Sarah ordered. As they came closer, Dyami could see the dark resonating aura under the sand.

"It's just below the surface of the sand," Dyami explained to the crew and the nearby Scanii.

The others could also see the aura within the shared vision. The shared vision experience was similar to looking into a rearview mirror. Sarah could feel the visual information was being shared, but unless she focused her attention, it was unobtrusive to her current focus.

One of the hunters plunged the long-hooked blade into the sand. There was a muffled screech that then fell into quiet. The warrior pulled the blade from the sand using the curve to pry it free, hooking something buried. As the edge rose, the small Axén lay dead, encapsulated by the soft shell of an egg. Dark green oozed from where the blade penetrated the unhatched creature. Although the creature was still unborn it was over half the size of the Axén that had attacked the camp last night.

"There are three more eggs down there," Dyami said as he indicated the spots.

"Are these their children?" Kiah asked.

The shock of this realization left a pit in Sarah's gut. "How big do they get?" Sarah wondered aloud.

"We should collect one of the eggs," Ben said.

"Are you sure that is a good idea?" Kiah asked.

"Will that dead embryo be enough? I don't want to risk the ship by bringing a live one aboard." Sarah asked, indicating the specimen they just killed.

"Alright, let's move it into the second tank with the other body for now. If I collect some samples for comparison, I might be able to determine the growth of these Axén," Ben said.

Sarah nodded in agreement. Sianda, who was taking up a close position on the starboard side of the Pegasus, nodded to the warrior who had extracted the creature from the sand. As Ben left the bridge to secure the new alien specimen, Sarah turned to Sianda and asked, "Are we too far to turn back?"

"It will take us another four hours of travel to get beyond the dunes, but if we travel along the surface during the remaining light, Dyami can help us visualize any threats. I still think that we can make it," Sianda replied.

"Alright, then we need to move," Sarah said. The convoy continued its trek deeper into the dunes. Everyone on the bridge remained quiet, helping Dyami concentrate on his meditation. The convoy moved as silently as possible to avoid drawing any unnecessary attention, and no Scanii broke the water's surface as they trailed behind the Pegasus. After another hour of travel Dyami seemed to relax a bit.

"I'm not seeing any more signs of Axén beyond that first egg cluster," he reported as they continued to travel. After another hour, Dyami wondered if that first cluster was all there was. The convoy took a short break to rest in the quiet of the day. The crew started to relax as they began the final leg of the journey over the dunes. Above the surface of the water, a light rain began to fall. The crew had seen a glimpse of the enormous storm approaching overhead from the oceanic scanning satellite that was still in orbit. The seas might be rough, but they could manage even if they encountered a sharp shift in the currents.

Just as they started again, Dyami pointed out another Axén egg cluster buried beneath the sand. They gave the cluster a wide berth. Then Dyami pointed out another just as they finished avoiding the latest clutch. As the convoy continued moving, the egg clusters became more frequent and condensed. There was no avoiding them now. They had to push through.

"Sarah, the egg clusters are everywhere," Dyami reported. Sarah saw the reason for the dread in his voice as the Scanii shared his vision with her. The scene writhed from their movement, and she gasped as she saw the situation. The Axén stirred within their shells as the auras twisted in a hypnotic pattern beneath the sand.

"We need to hurry. We can't get caught here at night, and I don't want to see what happens when these things hatch," Sarah said.

Every minute started to feel like an eternity. The nervous tension on the bridge seemed to manifest in the oppressive storm clouds that now blackened the sky above. The stars' light faded with the immense amount of water that now fell from the atmosphere. They continued forward, the pace picking up as the deafening sound of thunder erupted through the water.

Then there was massive turmoil in the currents as the storm head approached. Sarah watched in horror as the dunes writhed, and through the bridge's magnified image, she saw the Axén awakening. Sand clung to thousands of newly born bodies. Many Axén were caught up in the intense current, but many more seemed to swim efficiently, even moments after their birth.

"Holy mother of creation!" Dyami exclaimed.

The wall of the storm and the twisting sand was now rushing toward the Pegasus. A cloud of Axén was forming and could be seen, even with the naked eye. Their development was not quite to the point they had complete control over the chromatophores in their skin.

"EV, move parallel to that storm wall and get out of the dunes!" Sarah shouted as EV pulled hard on the controls. The Pegasus pulled hard to port. Emergency seat straps deployed in response to the sudden g-force encountered during the maneuver. The gravity decking took only a moment to adjust, but Sarah was still thrown back against her seat as they flew through the water on the new course. The main group of Scanii swam hard toward the possible safety beyond the dunes.

Dyami pointed at a spot along the horizon, "Go! There!"

"EV, GO!" Sarah ordered a split second before the ship changed to the new heading.

The Pegasus raced forward along the storm, and Sarah could tell they would meet the storm wall in moments. "Dyami?" Sarah wanted his confirmation in an instant, the question with just his name.

"Keep going! EV, get ready to change course to match the current!" Dyami replied.

The first wave of sand washed over the hull of the Pegasus, and a few Axén spawn slammed into the hull by the force of the current. NIC material held firm with the sharp impacts. The current suddenly shifted, and EV quickly adjusted the course to match. The Pegasus slipped into the underwater wave as forceful ocean water executed its will. The wave pushed the Pegasus toward the ridge of an underwater cliff. Sarah just hoped the drop would disperse the second part of the wave closing from behind. The writhing mass of tens of thousands of Axén could be seen swimming within the current.

The shrill sound of an alarm rang out across the bridge as a hull breach warning flashed across all of the screens. Ashley shouted out, "Hull breach deck two, hydroponics! Bulkheads are sealing the area!"

"The bastards ate through the damn hull!" Ben shouted over the com.

The Pegasus started listing and gradually slowed in speed. EV punched hard at the console and attempted to compensate for the new water weight within the ship. With a sudden burst, the Pegasus flew over the edge of the underwater cliff, the Axén horde in hot pursuit. It took a few more moments before they saw the new threat. A tyrant rahav came into view from just under the lip of the trench as it extended toward the ocean floor. With a roar, it followed the Pegasus.

This particular rahav was young and looking to stake a claim on his first hunting ground when the Pegasus suddenly appeared on the menu. The bridge view swiveled as the camera tracked the young adult rahav as it started its pursuit. Then the Axen horde caught up with the rahav. With a sudden awareness of the danger in the situation, the tyrant screamed as it was overwhelmed by the feeding Axén horde. The rahav was torn apart and eaten alive by Axén as this young predator was too late to realize the dangers of this new territory.

As blood poured from the dying tyrant, the remaining Axén broke off pursuit of the Pegasus to feed on this new source of fresh flesh.

DAMAGE CONTROL

The Pegasus was wounded and needed to be repaired. The hydroponics bay had completely flooded, and the ship became next to impossible to control. The hull needed to be resealed, and the ocean water pumped out. The Scanii convoy had suffered several casualties, many of which were older individuals who didn't have the speed to keep up when the wave of Axén attacked. They had also been forced to abandon their belongings during the flight from the Axén.

"Dyami, are there any indications of Axén?" Sarah asked.

"Yes, but I can't tell how close they are. We need to hurry!" Dyami said.

Sarah nodded and keyed the com to the moon pool dock, "Ashley, seal off the leak in hydroponics and be careful out there."

Ashley keyed the controls, and the cover retracted from the moon pool. She held the laser cutter and NIC glove as she leapt into the cool water. She took a moment to orient herself, and swam along the hull toward the stern of the Pegasus.

"I'll keep watch for any danger," Sianda said as she swam up to Ashley.

Ashley nodded. As they approached the damage, Ashley clearly saw the large ragged hole in the hull where the acid had burned its way through the NIC material. There was no time to waste. Ashley began cutting away the melted material using the laser, allowing for a clean edge to start her rebuild. As she worked, she felt a chill run through her. She had never seen anything eat through NIC material so quickly. Ashley kept seeing flashes of the endless Axén horde that was still out there.

"Sianda, how do we survive against the event that we witnessed today?" Ashley asked with a prominent layer of fear.

Sianda frowned as she spoke, "I do not have an answer. That many Axén will consume this world until there is nothing left. What we saw was death..."

Ashley discarded the melted and contaminated material and stored the cutter on her back. She then tapped the controls on the back of her right NIC glove to begin the repair.

There was a sudden crackle across the radio as Dyami's voice rang out across the com channel, "Ashley, there is an Axén in the hydroponics bay!"

Ashley saw the movement in the dark recess beyond where she was working as the creature regained consciousness, and then it vanished. Ashley knew the Axén was there, but still couldn't see it any longer. Sianda drew her knives, and Ashley retreated behind her.

The opening in the hull was just large enough to squeeze through, and Sianda proceeded cautiously into the flooded bay.

Dyami's voice cracked across the com channel again, "It's in the corner. Sianda, it's stalking you from there."

Sianda couldn't see it with her own eyes. Its camouflage was perfect, just hours after being born. She carefully made her way across the room, eyes fixed on the vague aura that Dyami was sharing with her. With a sudden flash of ink, tentacles shot forward. Sianda dodged the attack and grabbed the tentacles with one clean move. The Axén screamed and lunged forward with its sharp beak, pulling itself forward by retracting its tentacles. Sianda sliced down across the tentacles with her knife cutting clean through.

The creature's maw still bit deep into Sianda's shoulder, and a sharp pain ran through her body. She stabbed the Axén through what looked like an eye, and the spawn let out a death cry and fell away from her, leaving a coating of gel-like acid within the laceration. Suddenly the pain intensified, and she felt herself nearly pass out, as she cried out in agony, from the fierce burning deep within her flesh.

Ashley could tell they needed to get Sianda immediate medical attention. "Ben, Sianda's shoulder was bitten. We need something to neutralize the acid. Quickly!"

Ashley helped Sianda pull her body from the flooded compartment. Her arm was completely limp. After pulling free, Sianda swam toward the moon pool dock.

"Finish the repair. We are not going to have much time," Sianda said. Ashley saw blood was already in the water and knew they wouldn't be safe here for long. She nodded. Delicately she removed the Axén corpse and continued her repairs.

Ben was waiting at the moon pool dock with a neutralizing agent and warm soapy water, ready to flush the burn until he was certain any reaction had stopped. He observed that the compound was water resistant from his work in the lab, and the soap would help to break down and clean off the digestive ooze. He would then use the agent to neutralize the acid. He hoped that this combo would be enough. Sianda pulled herself from the water with her one good arm. Ben could already tell he would have his work cut out for him.

Ashley wasted no time and completed patching the breach.

"Bridge, the hull is sealed. Start pumping out the water, and I will make sure we don't have any more leaks," Ashley said.

"We are trying it now," Kiah responded.

Ashley looked to see if she spotted any bubbles that would indicate any additional breaches along the hull. Once she was satisfied that the repair was solid, she made her way back aboard the Pegasus.

"Repairs are finished," Ashley said as she pulled herself out of the water. As soon as she reported, she felt the Pegasus begin to move again toward Tirilean. Ben was still working on Sianda's arm in the moon pool area, and Ashley could see she was still conscious and in tremendous pain.

"Ashley, good. Please help me out. We must find a way to keep Sianda's skin moist while I work on this arm!" Ben explained.

"I'm on it," Ashley responded.

"Sianda, I'm going to try saving your arm," Ben said.

Sianda looked at the injury, and through her pain and fear, she replied. "There is nothing there to save."

"I have something I can do. Will you trust me?" Ben said. Ben was thankful he had taken a few voluntary biometric scans of the Scanii and had conversed with one of the group's healers. Now he would be tested on what he had learned.

Sianda looked at him with pain and uncertainty but nodded. Sianda was the first Scanii Ben had ever treated, but he had learned enough about Scanii physiology to help. Within a few minutes, Ashley had an arm full of tubing pulled from the wall and began pumping clean ocean water to where Sianda was being treated with an additional tube removing the water from the work area. Ben was afraid to use anesthesia and just used localized painkillers. Mercifully Sianda started breathing easily and passed out when she saw the situation was under control.

The night was brutally long. Ben began the meticulous process of reconstructing Sianda's limb using regenerative techniques. It would still take months to grow and heal fully, but he had saved her arm. As Ben tirelessly worked, the rest of the crew limped the Pegasus toward the city as the water was pumped and drained from the flooded compartments. Time was frighteningly slow as everyone constantly worried the Axén could appear from anywhere.

Sarah held her breath as the dawn's light peeked through the water. They had survived the night and would be at Tirilean in just a few more hours. Richard would try to meet them there, but if he succeeded, his life would be in danger too. No one had ever experienced a biological terror as powerful as the Axén horde. After witnessing the past few hours, the Axén were not here to fit into the ecosystem but to devour everything they could of this world.

DECOY

After several days of hard work, the Europa team had transported a massive amount of NIC building material to the bottom of the ocean and had placed it adjacent to the clearing where the crescent ring gate lay in wait. The team kept a constant vigilance for the horn-heads as they individually left their den in the control room to hunt. One individual always stood guard over the lair, and Richard wondered what they might be protecting. Whatever it was, he knew they needed to use the control room to operate the galaxy traversing gate. They had been monitoring the activity of the horn-heads using a video drone since the construction of Paradise Base. The horn-heads used the automated bay door as they entered and exited the control room, and Richard and Anya carefully observed, trying to find an opening. He just hoped his plan would work.

The two drones sat side by side in the frigid ocean, awaiting commands. Bobb had silently watched as Richard had constructed the Glow drone over the last few days as a one-of-a-kind creation. During the tests, Glow sparkled with a prism of colors and patterns, her impressive tests even gaining the attention of several nearby loopens. Glow was built for one purpose, and her first mission was likely going to be her last mission. Richard and Anya piloted the drones from the Crichton, hidden behind the stacks of NIC material, ready for their trip across the galaxy.

"Richard, I think this is our shot. The big alpha has left to hunt, and only two are left in the room," Anya said.

"Alright, I'm ready to go with Bobb. I need you to distract them for as long as you can. Remember, we need to get both of them out of the room for this to work," Richard replied.

Glow leapt forward as Anya keyed the drone's commands, leaving Bobb in the cold dark sea.

"I will give you as much time as I can. Glow's performance will be spectacular with the new speaker we added," Anya said.

"I am sure the ruckus will grab their attention, let's just hope she is fast enough to keep them busy for a while," Richard replied.

Glow slowly approached the control room door, and the doors began to part. With the flip of a switch, Anya turned on the lights, and Glow began to sing with pre-recorded animal distress vocalizations. She brought the drone about as she prepared for the chase. Inside the room, two massive red creatures stirred from their slumber as the performance began.

After a single moment, it was obvious that the beasts were going to chase as they unfurled their bodies and engaged with this new glowing menu item that had appeared in their home. Anya punched the throttle, and Glow shot away from the danger of the now pursuing horn-heads. Anya could already tell that the great beasts had the advantage of speed as they surged toward the now fully illuminated Glow that was putting on a light show that rivaled the best rock concerts. She would need to use Glow's agility to keep them busy.

"The room is clear, Richard. GO!" Anya exclaimed.

Richard slipped Bobb into the control room and headed directly to the gate controls, the doors remaining open during their five-minute cycle period. The control room was well preserved, and Richard had a strong feeling of déjà vu. With a shake of his head, he refocused as Bobb's light shined across the ancient panels. Bobb's small finger-like probe extended and touched one of the panels. It immediately came to life, and the room was illuminated with a blue glow.

"Alright, I'm at the controls. Just keep them busy for a while longer," Richard said.

Richard quickly started tapping the Scanii controls using Bobb. He remembered how Rux had set the inputs from the computer's saved destination list. After another moment, Richard could see that the computer was processing his requested location and was calculating the current positioning that would see them leaping across the galaxy to the site on Violatis. He anticipated that such a complex calculation could take a minute, even for this marvel of alien technology. Suddenly from behind him, Anya shouted, "They killed Glow and are on their way back!"

Richard sharply exhaled as he felt his tension rise. The calculation was still processing and needed more time as the great beasts now appeared back at the door. They moved swiftly across the room toward the now glowing controls that illuminated the room and closed on Bobb with frightening speed.

Richard pulled back on the controls for Bobb, and the drone backed away from the console as the nearest horn-head was bearing down. This sudden movement made the horn-head re-evaluate its target, split between Bobb's movement and the light from the panel. It surged between Bobb and the console, whipping Bobb across the room as its tail made contact with the drone.

"NO!" Anya shouted as the camera spun wildly on the feed from Bobb. She felt helpless as Richard struggled to regain control of Bobb again.

Richard felt the sudden strike of panic, and it took all of his experience and concentration to stay focused. He steadied the drone and pointed it back toward the control panel. With a flash, they saw the ready indicator light blink on the Scanii console across the room.

Anya held her breath as she watched Richard maneuver Bobb. She wanted to shout but knew to stay silent as Richard concentrated. All she could do was watch and pray that Richard had the skill to pilot Bobb through the danger.

The second horn-head surged toward Bobb as the first circled for another attack. Richard pounded the controls, and Bobb ascended and rushed forward. The beasts gaping maw barely missed because of the unexpected movement, jaws snapping closed without making contact. Richard held his breath as the console filled the video display. Bobb was almost to the control that would send them across the Milky Way, but he knew another attack was imminent.

Suddenly the only thing Bobb's camera saw was teeth as the horn-head grasped the drone in its jaws. The video feed went dead, and Richard felt his heart sink into the pit of his stomach. Bobb and Glow had been sacrificed; their final mission was unsuccessful. Richard would need to remake new drones to try again, and there was no guarantee of success. The failure was a disappointing setback and would likely cost them days.

Without warning, the gate activated. The rings crested up in the clearing as they prepared to transport everything in the area, sending Richard and Anya across the galaxy, held in the safe embrace of the Crichton. The massive load of NIC material would be coming with them on their journey to a new world of Violatis.

Richard felt himself fall through the rift. So many paths in his life he had not taken passed before him in a moment. Only this path had led him here, on this journey. What lay beyond this path was beyond his current vision. However, there was still something else he noticed. Kite, the loopen, had joined them, coming on this journey.

REUNION

The ancient ship that had rested over two thousand years ago was at the neck of the hourglass in the splendid underwater city of Tirilean. Living stone grew around the huge grandfather Scanii ship, and Sarah guessed that thousands lived in the structures created above and below the great vessel. Spires connected the top and bottom architecture, forming intricate patterns that cradled the upper part of the city. Suns' light peered through holes, many reaching through to the ocean's surface. Green underwater plants seemed to grow and twist through the holes and the stone structures. Light reflected off their leaves, illuminating the whole capital in pale green diffused light. Sarah noted the homes and more prominent areas that looked like gathering and working spaces as they traveled deeper into the structure.

The Pegasus flew straight to the heart of the capital, escorted by Syuk. Sianda had sent word ahead about these visitors, and the news of their arrival spread quickly throughout the city, drawing significant interest. The rest of the Scanii group with whom they had traveled had a designated camp outside the city. Sarah had watched as the Scanii there had warmly greeted their family and friends, but the greeting was often short-lived as many watched the approach of the Pegasus. None had ever seen this type of lifeform or technology before, much less one visiting their world from so far away. Many also watched Hot Wings as he gracefully swam by. This encounter was the equivalent of seeing a unicorn for many who were transfixed in fascination.

The Pegasus glided around the spires of Tirilean, moving toward the grandfather ship and the great gathering chamber within. Syuk had told the crew about this chamber where the crew could meet the leadership of the Scanii. As they approached one of the inner spires, they were stopped by a checkpoint patrol. The patrol cautiously approached and was armed with gray metal spears and intricate armor. Sarah had learned from Syuk that the metal was a form of carbon steel alloyed with another material that made it light but tremendously strong and never deteriorated in salt water. They called the metal kigor.

"Syuk, is that who I see before me?" a huge male Scanii said as he swam up. He seemed to relax a bit as he recognized his very old friend.

"Dac, you old ranger!" Syuk held a massive smile as she touched out with the end of her fluke to his.

That was a very warm greeting, Sarah thought and tried to calm some of her nerves. They still needed these Scanii to help them, especially now that a large portion of the crew's grown food was destroyed by the flooding of hydroponics. She needed friends now more than ever. Especially since Richard's plan was to arrive with a freighter worth of supplies to start building a gate, she had told Sianda about the plan to create a new gate with Richard's help and that the wheels for that plan were already in motion. Due to their limited communication with Richard through the loopen connected consciousness, Ashley and Jake decided to proceed before gaining the Scanii's permission. Sianda had agreed to help smooth things over with the Scanii leadership if and when Richard arrived. Most humans would never have been this kind to alien outsiders.

Dac looked as if he wanted an explanation for the alien craft looming before his patrol. "Syuk, I'm going to need some answers regarding this," Dac gestured by waving both his hands at the Pegasus. "Also, where is Sianda?" he asked.

"We need to report!" Syuk insisted. "There is too much at stake now. The gathering must know about what we have seen!" Then Syuk produced a white object that looked like a spherical shell. It was Sianda's orb of trust.

Syuk looked at Dac, "Sianda is ok. She is in there." She nodded to the Pegasus. She squared his gaze now as she said, "These people saved her twins, Dac."

With that, Dac nodded with comprehension. He relayed a communication with his thoughts, and waited for the reply that occurred after a few moments.

Once he received confirmation Dac said, "You may go and speak. But the ship needs to remain here for now."

"These humans and loopen are coming with us," Sianda said as she swam up. She was still severely injured, but she insisted that she was joining them. She was needed, here and now. She would need to con-vince the gathering of the importance of helping these people, especially in the face of the Axén threat.

Sarah, Ashley, and Hot Wings swam behind Sianda as she nodded to Dac. He nodded and replied, "If you would follow me."

Dac led the way as the group and escort guards swam slowly into the center of the city. Sarah ran over the facts in her mind trying to calculate what needed to happen next. She had a nervous feeling she was holding in check as she wondered what something called the gathering would look like. Public speaking wasn't something she feared, but the massive gravity of the situation and how it would affect the future was consum-ing her thoughts.

Soon the group was inside the hull of the grandfather ship. They made their way through the corridors of the great vessel. Sarah marveled at the metal grandfather still standing strong in the face of time. The whole structure was made from kigor.

Soon the group swam into a room that was large and round. Syuk swam into the middle of the space, helping Sianda. Sarah could sense how much pain Sianda felt as she moved. The wrap around her arm was there to help it grow back and to protect it. The two stopped as they arrived at the center of the room. The rest of the group entered and swam to Syuk and Sianda as the door shut behind them. The room was dark momentarily before a bright beam of light came from above. The ceiling opened, and the room was lifted as the group floated up and was presented on the main floor of the gathering chamber. The room had reflected sunlight that was focused on this stage, while massive caverns of space wrapped around them and far into the shadows beyond. There was a great silence. Nothing made a sound or disturbance in the water beyond the lifting platform.

Then a voice seemed to echo in everyone's mind, addressing the gathering. "Sianda, the gathering hears your words," the voice seemed to fill the space as it spoke. As she swam forward, Sarah saw an individual figure illuminate in the gathering chamber. It was a Scanii female, and the light seemed to shine on her as she addressed the chamber.

"Thank you for listening," Sianda spoke to the entire chamber as she sang her words. "I assert my position here with these friends. Their ship and crew were recently lost here on Violatis, transported here unexpect-edly, not by their own choice. One of my kin, Syuk, had been observing these newcomers that traveled with a loopen. When they needed aid, she stepped in and saved a member of their crew. When I first heard about these aliens in our world, I was also skeptical of their intentions. But after meeting them and witnessing their actions, I found that each one of them acts with honesty and integrity. Then we were attacked by a group of Axén, and several of my kin were killed, including my cherished Yamala. My twin boys would have also perished that night if it was not for this crew's intervention. Their captain sacrificed himself so that they would live on. I have not come here today just to discuss our human and loopen friends. On our way here, we were attacked by countless Axén spawn that had been hiding beneath the sand of the dunes. The Axén themselves are new to us, only having appeared in the last few cycles, and we have only ever observed small numbers of them as they attack and kill Scanii in our caravans." Sianda paused and emphasized her following words. "This new Axén horde is a wave of death and will be coming for our loved ones." Sianda projected an image of the Axén wave with her thoughts. "We need a plan to protect our kin and our city. If we work together with these humans, we both have a chance to survive. Any other concerns must be set aside until we protect this city."

Shadows now revealed Scanii shapes. Hundreds of Scanii sat in the audience of the chamber. Private debates and observations were now taking place by all. The gathering's next question would be asked as a unified group.

"Current leader of the humans, please swim forward," the chamber seemed to echo. A new figure appeared in the light cast into that space in the chamber. "Sianda is well respected and presented her orb of trust in this matter. But before this gathering can support an alliance with your species, you must show us you can be trusted. Do you have a way to do this?"

Sarah swam higher as she addressed the individual that had presented the gathering's question. Her rebreather mask was still connected to a com feed linking to the Pegasus. "Sianda and Syuk have been helping us since our first meeting, even before they knew us as individuals. Syuk's first encounter with humans ended after she had saved one of my crew. Your kin has already shown us great compassion, and we deeply appreciate your species' benevolence. Our captain, Jake, gave his physical life to save Sianda's twins because he was honorable and would not allow her children to perish. We have bled alongside Sianda and Syuk in our effort to reach this city, not only to warn you of the danger but provide our assistance. You want to know the truth, and I will share it. Jake's mind still exists. Ashley can still speak to him through a connection with this loopen." Sarah paused as Hot Wings seemed to cue his entrance. "We have found a computer with plans for a crescent ring gate, and more humans are coming to help us construct this gate. But our goal of returning home will only be addressed after we deal with the Axén threat. We will stand with your kin and fight at your side. That is the type of ally we are, and we will only rest once everyone is protected," Sarah projected her thoughts for all to listen in this grand space.

"We also brought this." Sarah held up the Solo Blade. "This was Rux's blade! I have been told its match is mounted in this very chamber. As a symbol of hope for all Scanii." That is when Syuk swam to one of the back walls. "This blade belongs to your kin, but I would hope that just as these blades are now re-united, you will see that we can unite with each other." Syuk retrieved the other blade that was hung on the wall as Sarah spoke. Sarah handed the second Solo Blade to Syuk. The two Solo Blades henceforth would be known as the Reunion Blades.

"We will face the Axén with you," Sarah finally said.

Sarah felt relief for a moment, but then the chamber remained silent, and she felt her tension return. "Very well, we will help each other," a voice sang out. This voice was speaking for almost all of the Scanii in this gathering.

Sudden words echoed in the chamber, "Something just came through from Europa!"

The chamber illuminated as reflective mirrors were repositioned, and the room started to empty. Sianda, Syuk, Sarah, and Ashley followed the crowd's direction. Richard always has the best timing, Sarah thought as she felt elation from what had just occurred. She had secured the Scanii's help, and more than that, she had secured their trust. She had mixed feelings that Richard might just have sealed his fate by leaping to this place that might be overrun by Axén soon. However, she pushed the thought aside as anticipation built. She was about to see her father again, and they too would be reunited.

The group swam through the corridors until it opened onto a platform just outside of the grandfather ship. There was a massive stack of NIC cargo boxes and a petite utility sub with the word Crichton printed across the starboard side facing them. The cargo had fallen a bit in the water and was loosely scattered on the platform. Sarah swam as hard as she could toward the sub. The large crowd parted around her as she did a butterfly kick toward the Crichton, her legs pushing with excited energy. Ashley and Hot Wings were in close pursuit.

Even before she arrived, Sarah saw Richard's face with Anya right by his side through the NIC glass. He was really here.

"Look who joined the party," Sarah said as she changed to the new local com channel.

"Sarah! It's good to see you!" Richard said, as he saw his grown daughter swim into view. She had become so much more in her life than he ever dared to imagine. Richard always tried to protect Sarah from his shadow, being a council member of Earth Initiative. But here she was, now a captain on a critical mission for all of humanity. She had gained support from a sentient alien species in a first contact scenario and had done so despite Jake's death. Richard marveled at the gathering alien crowd forming around the Crichton. Richard was here to help, but Sarah knew how best to approach the current situation.

Sarah felt the strong urge to hug her father but realized this would be difficult with them separated by NIC glass. "Hey, Dad!" she smiled. "I'm so glad you're here! I have some very good news, and I have some very bad news."

Richard always wanted good news first. "Give me the good news!"

Sarah looked around at the many faces surrounding them. "These are our friends. They have agreed to help us." Syuk swam up beside Sarah.

Sarah's face appeared as stone as she added, "The bad news… We might all be facing annihilation. Many thousands of invisible creatures called Axén are coming, and we are not sure when. When they come, they will try to consume the people of this city. We are going to help them!"

"Jake had told me about the Axén," Richard said. Sarah realized that Richard, now connected with a loopen, could also interact with Jake. She nodded. On cue, Kite swam into view, and Sarah couldn't prevent the wide smile that spread across her face.

"Dad, I would like you to meet someone. This is Syuk," Sarah said as she turned toward her friend.

"You are the one that saved Ashley!" Richard exclaimed.

Syuk nodded once in affirmation, "Ashley would have done the same for me."

"It is amazing to meet you, Syuk!" Richard said, realizing that he had made it to this new world. He was here. The city shined around him, and he tried to take it all in. This warm arrival was followed by dark news.

"Syuk, this is my father, Richard. He always seems to come through when you need him," Sarah said.

"If you are anything like your daughter, then I am sure we will be great friends," Syuk sang.

Syuk was then joined by another Scanii, the individual that had addressed them in the gathering. "This is gathering member Jenn," Syuk addressed the group.

"It is pleasant to meet you all, but if the situation is as bad as you say, we must get started immediately." Jenn sang. "We have allowed your ship to rendezvous with us here."

That is when the Pegasus glided into view.

"It's good to see you, Sis," EV's voice carried over the local com channel.

"Well, traveling across the galaxy to save your backside should make us even now," Anya replied.

"I agree. I am glad that you are here!" EV said.

"Thank Richard, he's the one that got me involved in this crazy party," Anya said. "It sounds like we need to prepare."

PREPARATION

Jenn would act as the liaison to the current mission with humanity. She relayed the emergency preparations that would take place, informing the crew of the Pegasus. The Scanii would evacuate the outskirts of the city, planning to barricade and defend the inner core of the grandfather ship. This was the only defendable location, and they would need to stand against the Axén here. After being told about the Axén horde, nearly all the mobile Scanii camps departed, heading away from the dunes and the city. However, a few warriors did stay and vowed to protect the city.

Ben had spent his time studying the Axén. He compared the differences between the unborn Axén that was killed on the dunes and the Axén that Jake had killed the day before at the Scanii camp. He ran the tests twice to verify the growth patterns. What he saw scared him. From his observations, the Axén that Jake had killed was just over two-hundred kilograms. The infant was a little less than half that size. However, it appeared their age was only a few weeks apart. These things grew big, and they grew fast. He now shared his findings with the crew and with the new additions of Richard and Anya. Syuk and Jenn also joined them. After docking with the Crichton, they met in the briefing room aboard the Pegasus.

"What are we talking about in total size?" Sarah asked.

"It is hard to estimate, but they could grow to be several hundred kilograms and possibly twenty-five meters long from head to the end of their feeder tentacle," Ben said. "If they grow that big, we might have new problems."

"We have never had a report of them growing that large," Jenn commented.

"Well, it is just an estimate, but the growth pattern and egg size suggest an enormous animal after they fully mature," Ben responded.

"What else have you found out?" Sarah asked.

"These guys are good at blending into the background. Their skin even has a sort of heat and electrical dampening, which is why we can't pick up these things on sensors. Layer that with the ability to replicate a perfect image of the scenery behind them using the chromatophores in their skin, and their camouflage is complete," Ben continued. "I started to think that these camouflage combinations with the accelerated growth were almost too perfect. So, I dug a little deeper."

"What did you find?" Sarah asked.

"They are not natural. They were genetically engineered," Ben said.

Syuk eyes widened, and she asked, "What do you mean?"

"They are built to destroy worlds like this, engineered to kill," Ben said.

Sarah's mind raced with this new information. "Could this be some type of bio-engineering by a rogue faction of Scanii?"

"There is absolutely no way," Jenn firmly responded.

"I have no indications that they originate from Violatis," Ben confirmed. "But that does bring up a whole new line of disturbing possibilities." There was a brief pause while everyone processed that bit of information.

"I have some good news to share also," Ben said.

"Please," Sarah nodded to Ben.

"The purpose of the ink substance Axén use just before they attack is to incapacitate prey, specifically when processed through gills. The Axén we encountered were clumsy with their use of this substance and gave away their positions before striking. With more mature animals, my guess is that they will have much better control over this function of their bodies," Ben said.

"I'm still waiting for the good news," Sarah said.

"Even before this substance is deployed, I believe we can detect the traces in the water," Ben explained. "You would need to be fairly close to the creature, but it would likely be possible to pick up chemical traces before an attack."

"How close are we talking?" Richard asked.

"It would depend on the water conditions. But you might be able to detect them if they were within one to ten meters of the source," Ben responded. "It's just a guess without more testing."

"They are extremely deadly from that distance. How would we use that to our advantage?" Kiah asked.

"Is it a compound trace in the water?" Ashley asked. Sarah could already see the wheels turning in Ashley's brain. Sarah hoped that whatever she came up with would be enough.

"Yes," Ben replied.

"Then I think I can modify a drone to detect these things," Ashley explained.

"We could create a drone detection cloud," Richard responded. "That's a good idea."

"More than that, I think we could arm the drones," Ashley said. "Would the compound concentration be traceable back to the origin?"

"Yes, that might be possible," Ben said.

"If we set the drones to seek the highest concentrations, it would lead back to the animal itself. The drone cloud could help to triangulate and target the individual Axén based on the chemical signatures," Ashley explained.

"I don't think we have enough NIC material to make a probe for every Axén, and we do not have any explosives," Richard replied. "Even after we reestablish communications with Earth, I don't think Earth Initiative would be able to get us any material shipment soon, even if I convinced them to intervene."

"You're right. That is why I was thinking about a replaceable blade clip at the front of the probe?" Ashley explained. "We track the traces with the probe, then impale them. If the blade doesn't come free, we program the drone to eject it and replace it with a new blade. That way, we are replacing easily printed blades and not replacing drones."

"That is the best idea I have heard so far," Anya commented.

Sarah nodded, "How soon would something like this be ready?"

"Modifying the drone and fitting the regenerative blade will take me several hours. After we complete the blueprint, we could probably make five drones an hour, or about one hundred and fifty drones per day. That is with the resources available on the Pegasus and the Crichton, including two people using the NIC gloves to create the drones," Ashley said.

"Well, it's something," Sarah said as she turned to Jenn. "Would this plan interfere with the Scanii defenses or any of your forces?"

"We will need to coordinate the deployment of these devices across the city and use them in coordination with our patrols." Jenn paused a moment in thought. "Would it also be possible to equip our patrols with these sensors?"

Sarah turned to Ashley. "Can you also see about making a handheld detector for their patrols?" Sarah asked.

"Let me take care of that one," Richard stepped in. "Let Ashley focus on getting the drones to work. I can help get the Scanii patrols outfitted with detectors."

"How many patrols will you have around the city?" Sarah asked Jenn.

"We have just over one hundred armed patrols at any given time in rotating shifts," Jenn explained. "We have five hundred kin ready to protect this city."

Sarah nodded. She hoped that would be enough. She found the fact that these creatures were genetically engineered to be very disturbing. If it wasn't a Scanii who engineered these Axén, then who built them and why?

"We also have many volunteers that want to train with Dyami on seeing the auras of these creatures," Jenn added. "We need to work on multiple fronts!"

Sarah shifted to Dyami, "Is that something you can take care of?"

"There is just one thing that I must do first. Then, I will start their training," Dyami said.

Hydroponics was in shambles. *At least it's no longer filled with ocean water*, Ben thought. Many of the plants were dead or dying, and a robust rotting ocean smell filled the space. Then he saw Dyami was already in hydroponics and helping clean up. The hull damage had also been permanently fixed.

Suddenly, the fact that the lab was wrecked did not hurt so much. Ben used the positive moment to turn his mindset around. This situation was challenging, but Ben had a friend that was there when he needed him. "Hey, Dyami," Ben softly said as he stepped over a pile of dead plants.

"Oh hey, I thought I might help you get set up again," Dyami said casually. "I asked Richard to use the Crichton to patch us up quickly," he nodded to the repaired hull. "I know you have been busy with the Axén research."

"Thanks. I appreciate that," Ben replied.

Dyami nodded and said, "You will have to thank Richard. From what he said, we could hear from Angi in a few days."

"Yeah, keeping busy has been helping me to not think about that constantly," Ben admitted. "Every second, I'm waiting for her to call. Even when I am not thinking about her, I'm thinking about her."

Dyami laughed a bit, "Yeah, I can see that."

"I just need to see her one more time. To tell her I love her before… whatever happens next." There was a deep longing in Ben's voice. She was the light that kept him going, and she deserved more than he could ever repay her. He could not bear the thought of never seeing her again.

Dyami nodded once with a knowing look. "She knows, Ben. She is on Europa right now trying to rescue all of us, and you are doing everything you can to get back to her. Just trust in that," Dyami shrugged. "There are still reasons to hold onto hope."

That is when Kiah and EV walked into the hydroponics lab. "Aw, see, Ben beat us here," EV said.

Ben looked to Dyami, "You invited them too?"

"Actually, this was Kiah's idea," Dyami admitted.

"Hey, I like to eat too. You didn't think I was going to lose all that food without some intervention on my part!" EV joked.

Kiah looked sternly at EV because he blundered into the conversation before she could respond. "Ben, we all need reminders of home. Things we can hold onto through the challenges. We all appreciate your efforts down here and want to help!"

Ben nodded, "Thanks, Kiah."

Dyami shrugged again. "We were lucky we had converted part of environmental to food production. Just have to reverse the process to rebuild this space."

After several days of hard preparation, there was still no sign of the Axén. The crew had created and tested the replicating blade-clip drones. EV started calling them clippers, and of course, the name stuck. They were remarkably effective in the tests and already had an ever-growing cloud of machines. Ashley had recommended that one of the reconnaissance teams should test the drones before relying on them to protect the city. They just needed to know where to look.

Dyami had begun to train some Scanii in how to visualize auras. He found that a few of the Scanii individuals could see the energy patterns the way he did. Many of them simply didn't know there were others out there with that same ability. Many of the Scanii that lived in the city had never encountered an Axén since the Axén attacks had only started to occur in the last few cycles, and they had only attacked smaller caravans before. So the ability had never been used before to try to detect them. Kydar was a young host with just such an ability, and Dyami was amazed by their even and calm demeanor. The youth seemed to understand things and asked many questions that showed their comprehension of the methods taught to them.

"How did you find out that you had this talent?" Kydar asked.

"I could see auras ever since I was a child, but many people told me they weren't real. My family always seemed to believe I could see them. However, it wasn't until I was an adult that I found I could trust what I saw and had some understanding of their meaning," Dyami said.

"What do they mean?" Kydar asked.

"I believe what I see are the connections between life. I think that might also be why the Axén appear as a dark cloud, like a void. It is because they are not a natural part of the life here on Violatis," Dyami explained.

"Why are they here?" Kydar asked.

It was a good question, and Dyami wished he knew the answer. If the Axén were truly not created here, then that pointed to an outside presence deploying a genetically engineered weapon. *What reason would they have to deploy such a weapon in this world?* he wondered. "I wish I knew Kydar, and I promise I will do what I can to find that answer," Dyami said.

"What will we do when they come?" Kydar asked.

Dyami saw fear in the youth, but he would not lie to him. "Kydar, we will ALL do our part to protect this city and this planet. We will each play a role when the time is right. Trust yourself that you will make the correct decisions, because I trust in you."

Kydar's face was grim, "Will we make it?"

"There is always hope," Dyami touched the glass that separated himself from Kydar. Dyami spread his fingers wide as he held his hand on the glass. He wanted to convey some calm to assuage Kydar's fear, "I will do everything I can."

Kiah was reviewing the sensor data, still trying to optimize sensor inputs and executing and rewriting precise drone control functions. With the lack of real-world tests, her control adjustments would have to be as accurate as possible to ensure the plan had the best chance of success.

She had loaded the three-dimensional scans of the Axén bodies and matched the camera recordings from their encounter with the Axén wave, predicting how they moved. She then marked out areas on the body where fatal stabbing locations could be found. She noted the position of the glands that secreted the detectible substance in the water.

Matching that information with the refined specifications for the new armed drones, she modeled the potential trajectories and different sizes of bodies. She ran the simulations again and again. Adjusting each time how the water flowed, how the probe moved, multiple creature sources, and different potential detection models. She ran billions of scenarios in rapid succession as she refined the functions and redefined the parameters within the system. Every day she seemed to think of potential variables to add or adjust.

She would upload the latest firmware to each drone refining their capabilities as data was processed and controls refined.

The real test would be on a reconnaissance mission. Kiah hoped it would work. It had to work.

RECONNAISSANCE

Dawn broke, and Syuk could tell something did not smell right. There was the slightest trace of blood drifting on the current. It was Scanii blood. The most troubling part was it was not coming from the direction of the dunes. It was coming from where Tirilean was expecting its next convoy of food. If the city came under siege, it could be the last food the city was expected to receive for a while. Syuk had smelled blood in the water many times, but only a few times had it been Scanii blood. She could already see that others had noticed the same trace, and warriors gathered defensively in the direction of the current as it pushed swiftly into the city.

Syuk saw Xieb, captain of the Tirilean Rangers. Xieb was assigned to lead the ranger squad for this reconnaissance mission. Syuk did not always agree, mind to mind, with Xieb, but she deeply respected the ranger. Xieb was true to her word and showed many times she could complete the difficult tasks assigned to her. When Xieb asked Syuk if she would fulfill the scout role on this critical mission, Syuk felt it was a request coming from all her kin. The current now pointed them in the direction of what was likely an Axén attack. Even a great rahav never left a scent like this on the current. It was the smell of death.

Syuk had been a scout for all her adult life. The skill had been an essential part of her growing up. Syuk's natural kins were killed before she had any memory. The larger group raised her, but a particular Scanii did take her under their wing. Viv was a host and the scout for the group, and Syuk was always fascinated by their abilities and stories. Syuk eventually learned the trade, developing the ability to survey and evaluate areas of the ocean very quickly. Syuk had honed her ability to detect trace scents in water. Even humans had a particular smell, even detectible through their wetsuits. Using these scouting abilities, she found the humans and saved Ashley on that first encounter.

Syuk recalled Ashley and Kiah's update on the clipper drones. They needed a test of the new weapons. These drones would engage and destroy any Axén if the group encountered them. Syuk thought about the possibility that they might encounter the horde and shuddered. Death already surrounded this mission, and there was a strong possibility Syuk could face this violent adversary.

Syuk's mind wandered to her earlier conversations with Sarah. She had shared very personal experiences with this human alien. Her features are so much different from the Scanii. The tone in her words, and the way in which she spoke. It was strange but... *What would it be like to speak like that?* Syuk thought.

Syuk was pulled from her reminiscence as she saw Dac as he approached.

"What are you doing here?" Syuk asked.

"I am trying to talk you out of going. From the stories I hear..." he shuddered. "I just don't want to lose an old friend." Dac's face showed the fear he had of losing her.

Syuk looked at him carefully. "This is larger than you or I." Dac saw her resolve was firm by the look that reflected deep within her eyes.

From over Syuk's shoulder, Xieb waited patiently.

"Promise me that you will return," Dac's tone was smooth in mind.

Syuk nodded. "I will."

Dac swam back as Syuk turned to greet Xieb.

"Syuk, I need all your senses for this one," Xieb said after greeting her with a cross-finger salute. The greeting was for a respected comrade.

"Xieb, I will do everything in my power. Countless Axén are out there, and I hope you brought someone along that can see this threat," Syuk responded.

"I did, her name is Onasa. She can see the auras, and Dyami seems to trust her ability," Xieb said. That is when Kiah and Dyami swam up, followed by a slender and somewhat frail-looking Scanii female. A set of six clipper drones flew in the ring formation around a long-range primary control drone. Ashley was flying the entire formation through her console on the Pegasus. She would manually pilot the control drone circled by the clipper drones that would be released on a tracking trajectory when hunting Axén. The clippers could also be manually called back to the formation by Ashley. Syuk noted the blades on the drones were currently retracted. Tension was set behind the blade to spring forward just before a strike. The blade and outer shell of the drone also could become electrified as a defensive and offensive capability.

"Syuk, let me introduce Onasa," Dyami said as they stopped the Sea Wing's forward motion. "I think she is your best hope for seeing what's out there."

Onasa crossed her fingers with respect for Syuk, "It is pleasant to meet you." Onasa was wearing an old set of goggles with lenses to correct her vision.

Syuk returned the gesture.

"I will remain at Tirilean to keep an eye on the city," Dyami said.

"These drones have the latest updates for the tracking software, and Ashley can manually control each if needed. The com channel will be open, and there will be a Scanii translator on our side," said Kiah, then she gestured to the center camera drone as she looked at Syuk. "So, you can keep us posted by communicating into the drone. I wish I were going with you."

"It would be an honor to have you along, but you would not be able to keep up with your artificial fins, and the vibration of a Sea Wing might give away our position," Syuk sang softly.

"I understand. You be careful out there!" Kiah said.

"I will," Syuk sang. Syuk felt a sense of solitude at that moment. "We must hurry, come Onasa."

With that, the group left and started following the blood, becoming more prominent in the current. Swimming against a current this strong would wear on the group. *At least the Axén will not smell us coming,* Syuk thought.

The squad of fifteen Tirilean Rangers found the raft adrift in the current. The raft was untouched, floating on the top of the water. All the pulls for the raft were slack and drifting loosely along the surface. Syuk could still smell the traces of blood in the water, but no survivors or bodies were in sight. The Scanii in the caravan was gone. Xieb mentally reached out to communicate with any Scanii in the area that extended out a few kilometers. Syuk opened her perceptions for any signs of survivors. There was no response. There had been hundreds of Scanii here…

the water held a chill as the horror set in. Syuk squeezed her eyes shut, focusing her concentration, trying to determine if there was even a faint thought from another Scanii in the area. Xieb sang out again, looking for anyone. Still, no one responded.

"Syuk, I don't sense anyone here. We need to get this food back to the city," Xieb called as her squad formed up along the pulls for the raft.

"Yeah, I just have a bad feeling," Syuk responded. "Onasa, do you see any auras?"

"Nothing," Onasa said, peering through her lenses.

Xieb gave the order, and the group started to move the large raft of food supplies. Despite the weight, the Rangers could move the supplies along the water's surface. They acted as a tug as they gained speed and started guiding the craft to Tirilean. Syuk's intense tension never subsided as they moved toward the upper outskirts of the city. Onasa was the first to cry out, "Axén are coming!"

As Syuk turned, Onasa projected the auras of the Axén to the team as they closed fast! There were at least two hundred or more. Syuk felt the sudden rush of fear. These Axén were already as large as the specimen that had killed Jake, and it took great effort for Syuk to keep her anxiety in check. They would need to make it back to the city! Although they could see the Axén auras, this group of Tirilean Rangers would not survive in a direct fight! They were vastly outnumbered by over thirteen to one.

"Xieb, we need to get the Rangers back to the city! Make a break for it!" Syuk shot out her call.

Syuk saw the primary drone reposition, and it was apparent the clippers were preparing to engage as they peeled off to attack the threat.

Syuk pulled Onasa's arm toward the city, "We need to go now!" They were going to make a run for it. Axén howls rang through the water as the chase began. Onasa kept her concentration and gaze on the approaching threat, relaying her vision to the other Rangers. Syuk locked arms with Onasa, back to back, swimming with her, the beats of their tails unifying as Onasa held her aural gaze on the Axén.

Syuk swam hard as she kept an eye on Onasa's vision. Syuk thought about it like staring into a mirror pointed over the shoulder. Her concentration was on the mirror, but she also could refocus with her own eyes. The moment slowed as she saw the drones were about to engage the Axén. The distance between the target Axén and the clipper closed.

Syuk's mind was etched with what happened next.

Blades shot forward only moments before the drones made contact with the Axén, stabbing the beasts before giving one lurching, tearing stroke then trying to spin free. When a blade was wedged deep within a creature, it would eject, and thousands of barbed hooks extended, bleeding out the beast. Blades were only lost when they did not rip free from the flesh. Syuk saw as five of the six drones killed their target outright. The Axén, subject to the attacks, writhed in death spasms. The sixth drone had missed only slightly and had torn the hooks straight out of the Axén's skin. The beast howled and stopped swimming, blood indicating the location of the injured.

Syuk saw several other Axén break off their pursuit to eat the dead and injured Axén. They ate their own, never wasting an opportunity to consume and to grow.

The drones reset their pattern and broke into an arc to cover the escape further. Syuk swam in rhythm with Onasa as they raced through the water toward Tirilean. Over a hundred Axén were still overtaking the Rangers' retreat. Drones started to drop second and third targets. Twelve Axén already lay dead from drone kills, and more delayed to feast on the dead.

Syuk could see reinforcements coming from the city. Fifty warriors were swimming out to meet the threat and cover the escape. Syuk spun away as the closest Axén shot its feeder tentacle toward her. Onasa then lost her concentration on the auras as the pair spun in unison to avoid the attack. Syuk was impressed by the pinpoint coordination with her swimming partner but knew Onasa needed to keep processing and sharing the vision, if the Scanii had any hope of defending against this group of Axén.

Syuk held the position of the nearest Axén in her mind. With one motion, she separated from Onasa and slipped her blades from their sheaths. Syuk coiled her body and shifted directions. Onasa regained her focus just moments before Syuk plunged her blades into the closest Axén. The beast writhed and screamed as the blades struck deep, killing it within moments. Other Axén surged forward, and she could see them clearly through Onasa's vision. Syuk saw herself dodge and grab the next attack from feeder tentacles, dropping both knives into her right hand. She pulled the beast close before hooking her blades into the creature.

Syuk released the body and swam for Onasa. She could see the next beast as it lunged forward toward Onasa. Syuk pushed herself forward to get to Onasa, who was still concentrating on projecting the auras. Just then, Syuk saw a drone engage and lock onto their pursuer. The drone tore through the Axén, leaving a hooked blade behind for the Axén to die on.

Syuk swam again in tandem with Onasa as they pushed toward the Scanii defenders. That was not the only thing that was coming, Syuk realized as she focused forward. The Pegasus, surrounded by drones, was now also on approach. "Hold tight. We are coming!" she heard Sarah's words in her thoughts.

The cloud of drones advanced from the Pegasus toward Syuk's position, preparing to cover their escape. Syuk and Onasa swam hard toward the Pegasus. The drones were skimming past Syuk, locking onto Axén targets. Death cries of Axén could be heard as more fell to the larger cloud of drones. After only minutes, the fight was over. The clipper drones effectively destroyed all of the remaining Axén within the area.

Syuk and Onasa had lived. However, Syuk discovered that five Rangers, including Xieb, had died, forming a phalanx to allow them time to escape. *Xieb and her Rangers sacrificed themselves to save us,* Syuk thought.

The day had been won, and the few damaged drones could be repaired, but irreplaceable lives had also been lost.

LONG DISTANCE

Ben had fallen asleep on a console in the marine lab. His exhaustion finally manifested as a restless sleep. His mind still wrestled with the realities that the crew now faced. Ben had been pushing himself, grasping at any semblance of control over their situation. As a medical doctor, he was used to dealing with emergencies and long hours. In those situations, he often felt a certain level of calm, even with the chaos surrounding him. He had mastery over those situations, and once his work was finished, he returned to his life… to Angi. These circumstances were different, and the odds continued to mount against them returning home alive. Ben had spent every waking moment focusing on his tasks. Still, despite all his efforts and contributions, he felt like he was failing. He felt as if his life was slipping away with every tick, and he might never get back to the people he loved and who loved him.

Sarah found him lying against a panel with an analysis progress bar still processing. It was apparent the pressures that he was putting himself under. She could tell his mind was unsettled as it grasped for the sleep he so desperately needed. Should she wake him to send him to his bed? Or just let him get sleep anyway he could get it? Sarah had noticed the slow torment that Ben had been putting himself through. She was here to check on him and see if there was anything she could say or do that would help ease the pressure she knew he was under. Sarah stood there for a minute and watched as Ben slept. A slight groan escaped Ben's lips as his mind repeated another loop in his fevered dream, grappling with a problem that might not have a solution. Sarah decided she would let him sleep but would bring him back a pillow to make the desk less cold and hard.

There was a sudden chime as the intercom cut in from the bridge. "Sarah, Earth Initiative is on the channel. They just reestablished communication! The Secretary of Council is asking to speak with you immediately," Kiah said.

Ben's eyes opened, and he peeled his head away from the panel. "The Secretary is calling… from Earth?"… his brain was still in a fog. His eyes snapped to Sarah standing in the marine lab doorway. Sarah saw with one look what Ben's question was. "Angi?"

Sarah returned what she hoped was a reassuring gaze. "I will be sure to check, Ben."

Sarah tapped the com on the doorway, "Kiah, send the call to the briefing room."

"Already done. Richard is on his way there now," Kiah said. Sarah heard the slight edge in her voice.

Sarah refocused her thoughts as she entered the briefing room. Richard was already there. The display was already lit with the face of the elected Secretary of the Earth Initiative Council, Luthor Hymoon.

"Captain," Luthor formally addressed Sarah.

"Secretary Hymoon," Sarah returned the formal gesture. She had met with Luthor on a few occasions, but each one of them was at a public event or ceremony. Sarah looked to Richard for what his reaction might tell her about what she was in for. Since Richard was on the council, he might have had a clue as to what to expect. Sarah saw his expression was very neutral and felt a sense of unrest sit in the back of her mind. She wondered what words had been exchanged before she had entered the room.

"Captain, I'm going to be straight. Your father's mission was to bring you back, not follow you to the ends of the galaxy, and he neglected to mention his intentions before doing so. He is obligated to the Earth Initiative Council, and his failure to mention that important detail in his report was unacceptable!" Luthor had an edge in his tone. "By the way, that first long-distance call that knocked out the Earth Dock communications system had the side effect of informing every living human of the fact that your team is off on some distant alien world. Rumors have been rampant, with everyone wanting to know what happened to their beloved Sarah. Actual facts have been few and far between. Everyone wants to know what is happening, and you will tell me. Report!" Luthor's gaze hardened as the final words left his lips.

"Luthor I…" Richard was cut off by a sharp look from Luthor. He returned his gaze to Sarah.

Sarah needed to show her lived truth in this situation. She knew the conversation was being recorded, and all of humanity would see her response. Her team had been the first to make contact with any intelligent alien species. With their present situation, she had almost forgotten the greater magnitude of first contact with the Scanii. Since that point, so many events had transpired. Her crew and the entire world of Violatis were now in danger. The enemy they faced was still shrouded in mystery and shadow. Earth Initiative needed to be convinced to support their current situation and nurture the relationship they had forged with the Scanii. They needed to be convinced to stand against the enemy that had created the Axén horde. Their support rested on her following words.

"Secretary, we have met a race of sentient, intelligent, conscious beings," Sarah let the statement sit for a moment. "During our first encounter with them, they saved the life of one of my crew." Sarah wanted to make that fact clear. "Our former captain, Jake Riley, also gave his life to save Scanii lives. The two lives he saved belonged to the children of Sianda, a leader of one of the Scanii groups. Now, there is a grave threat to these beings and to my crew."

"Go on," Luthor held a neutral unblinking stare.

"There are these creatures, called Axén, that have been engineered to kill all life in this world," Sarah explained.

"Engineered?" Luthor cut in. "By whom?"

"I only have a hunch," Sarah replied. Luthor saw in Sarah's face that she had an idea but did not have any proof yet.

"Luthor." Sarah used his first name to gain every fiber of his attention. "Based on the stories they have shared, these people escaped from an empire. Now these weaponized creatures suddenly appear in their world. The stories of this empire are thousands of years old, but perhaps that wound never healed."

She saw the realization wash over him. Then his face turned firm. "How much proof do you have of all this?"

"I have a few Axén bodies stored in our marine lab," Sarah said. "The Scanii language doesn't directly translate over the com channel. They communicate with us telepathically, and we can have a crew member translate on our side. But any of them would be happy to speak to you directly about our situation. We are going to need more help!"

"Captain, I admit, I'm not comfortable with the facts that you just admitted to me. You're saying these beings have been in your mind?" Luthor frowned at the thought.

"We only hear the translations of their speech. It has been nothing more," Sarah explained. "There are more pressing matters at hand." Sarah didn't mention the loopens. She was not sure what his reaction would be to hearing about their abilities right now.

"Well, you'll get your shot to tell the world. Too many people know about this, and too many people know we are testing the new communication array system now. What I need to know now is all the details. You need to explain everything."

Sarah started from their first encounter, "Syuk was the first Scanii we met."

As she explained the sequence of events that led them here, Sarah could tell that Luthor wasn't totally convinced about every detail. After he saw the physical evidence that Sarah had, from the camera footage to the dead specimens, he started to look pale. The Pegasus transferred all the relevant data back to Earth Dock.

"The thing I'm very concerned about is we might be getting into a war, and we don't even know who is on the other side." Luthor gave his straight answer. "Did you find any hard evidence of who is behind these Axén creatures?"

"Not yet," Sarah admitted. Despite all they had been through, Sarah wished she had a better lead than stories of an old empire that might have died thousands of years ago. Or perhaps another ghost from the Scanii's past? There were far more questions than answers about the source of the Axén.

"And you are still stuck on that world until this…conflict with the Axén is over?" Luthor questioned.

"Yes, it could take many months to build the gate, and our immediate threat is the Axén. With their numbers, they could easily overwhelm the city, and despite our recent success, I'm told they can grow quite large. The longer they wait, the larger they become as they consume the environment around them. Ben has found direct evidence of this. Ashley is looking into larger drones to combat larger creatures but is still prototyping and testing the larger design. However, we only have so much material and have used much of it for the current drone cloud defense," Sarah said.

"Alright, let me take this information back to the council. The public will need some explanation too. Like I said, too many people already know you are not on Europa anymore. The council will convene again immediately after this debrief," Luthor explained.

"Is there anything else to report, Captain?"

"Secretary… Luthor, my doctor, would like to speak with his wife," Sarah addressed him personally in this crucial matter. "He needs this. This has been a hard mission, and I need him at his best."

Luthor looked at Sarah through the com, and she saw the resistance in his face. "She is still on the Europa team. I will make arrangements to have her call him soon. Anything else?" Sarah picked up the vibe, knowing she didn't want to ask for any more favors right now. She shook her head. "Luthor out," he said, terminating the com.

Sarah was left standing there with Richard. "You didn't want to tell them about your trip here?" Sarah finally asked.

"I couldn't leave it to chance," Richard replied. "The decision to come and save my daughter was the only choice. Red tape wasn't going to get in the way of that decision."

"What about the consequences?" Sarah asked.

"Those have yet to be decided," Richard replied.

"You mean if we find a way to live through the end of this world?" Sarah responded.

"That, also, has yet to be decided," Richard said softly. His eyes dropped for a moment. "Taking command like this could not be easy. Do you want to talk about it?"

"I'm not from Earth Initiative. Now I'm leading the first contact, and I'm in command of this mission. How is Luthor going to take that?" Sarah asked.

"It was a good sign he was addressing you as Captain. I'm not sure he likes the reason I failed to report my trip here." Richard explained. "Sarah, you know the crew here has your back. From the outside, you have said and done all the right things. Just let me know if you need to talk about the layer underneath that exterior." Richard paused for a moment. "I know from experience the pressures of command, and that was before you add the horrors of the current situation."

"Dad, I'm well aware of your resume. I'm glad you are here." Sarah let the words resonate with a slight sense of relief. She felt her own tension as a knot located in her right calf muscle. Whenever she was sick or stressed, it seemed to ache. It had been tight for a few weeks now. "I think I'm going to try to get some sleep. I will catch up with you once I have a clearer head."

Richard walked across the room into his daughter's embrace. "Alright, Starlight. Get some sleep."

The call from Europa came in about a day after Sarah spoke to Luthor. Kiah routed the video feed to the Marine Lab, where Ben was apprehensively waiting.

Angi's face filled the screen, and Ben felt the warm ocean of elation wash through his tired soul.

"I love you!" Ben told his wife the most important thing first. The thing he had promised himself he would say when he saw her again. The words were thick with relief, excitement, and exhaustion that ached in his bones. They were all carried by the tone in his deep voice. Ben felt the exhilaration from the moment.

"I love you too!" Angi said the most important thing first. She always did.

IT'S HER! Ben felt a wave of tension fall away from his being. Just the sound of her voice was like a blanket of hope that Ben wanted to wrap around himself. It gave him renewed strength to keep on pushing, to keep on moving forward.

"Ben, I'm here, baby!" she regarded her husband closely. Her face was the most beautiful thing he had ever seen as she looked at him across lightyears. "My poor Ben, you don't look like you have been sleeping much," Angi's voice was so very smooth as she spoke to her husband. She was always there when he needed her most. Here she was again, just when Ben needed her. She had found a way. She would always find a way.

Ben cracked a weary smile. The last few weeks were taking their toll, and the stress was coursing through his head. "How long do we have?" he found the words in the jumbles of his thoughts.

"We have fifteen minutes. At least for now," Angi explained. "Sending a communication across the galaxy requires another level of power. They are still telling the public that they are running tests."

"Angi, did they tell you anything about our situation?" Ben asked.

"EI told me that this communication would be monitored and recorded. They have been tightly controlling the publicly released information surrounding this entire mission. I had to agree to a new level of clearance just to speak with you. There was some information that they passed along to me about contact with an alien race, but they had very few details within the material. They said lives might be at risk. What's going on, Ben?" Angi's voice was steeped with concern.

"Baby, there is something out here. There is a chance the crew might not make it." Ben felt the words topple from his mouth. The truth lay there as he saw the realization wash over Angi's face. "I'm not sure you want to know the details."

"Ben, I need more. You can't just let my imagination run wild on the idea of alien sea monsters." As Angi spoke the words, the expression on Ben's face told her she had hit the truth.

"The type of creature that killed Jake, well it turns out there are a lot more of them," Ben said.

Angi paused for a moment. "What are your chances?"

Ben shook his head. "I don't know, but it seems pretty grim."

"Now I know why you have not been sleeping," Angi said as she looked into her husband's eyes. The video feed still captured the kind brown eyes she had fallen in love with so long ago. "I will do everything I can to bring you home." Ben knew the depth of that promise. The couple had seen their share of trying times, and they had always been there for one another.

"You're still on Europa?" Ben asked.

"There are a few of us here. Rafter was put in command after EI discovered Richard was gone. He seems… green. Malcolm has been handling the logistics for the mission here. Without him, we couldn't have sent you the NIC treasure trove Richard brought. Are you good on that, by the way?"

There was something that Ben recognized at that moment. His wife already had another card in play. "Do you have something in mind?"

"Not yet. I will try to come up with something," Angi winked at her husband and adjusted the strap on her bra. Her finger lingered for a moment and casually pointed to her lips. Ben received the message clearly. She was not going to talk about it openly, but he knew she had a backup plan.

"I'm so glad to see you," Ben let the words flow from him as he nodded. The relief was apparent on his face.

"Have you spoken to the kids?" Ben's eyes welled as the thoughts of his children rolled over him.

"We connect when we can and have been sharing video messages every day," Angi replied.

"You have?" Ben's voice cracked. The shock from what he had missed washed through his mind. Kasidy's birthday wasn't the only missed occasion. Ben would remember Tyler's seventh birthday very well as the day he witnessed the Axén horde spawn.

Angi nodded. "Ben, are you ok?"

"I'm working on it." Ben's face looked tired, but he managed to crack a smile.

"Your work?" Angi knew that was the cause of her husband's lack of sleep. He always threw himself into the fray when lives were on the line.

"It's keeping me busy," Ben nodded.

"Baby, you need to take care of yourself. If you break, you won't be able to help anyone. I need you not to break for me." Angi's words held wisdom, caring, and love. She hoped hearing them would, in some small way, keep Ben safe from the darkness she imagined existed within the universe.

"I'm working on it, Angi, my darling." Ben's words were as reassuring as he could make them.

"Do you want to see the kid's birthday videos?" Angi asked.

Ben's mind was delighted at the prospect of seeing his children. He nodded as a tear rolled down his face, and he cracked another weary smile.

"I thought you might. I have some video clips. I know you want to watch them with me." Then Ben caught the hand signal, signifying the number THREE, followed by the increment DAY. It was a family code that had been passed down for generations.

Angi played the video of Tyler's birthday. Ben set the information aside for now as he relished the clip. Ben could already tell that Tyler got tickets to see the Highflyers game. "Dad, Mom, I know you are off on something very important. So, I thought that I would record the day for you. Enjoy!" The camera shook around as Tyler tried to reposition it. Ben could tell the camera's lens was about fifteen centimeters off the mark. He was staring straight into the back of some lady's baseball cap. The video traveled hundreds of thousands of lightyears to show the back of this one lady's head. Ben chuckled a bit at the thought and the now-shaking camera as Tyler clapped with the crowd. There was silence in the video as Ben imagined the pitcher setting up on the mound.

Crack! A film-making miracle happened next as the camera was raised above the head, and Ben saw something spectacular. The Highflyer's own Muggzy, at least that is what the real fans called him, leapt forward from right-center and caught the ball as he landed on the ground. Then using his forward momentum, he somersaulted into a strong throw, picking off the runner that had attempted to retreat to second base, saving a run and getting two quick outs.

Ben found that his jaw dropped.

"He thought you would like that!" Angi said as she smiled at Ben.

"He captured that shot?!" Ben found the energy that he needed. He felt so happy and overwhelmed with a deep heartache that he was still out here and in mortal danger. He needed to see his son and daughter again.

"It is a damn miracle if you ask me. Most of his videos look like they were actually shot by a squirrel falling out of its tree!" Angi exclaimed.

Ben laughed. "I'm familiar with his work."

"It looks like a good time. Next time, we should all go." Angi looked at her husband. Angi never watched much baseball. She only liked it when it meant spending time together.

"I will do everything to get back there," Ben promised.

The screen changed, and Ben saw his daughter, Kasidy. She was at an aquarium, standing beside a whale shark swimming just beyond NIC glass. The great beast swam just behind her head in the frame. "Hey guys, it's Kas. Just chilling with my new friend here in Monterey Bay. This place is pretty chill. The grandparents follow us around and are generally very nice to us. I miss you and can't wait to spend time with you both. Oh, and this big guy. I just nicknamed him Philip. I'm not sure what his real name is, but he came over when I said Philip, so maybe he just likes that name or something."

Ben watched as she panned the camera around the aquarium, paying extra attention to Philip. Angi had also missed this day, and regret was apparent on her face.

"Hey Kas, are you ready to go get something to eat?" Angi's mother filled the frame.

"Just give me another minute with Philip. He was just telling me about his sister." Kasidy turned the frame again to the majestic whale shark.

The time was nearly up.

Angi shut off the videos from her feed. "I will keep up my end, but you need to return safely to me. That is your part of this deal."

Ben just nodded. "Let me record something you can send back

to the kids."

Angi gave a stiff nod seeing how quickly the time had gone.

"Hey guys, I love you both. Your videos reached me across this galaxy. Just know that your family will always be there and look out for each other. I am working on getting home as soon as I can," Ben said.

The video feed displayed a low power indicator and then shut off.

EI SUPPLIES

At first, many Scanii thought fleeing the city was the safest idea, keeping themselves and their kin moving away from the danger. Maybe that had worked for some, but a very small number were returning to the city with devastating reports of mass predation events by the Axén, destroying entire family groups, convoys, and tribes of Scanii. These horrific stories took their toll on everyone's morale and mental well-being. Now, no living soul arrived from outside the city. Was anyone still alive out there?

Despite the vast NIC supply cache that Richard and Anya brought from Europa, they were running out of materials for new clipper drones. Ashley had created a cloud of drones, which were a vital aspect of the city's defensive strategy. They proved effective in early tests, and Ashley had made a new series of larger drones to combat larger Axén. The clippers needed no sleep, and only after several patrols did they need to recharge at a charging station Ashley had constructed. One crew member always stood the watch with these bladed sentinels as the city clung to existence.

"What is our status?" Sarah's voice, over the com, bounded off the walls in the Crichton's tight cabin.

"We have enough material to finish this last one," Ashley's voice sounded thin, even in her own ears.

Ashley, Richard, and Anya had been printing the clippers non-stop and were just about out of material. The larger clipper variants were put together piece by piece using the Crichton. Ashley hoped that within the next day, they might receive more material. At least, that is what Ben said might happen. He had indicated his wife, Angi, had a plan in the works, but the details were vague. Despite Richard and Anya's successful journey to Violatis, Ashley still had a hard time thinking that more material might just show up from the Sol system.

Ashley finessed the NIC manipulator arm of the Crichton as she finished assembling the last large clipper drone. Ashley keyed the control in front of her, establishing a computer handshake between the new clipper and the rest of the network. The panel display shifted to the clipper formation visuals, and she established the new clipper's position within the defensive cloud. Ashley had refined the design, and they had been able to print more drones than they had initially calculated. The process had gone smoothly with Ashley's ability to rest within a few seconds from her connections with Hot Wings. She thought about how she might want to refactor some of the older drones in the cloud to reduce their overall material and recycle it into just a few more drones now that she had further optimized the designs. For now, she would report that the task was completed and talk to Sarah about her plan to reconstruct some of the earlier models when Sarah was available.

"Sarah, the last one is ready," Ashley reported.

"Thanks, Ashley. Meet up with the Pegasus. Kiah and Ben need some help with a backup plan they have been working on," Sarah said, voicing her appreciation for Ashley's hard work. Ashley wondered what the pair were up to as she maneuvered the Crichton toward the nearby Pegasus.

After docking, Ashley slipped back to her quarters. She needed to take a few minutes to recharge. Sleep and seeing Jake were her priorities. Time in the outside world crawled forward while she was in the mind space. Evaluating how much time had passed didn't seem to be linear. Sometimes Ashley would feel like ten hours had gone by while she was in the mind space, but the outside world had only moved a few seconds after she returned. Other times she would feel like only an hour had elapsed, but in real time a full two or three minutes had gone by. Ashley realized with some growing awareness that the reason was an organic one. It depended on the times and frequency of her visits to the mind space. Hot Wing's concentration during each session affected the time dilation that was experienced.

The more time between her visits, the more time seemed to slow, and she wondered if it was related to Hot Wing's mental focus at that moment. After discussing it with Jake, they came to the conclusion that Hot Wing's focus might be responsible for the time dilation. Neither of them was sure if the effect was intentional. Was he trying to slow time when Ashley was connected? Was he allowing them to use this power?

The time dilation effect also seemed to operate differently when both loopens were in the mind space. Kite was always there when Richard was there. It almost felt like the loopen was escorting Richard during those periods. However, Ashley still seemed to have her own strong connection to Kite from their first encounter on Europa. She wondered if that was how Richard was able to communicate in the mind space, to begin with. Were they both connected to Kite in the same way? Sometimes Kite would be present in the mind space, and Richard was nowhere in sight. Time hovered close to the brink of total suspension when Kite was present with Hot Wings. Were both of the loopen minds combining to slow time even further?

Ashley started to wonder if Kite was less willing to connect to Richard, and that is why she rarely saw him in the mind space. She would need to ask him about that.

Then Ashley had another thought. *What happens if my relationship with Hot Wings changes? What would happen to Jake?*

"Secretary Hymoon, it is nice to see you again," Sarah stood in the briefing room. Luthor's call gave Sarah a sense of anxiety. She had kept the feeling in check until the call had come in, remaining focused on her duty and crew. But now that Luthor was on the line, she wondered what the outcome would be of EI's impending decision.

Richard came into the room as Luthor began to speak. "Captain Triv, I am not going to lie. Many of the council didn't see this situation *your* way. There are some serious questions that, at this point, can't be answered. The council wants to avoid sending more resources that might, in effect, start a war. They simply can't throw support behind that before we know what we are dealing with. There are too many variables."

"Secretary, we are already in it," Sarah pleaded. "We are talking about our lives out here and our relationship with the most intelligent race, we, as humans, have ever encountered."

"That's what I argued. So, there was a compromise," Luthor shrugged. "Richard, you owe me a favor." Luthor's tone was clear that he expected repayment of that debt someday.

"I understand. That is… if we come out on the other side," Richard said dryly.

"We are sending you more NIC material. We can't send you any explosives, and we can't commit any military resources or personnel. Sorry, but that is how the politics have played out on this one. EI's actions in this situation can't be on the books as a military engagement. We must maintain some plausible deniability, and military authorization would require more votes than are available. The diplomats still want their wiggle room if they need to negotiate peace with a foreign alien empire or if something goes wrong and they need to clean up the PR," Luthor shrugged again.

"Well, I guess that is something," Richard said. Sarah couldn't tell if the tone was grateful or sarcastic, but it seemed to have some effect on Luthor.

"I'm still working on anything beyond that, but you know that will take time. There is no getting around the debate this situation has caused. Some want to avoid any action against the Axén that could lead to a war with an unknown enemy. Even sending more NIC was a hard sell to them. Others believe we must go to any length to bring the Pegasus home, including military options. They are afraid of public backlash if your crew is lost. Both sides have strong points," Luthor explained.

"Well, I'm glad they care about us," Sarah said sarcastically. "When can we expect something?" Sarah felt her words catch a bit as she spoke.

"A day. Apparently, Mrs. Rapner has been busy on that front, already sending down a few more supplies. She revealed her plan only after we said we would try to send something. We have a special shipment on the way. If we can get this ring gate to work again, you should have your supplies then." Luthor paused for a moment and became hesitant with his next words. "They are also sending another research team to Europa to investigate the loopens further. From your reports, we need to learn more about these creatures and the possible dangers of these… mind connections."

Well, that sounds ominous, Sarah thought to herself. "Everything alright?" Sarah stared at Luthor, trying to read his expression. She could tell she wouldn't get anything else from him.

"I did what I could," Luthor seemed to hold some resentment in his words.

"Thanks… Luthor," Richard's voice cut through sharply but ended softly.

Luthor nodded at that. "Don't get yourselves killed. It would be bad

PR if we had to report that you all died. I will be in touch again during our next window."

With that, the channel was cut. The screen darkened, and the briefing room fell silent for a moment as they both processed the news.

"What was that all about?" asked Sarah as she turned to Richard.

"I'm not sure, but confronting him directly was not going to provide the answer," Richard explained. "Besides, right now, we have more important matters to worry about. Kiah and Ben are..."

The statement was interrupted by the alarm. A low pulsating alarm and the red-light indicators on the terminals meant one thing, the Axén were coming.

AXÉN

Darkness crept through the water as the Axén chose the cover of night for their lethal assault. The daylight faded as the residents of Tirilean clung to any glimmer of hope. Sarah entered the bridge, and Dyami was already waiting. "They're coming!" he exclaimed.

Like clockwork, the current had slowed and shifted direction nearly an hour ago. The sensors on the clippers had picked up the Axén approach through trace chemicals drifting through the current. They were closing from the west, and now Dyami could see the dark void on the horizon.

Sarah Triv, Captain of the Pegasus, resolute in the value of life, would confront an adversary threatening every living soul in this world. The crew was at their posts, steadfast in their commitment to her and to one another. They would fight side by side with the Scanii for the right to survive.

EV sat at his post, ready to guide the Pegasus into battle. Anya reported to the front right station, keeping her eyes on the sensors and life readings. Ashley commanded the clippers from the engineering station, and Kiah sat beside her tweaking their behavior and patterns. Richard sat quietly at the science station next to Dyami, who was gazing into the void as the Axén approached.

"What do you see?" Sarah asked Dyami as she walked up next to him.

"There are enough of them for a hell of a fight. By my estimate, there are over a hundred thousand out there. They are separating into three different groups," Dyami reported.

"It's just as we feared. This is a coordinated assault by the Axén. They are communicating and dividing to topple the city. Their attacks are not random or mindless. Ashley, are the clippers ready?" Sarah asked, firm in her resolve.

"We are ready," Ashley replied. She nodded as she keyed the controls.

Sarah could see the Scanii were sealing the core of the city inside the grandfather ship. Most of their warriors would defend the ancient vessel against any breaches and protect the civilian populations. However, a group of Tirilean Rangers would be sent to help the Pegasus and the clippers with the offensive. Their primary objective was to preserve Scanii life by neutralizing the Axén. Tirilean was the only city on Violatis and was the key to survival.

"I want you to hit and run. Pick off as many as you can. We are vastly outnumbered and can't afford to lose those clippers," Sarah let her doubts fall away as she prepared for battle with the lurking shadows. The clippers were ready, and hopefully, there would be enough of them. The fate of every life within this world would be decided this night.

Ashley keyed the controls, and the drones broke into attack formation as they headed toward one of the smaller groups of Axén predators. Ashley watched as the sensor readings visually displayed the drone positions moving toward the dark waters ahead. To the naked eye, the Axén were invisible. However, everyone could sense where the Axén were because of the shared images by aura-sensitive Scanii. The crew could visualize the location of the Axén horde with the array of images shared within their minds.

"EV, make sure to keep us well away from any of those groups, evasive echo three. If they want to chase us, it will cost them," Sarah's command was executed with quick effect. She could feel the ship's engines working through the humming in the hull. The Pegasus glided around, ready in case of a chase. Only a small handful of drones had remained behind to escort the Pegasus. The mission was to stay alive and destroy the Axén horde.

"Clippers engaging now. LOOK SHARP!" Ashley called. On the main screen, the magnified image of the weaponized drone cloud showed the exact moment of engagement. Sarah was holding her breath as over twelve-hundred clipper drones coordinated attacks against different targets.

Even against the smaller group, the drones were still outnumbered almost five to one. The clippers proved effective again, easily killing or wounding every initial target. Alien blood filled the water as the vanguard of clippers retreated. The Axén could be briefly seen as the green blood changed the immediate clarity of the ocean water, looking like ghosts in the dark. The horde lunged forward after the vanguard group, destroying only two clippers with their attack. A second clipper group attacked the flank of the horde. Each of them killed a target of opportunity within the Axén ranks. Despite this initial success, Sarah knew they had barely scratched the dark cloud of bodies that loomed before them.

Bursts of black chemical clouds erupted from the Axén as they lunged after the drones. Feeder tentacles appearing through the ocean fog shot forward only to come up empty. Axén were fast, but the clippers were faster. The drones circled the horde and picked off easy outside targets. Each wave of clippers changed the direction of the attack throwing the alien swarm off-balance. The drones shot through targets as they shredded the Axén they came in contact with. It was apparent Axén were used to attacking with an element of surprise but were realizing this enemy could see through their stealth.

Meanwhile, the fifty thousand-strong group of the Axén pushed forward toward the city and began to spread out. Their auras appeared as a dark void as they descended upon the city. Hopefully, Jenn was right, and Tirilean's defenses would hold against those kinds of numbers. Sarah had seen how the gathering chamber could be sealed and defended even after the main defense line broke. She had to hope it would all be enough. She had to focus on helping to thin the Axén numbers. As planned, the five hundred Tirilean Rangers attacked the main force from afar, hurling several harpoons through the water. They would attempt to hit and run and keep some part of the horde away from the city's core.

"Those brave souls…" Kiah said as she watched the Scanii charge.

Despite the lack of any electronic technologies, Scanii did possess some very brilliant mechanical devices. Sarah marveled as the thrown harpoons seemed to return back to the thrower, allowing reuse. Then Sarah saw many harpoons had hit their target, and individual Axén were pulled, bloody and impaled, from the horde. A line was attached to each harpoon. The Scanii exerted tremendous pulling force as they reeled in the line from within their armor.

Could this work? Will I kill wave after wave of Axén until nothing is left? Our success here means hundreds of thousands will die by my hand. Despite the fact they are engineered, they still feel pain. At one point, were these creatures once more than just a weapon? Sarah thought to herself.

"Captain, that last group looks like it is coming after us!" Dyami said sharply.

"EV, back us off!" Sarah ordered.

"Aye, Skipper!" The Pegasus came about and headed away from the approaching horde. Ashley was furiously entering commands as the drones disengaged from the first target group and headed to cover the Pegasus. Sarah's move wasn't one of desperation and was executed with thought and strategy.

The horde rushed after the Pegasus as it reached its maximum speed. Sarah could already tell that the horde was moving faster than the Pegasus and would overtake the ship in just a few moments. The size of these Axén were only five meters long, and Sarah was relieved that Ben had been wrong about their enormous size, at least at first. These Axén were fast, and it would not be long before they would catch their target, the Pegasus.

Sarah tapped the com channel on her chair. "Ben, we are out of time. Are you ready down there?"

"Captain, I'm ready when you are," Ben's voice came over the com.

Even with all the hard-earned mutual trust Sarah had built with Ben over the last few weeks, she was not sure this would work. She pushed that aside and focused on the task at hand. "Release on my mark," Sarah said.

"Captain, they are almost on top of us!" Dyami exclaimed.

The void started to overtake their position. Sarah waited that extra moment, then cried out, "MARK!" Sarah felt adrenaline and a cold chill rush through her system. If this did not work, this might be a very short fight.

The Pegasus opened exterior compartments along the hull, spilling their contents into the water. The water turned milky as the compound was released and began reacting with the ocean. A giant cloud now rapidly expanded behind the Pegasus. The pursuing Axén were suddenly trapped within a thick viscous slime, covering their bodies and sticking them together in a twisting mass.

"Kiah. Now!" Sarah ordered.

The lights dimmed as a massive electrical discharge built-up within the Pegasus's BRIL reactor. An accelerated hum seemed to quake through the hull as a bright blue surge of electrical lightning was directed into the super-conductive slime. Sarah could see the bolt arcing gracefully through each Axén as they were instantly slain. The pursuing Axén were electrocuted, encased in the lightning-encrusted slime. That plan had worked! Ben's slime and Kiah's spark had saved the ship.

"HELL, YEAH," Anya shouted from the engineering station as the entire crew saw countless Axén fall to the ocean floor all at once.

Relief washed over Sarah as she realized they had neutralized the immediate threat. The clippers came screaming in, picking off the few stragglers that had escaped the electrical surge. Thirty-thousand Axén corpses now fell into the depths.

"Great job, but this is far from over. EV, head back to the city. We need to help our friends!" Sarah ordered.

The Pegasus glided in a smooth arc as it came about, powering back toward the city. The clippers took point as they returned to the battle.

"Ben, do we have any slime left?" Sarah asked.

"I released the entire batch we had, Captain," Ben reported.

"That strategy was brilliant, Ben," Sarah said.

Sarah wished they had more slime. The tactic proved more effective than she could have ever imagined. Her thrill turned into sudden horror as they entered the city limits. Only a handful of Rangers were left. The speed of these Axén had outmaneuvered them. Sarah could tell their situation was dire. The mortality of the situation hit Sarah then, and a flash of horror made her freeze. She struggled momentarily to push the fear from her conscious thoughts and regain control.

The largest horde was descending on the grandfather ship, but the Axén were having difficulty finding the cracks in the armor. Sarah could hear the Scanii communication coordinator in her mind and knew that the city was still holding firm, at least for now.

Sarah had made up her mind. "We need to help those, Rangers!"

Ashley keyed in the command, and the clippers shot away to cover the ranger's retreat. To Sarah's shock, the Axén broke off their pursuit of the fleeing Rangers and turned to face the incoming clippers. Sarah saw, with horror, fifty clippers suddenly go dark.

"What happened?" The words escaped Sarah's lips as a new image was sent to her mind. She saw with a shock that the Axén had used their acid to melt the casings on the drones. They no longer responded and were cast to the ocean floor. Ashley let out a shocked gasp. The crew had all seen the same thing. Sarah felt her stomach sink at the sight of the broken clippers. This fight was a numbers game, and they were on the wrong side of that equation. Losing a few drones was expected, but losing so many and so quickly would mean their eventual defeat.

Sarah reached out with her mind and tried to contact the Rangers group. To her surprise, a familiar voice communicated back. "Syuk!"

"Sarah!" Even in Sarah's mind, Syuk's tone quaked with suppressed fear. Sarah was shocked to find Syuk fighting on the front line with the Rangers. She thought Syuk would fight by Sianda's side. With her injury, Sianda was fighting with the civilian militia. Syuk had never mentioned she was going to be on the front line. Sarah would have remembered that. She felt a cold grasp of fear in her heart as she realized the danger her friend was in.

"Ashley, continue the assault on that group of Axén! Syuk is out there!" Sarah's voice was sharp as the order rang out.

Richard's voice cut in from the back of the bridge, at a seat near the engineering station. "Captain, those drones are all we have. We can't afford to lose too many of them. You saw what happened!"

Sarah shot her father a hard look. "Syuk's selfless actions have saved members of this crew, and we are not going to leave her out there to die."

"Sarah, think of the good of the many," Richard said.

"This is not a debate! Ashley, you have your orders!" Sarah barked.

Ashley nodded. The clippers were in full engagement with the horde. Now less than a thousand clippers were in full operation and engaging the writhing mass. The death of Axén and the destruction of drones littered the homes built up from the ocean floor.

"Captain, I think I can help make our drones more effective in this type of engagement!" Kiah shouted from her station. "I programmed them with an alternate set of tactical patterns that I think will work for this situation."

"Do it!" Sarah ordered.

After a few more minutes, it appeared that the destruction of the clippers had slowed, and the Rangers had retreated to where the Pegasus had repositioned away from the conflict between the clippers and Axén. Sarah felt a wave of relief as Syuk swam by, but her eyes reflected the horror and anguish she had witnessed. Syuk didn't seem to focus on anything in particular and was in an apparent state of shock. Sarah recognized the look of someone struggling to deal with witnessing the violent death of a friend.

Sarah couldn't focus on that now. She pushed past the moment and turned her attention to the raging battle before her. Every decision she made now had to count. Clipper signals faded as they were lost, dying with every tick of the clock.

"Pull back the clippers. EV, hold position, but be ready to evade on my order. Ben, get down to the moon pool; we have wounded incoming." Sarah's heart was in her throat. The next move would be up to the Axén.

The Axén, free from the clipper onslaught, selected their next target, heading straight toward the Pegasus and the retreating Rangers. They were going to finish the fight they had started.

"Ben, we need to run! Tell me when you have the injured Rangers aboard!" Sarah ordered. The next ten seconds felt like an eternity as she waited for a response.

"They're coming! We need to go!" Richard shouted.

"I have them, Captain!" Ben's voice cut across the com channel.

"EV, GO!" Sarah jumped from her chair. Sarah's mind started keeping track of every moment as they fled.

"Ashley, re-engage the drones to attack from behind. Kiah, revert to the hit-and-run tactical patterns," Sarah ordered.

Most of this group of Axén were smaller individuals and were not as quick as the previous horde. Their smaller size did not stop them from closing the gap as they chased the Pegasus and the retreating Rangers. The clippers continued their assault, killing all the Axén that fell behind the main pack.

"They are going to catch us in two minutes," Kiah reported.

"Options?" Sarah asked.

"Maybe we can use this!" EV shouted. He flashed a map and an external camera to the main display showing a nearby crater dropping through the ocean floor. Even in the darkening water, Sarah could see large columns of steam bubbles rising from several deeper holes within the crater itself. From the sensor readings, the site didn't appear to be tectonic in nature, but whatever was creating the super-heated steam columns was incredibly powerful. The Pegasus was just small enough to squeeze into the crater entrance.

"Where the hell is all that heat coming from?" Anya asked.

"Captain, we would need to bring the Rangers on board. According to these readings, the water temperature at the crater mouth will cook just about anything," Kiah said.

"Anya, get down to the moon pool. We are going to need to bring the rest of the Rangers on board on the fly!" Sarah shouted. Sarah knew it would be tricky to bring the Rangers aboard while in motion, but she also knew the Scanii would not survive the near-boiling water temperatures.

Sarah then shot the thought to Syuk, "We have an idea, but you will need to bring you and your kin aboard the Pegasus." Sarah felt the long two seconds before Syuk's response.

"We are coming," Syuk replied. "I trust you, Sarah."

"Head for that crater," Sarah said to EV and told Syuk in thought.

The Pegasus made a graceful arc toward the rocks as the bottom seemed to rush toward the ship. She made her descent. The Axén continued to close in. Through the shared images, Sarah could see the Axén were getting much closer to her ship. The closest Axén lashed out with its feeder tentacles. Syuk cried out in Sarah's mind. Sarah then saw the Axén feeder tentacles had been cut. The blood squirted into the water, and again briefly, the Axén could be seen by the naked eye.

Anya's voice cut in through the com channel. "We have all the Scanii aboard. CLEAR!"

"EV, get us in there!" Sarah ordered.

The Pegasus burst into the wall of super-heated ocean water. Then the siren of a hull breach blared through the entire ship.

"HULL BREACH, DECK TWO!" Ashley shouted. "It's the corridor right outside the medical lab. Bulkheads sealed! The corridor is filling with the super-heated water from the outside."

Sarah felt sudden panic as she realized Ben had likely been transporting the wounded to the medical lab. "Ben! Report!" Sarah looked sharply toward the com on her chair.

"Captain, the doors sealed in time, and no one was in the corridor, but we are cut off from the rest of the ship," Ben reported.

"Anya?" Sarah asked.

"We're good at the dock," Anya said.

The Axén outside didn't stop at the crater entrance. A great many dived after the Pegasus into the super-heated water. They writhed with aggression and pain as the water started cooking them from outside to inside. The remaining Axén pulled out of the chase to be ruthlessly flanked by six-hundred thirty-two lethal clipper drones, further thinning their numbers and starting to even the odds.

"Well, if the cause of the breach was an Axén, it's dead now!" Sarah said. "How long can we stay in here?"

"Well, that might depend," Ashley stated. "The Pegasus hull can take the heat. That is the good news."

"What is the bad news?" Sarah asked.

"We can't send anyone outside to repair the hull damage while we are here," Ashley said.

"Captain, I have some bad news," Ben's voice came over the channel. "We can't cycle any fresh ocean water to medical right now, and we have two Scanii wounded down here! I think it's related to the damage in the corridor."

"Ben, how long?" Sarah asked.

"We have maybe fifteen minutes. These individuals will not last long without water," Ben said.

"Ashley, how long will it take you to repair the corridor once we clear this crater?" Sarah asked.

"I would need to look at the damage. Likely, more than fifteen minutes. However, I do have an idea to help the Scanii in medical," Ashley said. She seemed to nod to herself. "Ben, you still have that laser scalpel?"

"Yeah, we always have one in medical," Ben replied.

"There is a connection to the refugium for Hot Wing's aquarium. If you cut a small hole, you can likely access the piping on the other side of the wall. I can walk you through it," Ashley said.

"Alright, give me three minutes. I need to finish stabilizing one of the patients. Then, I need you to walk me through it step by step," Ben's voice was overlayed by songs of agony escaping Scanii lips.

Outside the crater wall, the battle between the clippers and the Axén raged on. There were now less than two hundred of each. Sarah remembered they still had to deal with another fifty-thousand Axén that were still attacking the city, the last of the three groups. She was unsure how long the city could hold or how many Axén the Scanii defenders might be able to kill before being overrun. But if they lost the clippers here, how would they fight on in that battle?

Deal with one crisis at a time, Sarah thought to herself.

"Alright, Ashley, tell me what to do." Ben's voice came through after another minute.

"Ben, inside the right cabinet that faces the bow of the ship. There should be a spot on the bottom shelf in the right corner. Cut a twenty-centimeter square in the back wall. Be careful. You just want to cut through the wall but not the pipes. You might be able to tell exactly where they are by touching the back wall with your fingers," Ashley said.

"There is an inflow and outflow. Just connect your water pumps through those feeds. You got it?" Ashley asked.

"Yeah, I'm on it." Ben's voice sounded confident, with a hint of annoyance at the situation he was now facing.

Sarah noticed something strange. She kept seeing Axén suddenly stop and hold perfectly still, and most shockingly, they visually appeared. Their mirrored skin faded to a deep red as they revealed themselves. Clippers adjusted for the pattern and wiped out the last hundred Axén. As they fell, the Pegasus emerged from the super-heated crater, sluggish from the flooded compartment but still in one piece.

They were down to just thirty-three clippers total. Sarah took over the clipper controls as Ashley raced to the emergency airlock to start her repair of the hull. The path to the moon pool had been blocked by the super-heated water in the flooded corridors, but there was a single mask and tank with a NIC glove adjacent to the lift at the back of the bridge.

Ashley emerged from the emergency airlock and looked around. Dyami had said there were no Axén outside, but she knew sometimes they would suddenly appear. She pushed through her fear and swam hard toward the damage on the starboard side of the Pegasus. She didn't have the luxury of time, and the longer she delayed, the more likely deadly aliens would appear. As she rounded the hull and saw the damage, she smiled a bit.

The damage was a fist-sized hole in the hull, but that was not what Ashley looked at. Plugging the hole was a crispy Axén body. It was very dead.

"Well, I don't have to worry about you," Ashley told herself.

Ashley used the NIC glove to rearrange the material and reseal the hull. She was pulling particles from here and placing them there. Her skin began to crawl after a minute. Ashley could feel a presence behind her, but when she looked, there was nothing. Another minute went by. Ashley looked again, and Hot Wings was there. She felt a sense of relief and gave her full focus as she completed the repair. She was done in under five minutes.

"Bridge, you may begin pumping the water out of the corridor," Ashley reported.

"Acknowledged," Sarah said.

Ashley waited for a moment looking for any further damage before swimming toward the moon pool.

Sarah could wait no longer and needed to know. "Syuk, are you alright?" Sarah asked through thought.

"No…" Sarah could sense the weight of the death that Syuk had witnessed. "Dac.. He is dead… He was here because of me. He said that he could not let me fight without him there to protect me," Syuk's tone was low. Sorrow filled her thoughts.

There is a high level of empathy for the emotions shared through thought. Sarah could feel the deep sadness for the loss of a lifelong friend. The friend was not Sarah's friend, but she shared the pain with Syuk.

Sarah used every fiber of her heart and tried to send a sense of comfort to Syuk. "His death will not be in vain!"

"Sarah? I…" Syuk's thought was interrupted.

A thought rang out across the sea. The city had been breached. The Axén had found a way in. The Scanii communication coordinator was showing the civilian retreat to the gathering chamber. There was not much time left.

Ashley was almost to the moon pool when she saw Syuk and the other Scanii exiting. Syuk's fore arm was wrapped in a regeneration sleeve. Ashley looked and saw there was still a spark in her gaze. Syuk nodded to Ashley, acknowledging her.

"You ready for this?" Ashley asked.

"I am in this until the end!" Syuk replied.

SUPER POWER

"Sarah, I don't want to leave you," Richard insisted.

"The plan won't work without the Crichton, and I need you backing me up," Sarah said.

Richard sighed.

"If you have a better plan, I need to hear it," Sarah declared.

"I don't, but if this doesn't work, there will be no second chance," Richard said.

"If we don't take action now, we will lose the city. If we lose the city…"

Richard nodded. "I know. We will be right behind you," Richard said.

"Thanks. I love you, Dad," Sarah said.

Sarah could see the airlock cycle as the Crichton autonomously docked with the Pegasus. Anya stepped off the lift, entering the docking area as the hatch popped open between the two ships.

"You ready to go?" Anya asked Richard.

"Yeah," he replied.

"Then let's go. We can't waste a second," Anya said as she boarded the Crichton.

Richard looked at Sarah. "I love you, Starlight."

He stepped through the lock, and the hatch sealed behind him. Richard found his seat quickly and keyed the dock release.

"You're not sure this plan will work," Anya observed.

"We are putting it all on the line with this," Richard replied.

"Everything is already on the line. This is our chance to end it," Anya said.

"I hope you're right. It's unbelievable we made it this far… Thanks for sticking with me." Richard cracked a weary smile.

"No problem!" Anya exclaimed.

Richard nodded. "Alright, then, let's back them up."

Anya leaned over and placed her hand on Richard's shoulder. She softly squeezed with encouragement. "Sarah's got this!"

The Axén horde was systematically breaking through the outer rooms and corridors as they pushed the Scanii deeper within the fading sanctuary of the ancient ship. Many of the wide corridors now coursed with Axén as they flooded in. Sianda held her position behind a bulkhead, sealing the next ring as she retreated deeper with her two children and a few conscripts. The conscripts were only armed with sharpened metal spikes. These crude weapons were all that remained for many of the civilians inside. Her children were not fighters, and Sianda was not going to leave their side this time.

The door shuddered as the horde pounded their bodies against the great metal frame. Shouts rang out from behind one of the outer walls as a wave of Scanii defenders retreated, Rynan being one of them. After their last encounter, Rynan and their children remained with Sianda. The family was still grieving the death of their host Yamala. Now, a thick layer of metal separated the pair as Rynan and Sianda stood on opposite sides of the sealed barricade. Sianda realized with horror that the defenders had been fleeing from the grasp of death. Thousands of Axén had followed them here, and now they were pinned between the block and the executioner's axe.

"Rynan!" Sianda cried out.

She felt everything he was feeling at that moment. He sensed his demise was imminent. The next few moments would be his last. She would lose him to the Axén, and he would join Yamala as energy. Filling his mind with a sense of peace, he reflected on the time the three lovers had spent together, raising their children within this world.

"Sianda, take care of our boys." Sianda could hear the defenders' charge as they sought to preserve every precious second for the individuals inside. Rynan didn't hesitate, even as an unholy cry rang out in response. The horde showed no remorse as it swallowed the father of her children. Death was everything except silent.

Sianda gasped as she heard Rynan's mind screaming out with his final thought. Then her love's mind slowly faded away.

Sianda felt numb. Her children no longer had a father.

"Hang on! We are on our way!" Sarah's voice cut through the chaos. "Get everyone to the middle of the gathering chamber and lock the doors! Swim to the very center of the chamber! Touch nothing!"

Sianda looked at Ven and then at Zovair. She fought through the emotional shock and pain. "We need to go."

"Captain, we are approaching the grandfather ship," EV yelled. Sarah watched as the Pegasus approached the mayhem through the glass. The Pegasus' main display magnified the target destination within the enormous frame of the ship.

"Captain, we still need to get through. Almost all the Axén are in the ship already, but a few are still out here!" Dyami exclaimed.

"Ashley, provide some cover with everything you have left. EV, bring us in full throttle!" Sarah ordered.

The Pegasus dove toward the grandfather ship, pushing everything into the engines that she could spare. The clippers flew out in front and again engaged with the small group of Axén that remained between them and the grandfather ship, clearing a path for the Pegasus. The thirty-three clippers reconfigured, acting as a spear while the Pegasus dove toward the ship.

The spear point plunged through a ragged tear the Axén had made in the grandfather ship. The Pegasus slowed just before making contact, scraping the ancient ship's hull. EV held firm as he expanded the surface area of contact. Sarah could hear the shrill sound of metal grinding against metal, creating a bridge between the two ship frames.

"Kiah, dump everything now!"

An audible overload rang out as the BRIL reactor restrictors were removed. The raw power from the reactor surged through the skin of the ship as the tremendous stored energy was released all at once.

"Contact!" The reactor released every drop of energy as a massive surge erupted through both ships. The electrical shock struck the superstructure erupting in electrical lightning that surged through the old ship's frame and all its corridors. Sarah watched as the energy tore through her ship's systems. Acrid smoke and the smell of burnt wiring sizzled from the bridge's consoles. Every system on the Pegasus went dark as every last spark burst through the hulls of both ships.

The Pegasus was completely without power. The bridge was swallowed by darkness. Even the emergency lighting system had been damaged and was without power.

"Everyone alright?" Sarah asked within the darkened bridge.

Everyone was still alive as they checked in. The stations on the Pegasus had routed the surge around the crew members. They had equipped wetsuits for extra protection and had their rebreather masks, with lights, on hand. Everything fell quiet as the crew held their breath, listening for any sign of a living Axén.

Sianda had led the Scanii to retreat to the dark gathering chamber, illuminated only by the bioluminescent plants growing along the timeworn frame. "Swim to the very middle of the great hall. Stay as far as you can away from the walls," she sang. The pain of her loss was still fresh, but she pushed it aside as she fought for the remaining Scanii's survival.

She knew the plan. They would need to stay away from the structure of the great ship, the water surrounding them would be their only insulator against massive electrical fury. Ocean water is a horrible insulator but was still significantly less conductive than the frame of the great ship. Sarah had communicated the final details with everyone. As they barricaded the doors, Sianda had the strange sense of leaving the fate of their lives in the hands of a single person for a single moment. Despite Sarah being an alien, Sianda trusted her, even in this unforgiving circumstance. How ever this ended, she would remember this decision, this moment, for the rest of her remaining life.

A massive thud reverberated through the water as the Axén slammed their collective force on the doors of the gathering chamber. Sianda heard the horde writhing at all the doors of the massive chamber. They packed the halls just outside, raging as more bodies spilled blood into the water. They were feasting on the corpses of Scanii and Axén alike. The horde loomed just outside this last point of sanctuary.

Sianda heard one final scream as she realized another of her kin would never make it.

Then she heard the shout in her mind. "They are in the chamber!"

Sianda turned and saw several Axén racing for the group at the chamber's center!

Without a second thought, Sianda put herself between the Axén and her children. The Axén had already killed Yamala and Rynan. She would not let them take her children while she was still alive!

Sianda sensed already it was too late. A wave of Axén poured through the door now. Despite the pain coursing through her injuries, Sianda faced the darkness. She was going to push with everything she had left.

Sianda made peace with all the choices she had made in her life. She absolved herself of her regrets and thought about her return to energy. She saw her two sons, Zovair and Ven swimming just behind her. She, as a mother, had to protect them.

Then, a brilliant burst of sparks flared through the hull of the grandfather ship. The hull ignited in blue electricity. Sianda watched as most of the Axén were killed with the swift bolts of fury. The energy seemed to pour over the entire hull. It was more energy than she had imagined possible. The energy reached into most of the space in the gathering chamber, but it did not reach her kin. Her excitement was tarnished as she realized a handful of the Axén were still alive.

She gripped her spear as her knuckles paled. Then she saw Zovair and Ven swimming at her side. Their gaze held hope and resolve.

"We fight together!" Ven exclaimed.

"I agree. We hold here!" Zovair asserted.

Sianda felt her heart come back to life. Despite their losses, they would all fight to keep what they still had. She realized they were not alone. As they charged together, the civilians joined the fight. Just before they got there, the last few Axén turned visible and seemed to go limp.

They finished all the Axén left in the chamber.

The stillness held. Then Sarah heard Sianda's thought to all. "They are dead!"

In the darkness of the bridge, the crew let out shouts of relief and triumph. The clippers were still picking off a few Axén, but they were only stragglers. The Crichton pulled up behind the Pegasus.

"Sarah... I... That was incredible back there." Richard's voice reverberated with his amazement, even through the com channel that was echoing in Sarah's rebreather mask. The suit com was the only equipment still working on the Pegasus.

"Anyway, need a jump?" Richard laughed.

Sarah replied, "Yeah, that would be great." Her voice was shaky, with her emotions still running high.

"You pulled it off, Sarah! I am proud of you," Richard's voice cracked. "You did what I thought wasn't possible."

Sarah felt her father's words roll over her like a tide. She knew the words had a deeper meaning than what he was revealing. At that moment, she felt a lifelong trust form with her father. They were still standing.

"Sarah…" Dyami's voice cut across the bridge.

Then she saw the massive Axén, now arriving. They were fully visible, adding to the horror as they descended on the city, relishing in the death around them. They fed on the dead and were even larger than Ben had predicted. Sarah realized they were now totally defenseless against these new monsters.

After everything, there were no more moves left. The Pegasus was dead in the water, and the charge and restart would take longer than they would live. The Crichton could not outrun them. This was it. Checkmate.

Then, the darkness was broken by a flash of light.

The light shimmered as entities crossed the great Milky Way Galaxy. This was their moment in time. They felt the pull. This was where they were needed. The Europa crescent ring gate was just a tool for the loopens. Their will had brought them here to Violatis.

The behemoth Axén turned to face this new food source. They killed anything they wanted, and these new arrivals would be no different.

"NO! We need to stop them!" Ashley screamed as the behemoth Axén charged the loopens.

The loopens held their distance.

"They are distracting the Axén. We need to escape and regroup," Dyami suggested.

The thought raced through Sarah's mind as she calculated their next move. "Everyone, get to the…"

Then through the NIC glass, the crew saw all the Axén stop. Every one of the hundreds of behemoths, every one of thousands of Axén across the world that still were hidden, all stopped.

At first, Sarah thought the Axén were creating terror with their delay. They didn't move and remained motionless.

"Why don't they attack?" Richard's voice came in over the com.

"It's the loopens!" Ashley said as she returned from the connected space with Hot Wings between seconds. Suddenly it all made sense. "The Axén don't have a defense against the minds of the loopens."

"You mean they are trapping the Axén within their own minds?!" Sarah asked.

"That is exactly what's happening!" Ashley exclaimed.

"Whoa! That's… WOW," EV gasped.

The Axén remained frozen in the unbreakable trance. Although the night had been long, the task of killing thousands of motionless Axén still lay ahead.

RECOVERY

"So, the loopens are able to trap the Axén in this trance? For how long?" EV asked.

"Apparently, for as long as it takes. Jake told me that a small group of them are responsible for Axén stasis, and the loopens are collectively sharing that responsibility," Ashley said.

"We will need to work on eliminating as many as we can find. They don't belong here and are still a threat as long as any are left alive," Sarah said.

"The good news is that they are still organic beings. So, if they can't eat, they will starve to death after a few weeks," Ben added.

"That seems like a brutal way to go," Ashley said.

"Maybe it's not so bad if you're a horrible monster," Ben said, showing very little sympathy.

"There is still something that I don't understand. We saw loopens being hunted on Europa. Why didn't they stop the horn-heads from hunting them?" EV asked.

"It's an interesting question. I'm not sure of the full answer, but we did observe that the older the horn-heads became, the less effective they were at hunting loopens. They had both experience and speed on their side, but the larger animals never caught any loopens. In fact, we never saw any of the adults by the nest at all," Sarah explained.

"So, the loopens eventually wore through the minds of the older animals?" Kiah asked.

"Your guess is as good as mine," Sarah said.

"What do horn-heads have that the Axén don't?" EV asked.

"That is also a good question. Maybe thousands if not millions of years of evolution?" Sarah speculated.

"So, where do humans fit on that scale?" EV asked.

"Based on what I have seen, we are at the whim of the loopens,"

Ben explained.

"I guess we need to stay on their good side then," EV chuckled despite the frightening truth in his words.

Sarah felt overjoyed when she saw Syuk again and swam hard toward her. Against the odds, Syuk had survived the attack, and the fact that she was alive filled Sarah with elation.

Syuk felt Sarah's approach and didn't hesitate to embrace her. The two floated within the violet ocean, neither letting go of the other. Hell was behind them, and they both knew that challenges were ahead, but they relished this serene moment.

Sarah was the first to speak. "I was so worried about you when I saw you were on the front line… I am so sorry about Dac."

"I had an obligation. I did not tell you because I did not want you to focus on that. You had your crew to worry about," Syuk responded.

"I understand. I just…" Sarah could not find the right words.

"Sarah, thank you for saving my life and the life of my kin," Syuk's words were filled with gratitude.

"I know you have lost so many friends and kin. Are you going to be alright?" Sarah was a bit nervous to touch on the subject but deeply desired to help in any way she could.

"Eventually," Syuk's pain was fresh, but she knew it would fade with time.

"Syuk, I'm here for you, and I promise to help you and your kin in any way I can," Sarah said. "I am not going anywhere."

Ashley couldn't wait to get out of her wetsuit. She had been in it for forty-five hours trying to get the Pegasus reactor to charge and restart. Even with her breaks to sleep and see Jake in the mind space, her suit was now itching like crazy all of the time. After the Axén attack, Ashley set to work on resurrecting the Pegasus reactor. However, many of the survivors, including Sarah and Richard, had the grueling task of killing every last Axén in sight with the remaining clippers. Some of the rotting dead began to rise as putrefaction gases made the bodies buoyant, time taking its toll. Ashley had never been so glad to see ocean scavengers. In comparison with that task, she figured restarting the stubborn reactor and repairing and rebuilding the massive electrical damage was the better choice.

After printing and replacing almost everything using the Crichton for power, the BRIL reactor needed an infusion for it to restart the chemo-synthesis process. Luckily the Crichton had that answer, too, carrying the seed that would spark the Pegasus back to life. The hyper-compressed archaebacteria were carried through the cylinder that Ashley now held in her hand. She inserted the new material with a click. This was the third attempt, and they had already needed to produce more archaebacteria to even get this far. On Violatis, they also had another advantage over Europa. Both ships came printed standard with photovoltaic skin, allowing them to convert sunlight into energy. Of course, this only worked during daylight hours near the ocean surface. Now that the suns were rising high in the sky, Ashley hoped a bit of charge in the ship's batteries would be the key to her reactor restart puzzle.

"Alright, I'm giving it a try again," Ashley said.

"I'm ready on this end, on your mark," Kiah's voice came through the com.

"3...2...1...mark," Ashley called as her body tensed.

There was a thud before a soft whir. Then, the BRIL reactor came to life and arose from the ashes, the room filling with a comforting red glow. Power returned to a few critical systems Ashley had rebuilt for this very occasion, including full life support and water, hot water.

Ashley smiled to herself. "Looks like we got it!"

"Yeah. Didn't you say that you were going to fix the water heater control too?" Kiah asked. Ashley had been thinking the same thing.

"I did indeed!" Ashley exclaimed.

"Please have the first crack at it. I can wait for a bit," Kiah said.

Ashley's thought of a hot shower made her muscles burn with anticipation. Her body still needed rest outside of the mind space. Even though her mind could rest there, the physical toll was accumulating, and her body needed to recuperate.

Ashley felt weak after all the long hours. She looked down at her still-toned stomach, remembering her child with Jake was growing within. The child's presence had become more defined as time progressed, but still remained as an unborn mind within the connected space. Ashley wondered when their offspring would become conscious. Would it happen before the baby was even born?

Ashley finally made it to her quarters. All the lights and paneling remained off as she entered. The only light was sunlight washing through the NIC glass, casting purple ripple patterns across the walls.

With a grunt, she peeled off the wetsuit that had stuck to her skin in every way that it could. She stood there naked for a second giving her skin time to adjust to the cool air. She savored a breath as her tension began to subside. Now was her chance to see if the hot water worked. She crept into the shower as the water warmed. She had to make extra effort not to fall over after the many hours of constant use of her muscles.

Ashley did nothing but stand there for a long while, letting the water work through her tension. She was alive. The warmth danced across her skin. After her fingers began to prune, she finished her shower and put on her most comfortable pair of shorts and a shirt.

She lay on the bed and felt herself drift into sleep.

After ten hours, Jake woke Ashley with a kiss. After resting, her unconscious mind had wandered back to him in the connected mind space.

She felt his warm lips touch her back as she rolled over to face him. She could feel their child's energy, and the three seemed to bask in this moment of peace. If this were their life from now on, Ashley would cherish it. They would lead an extraordinary life tied to the extraordinary Hot Wings. They would be truly happy for as long as they were allowed to. Countless lifetimes would be possible in the mind space.

"Is it wrong to enjoy this?" Ashley remarked.

Jake looked at her, "What do you mean?"

"After all the trials, after all the sacrifice, you and I still have each other. Our futures are still in front of us. I feel the grieving all around us, but don't share in their deep personal pain," Ashley said softly.

"Ashley, this is not something you should feel guilty about. I see a person that is empathetic to the pain of others but is living in this wonderland," Jake looked around at the vast beach that now surrounded the bed they lay in. Jake looked her in the eyes. "It's ok to feel whatever it is that you feel."

Ashley nodded. "I just want to focus on our now."

Dyami was glad to see that Kydar and Onasa had survived the attack as his pupils approached the large port in the galley. He smiled as they swam up, just outside of the NIC glass. A stream from a single tear trickled down his face as his worry turned into joy.

"I am so glad to see the two of you…" Dyami said.

After the siege, all their emotions were raw and worn thin through the event. However, they had survived, and there was still life, still hope. Putting the Axén assault behind them was going to be a long road of emotional rebuilding. Surviving the ordeal was one thing, dealing with the years ahead as someone who had lived through that night, was going to be another. Dyami would be there for them, and they would get through it together. He sensed they would not be able to survive alone.

Kydar saw Dyami's tear. They knew that water was precious, water sustained all their lives, and Kydar nodded, understanding what it represented, even without ever being able to cry themselves. "We will make it." It was all they sang. Dyami marveled at the bright young host and the hope that surrounded them.

Onasa's face seemed to melt with emotions at that. She embraced Kydar, and Dyami touched his hand to the glass, wishing he could do the same in that moment. After several emotional seconds, they turned to Dyami.

"We would like to continue to meditate with you and learn more about the auras," Onasa sang.

"Of course, I'm not going to leave you two." Tears began to pour from both eyes now. "I'm here for you as long as you need me."

"That will be forever," Kydar replied.

Sianda returned with her children to their tribe's camp. The camp was littered with dead Axén and parts of clippers. It was almost unrecognizable except for a few patterns woven into the structures. Sianda felt deep sorrow for the loss of her mate Rynan and her host Yamala. However, mixed with that sorrow was a greater appreciation that her two boys were still alive.

Zovair shook his head. "Mother, what will happen to us now that Father is dead?"

"I am going to take care of you. I will never leave your side, ever again," Sianda embraced them both. She would always be there to protect them.

Ven was still processing their new reality. When he finally spoke, he sang out softly. "Father has returned to energy?"

Sianda nodded. "All life returns to energy, but he exists with us in our memories, and that can never be taken away." She knew that was a hard reality, but the reality that they had to deal with.

"Did he rejoin Yamala?" Ven song was almost a whisper.

"He did. They no longer have any need to separate," Sianda called back.

Sianda cleared away pieces of wreckage as she uncovered their home. There were only a handful of their tribe's kin that had survived. They would remain here now, in Tirilean. She was unsure who was behind the Axén, but she felt this was not over. The Scanii would no longer be able to stay hidden in what used to be paradise. They would need to embrace technology again, and they would need to be ready for what was next. She needed Sarah's help. She knew deep within her heart that Sarah would support them, and that realization gave her hope for the future.

CONNECTIONS

Richard could tell Luthor was only slightly pleased that he was still breathing.

"So, you guys neutralized the alien threat. Great job, Richard…" Luthor seemed to say it like he was reading boilerplate text. "Now, I need you to get your ass back here. How long will it take for you to build the gate?" Luthor looked as if he wasn't going to wait for the response.

"Luthor, we have tons of repairs and cleanup to complete before we can get started on the gate," Richard explained.

"So, next week sometime?" Luthor pressed. It was unreasonable, and Luthor probably knew that but didn't care.

"This will take months if I can get it to work at all with just NIC printed materials. Even with the help from Europa's gate research teams, this is no small undertaking," Richard responded.

"Richard, you own me one. Remember? How can I collect that debt if you're on the other end of this galaxy, sitting on your hands?" Luthor was not going to give an inch. Richard then thought, *What can he do from there? It was going to get done when it gets done.*

"Well, you could send me more material instead of us having to figure out what we can reclaim here," Richard said with a half-smile.

"Absolutely not. We are already way over budget on this one," Luthor said. Richard knew the money was not the obstacle here.

Richard decided this was his time to drop a bomb over the com. "Luthor, I will come back and pay my debt, but the Pegasus and most of her crew are staying here!"

"NO! THAT IS NOT AN OPTION!"

"Oh, I think it is an option. You see, we already got the message out to Sol TV, and they are excited about exclusive interviews with Sarah and the crew here exploring this new world." Richard let his words sink in a bit. "This is the biggest story ever for humankind, and they have some very critical details. They are going to run the story with or without your help. We set this up with your name on it!"

"There was no communication sent. How am I to believe anyone there contacted them?" Luthor barked.

Richard smiled. "We have some of the best scientists working on this mission. You don't think we know how to drop someone a message from across the galaxy?" he asked.

Luthor smirked at that and saw the point and the political advantage he dared not squander. "So, you do know how to play the game. Alright, you win. Just get back here when you can, and I get to dictate the narrative to the news organization," he said.

"Luthor, the narrative will be the truth, but you can operate within that," Richard said.

Luthor's face twisted slightly at that, "Alright, fine." Luthor knew he would get what he needed from Richard later.

Loopens are a bridge that brings conscious minds together. Perceptions can be shared and are fluid in the connected experience. Words are just the beginning of communication, and loopens thrive within the deeper connections that go beyond simple words.

It was a strange sensation, but Sarah was getting used to the control she had over the mental space. Her loopen had connected with her in a dream, and she recognized the connection, letting her mind accept this new presence.

Spirals of blue silk seemed to flow through the sky. This was a place she had dreamed of as a child. Patterns of light played off the floor where she stood, changing with the shifting fabric above. She saw pools of water that floated by in perfect spheres. Each held a myriad of tropical fish she had studied as a child. Above her, she could see an orca swimming through the waves of blue fabric. He was an individual she recognized before vanishing behind the blue silk veil.

At first, Sarah thought she was present with a single loopen in this grand space. Sarah had tried to recognize each loopen in the physical world, but other than Hot Wings, with his distinctive red coloration, and

Kite, with his recognizable mark, she had a hard time telling them apart. Loopens came in a variety of sizes and patterns, but to the untrained eye they look similar. However, here, the loopen she had connected with seemed to radiate a kind of energy that was distinct. Her heart seemed to fill with warmth as the creature playfully swam by. The name Radiance seemed to fit this peaceful creature.

Then another loopen appeared. The two loopens seemed to dance and play in the silk waves. Sarah marveled at their grace and felt a sense of great comfort as she watched. Someone else then appeared.

The person walked toward Sarah, and at first, Sarah did not recognize the stranger. Her features were familiar, but Sarah's mind struggled to remember any person that walked with such grace and beauty. Then the realization hit her like a bolt of lightning. It was Syuk. Her tail had been replaced with gorgeous legs and she was in a human form.

Sarah gasped as she realized what she was witnessing. Syuk was here and had taken a form of her choosing. Sarah felt her heart skip as Syuk sublimely moved toward her, an evening gown flowing across her elegant body.

"What do you think?" Syuk asked.

Sarah was struck speechless.

"That bad, huh?" Syuk teased.

"You look amazing," Sarah finally blurted out. Her mind still was spinning from what she saw, and she could not find any other words.

"Thank you," Syuk said. Her voice was as sweet as anything Sarah had ever heard, and her words flowed with perfect tone. "I wanted to try walking and talking like you do."

"You make it look so…" Sarah could not find the right word. She finally settled on the word "amazing" again.

Syuk seemed to smile at that.

"Sarah, I need to tell you something…" Syuk's words flowed together in perfect English.

Sarah's heart nearly leapt out of her chest. Sarah had not dared to wish before now. Every fiber of her being knew the words she wanted to hear. Every fiber of her being was anxious about what Syuk might say next. Syuk seemed to pause for a long time, and Sarah felt so much tension that it seemed to stretch on forever.

"Sarah I…" Syuk stopped again. Sarah could see she was struggling with her feelings. At that moment, Sarah could tell what was there. She had felt that same way only one other time in her life. Sarah made the leap as her lips met with Syuk's.

Sarah felt Syuk's very brief moment of surprise at the act. It quickly melted away into passion as she felt Syuk kiss her back. The embrace was exquisite, and Sarah felt a connection she had never imagined. She caressed Syuk's cheek with her hand as the kiss lasted longer than any in memory. Sarah knew now that anything was possible. After the longest moment in the history of time, the kiss finally stopped.

"How did you know?" Syuk asked.

Sarah smiled, and she kissed her again. Outside of the mind space, time stopped. Energy radiated from the two loopens as they facilitated this bond created from love.

"Syuk, I…" it was Sarah's turn to lose her words. She was over-whelmed with happiness. This experience was beyond anything she had ever dared to dream. Sarah felt Syuk's breath lap against her skin. She had always been attracted to Syuk's mind. This new way to touch, this new way to shift forms, this new experience had opened the floodgate in Sarah's heart.

"I guess it is possible for us in this universe," Syuk's words were like sapphire.

Sarah's gazed deep into Syuk's eyes. Many of her features were human, but she had the same generous eyes. They were here. Nothing could take this moment from the pair. This feeling would be remembered forever.

"Yes, I'm not going anywhere," Sarah reassured her.

"I am delighted to hear that. We need you here, Sarah," Syuk paused perfectly. "I need you here!"

Sarah just smiled and hugged her. "You have me!"

CRATER

"Alright, this has been bugging me. What the hell is generating all of that heat within the crater?" Anya said as she and EV combed through the recorded video of their fight against the Axén.

"Well, it saved our ass back there, but I haven't seen anything like this," EV said as he scrutinized the footage. He shivered at seeing a living Axén again, even through a holorecording.

"The Scanii told us that it appeared about six cycles ago. They presumed that it was some volcanic vent releasing pressure and the temperature would fall as time passed. They didn't have the tech to investigate deep within the chasm. I just don't buy that natural volcanic activity is causing this. The sensor readings do not match that theory," Anya said.

"Oh yeah, what is your grand theory, Sis?" EV snickered a bit, just as he had done since they were children.

"Well, rather than just guessing, let's find out! But, if I had to guess, whatever it is, it's artificial," Anya said.

EV knew it was in the cards to investigate the steam crater at some point but now understood Anya's concern. "You think it could be related to the Axén?" He shivered just with that thought.

"As they say, there is only one way to find out! Sianda did say the Axén have only appeared during the last few cycles. Based on the timing, I think it might be connected," Anya replied.

"Oh, shit… did you already tell the Skipper?" EV asked.

"Yeah, she knows," Anya nodded with conviction.

"Why am I always the last to know?" EV suddenly felt out of the loop.

"I just told you, didn't I! You're helping me on the damn project, aren't you?" Anya barked at him.

"That is why you needed my help?" EV asked.

"Well, Richard, Kiah, and Ashley are working on the ring gate. So, you were actually my fourth choice," Anya explained.

EV feigned an injury to his heart. Anya could not help but smile a bit at that.

"Evengii Balabanov, I'm not going to let you get out of this project that easily!" Anya exclaimed as she scolded him.

"Alright, what are we doing?" EV rolled up his sleeves.

"Well, we are going to do what we do best! We are going to build an exploratory drone," Anya explained.

"I can see why you wanted Ashley on this," EV commented.

After a few test runs, Anya and EV were finally ready for the Steam Runner's maiden voyage into the deep vents that extended further down into the crater. The crew had joined them on the bridge, and Syuk swam just outside the NIC glass as they prepared for this expedition into the unknown.

The drone pushed through the wall of steam and into the depths of the first hole. The walls narrowed as the Steam Runner descended into the turbulent vent. Descending further into the hole proved problematic against the pressure of the rising gases, and the drone struggled against the surge despite their preparation. Anya relied on the array of sensors that had been packed into the drone to navigate the twisting tube as the bubbles obscured the camera's view.

Sister and brother stared into the screen, waiting for anything to appear through the visual turmoil. Suddenly, an object came into view, and Anya saw with horror that her prediction was correct. There was a round artificial vent made of black metal with a series of small round holes. Each hole was about the size of a small coin, and steam escaped through them. "Oh, shit!" Anya felt the words in her gut as much as she said them. She could feel her stomach turn over and immediately regretted that her prediction was correct. They would need to cut their way through the vent to investigate further.

"Can we cut through that?" Sarah asked. Her face had a look of grave concern.

EV looked back and nodded. He had suggested modifying the cutting torch to add extra power, and now Anya was glad he had made those modifications.

"Alright, let's do it," Sarah confirmed.

EV made the cut, struggling against the steam still pouring from the vent. Eventually, he made a hole large enough for the body of the Steam Runner. The drone didn't get much further into the hole. Hundreds of smaller channels seemed to interconnect just before the vent. Sarah tried to imagine what she could be looking at.

"EV, let's see if we can cut our way through," Sarah ordered. She didn't see another way. Other than this vent, the steam tube itself was solid rock.

This time EV cut through the channels, trying to clear a path through. They seemed to be a twisted maze as he worked against them. The steam pouring from the channels was the source of the heat, and the alien material proved to be resistant to the torch. Then, they began to break through. Cool water poured out from the new opening.

The space they cut into was about the size of ten shipping containers, and it was immediately evident what it was. At the center was an Axén. This one was different than any they had seen before. It was a behemoth, connected with dozens of alien probes. It seemed to hang in the center of the room. The crew watched as the features seemed to shift slightly across the head. Sarah could tell that it was not yet dead, but like so many others they had seen, it appeared to be held in the trance by the loopens. A ripple seemed to walk across the silvery-red beast's skin.

"What are we looking at?" Sarah was the first to speak. There were no signs of any controls or panels in the chamber.

Ben was staring at the images on the main display with horrific fascination. "I think that we are looking at what built the Axén. Even now, it is trying to modify them to be better killers." The features of the creature shifted slightly again. It seemed to be minor changes, but over time they equated to something even more deadly than the previous iterations.

Suddenly the connection with the drone was lost.

"EV report," Sarah barked.

Then a massive thud could be felt through the entire Pegasus frame. Water pushed against the ship's hull as a dispersed shockwave hit the ship. The impact was significant despite the several hundred meters between them and the crater.

"It's gone!" EV said when he finally found the answer.

Sarah felt her stomach twist with anxiety and fear as she thought. *What the hell happened?*

"Steam Runner was destroyed?" Sarah asked urgently.

"All of it is gone," Kiah was in awe as she looked at the readings. "There was some type of energy surge and explosion at the site."

"Captain, I detected a transmission sent before the explosion!" Ashley exclaimed.

"Do we have the content of that message?" Sarah asked.

"We have something, but we currently can't decrypt or translate it," Ashley said.

"Was it reporting back?" Syuk asked.

"Probably," Ashley said.

"Then they will be coming," Syuk sang.

"The gate will be our ticket out when we need it. It must be built and soon," Sarah stated.

"The loopens will show us the way," Syuk sang. A group of loopens swam past the Pegasus toward the destroyed facility. "This planet has been our home for thousands of cycles. But they have shown us the way before." She nodded at the group swimming quickly along.

"Well, let's go see what the loopens are trying to show us. Ashley, how is Old Rusty?" Sarah asked.

"He is still leading the clippers," Ashley said with pride. Old Rusty had taken some damage during the defense against the horde but had never quit. After a small patch and a punk graphic, Ashley had sent him back into the action.

"Have Old Rusty lead on. Let's have a look at what is left," Sarah ordered.

There was nothing left except a hole. Sarah could tell that the entire structure was vaporized just from the footage on the Pegasus main display. Then she saw something she didn't expect.

NEW NEST, OLD NEST

After a busy first few hours, the loopen nest was coming along nicely. They were building their homes on Violatis, right in the newly formed crater where the Axén genetics lab had been. The Scanii saw it as a sign they could stay, at least for a while. Hopefully, they would have enough time to say goodbye to this beautiful world they had called their home for so many centuries.

After many days, the ocean scavengers of Violatis had the cleanup almost done. The city of Tirilean was being refreshed. It was just in time. The remaining Scanii returned to the city now, but many more had died. Entire tribes were lost, never to be seen again.

At this point, Sarah could tell this loopen nest was more elaborate and complex than the one they had seen on Europa. The nest did contain the same pods as before, but their structures seemed to grow differently in the light. The loopens seemed to relish the warmth of the water and the suns' light, and Sarah began to wonder if they were even originally from Europa. They seemed to find a home where ever they went.

Hot Wings always stuck out in the crowd, but now Sarah suddenly started recognizing each loopen by their personalities as much as their unique skin patterns, especially her loopen, Radiance. Despite their deepening connection, there were still so many loopen secrets that Radiance did not reveal to Sarah, and Sarah found them even more fascinating. Sarah also had been reunited in the mind space with the orca she knew as Keenan. At first, Sarah thought it could be just memories she had of the whale she had known for years, but as the days went on, it became increasingly evident that he was his living self, dropping by on his own terms. Sarah was unsure how this was possible since no one had ever seen a loopen on Earth.

The ring gate construction was now underway, still months away from completion but a solid start. Ashley and Richard had devised a reclamation plan for the destroyed drones, and most of their material was reformed into the growing crescent structure. Richard kept saying there was no way to know if it would even work, but Sarah knew her father would find a way eventually. As fantastic and horrific as their adventure had been and how close the crew had become, Sarah started to face the reality that not everyone would stay with her crew after completing the gate.

"You're going back to Angi and your children. Aren't you?" Sarah asked.

Ben nodded. "Yeah, as soon as we finish the gate and get a replacement here." He looked at her for a moment. Sarah could tell in his eyes that this was not easy for him. They had all survived great hardship and forged relationships that would last their entire lives.

"We are going to miss you," Sarah said.

"I know. But you have to hope you can get someone better, right?" Ben asked.

Sarah could only shake her head. Ben had been one of the finest individuals she had ever known. Just the thought of him leaving tore at her. "I'm going to miss you." Sarah hadn't known him before joining this crew, and now she could not imagine the Pegasus without him. He had become one of her greatest friends, and she wasn't alone in that feeling. His work, knowledge, and dedication saved many lives, including every life aboard the Pegasus.

"I will stay in touch," Ben said.

Sarah only nodded. She was not going to stop him. He was returning to his family, and as much as she needed him here, she wouldn't ask him to stay and possibly never see them again. That was not a sacrifice she was willing to ask of this man that had fallen into this situation. "Thank you, Ben..."

"I heard EI was thinking of sending Dr. Nidal Rossi. From what I have heard, he is amazing at his work," Ben said.

"I'm sure we will be in good hands with him. When you return, please hug your kids for me and tell them how you saved the Pegasus. You helped to save this entire crew and planet... they deserve to know," Sarah said.

Ben smiled a bit at that. "I will be sure to tell them the truth."

"So, you're just ditching me on this world," Anya accused.

"Hold on there. You could come back to Europa if you wanted to," Richard explained.

"Pfissst.. Why would I do that and miss all this fun?" Anya asked.

Richard just gave her a look.

"What does that asshole Luthor think he has on you anyway?" Anya asked.

"He went to bat for us at the council. It's a debt I owe him. They got us help when we needed help. Maybe they didn't intend to send the loopens, but without them preparing the gate for another transport, we might not have survived," Richard said. He didn't like the man either, but facts were facts.

"So, you're just going to go back to do what he tells you to do?" Anya wanted him to stay but was being cagy about it.

"I will, within my morals, yes. Luthor knows that," Richard responded.

"So, I guess we are back to you ditching me on this world!" Anya pressed.

"I am sorry for leaving you here," Richard sincerely apologized.

"Alright, fine. I guess you are off the hook," Anya conceded.

"Anya, you are rough around the edges at times, but the fact is that I couldn't have done this without your help. You came with me on one of the most dangerous journeys a human has ever faced and asked for nothing in return," Richard said.

"Don't make me hit you," Anya said as she blushed a little.

Richard laughed, "It would be an honor."

With that sarcastic remark, Anya hugged Richard.

Kiah had been waiting on this call from Earth Dock. She had not spoken to Mel since she had left Earth Dock and was excited to reconnect with him again after all these weeks. While on this mission, she realized how important he was in her life, and she decided to return to Earth and accept his marriage proposal.

Kiah was torn about leaving the crew, especially Sarah and EV, who had been her friends and colleagues for longer than she could remember. But seeing the face of death, she began to realize how life could be extinguished in an instant, and she wanted more in her life than just the adventure. She could tell that Sarah was stricken by her decision to leave, but Sarah had never confronted her about her choice.

Kiah sat in the briefing room, waiting for a moment as the signal connected. The screen flashed, and Melindro was there, sitting in his home at Earth Dock, a vast star-scape stretched out behind him.

"Kiah! I am so glad to see you! After I had heard the Pegasus had disappeared, I had been so worried about you!" Mel exclaimed.

"I'm so glad to see you too! I have thought about you every day since we left! I love you," Kiah replied.

"I love you too, Kiah Spearman," Mel said and then paused. "EI had told the public that it was just a communication problem with your team, but it was obvious that was not the whole truth. On the day I was going to talk to you, they just said I couldn't. Then when the entire inter-stellar communication network crashed, they finally admitted that you were off in some far-away system," Mel finished.

"Yeah… This mission… I don't even know where to begin," Kiah admitted. "I am just so glad I can see and talk to you again."

Melindro smiled at that. "I am glad that you are safe," he said.

"Mel, I have seen some awful things out here, and it has helped me to realize what is important in my life," Kiah took a deep breath and let it out slowly. "You have always been there for me since we met, and all I have been doing is running away. I know I hurt you when you proposed, and I told you that I would have to think about it. It was nothing you did. I think that I was just scared to grow old with someone. Now, I realize that growing old with someone is something I shouldn't have been afraid of. Melindro Rubert Jones, it would be my greatest honor to be your wife. I will marry you!" Kiah said.

Kiah spent so many nights thinking about this moment, this chance to see him and tell him those words. She had imagined so many times the look of elation on his face, the shared happiness they would feel together at this very moment. Those images are what had kept her going, had kept her fighting through the darkness. But what happened next was not what Kiah had imagined.

The unexpected words spilled from Mel's soft lips. "I have had time to think about it too, and I think I was premature in asking you to marry me."

Kiah felt her heart twist with pain in her chest.

"Kiah, I felt so much pain when you left. Then they told me that I couldn't even speak to you. I have had so many sleepless nights wondering if you were alright. Wondering if I would ever see you again and, if I did, would I ever be a priority in your life. I struggled with this for so long now. The feelings that I have aren't your fault. You have been doing amazing things and have made a tremendous mark in history. I care about you so much but will the love I feel for you torture me? Is it going to stand in the way of your potential achievements? I'm not sure that I can live with that. You have so much to offer the galaxy, and I can't ask you to give that all up because of me," Mel said.

Kiah only felt the growing numbness as the words echoed in her mind. "Mel, I don't want to do all this alone. You said you loved me. Is that not enough?" she finally asked.

"Kiah, you never have done it alone. Your crew depends on you, and so does all of humanity. What you have done, what you have the potential to do… I am not going to be the reason you give that all up. I can't be that reason," Mel said.

"Doesn't the way I feel mean anything?" Kiah's voice cracked with deep hurt.

Melindro's face twisted with pain at that comment. He just repeated, "I can't…"

Every ounce of the joy left their interaction, replaced with pain. Kiah felt a deep emptiness now. She wanted to scream. She wanted to cry. It felt like part of her soul had been ripped away. She just shook her head and couldn't think of another word.

"Kiah, you need to live your life. I can't be the reason that you give all that up. It would be best if you stayed with the people that need you. I couldn't live with myself if I took that away from you," Mel said.

Kiah could not respond. She just stared at the floor as silent tears ran down her face.

"I'm going to let you go. Please talk to Sarah. I know she will help you get through this," Mel said soothingly. The tone did not even register with Kiah, and the transmission was lost after another moment.

SOL TV LIVE FROM VIOLATIS

"We interrupt our regularly scheduled programming with Breaking News!" The Sol TV news bulletin flashes across the broadcast with a red graphic.

Frank Stone appeared on the screen, "We just have received a historical announcement from our sources within Earth Initiative. An EI team has made first contact with an intelligent alien species for the first time in human history. The crew of the Pegasus facilitated this contact during the course of their latest mission! We are just receiving the details on this monumental discovery since the Pegasus was able to re-established communications with Earth Initiative. The crew reports they are currently safe, and this species is non-hostile." Frank seemed to be in a bit of shock as he read on, "This marks a tremendous leap for our understanding of the universe and the life inside it. Again, if you are just tuning in, an EI team has made contact with non-hostile intelligent alien life!"

The information was now public. This broadcast was going to be forever carved into history.

"Joining me now is Earth Initiative Secretary of Council, Luthor Hymoon. Thank you for joining us, Mr. Secretary," Frank said.

The screen split, and Luthor joined Frank on the broadcast.

"Thank you, Frank," Luthor said smoothly.

"Secretary, with news like this, there are so many questions. Can you give us some details and elaborate on what this news means for humanity as a whole?" Frank asked.

"Certainly, Frank. While on its mission, the submersible Pegasus and her crew unexpectedly traveled across our galaxy from Europa to another world. The crew had discovered a piece of technology on Europa, not previously known to man, that facilitated this long-distance travel. Our scientists, including council member Richard Triv, were able to re-establish communications with the Pegasus crew after they ascertained their position in our galaxy. At that point, we in the council learned that they had made contact with this new species, and the crew had already established a trusting diplomatic relationship with the alien species known as the Scanii. From that point, the council supported the Pegasus crew and further solidified our trusting relationship with this alien race," Luthor explained.

"That is amazing! I would have figured this type of relationship would take time. Especially communication between a new race and humans. How did the crew communicate and establish this trusting relationship with this species so quickly?" Frank asked.

"That is an excellent question, Frank. In this case, the trust was established as a circumstance of necessity. At first contact, an individual Scanii saved the life of one of the crew members. It was a selfless act toward a species the Scanii had never encountered. Later, the crew discovered the Scanii had a way of communicating with other intelligent life, including humans. The Scanii offered graciously to help the crew, asking for nothing in return. Later a perilous situation occurred, and Captain Jake Riley sacrificed himself to save the life of Scanii children. He made this decision freely, and the Scanii honored his selfless act. These events cemented a bond between the crew and the Scanii on the world of Violatis," Luthor replied.

"Secretary, tell me more about Captain Riley's death. How, in fact, did he die?" Frank asked.

"There was another predatory alien species present on Violatis. Both the crew of the Pegasus and the Scanii worked together to neutralize the threat presented by that species. Unfortunately, before they could do so, Jake lost his life. However, I'm glad to report that there were no further human casualties, and the remaining crew is safe," Luthor replied.

"Of course, there is still classified information regarding this mission, but is there anything else that you can share at this time about the Pegasus and their current situation?" Frank asked.

"Yes. The Earth Initiative council has convened on several occasions, and they have agreed that Sol TV can interview the crew of the Pegasus directly. I have also seen to it that certain videos and images are to be released to the public regarding the Scanii and the world of Violatis. I want the public to know what is going on. Of course, we still need to protect this crew, so more sensitive details will be omitted, but

I promise to share everything I can as we move forward with this mission," Luthor replied.

"So, they aren't coming back yet?" Frank asked.

"Our well-trained crew has proven their ability to establish and maintain a high level of trust and mutual cooperation with the Scanii. With the present situation, most of the crew will remain in place to continue forging that relationship with additional help from EI specialists. At this time, only a few of the original crew are planning to return to Earth, and it will be their choice to do so," Luthor replied.

"Secretary, it has been a pleasure to speak to you today, and I will be holding my breath with the rest of the world as we await the interviews with the Pegasus crew," Frank finished.

Luthor smiled and nodded with smooth politician practice. "The pleasure is mine, Frank. I will be in touch to arrange the interviews soon."

The broadcast fades to black.

"Now, Sol TV, in conjunction with the Associated Press, will be interviewing the crew of the Pegasus on the ocean world of Violatis," said the disembodied voice through the broadcast as images and graphics flashed across the screen. "Stay tuned for interviews with Captain Sarah Triv, Lieutenant Ashley Martab, and the Pegasus' pilot Evengii Balabanov." The broadcast shifts to the familiar presence of Ara Ayad as she sits comfortably on an interview couch across from a large display.

"Welcome all to this historic event. In just a moment, Sol TV will connect with the Pegasus crew located over thirty-one thousand light years from Earth on the world known as Violatis. This story of humanity's first contact with an intelligent alien species is wonderful. Remember, if you have missed any previous Sol TV reports, you can always re-watch the previous content on the Sol TV network."

"Joining me now via the com feed is the pilot of the Pegasus, Evengii Balabanov. Welcome to the program EV," Ara said as the screen splits, showing a grinning EV on the right.

"Thanks, Ara. Before we start, I just wanted to tell you I am a huge fan," EV said.

"That makes two of us. I have read the available reports, and what you and your crew have experienced and accomplished is incredible. I'm honored to be able to speak with you now," Ara replied.

"I'm fortunate to be a part of this crew. We look after one another," EV said.

"You have been serving as the Pegasus pilot for this mission. Can you tell us more about what that was like?" Ara asked.

"This trip has been something else! It has been beyond anything I have ever done, both captivating and frightening. I have seen many amazing things from my spot on the bridge. Communicating and sharing thoughts and experiences with the Scanii is beyond words. This crew is made up of the best of humanity, and that is how we did what we did. Sarah, Jake, and Ashley all contributed to the deep and peaceful connections we established with the Scanii in a very direct and real way. It is challenging to describe the intensity of the situations that we had to face. I did my best to pilot the Pegasus under the Skipper's guidance, and everything worked out," EV replied.

"You mentioned being frightened, was that fear because of Captain Riley's death?" Ara asked.

"It started with that, yes. I only met Jake Riley as we began this mission, but it was clear from the beginning that he was the right person for the job. When he died, it was horrific and shocking. I have served with Sarah for many years and knew she could lead this crew, but taking command in the face of such a tragedy was beyond challenging. However, Sarah has a strength of character that allowed her to fill the role and keep the crew together as we moved forward. We couldn't have survived without her leadership and guidance as we faced the darkness," EV said.

"The darkness?" Ara asked.

"The entities that took Jake's life. I apologize, Ara, I can't go into more details about that at this time," EV replied.

Ara nodded. "Tell us more about your interactions with the Scanii."

"They are a wonderful and generous race of beings! It was marvelous how quickly it all happened. We were able to communicate with them right away. We almost instantly saw how much we had in common with them, despite our two species coming from vastly different worlds and historical backgrounds." EV chuckled, "On top of all that, they are now the best swimmers I know and are fun to be around! I felt a strong connection to them," EV said.

Ara could tell that EV was not sharing something. Despite the positivity in his words and expression, she recognized an underlying pain in his voice. She knew that specific topics were off-limits for the sake of the interview, but her curiosity was piqued. Her following words were off from the original script.

"EV, what happened with the Scanii after Captain Riley's death?" Ara asked.

EV paused then, finding the words he could share. Earth Initiative clearly didn't want to disclose the story about the Axén horde or the potential threat the Scanii faced. That information was still considered classified since they didn't know more about the Axén and their origin. EI still held the position that they did not want to appear hostile in the face of this unknown adversary and didn't want to panic the general public with information they simply didn't have. For EV, the horror of losing so many was wrenching. He personally had felt connected to the Scanii and their ocean lifeline. New friends had perished, and he was still struggling with that reality.

"Ara, I… I'm not going to be able to answer that at this time," EV finally said.

Ara wanted to probe deeper, but his answer gave her more than she had expected. She could tell by his short response and facial reactions to the question that something more had happened and that it was obviously a painful topic beyond the surface layer he was allowed to share.

"My apologies, EV. Let's move on to the last question," Ara said, trying to shift gears. "Will you be staying on Violatis with the Pegasus, and do you ever plan on returning to Earth?"

"I will be staying with Sarah and other members of the crew as we continue to build a relationship with the Scanii. I feel so connected to all of them, and they have become my family. In addition to that, it would be hard to see my sister for the holidays if I left since she is also staying here on Violatis. This is where I belong," EV replied.

"That is wonderful to hear, Evengii. I wish you all safe travels!" Ara exclaimed.

"Thanks, Ara," EV replied

The broadcast fades to black.

"Welcome back to Sol TV. Joining me now is Lieutenant Ashley Martab from the Pegasus. Welcome, Ashley," Ara said into the camera.

Ashley appears on the screen and smiles. "Thanks for having me, Ara."

"We have already spoken with EV, but in your own words, can you tell us what it has been like on this mission?" Ara asked.

"Of course. I have had so many unique experiences since arriving on Europa that first day. Being unexpectedly thrown across the galaxy feels like just a small part of it at this point. This mission has reminded me time and time again of what it means to be alive. So many things I have experienced have helped reshape my understanding of myself and the universe. Meeting the Scanii, interacting with them and realizing how much they are like us, participating in how they live, and observing the peaceful path they choose. I have never felt so connected and hopeful as I do now," Ashley replied.

"You had a very unique experience when first contact occurred with the Scanii. Can you tell us about that?" Ara asked.

"Yes, of course. The first time the Scanii made contact with us, an individual named Syuk saved my life. I had been investigating an underwater cave when a sudden collapse trapped and damaged the Swift Sphere I was piloting. I swam toward the surface but was ensnared by underwater plant growth. She arrived just in time and cut me free. I would not be alive without her intervention," Ashley replied.

"What happened next?" Ara asked.

"After the first encounter, Syuk disappeared for a little while. We were aliens in their world, and they were unsure of our intentions. After all, they didn't know if we were friends or invaders. She later came back with another Scanii named Sianda, and they graciously offered to help our crew. They were the most sincere and selfless acts I have ever witnessed. Some humans are like that, but every Scanii I have ever encountered seems to radiate that same selfless sincerity. They work to live in peace and harmony and have done so for centuries. That fact is apparent by their actions," Ashley replied.

"So, you never felt any hostility or fear from the Scanii, despite being outsiders in their world?" Ara asked.

"No, every single Scanii I have encountered helped us, and I trust many of them with my life," Ashley replied.

Ara shifted her questioning. "You had served with Captain Jake Riley for many years before this mission. His death must have been tough on you. How have you been able to deal with that loss?" Ara asked.

"Jake is still with me. He is forever a part of me, and I will never let go of his spirit and wisdom for as long as I live. I find comfort in that as we continue on this journey," Ashley replied.

Mind altering, consciousness saving, and interstellar telepathic aliens were not something that Earth Initiative wanted to be public knowledge. A few images of the cute little loopens were released publicly with other pictures from the mission, but nearly all of the details of their abilities were deemed classified. To the general public, they were simply a new cute little alien from Europa that was overshadowed by the contact with the Scanii. Ashley was not permitted to explain her continued connection to Hot Wings and Jake to the public audience at this time.

"I understand," Ara said. She was not going to push that sensitive topic any further. "The Pegasus traveled across the galaxy, hundreds of thousands of light years beyond where anyone had traveled before. This was done without the aid of any other ship. How was this epic journey even possible?" Ara asked.

"We are still working to understand how the technology fully works. The traditional way humans have approached interstellar travel involves folding space but requires a set point on the other side to act as an anchor. With this method, the full distance still needs to be traveled by conventional propulsion, which takes time. Once the far point is established, it still requires a tremendous amount of power. The larger the hole and the longer the distance, the exponentially more power the journey takes for a ship or communication stream. That is why it is difficult even reaching tens of light-years from Earth. The new gate we found seems not just to fold space but somehow manipulates the very fabric of the universe," Ashley replied.

"Is that why the Earth communications system went down when EI first established a link with the Pegasus com satellite?" Ara asked.

"Yes, even though a communications link is just a microscopic fold in space, the thirty-one thousand light years was more than the Earth communications system could handle," Ashley explained. "It was a small miracle it worked at all!"

"Now you are in the process of building another one of these gates on Violatis?" Ara asked.

"Yes, we are. We hope to use it, to send some of our people home," Ashley replied.

"Is this technology something Earth Initiative will start using to facilitate all space travel?" Ara asked.

"It is too early to tell. We aren't sure yet if we can replicate this technology, and more testing will be required even if we can build another gate. We are still in the process of taking baby steps, and the use of this technology will depend on our results," Ashley replied.

"Once the gate is completed and if it can send you home, will you use it to return to Earth?" Ara asked.

"Ara, after everything I've experienced, I believe my home is with this crew. There might be a day I return to Earth, but not in the foreseeable future. I belong here," Ashley replied.

"Ashley, before I let you go, is there anything else you would like to share," Ara asked.

"I just want to share one last thought. I want to stress the importance of the relationship with these Scanii. Our relationship with them is precious and has been built on mutual trust. I know that in the past, humans have struggled to understand one another over minor differences. There was so much war and blood before we finally learned to live together. These Scanii are different from us in appearance and history, yes. But they have already extended to us their understanding and peace. I ask that we, as humans do the same. We can learn from our past and not repeat our mistakes," Ashley finished.

"Ashley, thank you for your time and wisdom," Ara said.

"Thanks, Ara," Ashley said.

"Coming up, we have an interview with Captain Sarah Triv. We will be back shortly," Ara said as the broadcast faded to black.

"We have already spoken to Evengii Balabanov and Ashley Martab, and if you missed those interviews, be sure to check them out on Sol TV network. Joining me now is the captain of the Pegasus, Sarah Triv. Welcome, Sarah," Ara said.

"Thanks for speaking with me, Ara," Sarah said.

"Sarah, I have had so many wonderful interviews with you over the years, and you have always been a great guest. Now, you have been thrust into this key position and aren't just leading the Pegasus crew but representing all of humankind in interacting with the Scanii. Just thinking about the implications of that boggles my mind. I guess my first question is, how are you doing?" Ara finally asked.

Sarah laughed a bit as she said, "Well, Ara, I am doing good. My crew has done an outstanding job with the challenges that we have faced, and they have performed exemplary. With their efforts and the Scanii's help, we have made it through some difficult times. We have had losses along the way but I'm very grateful to be here today with my crew." Sarah selected her words carefully. They had all experienced significant loss and tragedy with the attack on Tirilean, but she wasn't allowed to share any information about the massacre directly with the public. She was told that more facts would come out in time, but the sensitive nature of releasing such information could cause panic in the general public and possible resistance to the relationship with the Scanii. Public outcry and xenophobia needed to be avoided, and she would do her part to prevent that outcome.

"I'm sure it was hard for you to take over after Captain Riley's death. Can you tell me how that transition affected you?" Ara asked.

"This was the first time I had ever lost a crew member. It was agonizing. I felt a deep pain and a great void with Jake's absence. The realization that I needed to fill that role was intimidating," Sarah said.

"Your crew means a great deal to you. I know you have been on many missions with Evengii Balabanov and Kiah Spearman over the years. But Ashley Martab, Ben Rapner, and Dyami Swiftwater had not worked with you until this mission. How did they handle the transition?" Ara asked.

"I knew the crew was feeling immense loss and pain, and I knew I had to embrace the position of captain. I always knew EV and Kiah would stand by my side. But after the tragedy, Ashley, Ben, and Dyami each told me they trusted me, would support me, and wanted me to lead them. At that point, I knew we would make it through together," Sarah said.

"After speaking with EV and Ashley, I know they are staying with you on this continuing mission. What about the others?" Ara asked.

"Dyami has told me he has strong reasons for staying with us. Anya said she wouldn't be leaving. Ben will return home once we have a suitable replacement. I have already spoken to him about that. He has a family and needs to return to them. Richard is returning to his duties on the EI council on Earth. I will not speak for Kiah. This decision has so many considerations, and it is up to each individual to decide their own path," Sarah said.

"Speaking of paths, what are your plans for the future, Sarah?" Ara asked.

"At this point, Ara, I have found everything I'm looking for right here. There are people I will miss, including my father Richard, once he is gone, but I will never leave this crew. They have become a part of me. Staying is what my heart is telling me to do," Sarah said.

Ara nods. "So where does the mission go from here?" Ara asked.

"We still have many untraveled roads with the Scanii. We are working on a future where we can all live together and thrive because we rely on each other. History has shown us that total harmony is always an unrealized dream. But it's a dream that is always worth every ounce of effort we put in to attain it. With the Scanii's help, that dream is closer than ever before, and I'm going to dedicate my life to reaching that dream of harmony," Sarah said.

"Sarah, I want to wish you the very best this universe has to offer, and I hope I can speak with you again soon," Ara said.

"Ara, I'm sure we will speak again," Sarah said as she nodded.

The broadcast slowly fades to black.

FAREWELL

The light from the closest stars warmed Ben's face as he closed his eyes and let the moment wash over him. This was his final day on Violatis, his last day on this great adventure. For six months now, he had the overwhelming desire to return home. Now that his departure was close at hand, he recognized how much this trip had changed his perspectives on life. On this world, he had experienced great tragedy and death, but beyond that, great triumphs. Ben had formed unbreakable bonds, not just with people, but with beings from other worlds. His time here would be something he would never forget.

Ben opened his eyes and was still sitting on the spit of white sand that jetted out from the island he was on. The wind seemed to play across his hair as it gently pushed past him and into the vegetation along the shoreline. The stars' light played off the broad leaves, and the mixture of red and blue light made everything glow in an array of vibrant colors. Just offshore, Ben could see the Pegasus anchored and silhouettes of a few Scanii playing by the ship's hull.

This small chain of islands held many mysteries, and they were virtually unexplored. The Scanii lived their lives in the ocean, never venturing past the shore. These islands held a sense of awe and wonder. Ocean life was abundant just offshore, and coral structures provided countless creatures' homes. This breath of life was untouched by humans; however, each creature here was intimately known by the Scanii.

Ben saw someone approaching as he scanned the horizon. Dyami walked toward him lazily as the ocean washed against his bare feet. He smiled after seeing that Ben was watching his approach.

The smile was genuine, but there was a sense of sadness behind his smile that was reflected on Dyami's face.

"Hey, Ben," Dyami said as he walked up beside him, and their gaze wandered toward the ocean's horizon.

"Hey," Ben replied. He didn't know what else to say, and they stood silently for a moment.

"I bet you are excited to see Angi and your children again. This reunion has been a long time coming," Dyami said.

"Yeah, just a few more hours now. It feels like I have been gone so long," Ben replied.

"You nervous about going through the gate?" Dyami asked.

"Yeah, a bit. Richard and Ashley have tested it with other lifeforms inside the Crichton, but being the first human to be sent back through... It feels a bit like I am jumping from a cliff and hoping to grow wings on the way down," Ben said.

Dyami nodded. "It will be ok."

"Yeah, I trust them with my life," Ben replied. "I trust everyone here with my life... Leaving is not easy for me." Ben turned and looked at Dyami.

"I know. We will be sure to stay in touch. You will always be a part of this crew," Dyami replied.

Ben gazed around the pristine shore, "I'm going to miss this place. There is something... magical about this world."

Dyami wrapped his arm around Ben's shoulder and squeezed gently. "C'mon, we need to get you home." He smiled again at Ben, reassuring him that this was not the end. It was just a new beginning.

Sarah studied Kiah's face as she sat beside her at the dining table. After the shocking news that Melindro had ended his romantic relationship with Kiah, Sarah tried to do everything to support Kiah. Sarah had been the shoulder to cry on, but she knew Kiah needed room to find her path. This transition would be difficult for Kiah. After weeks when Melindro failed to contact Kiah, the relationship appeared to be over in a tragic fashion.

Kiah looked at Sarah before speaking, "Sarah, I'm still returning to Earth."

Sarah did not say anything and waited patiently for the full explanation.

"I know that it's probably over with Melindro, but that does not change the fact that I still want to have my own family and my own children," Kiah explained. "I just don't see how that is possible here. I know that if I stay now, I will never leave. Knowing the dangers out here, I would never be able to raise children in this environment."

Sarah gave a knowing nod. She gazed into Kiah's eyes and could tell the decision was final. Sarah had known this was a possibility, and she ignored the twisting in her gut. She would lose close contact with one of her deepest friends, and that reality was hard. "I understand." Sarah choked out the words trying not to reveal the hurt. It didn't work.

Kiah moved from her chair and hugged Sarah as a few stray tears rolled from both their eyes.

"I could come back someday," Kiah tried to reassure Sarah, but neither of them really believed that was a possibility in the future.

Sarah nodded but did not speak as the embrace subsided.

"Sarah, we have been friends for so long. This isn't going to come between us," Kiah said.

Distance often changes a relationship, and they both knew things wouldn't be the same. They would always be friends, but they would not see each other every day. That daily support would end.

"We each search for happiness in our own way. I know you will find what you are looking for, Kiah. I will always be your friend," Sarah finally said.

"So... you and Syuk?" Kiah asked.

The sadness evaporated from Sarah's face as she smiled brightly, thinking about Syuk. The last several months had been the most exquisite time in Sarah's life, and the blossoming relationship was beyond anything she could have imagined. She was sharing thoughts, sharing entire worlds, with someone who connected with her on levels she had never explored before. She was living a reality far beyond a dream.

"Kiah, I never thought anything like this would have happened to me. She just came out of the blue," Sarah said.

Kiah rolled her eyes a bit at the pun but immensely enjoyed it. "I know. You two will take good care of each other."

"Kiah..." Sarah's mind returned to the current topic.

"Sarah, you are like the sister I never had. We are family, and I will never let that go," Kiah said.

The crew's trip to the islands ended as Ben and Dyami entered the bridge of the Pegasus. They were the last to return, and now it was time for them to return to Tirilean and to the gate. Ashley and Richard were still there finishing the preparations on the gate and prepping the Crichton for Richard, Ben, and Kiah's departure home.

Dr. Nidal Rossi had arrived just over a week ago, traveling through the Europa gate. Dr. Rossi intercepted Ben before he could take his seat. "I reviewed your logs again, Ben, and I have a few questions for you. Do you have a moment to explain a few details to me in the lab?"

"Wait! While I have you all here, I need to tell you something," Kiah said. She stood there for a moment, gathering everyone's attention. "I'm going back to Earth with Richard and Ben. I have had time to think about this and decided to return with them." There were a few surprised looks but mostly understanding nods.

"Everyone here has become my family... except for Dr. Rossi. Sorry, Doc, I only have known you for a few weeks." There were a few chuckles as Kiah continued. "I just need another type of adventure in my life, and after what we have been through... I need a change."

"We understand, Kiah, and we all love you. You will be a great mother someday," EV said. After the words came out of his mouth, he flinched, afraid he had over-shared something personal. The look on Kiah's face told a different story, and it was undeniable that she was touched deeply by his words.

"Ben, shall we," Dr. Rossi insisted. Ben nodded. He took a moment to look at each of the crew. His eyes met with Kiah's, and he felt a wave of comfort, knowing she would be there with him as they passed through the gate together. He paused momentarily before following behind Dr. Rossi to the marine lab. A subtle emptiness fell over the room as he left.

"EV, set course. Some of our people need to get home," Sarah said.

"Everything checked out?" Sarah asked.

"Yeah, we are all set," Richard said.

"People that I love are riding on this trip," Sarah pointed out.

Sarah hugged her father. She wondered if this would be the last time they would be on the same planet.

"I love you, Starlight. You take good care of yourself," Richard said as the embrace continued.

"I love you too. Don't forget about us out here," Sarah said.

"I'm not sure how you expect me to forget my brilliant Sarah is all the way out here," Richard replied.

"We still should be able to see each other, right? I mean through the connections with the loopens?" Sarah asked.

"Possibly. They are living beings that have brought great wonders into our lives, but as you know, only they can control the terms of those connections. I have never been as connected to Kite as Ashley is with Hot Wings. I'm not sure what will happen when I return to Earth. The mind spaces have always been on their terms," Richard said.

"I know. If I have learned anything on this trip, it's that none of us know what the future holds," Sarah said.

"That's my girl," Richard said. With that, Richard gave Sarah one last look and crossed the airlock into the Crichton.

She watched for a moment as the airlock was sealed, and for a split-second, Sarah had the urge to return with him back to Earth, but then the moment faded. She turned and headed for the bridge.

As Sarah entered the bridge, she saw the remaining crew ready to give the Crichton a fond farewell from Violatis. EV was at the helm, and Anya was filling Sarah's old spot at the navigation and sensor station ahead of the captain's chair. Ashley had her usual spot at the engineering station, and Dyami sat beside her to Sarah's right. To the left was Malcolm Oliveira, who had made the leap with Dr. Rossi on the last gate jump from Europa.

As Sarah took her seat, Ashley said, "The Crichton is standing by."

"Open the com feed," Sarah said, and Ashley nodded.

"Pegasus ready. Have a safe voyage home Crichton," Sarah said.

"Acknowledged. We will call you from the other side," Richard said.

The crew watched as the Crichton reached the coordinates. A few loopens swam by the Pegasus, but none approached to make the jump with the Crichton. Sarah knew then that none of the creatures would be returning to Europa with Ben, Kiah, and Richard. She knew they could make connections over vast distances, but the connections to those people would become rare and precious. This moment was goodbye.

The gate shifted into position, and with a flash, they were gone, slipping through the fabric of the galaxy toward home. Sarah was left wondering. *Where will the universe lead us next?*

NOTE FROM THE AUTHOR

Thank you for reading the first novel that I have ever written. I am truly humbled by you, the reader, that cares enough about the story to be reading this note. I hope you enjoyed the tale of Pegasus and her adventures, and will continue with me along her journeys in the future. This book represents the beginning of my creative written works, and Sarah and the crew will continue their adventures in subsequent novels. I discovered that through the process of writing, I could explore a future where humankind had triumphed through hardship and embraced our differences. A place where society thrived, supported by understanding and consideration for each individual. I could manifest this environment and experience it with others by capturing it within the written word. I am so thankful we live in a time where I can to share this with you. We are each on our own path, and each attempting to find our own happiness and harmony within our lives. Thank you for spending the time and sharing this part of the path with me.

ACKNOWLEDGMENTS

Writing a novel is a long process, and I could not have done it without the support of my family and friends. I want to also give a special thank you to the initial beta readers, that took the time to read this work, and provide me their invaluable feedback and editing recommendations. Thank you, Jack, Ben, Beth, Allen, and Kathy. Each of you helped in making this story the best it could be, and your participation was greatly appreciated. I hope you very much enjoyed the final version.